ISLAMORADA

ISLAMORADA

E. HOWARD HUNT

DONALD I. FINE, INC.

New York

BOOK ONE

ONE

=====

THE FIRST time I saw her she was running along the beach, slippered feet indenting the moist sand, blond hair ruffled by the breeze. She was wearing an electric-blue Spandex halter and tight matching briefs, headband, wrist weights and dark wraparound shades. Appreciatively, I watched her perfectly proportioned figure diminish in the direction of Islamorada and then I resumed eating my juicy mango.

My stilt shack had been built off the south, or Atlantic, shore of Matecumbe Key. Its wooden deck was twelve feet above low tide level, nine feet at high, when water separated it from a bank of dunes overgrown with sea-grape shrubs and wild grasses. I'd chosen the place for its isolation, and the morning runner was only the fourth human I'd seen in the two months since I'd moved in. A walkaround balcony was railed by weathered two-by-fours, and from it I could view sea or shore as I chose. The shack had electricity, running water, a hot plate and a small fridge, to which I'd added a microwave oven and a charcoal grill. There was a cubicle for hopper and washbasin, and the bed's heavy timber frame supported a comfortable mattress. It wasn't a place for year-round living, especially during hurricane season, it was more of a fisherman's retreat. From the balcony I'd caught blue crabs, grunts, speckled trout, yellowtail, even chicken dolphin; all excellent eating and easy to prepare in my limited kitchen. Last winter I'd taken a 9 mm slug by my left shoulder blade during a drug-ranch shootout in northern Durango, and although the slug was gone some muscle damage remained. I was rehabilitating with swimming and light exercise, growing a beard and staying away from places where undesirables might recognize me.

After I'd tossed the mango rind to the crabs I felt a bump against one of the pilings and realized my snubbed boat was swinging with the changing tide. My boat by right of salvage, for I'd spotted it one dawn barely afloat some seventy yards away. In my two-man inflatable raft I'd paddled over, and with mask and snorkel gone down to find out why the boat was sinking. The coam-

ing was stitched with small caliber bullet holes, and below the waterline seven
.45 caliber holes punctured the fiberglass hull.

The boat was a Renegade and looked fairly new. It had a bow cubby for
stowage and a 250 HP Johnson clamped to the stern. I didn't know who the
boat had belonged to, but I suspected the previous owner wouldn't spend much
time looking for it. If any.

So I ran a line to the bow and very slowly towed it to my shack, shoulder
pain making me grit my teeth. With the boat tied to a seaside piling I cycled
to an Islamorada marine supply store and brought back a half-gallon of
water-setting fiberglass compound and a new battery. After plugging the
machine-gun holes I spent half a day bailing the boat before I could replace
the ruined battery. The pump sucked out the rest of the water, except for
puddles under the duckboards, and when I took them up I found a handful of
cartridge cases—.30 carbine and .38 automatic—sloshing around in bilge
goo. They had come from the MI carbine and Colt pistol that lay atop the
duckboards, both weapons too badly corroded for further use. I tossed both
seaward as far as I could. After drying the outboard's ignition system the
Johnson exploded into life with a blast of blue smoke. I had a fishing boat
of my own.

My years with DEA had taught me where to search for contraband and I
found it taped to the hull inside the covered stowage: plastic bags of white
powder, six keys in all. I slit each bag and emptied it into the water, dropped
the bags into the current, and felt I knew all I wanted to know about the boat's
provenance. A twenty-foot low-profile boat powered by an oversize outboard
was ideal for a fast shore run from an offshore mothership. Stowed under the
gunwales were four stubby billfish rods with large Penn reels, but any tackle
box with lures would have drifted away as the boat sank. The rods and built-
in baitwell were supposed to satisfy Coast Guard and Customs inspectors that
boat and occupants were engaged in recreational offshore fishing, a ruse that
occasionally worked.

For a serious drug merchant six keys of coke weren't worth the risk of
interception, so the boat had been involved in small-time smuggling by men
whose riddled bodies had been disposed of by sharks and barracuda. Their bad
luck had become my good fortune but I didn't want any blowback. So before
taking the boat to a nearby marina for supplies I'd unscrewed and reversed
three Coast Guard registration numbers on the bow—in case the originals were
on some Wanted list. Hauling supplies by boat was a lot easier than cycling
them from the highway 7-11 store.

The Florida Keys are a unique part of America. Curving down from the
southern tip of the Florida peninsula, the larger coral islands are strung together by forty-four bridges on the Overseas Highway's hundred-mile

length, from the mainland to Key West. The string's north side is Florida Bay, the south the Atlantic Ocean. There's diversity in dwellings, shops, restaurants, and among island dwellers whose common denominator is a loose, laidback lifestyle, which is what I was enjoying in my one-room elevated shack.

I hadn't thought much about girls or female companionship since last summer when Melody West had left me for a bronzed Italian diver she'd met in Barcelona during the Olympic games. I tried to be philosophical about it; we'd been together for three years while she trained for the Olympics and I did occasional jobs for Manny Montijo, once a DEA colleague and now a top supervisor in Miami's DEA office. Our separation intervals had increased until finally we were communicating mainly by telephone or scribbled notes. But I wasn't blameless by any means. In Guadalajara I'd fallen in love with Sarita Rojas, the Mexican film star who died while we were on the run from Mexican cops and drug *bandidos*, and I'd never been able to put Sarita out of my mind. So . . .

The next time I saw the running girl she wasn't running. Half-mango in hand I went out on the balcony and saw her kneeling on the beach staring at a washed-ashore gill net filled with dead fish. Choking sounds came from her throat so I cupped my hands and called down, "Can I help?"

Her face turned toward me and I saw that her cheeks were streaked with tears. "This your net?" she called back.

"Hell, no, they're illegal." I set mango on table and went down the board stairway to the sand. She was pointing at a small dead Ridley's turtle and shaking her head. "Whoever did this is a bastard. A real sonofabitch."

"Right."

"Just look. Baby turtle, yellowtail, permit, sea trout, crabs, all dead, all wasted." Slowly she got up and brushed sand from her dimpled knees. I said, "That's the third gill net that's washed up here this month. The netters set them at night so their dirty work won't be seen."

After wiping her cheeks she blurted, "I'd shoot those bastards if I could."

"Tell you what," I said, and gestured at my boat, "I'll haul this mess out to sea and sink it deep."

"Would you? I'd be grateful."

"After coffee," I added, really seeing her now for the first time. In her slippered feet she was about five-five, perfectly tapered thighs and legs, small waist, flat tummy, lean rib cage that swelled into firm-looking breasts that appeared oversize for her slight figure. Her hair was blond, as I'd noticed before, and arching eyebrows were a shade or so darker, accenting brown eyes. High, slanting cheekbones in an oval face, small perfect teeth, and a small nose with a very slight downcurve. Her skin was the color of wildflower honey, or maybe clover—somewhere between the two—but her features suggested something remotely Oriental or Indian in her genetic background. I swallowed and said, "Have coffee with me, then I'll go."

With a nod, she began walking toward the staircase in a fluid rhythm, and as she went up ahead of me I couldn't avoid noticing the play of her symmetrical pear-shaped buns.

On the deck she halted. "Live here alone?" she asked.

"I do."

"Drop-out?"

"Sort of," I replied, and walked in to my makeshift kitchen. "Name's Jim." Jim Nolan having been the name I'd signed on the shack's lease.

"Anita," she said, and stood with hands on hips looking around.

"Welcome, Anita. You're my first visitor." I tapped instant coffee grains into two mugs, got a pan of water boiling on the hot plate. While I was filling our mugs she said quietly, "I don't know why I get so upset over a bunch of dead fish, but I do." She sighed. "Life would be easier if I weren't so sentimental."

"Yeah, it can be sort of a curse." I offered the sugar shaker. "Milk?"

"No, I like it black, just a little sugar."

I took a second chair out to the balcony where we sipped and gazed at the reef surf line for a while. Finally I said, "When I'm up early I've seen you running along the beach."

She nodded. "Before the sun can burn me, while it's still fresh and cool."

"Live nearby?"

"I rented a place in town, but what you have here is more to my liking. Much more." Her nose crinkled. "Are you a writer?"

"Why?"

"I don't see paints or easel around. So you're either a writer or a recluse."

I smiled. "How about treasure hunter—waiting for Spanish gold to wash ashore."

She eyed me. "That would take more patience than I think you've got. No typewriter?"

I shook my head. "Guess that makes me a recluse."

"Well," she said after another sip, "you have your reasons and I won't ask what they are. But"—she hesitated—"are you married?"

I shook my head again, thinking I'd been a widower for nearly seven years, but why lay that story on her? "More coffee?"

"No, I'll be flying all day on this."

"Me, I'm a caffeine addict." Holdover from Navy days, but that was something else she didn't need to know. I stood up. "Come with me?"

"Have you got something I can use to cover myself? Sun's up now."

I gave her an unironed denim shirt, jeans and a floppy straw hat I'd found under the bed. "That do it?"

"Just fine." She got into the oversize clothing and we went down to where the boat was tied. I held the bow while she got lithely in and then I started the motor and nosed the boat onto the sand. The gill net was heavy with fish that had begun to smell. I waved away flies and loaded the net onto bow decking, then backed off and turned the boat toward the open ocean.

A mile offshore, at the hundred-fathom line, I tied heavy weights to the net and shoved it overboard. "That deep," I explained, "it won't do more damage."

Her brow wrinkled. "You sure?"

"Trust me. Too deep here even for crab pots." I gestured at the unbroken horizon. "No boats, *nada*."

As I turned the boat toward shore she adjusted the hat's brim to shade her face. "Fish a lot?"

"When hungry. I eat what I kill. Don't kill what I can't eat. And that includes predators like barracuda." I wiped light spray from my face. "If I got *ciguatera* I'd probably die in the shack."

"No telephone?"

I shook my head. I had a cellular cached away for emergencies, but why mention it? I'd probably never see Anita again. "Staying long on the island?"

"A while." She looked away. "I—I'm waiting for someone."

"Figures." She ignored the implication and fingered a bullet hole in the coaming. "This what I think it is?"

"Probably."

"Your boat—don't you know?"

"Wasn't always my boat."

"Why didn't I think of that." She peered up at me from under the hat rim. "Ever see me before?"

"Running? Sure."

"Walking. Sitting. With other people?"

I shook my head. "Should I have? Are you famous?"

"Never mind." She looked away.

"I don't have TV."

"What a blessing." In the baggy clothing she resembled a cornfield scarecrow. But I knew what the clothing covered and the vision warmed me. Her questions made me curious. I wanted to know more about her. Who was she waiting for? Husband? Lover? I estimated her age at twenty-four or -five, no more, and I didn't think I'd find her picture on any post-office wall. Maybe she was an actress, a model. She had the looks, the voice, for either and Miami's South Beach had become a magnet for foreign photographers and stunning models. Anita could easily be one of them. I wanted to ask how she passed her days—and nights—but didn't want to violate our tacit agreement to avoid personal questions. So, I'd probably never know.

Nearing the shack I cut the motor and drifted to a shoreside piling and tied up the boat. Tide was flooding the sand so I told her to get out of the scarecrow suit and I'd carry her to dry beach.

"Not necessary," she said, taking off her slippers. "I'll finish my run and wave to you on the way back."

"You know I'm here," I said, "so if there's anything I can do . . ."

"I'll come," she smiled. "And thanks for everything." With that she slipped over the side and waded to shore where she replaced her slippers. I went up the stairs to the deck and watched her pick up her easy running gait until she was lost from view.

What a girl, I said to myself, and my damn luck she's spoken for, fixated on some other guy. I rinsed her cup and made myself fresh coffee, turned the FM radio to 101.5 and listened to nostalgia stuff for a while. Then I took the boat to the marina, bought newspapers, two magazines, live bait, jugwater, a half gallon of milk and a liter bottle of Añejo to take the edge off the rest of the day.

Toward sunset I baited lines and anchored off the reef long enough to hook two nice mutton snappers. Then I went back to the shack for dinner.

The next three mornings I saw Anita jogging on the beach and each time we waved at each other. The following two mornings she didn't come and I realized that I missed her. Probably her man had arrived and taken her away to who-knows-where, I reasoned, leaving me with the memory of a brief one-time encounter and an empty feeling that was hard to ignore.

Late Saturday afternoon I cycled down the highway to the Osprey Bar & Grill and chain-locked my bike to a pole. Before going in I walked over to something I'd never seen before, a pink Jeep. Except for tires, everything was flamingo pink, even the roll bar. The paint looked factory-new, the waxed finish gleamed in the sunlight, and the odometer showed under four hundred miles. I wondered who the owner was.

Inside, the Osprey was a large low-ceilinged room paneled in dark cypress, with a long, waxed cypress bar, small dance floor and side tables of sectioned cypress surfaced with transparent polyurethane.

Toward one end of the bar a raised, large-screen TV was showing a baseball game. Bar stools and table chairs were turned toward it so patrons could munch crab sandwiches and fries, guzzle draft beer and mixed drinks. I found a small table by the empty dance floor and after a while a perspiring waitress accepted my order for fried oysters and a tankard of ice-cold Coors. "Good crowd," I remarked pleasantly. "Yeah, baseball season, always is." She wiped a hand across her forehead. "They'll get to bettin' an' turn rowdy. Oysters you say? Not clams?"

"Oysters. And Coors." She went away and I began scanning the bar customers thinking I'd find the pink Jeep owner on one of the stools. Now that my beard was pretty well grown I was less worried about being spotted for who I was and what I'd been so I wasn't packing iron, just a Boy Scout pocket knife with a well-honed blade.

As my gaze moved around the room I saw two tough-looking leather-jacketed *hombres* standing at a table. Their backs were to me so I couldn't see who they were harassing, but their voices were loud from too many beers, and I understood they were inviting an unseen female to leave with them. Their voices rose, coarsely and obscenely, and one of them grabbed at the woman's arm. Before he could jerk backward, the woman's free hand slashed down, the man yelled in pain and staggered back, pulling a fork from the back of his hand. His partner backhanded the woman's face, slamming her head against the wall. She screamed and whimpered, and then the wounded man yelled, "I'm gonna kill you, bitch!" He jerked away the table and hauled her upright and for the first time I saw the woman's face: Anita. She took the first blow on her shoulder, cowered as the punching fist drew back, and I raced across the dance floor. I kicked the back of his knees, and as he folded backward I chopped the exposed neck and he dropped. Anita screamed. The other tough grabbed me from behind and began bear-hugging me until I snapped my head backward and smashed his nose. His hands went to his face, I spun around and took his head-down charge with my right knee. I felt teeth on my kneecap before he fell forward. Stepping around him, I reached for Anita. "Let's go," I snapped, "outa here," then saw Shithead Two scrabbling behind his back for a pistol. He was thinking about the handgun, not me, so it was no trouble to kick his face and drop him. I jerked the pistol from his belt and thumbed off the safety. "That's enough," I snarled and looked around. The only sound in the room was the game announcer's inane chatter. "Great people," I told the customers, "swell folks," and pulled Anita toward the door. I paused long enough to dump the pistol magazine and eject the chambered shell, then tossed the pistol at the room's far end. I heard it clatter to a stop, then we were out of the Osprey and walking in searing sunlight. "Oh, God," Anita said hoarsely, "Oh, God!"

Suddenly I was sorry I'd gotten rid of the handgun, because I had only my bike for the two of us. "That's it," I told her, pointing at my chained bike. "Any better ideas?"

Wordlessly she opened her belt pouch and handed me a keyring. "Which car?" I asked, and she pointed at the pink Jeep.

As fast as I could I unlocked my bike and loaded it onto the Jeep, started the engine, and with Anita beside me, swerved out of the drive in a swirl of dust. But before I turned onto the highway I noticed two black-painted hawg bikes by the building's far end and drove to them. Their front tires were tough but my knife blade was sharp and within seconds both tires deflated. From the Osprey's entrance came roars of rage so I vaulted into the Jeep and we took off down the highway in the direction I'd come just a few minutes ago.

Her hand clutched my arm, road dust was caking her tear-wet cheeks. "Easy," I said, "just take it easy, Anita. You don't need to say anything." Her left cheek was swelling, the eye already bloodshot.

"Those bastards," I grated. "What the hell did they want?"

"*Want*?" she echoed in a tone of near hysteria. "They wanted to take me out and rape me—that's what they wanted!"

I felt my face flush. Me the idiot. Why had I asked so obvious a question? Things had happened so fast I'd gotten out of sync with realtime events. "I—" she began huskily—"I'm so lucky you were there . . . Oh, Jim, thank you, thank you, thank you—" she continued, the words running together on a rising note. "Hey," I said, "no thanks necessary," and patted her clenched hand to calm her down. She closed her eyes and leaned back, never asking where we were going.

Less than two miles from the Osprey I turned off the highway onto a rutted dirt road that lead bumpily through banyan trees and bamboo, sawgrass and sea grape until it ended at a dune. Turning off the engine, I handed her the keys, said, "We're safe," and helped her off the seat to the sand. Then I led her over the dune and pointed to my shack fifty yards away. "Thank God," she breathed, "I'm still scared, Jim; can I stay a while?"

"Long's you want," I answered and struck out across the sand. When she didn't follow I glanced back and saw her unbuckling leather sandals. She was in beige linen slacks and matching bush jacket, a harness leather belt around her waist. From her throat opening she drew out a flimsy crimson scarf and began dabbing her cheeks.

At water's edge I lifted and carried her through shallow water to the shack's stairway and she went up unsteadily. Inside I broke out glasses, ice and the Añejo bottle, and made her swallow two ounces before stopping. I downed half a glass and poured more, but she shook her head, coughed and looked around. She was noticing the unmade bed, so I suggested she lie down a while and rest, get over the shakes. She said it sounded like a good idea, and straightened the sheets before lying down. After a while she called, "I'm sorry, Jim, for all the trouble."

"You didn't cause it, honey. Thugs, beer and Saturday afternoon usually bring trouble." I sipped from my glass. "You've gone there before?"

"The food isn't bad, and it's a change from four walls."

"Quite a change," I observed dryly, "unless your place is crawling with hoods."

A shaky laugh was her response. I said, "Anyway, I'm finished at the Osprey, not that it's much of a loss. That C and W jukebox doesn't do a thing for me."

I thought I detected a low giggle, but didn't look her way. "This place is good enough for me," I declared, "though it hasn't been the same since you went away."

"I see. And how long ago was that?"

"Six days . . . um, eight hours and, ah, forty-three minutes. Anita," I said sternly, "you've put me through pure hell with your comings and goings, false promises and so on. Things gotta change."

That provoked a genuine laugh. "Oh, Jim, how you *do* go on. I'll be okay now. I'm okay. Just give me some ice for my face—and maybe a thimbleful of that heavenly rum."

I cracked ice in a washcloth and laid the pack across her left cheek; the eye was looking better. Her attackers would be feeling a lot more pain than Anita, and that was a satisfying thought.

I helped her get the glass to her lips so she could sip, and after a while she asked, "How bad is my face going to look? How long will it last?"

"Oh," I said, "it'll swell up like a humongous purple eggplant or rutabaga and just hang there for, oh, anyways—" I stopped. "How long's your lease?"

"Month."

"Month anyway. So you'd better stay right here where ol' Jim can doctor and feed you through this crisis."

"Would you? Really?"

Her question startled me. "Really would." Below the ice pack I could see her lips form a smile. Progress was being made. Helped by light banter.

"Now tell me," she began, "what *is* a rutabaga?"

"Like a loathsome turnip. Everyone knows what rutabaga is—everyone in this country."

"But, Jim . . . I'm not from this country. I only know South Florida and bits of California."

"Not . . . from . . . ?"

"Look, because of what you did today, and the other time, I trust you, so it's time I laid my cards on the table—as you Americans say."

I shrugged. "Not if you don't want to. No obligation."

She drew in a deep breath. "My husband is Claude Tessier, he's the man I've been waiting for. Heard of him?"

"No."

"He was my father's pilot—chief pilot. He's supposed to be released from prison. Soon."

"South Dade Correctional?"

She nodded.

"So, who's your father?"

Long hesitation before she answered. "He is—was—Colonel Oscar Chavez, the—"

"—Guatemalan dictator," I finished. How could such an evil man have so beautiful a child?

I went to the bottle and poured a double shot of Añejo. Turning, I gazed at her and now I understood the unusual, but beautiful, cast of her features. She was *ladina*, a Guatemalteca with a trace of Mayan blood. "Your father's dead."

"In a plane crash. Near Monterrey."

"What about his pilot, your husband?"

"Claude didn't fly him, another pilot did."

"What luck," I remarked, "and triple luck to have you waiting for him." I drank more rum. "When's he getting out?"

"Saul Hornstein says only a few more days. I saw him in Miami."

I knew Hornstein by sight and reputation. Probably the most famous—or infamous—drug lawyer in Miami. A big man with a black handlebar mustache and enough money to paper the Overseas Highway in hundred-dollar bills.

She said, "Do you believe Hornstein?"

"He didn't earn his reputation rainmaking so it's more likely you'll be a happy couple soon again."

She sat up, and the ice pack slipped away. "Jim, I'm not part of any happy couple, I never was. When Claude gets out we're finished. I've been waiting to tell him so."

Light at the end of the tunnel? I went over to the bed, picked up ice shards and dropped them in my glass. Outside the sun was lowering. Evening breeze swept through the open sides. A gull cawed in the distance. Bending over, I gently kissed the swollen cheek. "That's nice," she murmured. "Friends?"

"Friends." My throat tightened. "I've really missed you."

"Have you? I'm glad." She pushed a wisp of hair from her forehead. Dusk filled the room. "I feel so safe here, Jim, secure. My father's bodyguards were fast but, God, you were faster."

"And Miss Manners approves of how you handle a fork."

"Jim, does it make a difference that I'm my father's child? Be honest."

"We're not responsible for our parents' sins or achievements. Do I think any less of you? No. Do I think you're absolutely marvelous? Yes."

She turned my face and kissed my lips. Gently at first, then urgently. Her mouth opened and our tongues touched.

And that's how a deadly romance began.

TWO

MANNY MONTIJO drove down from Miami and met me at the Fish House on Key Largo. He was a short, muscular Hispanic with smooth skin that appeared lightly tanned, dark eyes and coal-black hair. A Californian of Spanish blood, Manny rebelled at being thought Mexican or Cuban. In DEA and FBI circles Latino employees were called *cucarachas* (cockroaches) despite orders banning the offensive term.

The Fish House was a low building that appeared to have been built with flotsam from the '26 hurricane. Inside, there was a raw bar, a refrigerated case displaying varieties of seafood, and maybe twenty wood tables. We were sitting at one of them gnawing Stone Crab claws and guzzling draft beer. Manny dipped a claw chunk in mustard sauce, bit into it, chewed and swallowed. After that he gazed down at his embroidered white guayabera shirt, checking for mustard spots. As usual when we got together for lunch we avoided business until after ingesting enough to sustain energy. Manny tilted his beer stein, drank, and set it down. "So why do I have to drive all the way down here, when it's the same distance to Miami?"

"I haven't got a car here."

He grunted. "A lot of money disappeared during that hacienda firefight, three or four hundred thousand. You got it, right?"

"Can't remember, Manny. I was in great pain from the shoulder slug. Delirious. Who's to say?"

He leaned forward. "Safe to say you can afford a car or two, *amigo*."

"I'm a frugal fellow. Remember?"

"Sure. I also remember paying you big bucks for undercover jobs—"

"—in which I risked my life on numerous occasions."

"Blown it all?"

I ignored the feeler, saying, "Let me tell you a little story that could be beneficial to you."

"Shoot—but what's in it for you? And is this gonna cost me?"

"We'll come to that. It starts with a beautiful young woman who jogs the beach in front of my shack. Name's Anita and she claims to be the daughter of the late Colonel Oscar Chavez.''

"Chavez, eh? You believe her?"

"I don't disbelieve her. Also says she's married to Claude Tessier, once Chavez's chief pilot. Expects Tessier to be released any day, thanks to Saul Hornstein's legal labors.''

Manny scratched his chin and stared at his stein. "After Chavez got kicked out of Guatemala he settled in Mexico. Took two years for State and Justice to arrange extradition. Chavez had enough smarts and money to hire Hornstein, who battled extradition every step of the way.''

I nodded thoughtfully. "While the Mexican Attorney General used every possible excuse to prevent extradition.''

"Yeah. Finally came down to Bush telling President Salinas to surrender Chavez and no more bullshit. That greased the skids. Our guys were all set to pick up Chavez at Brownsville but he never got there.''

"Plane crash, his daughter said.''

"So we heard. The Mexicans investigated the crash, declared Chavez, two bodyguards and pilot dead. Burned beyond recognition.''

"What do you think, Manny?''

"Case closed.'' He bit into a claw and chewed savagely. "If Chavez died that's a break for the US taxpayer. If the crash was phonied and he's off somewhere enjoying his stolen billions, who'll ever know?''

"His daughter?''

He sighed. "I don't want to get involved in the Chavez case, if there is one. Quite a few of us busted our collective butt getting evidence against him. The USA referred evidence to the grand jury, the extradition proceedings took forever, and we end up with six file cabinets of Chavez crap and a Mexican death certificate. Uh-uh. The office is overwhelmed with new cases and Chavez is history. That's the way it's gonna stay.''

I finished my beer and signaled refills. "Tell me about Tessier, the lucky pilot who was elsewhere when Chavez's plane went down.''

"Claude Tessier,'' Manny said slowly. "Dominican, if I remember right, and more than a plane driver for Chavez. We got phone intercepts of Tessier doing business for Chavez with narcos in Colombia and Venezuela. Arranging delivery schedules and payoffs. Once the drug loads were in Guatemala it was no sweat to fly the shit into Mexico.'' He shrugged. "From there, Uncle Sugar.''

"I understand. But what was Tessier jailed for?''

Manny laughed shortly. "Contempt of court, for God's sake. Refused to answer grand jury questions about his and Chavez's dealings. The USA tried to indict him with evidence gathered against Chavez, but the grand jury said no.''

"How's Hornstein getting him released?"

"Simple. The grand jury's term expires. Can't hold Tessier beyond that. Hornstein's intervention, if any, is redundant. But I'll bet he gets paid anyway. Plenty."

"But Tessier can be hauled up before the next grand jury, right? And if he refuses to answer, jailed again?"

Manny shook his head dejectedly. "Those things take time, *amigo*, and I doubt Tessier will stay around long enough for anything bad to happen."

"You mean, skip out?"

"Wouldn't you? Besides, he banked a lot of money for Chavez, and plenty for himself. It's sitting somewhere, just waiting." He eyed me over the stein rim. "His wife should know about that."

I waited until the waiter deposited fresh steins and took away the empties. "Says she's divorcing Claude as soon as he's free."

"Which doesn't mean she doesn't know significant things about her husband."

"Point taken."

He paused. "Married, she can't testify against Claude. But divorced . . ." He tilted his stein and drank. "Tessier could find that threatening."

"Guess he could."

"You like the little lady?"

"Fond of her, sure."

"Replacing Melody in your affections?"

"I don't want to talk about Melody. That's history, like Chavez. Can you get me background info on Anita?"

He nodded. "Her sister, too?"

"She hasn't mentioned a sister."

"Rita. We've got surveillance videos of both girls with their father in Mexico, some film footage from Guatemala when they were younger. Rita's married to a Spaniard, lives in Madrid but travels a lot."

"What about the Colonel's widow? Alive?"

"Believe so. Living in Rome or Paris, maybe Rio. Once a Paris showgirl. Natural blond. Marie spent time in Mexico consoling the Colonel before he, shall we say, died. Still a good-looking woman, maybe fifty."

"And she's got plenty of money?"

"They all have. Switzerland, Panama, the Caymans. Well stashed." He smiled suggestively. "Thinking of tapping into all that illegal wealth?"

"Not until this moment." I smiled back. "Is the Guat government trying to repossess it?"

"I've heard." He scanned the menu card. "Broiled yellowtail for me."

"Me, too." I gave our order to the waiter, who cleared away claw remains.

Manny said, "I enjoy time away from the office and a good meal, but beyond that what have I learned from your little story?"

"That Tessier's about to go free."

"I could have found that out—if I'd been interested."

"Yeah. Anyway, it's good to see you. I've stayed isolated."

"I love the beard. Natural disguise."

After drinking I set down the stein. "Manny, are we off the record?"

"We are."

"So you won't think I'm rolling in wealth, a big chunk of that hacienda money was queer."

"Surprise, surprise. You ripped-off, and got ripped-off. That's what I call street justice."

"Don't be so damn happy about it. And you can pay for lunch."

"Okay, Confidential Informant. What name are you using these days?"

"Jim Nolan."

"Got a phone?"

I gave him my cellular number and he wrote it down. "I'll phone you the readout later today or tomorrow."

"Appreciate it. Manny, I may not have wheels but I've got a boat. While the kings are running you should come down for some fishing. A day, a week, your call."

"Sounds good." His eyes narrowed. "You bought a boat?"

"Ummm. Not exactly." So while we were consuming garlic-flavored yellowtail I told him how I'd acquired the windfall boat and repaired it.

Irritably Manny said, "Ever occur to you we might have been looking for that boat? Or Customs?"

"Thought occurred but didn't linger. Anyway, law of the sea gives it to me. Try getting it back."

Manny chuckled. "Time was when you were a first-rate agent. Since then you've become a free-lance con man if not an outright thief."

"Flattery, flattery," I intoned. "Hard to believe you're not interested in Claude Tessier."

"I would be—if he'd talk. We'd love to have his rundown of narco contacts in Central and South America, shipment routes, money stashes. But as I said, he wouldn't talk."

"Had no motivation."

"Like what?"

"Wire-cutters nipping his balls."

"Jesus—you haven't changed," he said, appalled by my solution. "You've gotten bloodier than ever."

"Gotta survive in a cruel world, Manny. No place for sentiment."

"Especially if you're an ethnic minority-type kid." He ate a forkful of coleslaw. "We'll hafta do this more often, *compadre*. The *comida* couldn't be better."

"Why I picked the spot. Okay, you'll phone rap sheets on the Chavez sisters, right?"

"Right. Rita's the elder by a few years. Married name's Castenada."

"And Tessier?"

"I told you basically what I know. What's your interest in him?"

"He's the husband of my new girlfriend. Is he in the category armed and dangerous?"

"Absolutely. God knows how many he's gunned down—or shoved out of his plane without a chute." He shoved his plate aside and took a toothpick from the holder. Soberly, he said, "Have to wonder why Tessier didn't crash with Chavez—if Chavez was one of the victims."

"The question crossed my mind," I admitted, "only I can't think of anyone who might care."

Manny broke the toothpick and dropped it in the ash tray. "Just before Chavez dropped out of sight the Mexico City office got a report that the Colonel and a bodyguard were around town buying gems, mainly high-quality emeralds."

"So?"

"So—nothing. The information wasn't relevant to DEA interests."

"How much were the gems worth?"

"Oh, somewhere between one and two million dollars—small change to Chavez."

"But a succulent bribe for Mexican officials."

"Yeah, I guess they were passed out like Christmas candy. Anyway, the crash report didn't mention recovered valuables, and being carbon any gems would have incinerated." He shrugged. "Chavez—a circular story leading nowhere."

"Unless Tessier has the stones."

He eyed me. "Or his wife."

"You've indicated all Chavez females are richly endowed, Mom and both sisters. So if Anita's holding stones for her husband I imagine she'll return them." A thought occurred. "In exchange for divorce."

"That's family business," Manny said sternly. "I'd leave it alone."

"Plan to. I've enough enemies already."

On that note we left the Fish House and I walked Manny to his car. He didn't ask how I was getting back to Islamorada and I didn't tell him. But after he drove away I walked to the Holiday Inn marina and got into the Renegade.

Northeast breeze laid a slight chop on the ocean, so it took me more than an hour to navigate the fifteen miles back to my shack. I'd eaten too much food, drunk too much beer, and was tired from waves buffeting the hull. So I stretched out for a nap on the bed Anita had left at seven, and slept until the ringing of my cellular phone wakened me. I grappled it from under the bed and said, "Speak."

Manny's voice. "The girls are twenty-four and twenty-eight respectively. The elder likes fast cars and fast romance. No criminal activity except one shoplift in Hermès. That's Paris."

"I know," I said wearily. "Say on."

"Charge dismissed on payment for the merchandise. Her husband's an older fellow, ancient family financially shaky. Dabbles in Spanish politics, seat in the Cortes, their parliament, and lets his wife do as she likes."

"Sensible arrangement. Very continental."

"Yeah. According to untested sources if Rita had as many pricks sticking out of her as she's had stuck in her she'd look like a porcupine."

"Wiseass stuff, Manny, unworthy of you."

"Okay, the kid sister looks better. Went to Cal-Davis, kept to herself. Visited Guatemala from time to time, not after Dad was ejected. Married two years ago to the chap you mentioned. No one knows why."

"That it?"

"That's it."

I scratched my cheek where beard was itching. "Well, thanks," I said, "and for lunch."

"Let's not lose touch."

I clicked off the phone and suddenly realized that because I'd been talking I hadn't heard the stairway creak or noticed two shadows across the floor. Two men were in the doorway and one of them held a gun.

THREE

WITH THE sun behind them I couldn't see faces, so my first thought was they were the eraserheads I'd downed at the Osprey. But their builds were shorter, slimmer, and they wore light open-collar leisure suits with green-collared shirts. "What the hell," I said, "c'mon in. Drinks?"

The gunman moved two steps closer and I could see his face. It was thin, pockmarked, and a narrow mustache lined his upper lip. Black hair combed straight back from a high forehead. Briefly, I thought of reaching under the bed for the double-barrel sawed-off I'd taped there, realized it could be a major error.

"Didn't come for drinks," he said in accented English.

"Okay, so take the boat." I got up and stretched. My movement made him nervous. "It's fixed up, plenty of gas."

"Boat?" He looked back at his partner, who said in Spanish, "He's stalling. Tell him what we want."

Turning back to me, Pockmarks said, "You know the daughter of Dictator Chavez, *verdad*?"

"Met her. Why?"

"Her husband is a criminal, Claude Tessier."

"Criminal? Anita said she was married, yes."

"Nothing more?"

"Like what?"

The second man hissed, "Be direct, Pablo, tell him who we are."

Pockmarks said, "We represent the Central Bank of Guatemala. Our purpose is to regain wealth stolen from the people by Chavez."

"Sounds like a good cause," I remarked. "Can I help?"

"You can tell us when Tessier will be free from prison. And where the emeralds are."

"Can't help with that," I told them. "Didn't know the man was in prison, and the lady never said anything about emeralds." That part was true. I spread my hands emptily. "Maybe you should ask her."

"Where is she?"

"No idea. But I see her running on the beach most mornings. She's come up for coffee. No confidences exchanged."

The partner moved toward me and I could see a plump Indian face and a balding skull. A line scar angled down his left cheek and his teeth needed capping. Before he could say anything I said, "Give me a card and I'll pass it to Anita next time she comes by."

Partner smiled thinly. Pockmarks sneered, "You would do that?"

"I would do that." I smiled sappily. "If you want I'll ask about emeralds and report to you." I gazed at the handgun, .32 caliber revolver. Not much stopping power unless it hit a vital part.

"And why would you do that?"

"Because of what Chavez did to your country, your people. Now, for heaven's sake put away that gun. I'm not armed, and I'm not dangerous."

"Perhaps later. We know nothing about you. You could be a criminal, you could be part of Tessier's conspiracy. So I keep the gun where you can see it."

"That's reasonable." I walked slowly to the counter and poured jug water into a glass. "Dry throat," I explained and drank. "Tap water is lousy, tastes of sulfur and mold."

After they'd watched me Pockmarks asked, "Is she going to bring her husband to meet you?"

"I hope not. He sounds like a very ugly person."

The Guats exchanged glances. I said, "To clarify things, you're not interested in my boat?"

"No. We are not thieves."

Scarface said, "Ask his name." In Spanish.

"What is your name?"

"Nolan. Jim Nolan."

"You live here alone?"

I nodded.

"Why?"

"Well, I like to fish—and I've got AIDS."

Reflexively, the gunman stepped back, eyes wide.

"Not to worry," I told him, "unless you suck my cock."

He shoved the revolver into a hip pocket. To Scarface he muttered, "A waste of time. The *puto* knows nothing." He turned toward the doorway, Scarface shrugged and they walked out together. This time I heard them on the stairway and felt relieved they'd left without gunplay or bloodshed. I splashed Añejo into my water glass and gulped it down. I ought to warn Anita, I thought, but I didn't know where she was staying. From the window I saw the bankers climbing the dune before disappearing on the far side. How had they found me? I wondered. If they'd seen Anita's pink Jeep drive off at daybreak why hadn't they followed her and left me alone? Strange.

However inept the two bank reps were they could still be dangerous to Anita and me. Tessier I didn't care about. He was theirs if they could take him, but they'd need reinforcements. Against a stone killer like Tessier they were badly outclassed.

The sun was low. A Vee of five pelicans glided over the water. From the highway came the low hum of homebound traffic. I got a snapper filet from the fridge, marinated it in Key-lime juice, and loaded the grill pan with charcoal. Onshore breeze helped ignite the charcoal and I sat nearby, feet against the railing, deciding whether to go fishing after dark. The luminescence of a cold-light bar near the bait should attract some good-sized fish, and king mackerel steaks would be welcome.

As I sat there my mind turned back to evenings on my pier at Cozumel. I'd operated from that house for three years until banished by Mexican authorities, who resented my inroads into their narcotics traffic. The house had been confiscated as well as my little Fairchild Seabee amphibian, and I wondered where it was now, who was living in my house. I loved Mexico and Mexicans but not the men who ruled them.

About Guatemala I didn't know much except that it had a bloody history. One dictator after another, of whom Oscar Chavez was the most recently evicted, and who his successor was I had no idea. Probably cut from the same military cloth. Now I was involved with Chavez's younger daughter, marginally. Not much future there.

The charcoal was turning gray with ash. I stirred the briquets, went inside and flipped over the filet to marinate both sides. After dinner I ought to swim a while, strengthen damaged shoulder muscle. The alternatives were fishing, or a few drinks and reading in bed. Where was Anita? I wondered, and hoped the Guat pair didn't find her before I did.

While the snapper filet was grilling I boiled some rice, and then ate dinner on the porch. Afterward, I pulled on swim shorts and swam seaward for fifty yards, back to the pilings, seaward again, and so on for twenty minutes. I was pretty tired and my shoulder ached when I climbed the stairway but I knew I'd done the right thing. I was showering off saltwater when I heard someone hailing me from shore. Releasing the shower chain, I peered into near darkness and made out Anita waving at me. "Come aboard," I called, and began descending the stairway to meet her. Anita pulled off shoes and walking shorts and waded toward me in her panties. I reached down, took her hand and helped her onto the lowest stair, Her arms circled my chest and she hugged me tightly, then kissed me. "Hey," I protested, "you're getting wet, let's—"

"Oh, Jim, I'm so glad you're here. I have a lot to tell you."

"And I have things to tell you." We went up the stairway together and into the dimly lighted room. Turning to me, she said, "Good things, I hope, happy things?"

"Wish they were." I took her in my arms and felt her shiver. "You first," she said, so I told her about the two Guat bankers and described them. "Never seen either one," she told me, "but others have questioned me before. They all seem to think I know what my father did with his money."

"But you don't?"

She shook her head and looked around. "I could use a drink."

I poured Añejo into two glasses and gave her one. "*Salud*," I toasted. "And *pesetas*," she added before drinking.

"What's your news?" I asked.

"Claude—my husband—is being released tomorrow." She shivered again.

"And you don't want to see him?"

She walked to the bed and sat on the edge. "It's complicated, Jim. Claude was my father's confidant, his main man. My father insisted I marry him, and like a fool I agreed. Took me a while to realize the marriage was a device to prevent me from ever testifying against Claude."

"A marriage of convenience."

She grimaced. "Their convenience, not mine."

"Of course." I sat down beside her. I hadn't mentioned the emeralds the Guats had asked about. Her business, not mine. "Want to let me know where you're staying?"

"Didn't I? I have a bungalow at the Plaza Romana, that's near the bridge."

"I've seen it. Which bungalow?"

"Farthest from the road. I park the Jeep around back."

"Good idea. Around here it's unique."

I got up, went to the alcove and pulled off my wet trunks. Then I wrapped a towel around my hips and rejoined her. She smiled. "Hinting?"

"Maybe." I kissed her cheek, then her lips. She was a beautiful, exciting young woman, and I desired her. "Stay here tonight," I said. "Could be our last—"

"Oh, no." Her fingers sealed my lips. "I'll come back after—after things are straight with Claude."

"About the divorce?"

She nodded. "I'm afraid he thinks I know more about his financial dealings than I do, but I made a point of never getting involved."

"I don't know what advice Hornstein's given him, but Claude ought to get the hell out of the States before he's indicted for something else."

"That's what I'm going to tell him. But I'm afraid he'll insist I go with him."

"Will you?"

"If I can't avoid it. But I'll break away as soon as I can . . . come here if you'll let me."

"Gladly." I kissed her fingertips, unbuttoned her blouse and nuzzled her breasts. She gasped and shuddered, undid my towel while we were kissing, and took me in hand. "Easy," I warned, lay back, and pulled her on top of me. That delighted her, and for a long time we caressed and teased each other, finally climaxing spoon-fashion.

My arms around her, hands cupping her firm breasts, I said, "I'll miss you."

"And I'll miss you," she murmured drowsily. "Very much."

"So hurry back." I reached under the bed and showed her my phone. "Make a note of the number so you can reach me."

"Before I go," she promised, and then we slept.

During the night I felt her get up, heard the flooring creak as she moved around, and after a while she came back to lie beside me. Her presence and our lovemaking gave me a feeling of contentment that had been absent from my life for a long time. I hoped Tessier wouldn't give her a hard time, but whatever passed between them I wanted her back with me, the sooner the better.

When I woke at dawn she was standing naked by the window watching the sea. She looked so natural there, so innocent and unaffected that I felt my throat tighten and knew it was a moment I would always remember.

Naked together we swam beside the boat, touching as though by chance, until finally we embraced in a long, passionate kiss. Her legs flowed around my waist, my feet found bottom, and her hips moved until we were coupled and the rhythmic pressures of wave and current made our lovemaking effortless. In the aftermath she clung to me, cheek pressed to my shoulder, and as I stroked her glistening body I could almost read her thoughts: she didn't want to leave, didn't want the husband-hassle ahead. My thoughts were parallel.

While Anita showered and toweled her hair I fried bacon and eggs and was glad to find her appetite the equal of mine.

When it was over and she was standing at the top of the stairway, one hand in mine, I said, "I'm only letting you go because you're coming back."

"I am, dear Jim," she said huskily, tears welling in her eyes. We kissed a final time, and she went quickly down to the damp sand, walked faster until she was running, crossed over the dune without looking back, and was gone.

I heard the Jeep's throaty roar as she started the engine, the rasping whir of tires biting into sand as she spun her toy around and drove away. For a long time I stood at the railing, holding the fading thought that she would postpone meeting Tessier and come back to me, but she was truly gone.

At the sink I washed dishes, glasses and cutlery, fortified myself with a shot of Añejo from the bottle because I knew I was going to be very lonely until she returned.

By midday she hadn't telephoned—I hadn't expected her to—and loneliness was deepening into depression. So I ran the boat to Tavernier and went into a bar named the Dolphin, much like the Osprey but without the shithead bikers. Drinking alternate shots of beer and Añejo at the bar, I watched Atlanta pummel the Royals 9 to 1, and then the beer-and-baseball crowd thinned out and I went back to where I'd docked the Renegade.

After mooring the boat to my shack piling I walked to the highway and hiked half a mile south to the Plaza Romana. The office was set back from the road and fronted a two-story beige motel. Behind it a row of thatched cottages angled toward the bay. For the Keys they were an improvement over the usual CB blockhouses. Each cottage—or bungalow as Anita called hers—was white clapboard with peaked barrel-tile roof and frontal windows with flowered window boxes on either side of the door. A cupola shaded each doorway, and from where I stood in the hot sunlight I could hear the relentless straining of air conditioners. Behind them I could make out the mast and tuna tower of a pleasure boat moving along the edge of the bay: forty-foot Bertram or better. My face, throat and arms were streaked with sweat and road dust, and I envied the boat's crew, cool and remote from it all.

While I'd been absorbing visual inputs my mind was debating my next move: check out the last cottage for signs of occupancy or try calling her from the office phone. That seemed the better idea, so I trudged into the office, rattled a Sprite from the vending machine, and asked the clerk to ring the cottage of Mrs. Tessier. "That's the farthest one," I added after a long pull of cold Sprite.

"I know, I know," he said testily, a short, leathery senior with gnarled hands. "Who'll I say?"

"I'll do my own talking, thanks." Tilting the can, I drank most of what was left.

He buzzed half a dozen times, glanced at me and shrugged.

"Maybe she's sleeping," I suggested. "I'll see if her Jeep's there."

He went back to his swivel chair. "Had a visitor around noon. Mebbe left with him."

"Thanks for your trouble." I left the air-conditioned office and followed a crushed coral roadway past the identical cottages, until I reached Anita's. Without stopping I walked around the side, and there was the pink Jeep, patterned by shadows from the overhanging ficus tree. Should I peek in a window, or go boldly to the front door and ring? Having come this far, I was reluctant to leave without verifying her absence—or presence. Tessier, having been denied heterosexual play while in prison, would probably pull his wife into bed and keep her there. Did I want to play Peeping Tom and see the two of them making the beast with two backs? The sight would be hard to take. If I rang and Tessier came to the door, okay; but if Anita appeared and Tessier was within earshot she might blurt out something incriminating or indiscreet. Ungood for both of us.

As I walked away I realized I'd learned little for my considerable effort: her Jeep was there.

In the office I got another Sprite from the machine and opened it. Looking up, the old clerk wheezed, "Find her?"

I shook my head, sipped, and left the office with my canned drink.

As I hiked north, heat waves distorted the highway. Cars and trucks powdered me with fine coral dust, adding to my misery. When I reached the beach I pulled off my clothing and waded with it as far as the stairway. Then I ducked down and swam in the cool, refreshing water until I felt less like yesterday's roadkill.

After hauling myself up the stairway I showered, pulled on some khaki fishing shorts and sat on the balcony, watching a stillness settle over the sea. I sipped icy Coors, and reviewed the wasted afternoon. No, I reflected, not entirely wasted, for Old Leatherpuss had told me of a midday visitor. Had to be hubby himself, for who else knew her hideaway?

Saul Hornstein did. Had Saul or one of his gofers picked up Anita and delivered her to client Tessier? That was as reasonable as Tessier coming alone to the Plaza Romana cottage and spiriting his wife away for a second honeymoon. That would have been his expectation, though not Anita's if she planned to divorce him.

As an accommodation Hornstein's firm would probably represent Tessier in the divorce action; Anita could hire Roy Black or Neal Sonnet for parity. Or Tessier could skip to Mexico or the Bahamas, if he wasn't already there, leaving Anita unable to divorce him. And from what I'd gleaned of Tessier's background he wasn't likely to give her a divorce in exchange for the rumored emeralds; he'd beat them out of her.

But why was I preoccupied with what Tessier might or might not do? Because I was concerned over Anita's future. Not that I planned on marrying her—hell, I hardly knew her except in a carnal way, and that was no foundation for lasting happiness. It was more because she'd stayed untouched by her father's barbarities, and I could only imagine how difficult that must have been. Tessier I saw as the Colonel's accomplice and heir; equal to his leader in villainies, and Anita deserved far better in a husband.

Daylight was almost gone, the sun's last rays streaked shadows across the sand, whitened small surges of foam into phosphorescence. The tide was almost in. Fifty yards away I saw surface churnings and spattering as baitfish fled a feeding predator: wahoo, 'cuda or king. Reflexively, I went down to the boat, grabbed a live pilchard from the well and bent it on a hook. Then I steered toward the bait school and started trolling.

In about forty seconds a kingfish struck. It slashed at the leader wire and tried to shake the hook. Line screamed off the reel as the powerful king went deep and I let him run. When there were maybe fifty yards left on the spool I increased the drag and slowed him. My five-foot graphite rod bent into a half moon and my back and forearms began to ache. Every time tension lessened I bowed the rod and gained a few yards of twenty-pound test, then he'd rip it away. So we fought each other for a long ten minutes until I felt sudden slack. Bad sign because he could have snapped the line or slipped the hook, but I reeled frantically to regain line and suddenly it went taut and the rod tip dipped: he was there, all right, but not really resisting. I peered at where line cut the surface and saw it making slow circles as the fish orbited a hundred feet below.

Gradually, I reeled until he surfaced, floating on one side. I readied the net, figuring I might miss with the gaff, and raised the rod tip to bring him alongside. The king struggled as I drew him closer, then out of the depths erupted long wolflike jaws that clamped around the king's tail. Two vicious shakes of the 'cuda's head and the tail vanished. That portion wasn't one I cherished, so I netted three-quarters of an eighteen-pound kingfish and levered him aboard. He flopped around the duckboards until I drove an icepick through his walnut-size brain. Then he lay still, glistening in the moonlight.

I laid the carcass across the transom and sliced long filets from both sides before returning the balance to the deep. The 'cuda was welcome to it.

By now the baitfish school was long gone, along with its harriers. That was okay, because I had enough king filet for several sumptuous meals, at least one of which I hoped Anita would share with me.

As I headed the Renegade back toward my shack I was thinking of basting our broiling filets with a mix of olive oil, ground mustard, chopped green pepper and enough garlic salt to purify the blood.

While I was fighting the king, breeze and current had pushed the boat in a northerly direction. I made a course correction expecting to see the dark outline of my shack against the lighter background of the beach, but now there was a light in my shack. Had I left a bulb on? No, I hadn't needed one. Someone had turned it on. Anita, I hoped.

But I was no stranger to ambush, so I cut the motor and drifted in darkness, aware of wavelets slapping the hull as wind and current turned the bow northward. Kneeling on the duckboard, I peered over the coaming and watched my shack for movement. Except for a one-shot shark bangstick in the forward cubby I had no weapon on the boat, never thinking I'd need one. But in the shack I had the hidden sawed-off, and a Beretta pistol taped under the sink. Its fifteen 9 mm cartridges were enough to resolve any dispute I might be involved in. But it was there, and I was two hundred yards away.

A figure crossed the window and it wasn't Anita. Taller, and male. A second figure appeared. The Guat bank reps? No, these guys were burly. What the hell were they doing? My radio and microwave were the only items worth taking plus whatever cash lay about. Maybe the Osprey punks were trashing my place, only how had they located it? Both were armed, I knew, so I'd be taking an unacceptable risk if I tried to interfere.

Occasionally, I'd see the brief scan of a flashlight inside, then nothing but the dim yellow glow of the incandescent bulb. I'd drifted so far that I could no longer make out the shack in the deepening darkness. Stars were visible but low clouds screened the rising moon. That meant they couldn't see my boat, and must be wondering where I was.

After another ten minutes drifting I started the motor, heading slowly and quietly seaward and south of where I estimated the shack to be. Current would take me some two hundred yards from the shack, and while I was drifting, I was watching.

Half an hour passed. The boat was north of the shack when I saw the light go out. Presently, I heard the faint creaking of weight on the stairway, muffled voices as the intruders left. I started the motor and headed in the shack's direction, keeping well offshore. If they were waiting on the beach they might hear the motor but they couldn't see the boat. My immediate goal was to get surreptitiously to the shack and arm myself. Then I could appraise the situation realistically.

Gradually, I steered the boat in the direction of the shack, and when I was as close as I thought advisable I cut the motor and dropped anchor. Then I stripped off shirt and sandals, and went overboard with my snorkel mask. To spare my shoulder I breaststroked shoreward, helped by the current until I reached the nearest piling. For a while I clung to it, getting my breath, and then I took the stairway on my belly like a snake. Reaching the deck, I lay flat and scanned the beach. No visible humans, though the men could be on the far side of the dune, watching the shack. On knees and elbows I crawled through the doorway and stayed low as far as the sink. Reaching up and around, I felt the pistol and pulled it free of the tape. A shell was already in the chamber, safety on. Holding it, I sat and looked around.

The sponge rubber mattress had been pulled from the bed frame and overturned. Canned supplies and rice containers were strewn across the floor. Staying low, I moved to the toilet and found the top off the water tank. All my clothing had been turned inside out and left in a clump. Everywhere I looked there was chaotic evidence of a thorough search. My sawed-off lay under the mattress, shells missing: so was the nearly full box of Remington Number Fours.

If the trashing were senseless vandalism I'd have been madder than I was, but there was a motive for this act of violence. The intruders were searching for something—what, I didn't know and couldn't imagine. But it occurred to me that I'd been lucky not to have been present when the searchers arrived. Empirically, I eliminated the Guat bank reps and the punk bikers. Burglars would have made off with my microwave, TV and cellular phone, my double-barrel shotgun, leaving . . . ?

The original owners of the boat I'd salvaged. They'd spotted it on my earlier run from Tavernier, and wanted the six keys it had held. Not finding the boat moored, they'd searched my shack for the missing coke.

An alternate theory had them not as the boat's owners but the boat's attackers and killers of the crew. They'd seen the shot-up Renegade founder, and hadn't stayed to watch it sink. Today, spotting the boat afloat and running must have made them wild with delight. From Tavernier my course was observable by any motorist on US 1, and they'd followed, checking every cove, creek and mooring until they saw the Renegade. By the time they returned after dark the boat was gone, so they tore my place apart on the chance I'd stashed the keys in a safe place.

They'd come back—I was sure of that—to search the boat. Probably not tonight, or tomorrow, but soon.

I didn't want to kill them, and I didn't want to get killed, but I had to protect myself.

And I had very little time to prepare.

For a while I tidied up the place, made the Beretta watertight with a condom, and entered the water the way I'd come. I swam slowly to where I'd anchored the boat and pulled myself over the stern transom. Hauling the anchor aboard was more strain than my shoulder was ready for, but finally the job was done and the boat drifted free.

In the water again I kick-pushed against the stern, moving the boat slowly toward the beach. I wanted to see if the searchers would come out of hiding, so after the prow struck sand I stayed out of sight, Beretta in hand, Waited ten minutes and decided they'd gone. So I used the motor to run the boat to the shack and went up the stairway. After a quick freshwater shower I took a spool of nylon line partway down the steps and tied a tripwire, played out the line as far as my bed. There I looped three cans of refried beans, set them on a nearby chair and tightened the line. Anyone coming up the stairway would trip the line and drag the cans onto the floor with enough noise to wake me.

After that I dried off and got onto the bed, pistol under my pillow. Sooner than I expected I was asleep.

When my phone rang I had no idea of the time, just a sense that it was late. Groggily I answered, heard labored breathing before the thin, barely recognizable voice of Anita.

"*Help me.*"

FOUR

I FELT as if I'd been drenched with icewater. Clenching the phone, I asked, "Where are you? The bungalow?"

"Yes."

"Call the office," I told her. "I'm on my way." After pulling on shorts, sandals and a shirt I went down the stairway, remembering to avoid the trip-wire. I ran the boat flat out until I figured I was opposite the Plaza Romana, beached the prow and took off across the highway. I ran all the way to her cottage, surprised there weren't people and a paramedic van outside, but there weren't even any lights outside, or inside.

The door was unlocked so I went quickly in, calling her name, found a wall switch and got some light. She wasn't in the living room or the kitchenette. I found her on the floor beside the bed, telephone by her outflung hand.

Bedding was smeared by blood where she'd dragged herself to the telephone. She was naked but for translucent pink panties, and her eyes were staring at the ceiling. Her partly open lips were frothed with blood, smeared droplets at the corners of her mouth. There were half a dozen stab wounds in her torso and the dullness of death in her eyes. I pressed the carotid artery knowing there would be no pulse, though her flesh was still warm, then bent over and kissed her lips. Throat tense with rage and sorrow, I flashed the office repeatedly until a sleepy voice answered. "There's been a death," I said hoarsely. "Get an ambulance, police."

"*Police?*"

"You heard me." I replaced the phone as I'd found it and looked around the room. No knife visible; her killer had taken it. I looked at my wristwatch, estimated twenty minutes since her call, probably a bit less. Bloodstains on the bedding. She'd been knifed there, left to die, but managed to get to the phone. Her dying effort.

Help me. Her last words. I'd never forget she called me, and tears welled in my eyes.

Hearing footsteps, I turned, saw a large, shambling man in the doorway. "Who're you?" I snapped.

"Manager. Who the hell are you?"

"The guy who found her. Ambulance on the way?"

"Yeah. Sheriff, too." He was staring at her near nudity. Salaciously, I thought, but the guy looked like a moron. He scratched beard stubble and eyed me. "You do it?"

I grunted. "Would I have called you? Stayed around?"

He shrugged. "Where's the knife?"

"Maybe the cops'll find it." I started past him but his bulk blocked me. "You're stayin', pal."

"Not because you say so." I pushed him aside and went to the living room, sat on the sofa and covered my face with my hands. Poor Anita, my mind kept saying. Poor, poor, little girl.

"Robbed?" the hulk asked.

"Who knows? I just got here, found her, phoned you. I haven't touched anything. Maybe you better come here and wait with me." I wanted him out of the bedroom, wanted his obscene stare away from her body. He squinted at me, said, "I better get back to the phones." Just then I heard sirens in the night. "On second thought," I muttered, "you better stay right here."

A car pulled up fast, braked hard, and in moments two green-uniformed Sheriff's Deputies came in. "Where's it at, Jake?" the corporal asked, and the manager gestured at the bedroom. The corporal walked in and his partner moved toward me. "You the husband?" he asked.

I shook my head. "An acquaintance."

"Boyfriend?"

"I said acquaintance. Period." I thought the manager might yield a few clarifying words but he stayed silent. So I explained her call had wakened me and I'd come as fast as I could.

"She called you, eh?"

"Right." I glanced at my watch. "Half an hour ago. Said *Help me*, and I came."

The corporal reappeared, went out to the car and used his radio. While he was talking an ambulance ground up and two paramedics hopped out. They went into the bedroom and in a few moments came back. "Dead, all right," one of them said, "and not long."

"Figures," the corporal said. "We'll establish a crime scene and then you boys get the body."

"Like always. Shit! Another hour an' I'da been off duty."

"Shit happens," my questioner remarked and looked at me. "ID?"

"When the time comes. In connection with the statement I'm prepared to make."

"Let's save time, make it now."

"Uh-uh. Now, I've declined to answer questions and by law you stop asking them."

His smooth young face flushed. "You some smartass lawyer?"

"That's another question, but I'll answer it: no. But I've been in law enforcement. A sworn officer."

"Ain't that nice?" he sneered. "Do I cuff you or do you come peaceable?"

"Peaceable," I replied, "and for the record, I didn't kill her; I found her."

"Yeah, we'll see about that." He winked at the manager, said, "Jake, you can go."

Half-dressed cottagers were crowding around the ambulance. The manager paused to answer a few questions, pointed at me, and broke away, shambling off to his office. Already I was getting bad notices and the day hadn't begun.

A crime scene van arrived with a photographer and two forensic technicians. One of them said, "ME's on the way."

"Shit, the chick's dead," the corporal muttered.

"Not until he says so." They carried their death bags into the bedroom and presently the camera began flashing.

Outside, the car radio squawked and the corporal went to take the call. When he came back he stood in front of me. "On your feet, bud, let's go."

The Monroe County Sheriff's Office was and is at Mile Marker 88 on the west side of US1. The deputies didn't cuff me, but they led me inside between them. The main room was brightly lighted by overhead fluorescents. There were chairs, a reception desk, and an unfriendly looking deputy behind it. He had thick, nicotine-stained fingers and a mouthful of uneven teeth. Leaning back in his swivel chair, he ignored me and spoke to the corporal. "This the perp, Rafe?"

"That's him."

"Mean lookin' bastid," the receptionist remarked. "Sex pervert-killer?"

Corporal Rafe's eyes widened. "Her tits wasn't cut off if that's what you mean."

"Partly. Just partly." He leaned forward and picked up a pencil. "Anyway, Murder One. Right?"

"Why not?" Corporal Rafe smirked at me. I smiled back.

"Whatever happened to presumption of innocence, or doesn't the Constitution extend this far down the Keys?"

"And why don't you just shut up?" the receptionist snapped. "You there, Jesse, shake him down."

"I can see laughs all around," I told them. "Me suing you guys and the county for invasion of privacy, unlawful search, false arrest, and whatever else my lawyer comes up with.'' I scanned each face in turn.

The receptionist licked his lips. ''That's bullshit, we got a right.''

''You have a right,'' I said, ''*if* there's probable cause. You ain't got it.''

Rafe blustered, ''You was at the scene with the body.''

''And called in Jake. If I were the perp would I do that when all I had to do was walk away—as the killer did?''

My logic seemed to stun them. Looking at Rafe, the desk deputy said, ''He do that?''

Rafe shrugged.

''Why'nt you say so?'' He shook his head disgustedly, then looked up at me. ''You willin' to cooperate?'

''I'll give a statement on the record. Steno and witnesses.''

The receptionist—I now saw sergeant's stripes on his sleeve—said, ''Rafe, see if you kin get Subelle outa bed and down here, before this gentleman changes his mind.'' To me he said, ''Coffee?''

''I could use it. Black.''

''Jesse, rustle up two cups, full and hot. Have a seat, Mister.''

Outside, the first grayness of dawn feathered the horizon. A heavy tractor-trailer thundered past, hauling supplies to Key West's sybarites. I thought of Anita and her youthful loveliness, tried not to think of her bloody corpse. I didn't want to remember her that way. And as I sipped coffee I mentally assembled what I would tell the local law. If they took my prints, a fax check with Washington would reveal my true name and DEA background; even in the Florida Keys I had enemies. Or especially in the Keys, where an unhealthy percentage of law enforcement gonzos had been jailed for narcotics trafficking. The murder of Colonel Chavez's daughter was going to attract international publicity and I didn't want my name or photo appearing along with hers. I was sure Claude Tessier had killed his wife, but they weren't going to hear his name from me. In prison Tessier had had plenty of time to plan his moves, and by now he was probably airborne for Mexico or the Bahamas where his money would be more than welcome.

So by the time Subelle arrived with her steno equipment I'd developed a tale that would endure long enough for me to evade my interrogators.

Subelle Lanahan was a sixtyish lady with frizzed, purple-tinted hair, lined face, the lips of a smallmouth bass, red fingernails and an expression of resentment over being rousted before her usual get-up time.

To the muffled clatter of her steno machine's keys I said my name was Joshua Nottingham. I'd come to the Keys two weeks ago for the fishing, and was staying at the Plaza Romana, where I'd met the dead woman at poolside. Her first name was Anita, no last name given, and she hadn't told me why she was there or where she was from. I hadn't seen her socializing with other guests, and assumed she'd called me because mine was the only name she knew.

"Anything else?" the sergeant asked.

"I got the impression she was a cautious young woman. Fearful, maybe."

"She say why?"

I shook my head, then said, "No," to Subelle. "Just an impression. Maybe the manager knows more."

"Yeah, we'll ask him. You got any ID, Mr. Nottingham?"

I got up, pulled my empty pockets inside out. "In my room," I said. "After Anita called I got into the nearest clothes—not thinking I'd need ID."

"I'll have Jesse stop by and check." He grimaced. "Appreciate your co-operation."

"Thanks for the coffee." I glanced at Subelle. "Whenever the transcription's ready I'll come by and sign it."

"Tomorrow afternoon," she grumbled. "After two."

"Good. I'll bring ID."

He nodded. "Jesse'll take you back to the motel."

So I walked out into early dawn, inhaled damp sea air and got into the deputy's green-and-white car. He drove me the five miles in silence, let me out by the office, and drove away.

The paramedic wagon was still there, surrounded by other vehicles and a large crowd of onlookers. I went into the office, realized I lacked Sprite money, and left.

Tide had receded, so I had to shove the Renegade back into water deep enough to start the motor without damaging the prop. As I steered back toward my shack I saw early fishing boats heading for the Stream, a few crabbers, and two shrimp trawlers. The same peaceful scene took place almost every day of the year. Sure, Florida had hurricanes, but California had earthquakes, and with hurricanes you could count on a few hours' warning.

As my shack came into sight I realized that I hadn't resolved the challenge of last night's searchers. Assuming they were coke dealers determined to regain six keys, I knew they'd be back again. Targets: the boat and me. I couldn't replace the cocaine, but I could simulate it.

I steered to the nearest marina, filled the tank with gas, paid for it, and got permission to leave the Renegade for a while. From there I walked to a Burger King for an egg-and-sausage breakfast, then to a nearby Publix supermarket, where I bought fourteen pounds of confectioners sugar, a roll of masking tape and a box of gallon-size Ziploc plastic bags.

I took the boat far enough offshore to avoid onlookers and filled each of six bags with about two pounds of powdery sugar, adding a little more here and there until they all looked equal. After dropping the sugar boxes overboard I sealed the bags and taped them in the stowage cubby where I'd found the real stash. I got rid of the tape roll and dropped the Ziploc box into the bait well before continuing to my shack.

I went up the stairway, avoiding the tripline, and made coffee, reflecting as I waited for water to boil that the only significant information I'd withheld from the deputies was Tessier's name and my hard suspicion of his guilt. I didn't want to appear knowledgeable of Anita's affairs, and so there was no immediate way to tie Tessier to her murder. Besides, when one marital partner is murdered cops look for the spouse, so Claude Tessier would be sought without me voicing suspicion. Low profile was what I wanted, and to get a feel for the present situation I tuned my radio to a news station and listened to the eight o'clock news. The segment ended without any mention of an Islamorada killing, but Anita was identifiable through her driver's license and motel registration, and by ten o'clock word would be on radio and press wire service. TV and print reporters would flock to the Plaza Romana for whatever tidbits were dropped by other guests, and Jake—the manager—would get his quarter-hour of TV fame.

At nine o'clock I phoned Manny Montijo's office and told him I wanted a meet. "Have to be here," he said, "the day's booked full."

"Then I'll make it easy for you. Have lunch with me."

"Sure, but what—?"

"The lady was murdered last night, undoubtedly by her husband."

"You serious?"

"I found her, Manny, and it was pretty gruesome. So I'd like a copy of the felon's file and a photo or two."

"Well . . ."

"Look, the guy's probably fled jurisdiction in violation of whatever arrangement Hornstein made to free him, so your office and the Marshal's will be involved very damn quick."

He thought it over before asking, "What do you want the rap sheet for? You taking it personally?"

"You could say that. I liked her, Manny, I'd even thought of a possible future for us—after her divorce."

"I see. Okay, I'll get what I can. Where'll we meet?"

"You know Smitty's—Second Avenue behind Braman Cadillac?"

"I know it. What time?"

"I have to take the bus, so let's point for noon, okay?"

"See you."

From my limited, now wrinkled wardrobe, I selected jeans and a light blue guayabera shirt to go with worn Nikes. Putting them on reminded me of Anita's morning runs, and the realization of her death sickened me.

I waited on the Overseas Highway until a Miami-bound bus stopped and took me aboard. The driver said his destination was the 4th Street terminal and I paid accordingly.

Tension, stress and lack of sleep hit me with a combination punch after I was seated, and within a few minutes I was sound asleep.

I woke briefly when the bus stopped at Florida City, then slept until the driver shook me awake in Miami at eleven twenty-five. From the terminal I took a taxi to the deli-style restaurant, ordered coffee and settled down to wait.

When Manny arrived he slid a manila envelope across the table. "I notified the US Marshal of Tessier's probable flight, didn't think you'd mind."

"Good move. Anything public yet?"

"Radio flash. She's been identified as Chavez's daughter, so reporters will be bugging her mother in Rome—if that's where she is. Or Rio. The sister's probably in Spain."

"Rita Castenada."

"Your memory was always reliable."

I ordered Salisbury steak with mushroom gravy, mashed potatoes and string beans. Manny ordered same, and looked around. "Haven't been here in a while, guess the food's still good."

In addition to wall booths there were tables and a counter, all of which were rapidly filling. "There's your answer," I said, "and the chicken noodle soup used to be out of this world."

The waitress brought us two chilled bottles of Beck's beer and dripping glasses. After pouring, Manny asked, "So, what happened last night, *amigo*?"

Leaving out the trashing of my shack, I related how I'd been awakened by Anita's dying call, found her body and become a suspect. "For a while I thought I was going to have to call you for bonafides."

He grunted. "That would have given them real probable cause. You know how popular our office is in the Keys."

"That's why I didn't call. Managed to lie my way out of it."

"Give your prints?"

I shook my head. "The Sheriff's office doesn't know my name or where I live. So far."

"Must have been some amateur interrogation," he said drily.

"I avoided that by giving a statement—not under oath."

My cup of noodle soup arrived and Manny ordered one for himself. Then he touched the envelope. "Planning to work Tessier yourself?"

"I have as good a chance of finding him as the Marshals—especially if he's out of this country. Will you run a travel check? Commercial airlines and aircraft charters; he might want to fly himself to destination without leaving traces."

"He's a pilot, why not?"

"If I locate him," I said, "you won't have to worry about extradition this time."

"Like that, huh?"

"Like that."

After eating his Salisbury steak Manny went to the corner pay phone and talked while I corraled the check. When he sat down he said, "Marshal's office checked with Saul Hornstein, who was outraged by the implication his client might have left US jurisdiction." Manny smiled. "Outraged."

"I can see it now. Bet Saul didn't offer to locate Claude and notify the Marshal."

"He didn't—being too overcome by the preposterous allegation. So a travel check is definitely in order. Hear anything, I'll call."

"Thanks." I tapped the envelope. "And for this."

"Read and destroy," he told me, and I promised I would.

Sitting in the back of the southbound bus, I absorbed the Tessier file. He was forty-one, a onetime Dominican Air Force pilot, who was known to fly drug loads from Bolivia and Colombia in addition to being the personal pilot of the late Guatemalan dictator. Never jailed until convicted of conspiracy to import narcotics into the US, Hornstein had gotten him out on appeal after posting bond of half a million dollars.

He'd married Anita Chavez a little over two years ago, but the file held nothing further on her.

There were three fuzzy surveillance photos of Tessier taken in Mexico City and Cancun. One with the Colonel, the others with flashy-looking broads in string bikinis lolling under the shade of palm-thatched *palapas*. I estimated his height at six feet, an estimate borne out by a jail mug shot. His skin was on the dark side, he wore long, curving sideburns and a small triangular goatee. His lips were fleshy and the nose prominent. Eyes deep-set, staring hostilely at the camera. Weight at prison check-in, one seventy-two. Under *Remarks* I learned that he usually went armed, displaying handguns to intimidate whoever disagreed with him. Personal fortune said to be substantial, but no estimate given.

Anita, I thought sadly, must really have had to hold her nose when marrying him, even though it was at her father's demand. Or because of that. She hadn't had much happiness in her life, I reflected, and even that possibility had been brutally terminated.

My own viability, I was beginning to realize, was uncertain. If the investigators were halfway competent they'd drive Anita's pink Jeep up and down the highway, stopping at stores, bars and restaurants until they found people who recognized the Jeep and remembered the driver.

Some of those people would be found at the Osprey Bar & Grill, and those very people would recall and describe the stranger who downed the eraserheads and made off with the lady who owned the pink Jeep.

To that, I thought, add my appearance at the motel office and ensuing conversation with the sour old clerk. Maybe he couldn't remember to button his fly, but he'd be damn sure to remember the sweaty, casually dressed Anglo who had him buzz the cottage of Mrs. Tessier yesterday afternoon.

Would he also remember her noonday visitor? I wondered. Two to one it was Hornstein; a thousand to one, Tessier.

The file noted a Guatemala City address for Tessier that I assumed was nonfunctional, and two addresses in Mexico: one in the capital's posh Lomas de Barrilaco colony, the other in the Pacific resort of Puerto Vallarta. Doubtless he owned other hideaways, not necessarily under his own name, or in Mexico. And before I ventured into Mexico I would have to have absolute assurance of Tessier's location; only then would it be worth the risk. Like the late Parra brothers of Colombia, and the equally late Luis Quintana Rios of Mexico, Tessier would live in heavily guarded quarters. And wherever he lived Tessier would pay for the benevolent protection of the police. I tore out his photos and Mexican addresses and folded them into my billfold; the remaining sheets I'd destroy as agreed.

After the bus let me off I entered the access road cautiously and made my way through trees, vines and undergrowth until I had a clear view of the beach and my shack. Nobody on the beach or in my boat. The shack? A brown pelican was perched on the porch railing, and he wouldn't be there if there was movement inside. So I felt secure enough to wade out to the stairway. The pelican heard me, spread his wings and flapped away.

I went directly to the Añejo bottle, uncapped and tilted it, and as dark rum touched my tongue I heard a muffled clicking inside the bottle. I shook it, heard the same sound, and held the bottle toward light. At the bottom there were what appeared to be clumps of sediment. I rinsed my mouth, then emptied the bottle into a shallow pan. Light sparkled from the foreign objects. I lifted one and stared at its deep green glow.

An emerald.

Like the other eight.

FIVE

$\mathbf{A}$FTER RINSING the emeralds I set them to dry on a paper napkin. Five were emerald-cut, three baguette, and the largest marquise. I believed that they were some, if not all, of the emeralds Colonel Oscar Chavez had bought in Mexico City shortly before his death. From him they had passed to the hands of Claude Tessier by fair means or foul, thence to his wife. Or directly from Chavez to his daughter, who planned to trade them for a divorce.

The emeralds hadn't contaminated the rum, so I began pouring it back into the Añejo bottle. As I did, something rose from the bottom and settled back. I emptied the bottle and saw an oblong piece of paper with writing. No way to extract it, so I broke the bottle and picked up a laminated card. On both sides there was writing and eight-digit numbers. The writing abbreviated city names: Gen., Ber. and Zur.: Geneva, Bern and Zurich. The numbers, I reasoned, indicated bank accounts in those cities, seven in all.

I blotted the card dry and stared at it, realizing a key element was lacking: bank names. And I remembered waking that night and finding Anita walking around. She had been looking for a place for secure concealment and decided on the bottle.

Knowing my fondness for Añejo, she knew that eventually I'd notice card and emeralds, but at the time she expected to return and claim them, with or without my knowledge. Her purpose: keep them from her husband.

How much was the emerald hoard worth? A stone of average quality might go for as little as two thousand a carat and I estimated these as between eight and possibly twelve carats apiece. Of course, an emerald of the purest gem quality would be worth much more than an average stone—as much as a buyer was willing to pay. If the aggregate weighed a hundred carats I was looking at a minimum of two hundred thousand dollars in cut emeralds. But if their quality was especially fine they could bring four hundred thousand dollars, or more.

To me, that was a great deal of money, but in the world of narcotics barons and Latin dictators it was taco-and-tequila money. Or what a favorite whore might be tipped for a night's energetic entertainment.

So it was not for nine emeralds that Anita had been murdered, but for the Swiss bank accounts totaling hundreds of millions of dollars. Looted from the Guatemalan treasury, diverted from American aid programs, extorted in narcotics deals. Dirty money all.

Anita hadn't kept the bank list from her killer so she could keep the fortune for herself, but because telling where she'd hidden the list would have brought me lethal danger.

Or before the stabbing began Anita might have said she'd entrusted a package to me for safekeeping but didn't know what I'd done with it. That would account for the thorough search of my premises, and why my few possessions hadn't been stolen. The men were after much, much more. And if they believed I possessed list and emeralds they'd be back; this time to torture and kill me.

My impulse was to turn everything over to the repo men from Guatemala and get out, but there were two obstacles. I didn't know their names or where to find them. And until I saw authentic ID, I couldn't be sure they were legitimate. They could be treasure hunters; the Keys were full of them.

The facts, such as they were, plus my speculation added up to Anita's protecting my life at the cost of her own. Now I was less persuaded that Claude Tessier had murdered her, though he was ultimately responsible, having ordered it done.

It was now late afternoon, about two hours before sundown. If the killers were coming back it would be tonight. Until I had it out with them I'd live in fear, and I hadn't come to the Keys for that. First priority was to hide list and stones, then arm myself. I went down to the boat and retrieved the box of plastic bags from the baitwell, took it back and double-bagged emeralds and list. Then I dropped the sealed bag in the baitwell where it sank amid two dozen swimming pilchards and goggle-eyes. If I'd had a pair of water moccasins I'd have added the snakes to the baitwell. Where were poisonous snakes when you wanted them?

I ran the boat to the marina store and bought a box of 12-gauge Number Four shotgun shells, a six-pack of Coors and a frozen dinner. With all my problems I didn't want to add meal preparation.

Back at the shack I loaded my sawed-off and cocked both barrels, jacked a ready shell into the Beretta chamber, and stuck the pistol in my belt. Then I opened a can of Coors and sat on the balcony watching waves form at the reef line as the tide came in.

Just before darkness I microwaved veal parmigiana and spaghetti, ate inside from where I could watch the beach, and brooded over how tragically my brief affair with Anita had ended. By now the deputies must have learned no Joshua Nottingham had a room at the Plaza Romana, and must be plenty pissed off they hadn't taken my prints. The fact that I'd given a false name and address put me high on their list of suspects, so they'd be looking for me, full-court press.

If I survived the night I ought to locate another refuge, having worn out my welcome in the Keys. Well, I'd enjoyed some peaceful weeks, my shoulder had improved considerably, and in the Navy phrase I was combat-fit again.

As I looked around, I reflected that the isolated setting had been right for me weeks ago. Now, everything in the shack would be a constant reminder of Anita and that was too hard to take.

An evening news broadcast featured the murder of Colonel Chavez's daughter in an Islamorada cottage, where she'd been waiting the release of her husband, Claude Tessier. Attempts to contact Tessier had been unavailing; his whereabouts were unknown.

Surprise, surprise, I thought, and listened to a boilerplate summary of Chavez's dictatorship and his many crimes. From Rome his widow had no comment on her daughter's death, though an older sister, Rita Castenada, had fainted on being informed. It was not known where the murdered woman would be buried, or whether her survivors would attend the ceremony. Tessier's attorney, the well-known, highly paid criminal defense lawyer, Saul Hornstein, regretted the death of Tessier's wife but could shed no light on the circumstances. He declined to say if he knew Tessier's location, citing lawyer-client privilege.

Yeah, I grunted, and turned the radio to a Latin station featuring Afro-Cuban music. Then I dialed Information for Hornstein's office number and placed the call. As expected, the answering machine came on and a female voice invited callers to leave a message which would be answered during next day's business hours. At the tone I turned up radio volume, and over the beat of bongos and maracas I said breathily, "Saul, I'm a reporter and an admirer of yours so I want you to know there's a nasty rumor you're hiding Claude Tessier from the police. Before that goes public you better produce Tessier and let him answer questions about the murder of his wife. I'd like to leave my name, but can't trust it to a machine. You're a great lawyer."

That done, I opened another Coors and sipped while shadows lengthened across the beach. Maybe Saul would rise to the bait, maybe not. The anonymous message would trouble him and he'd be wondering if in his own interest he ought to get ahead of the curve and produce Tessier. As a lawyer of the predatory kind Hornstein would be trying to analyze the caller's motive. Why would someone, allegedly a reporter, phone him a friendly tip? He never crossed the street without being paid, why should anyone else? Hornstein had lived too long amid the mire of criminality to believe in the fundamental goodness of humankind; that was a lot of *dreck*.

Well, I thought, figure it out, Saul. And how do you like taking a chuck from your blind side?

As I sipped beer I remembered a week in the village of Coatzacoalcos on the Tehuantepec Peninsula. I was supposed to check on a cargo of hash an informant said was to be shipped out of the small port. The guest house had two rooms, both smelling of mold; the bed held a thin straw mattress badly infested with insects, large and small. Available food was tortillas, tacos and guacamole; small, hard oranges, papaya, rice and beans. Fortunately, there was beer and tequila as everywhere in Mexico, so I passed the first two days wandering around the docks, drinking Tres Equis and staying out of the sun. The third day I hired a small boat whose captain took me a few hundred yards into the river mouth, where I could see tarpon rolling. *Balao* bait wouldn't tempt them, not feather lures or jumbo frogs. Then, disgustedly, I dropped a naked, stainless-steel hook in the water and raised a hundred-pound Silver King. Repeated, and raised another and another, fished until back and arms were too tired for more. The rest of my time there I fished close enough to the port to watch boats coming and going, but none was large enough or sufficiently seaworthy to make the cross-Gulf run to the Keys.

Point being, I ruminated, you never know what kind of bait will work until you try. And sometimes the most unlikely bait will hook a victim.

The phone's ring interrupted my reflections. I got it from under the bed and heard Manny Montijo. "Travel lists negative, likewise private air charters."

"Hmmm. Could be using another name."

"The Marshals are looking, but he's not officially a fugitive. Could still be here."

I paused before asking, "Was that half-million-dollar bond in cash or securities?"

"I'll find out. Why?"

"Because the bondsman will either try to keep him from skipping, or bring him back if he goes."

Manny chuckled. "Midnight extraditions are out of favor. Remember that bigtime Miami embezzler who took off for Canada with his loot? The bonding company sent two strongarms after him. They brought him back and the embezzler sued the strongarms for kidnapping and civil rights violations."

"I remember—he won."

"And the strongarms did time. Crazy world, *amigo*. How you doin'?"

"Okay." I looked around the nearly-dark interior. "I'm thinking of moving on before the Sheriff catches up with me."

"Sound idea. Let me know."

"Will do."

As I replaced the cellular phone an idea occurred to me, so I gathered all my clothing and bundled it under the sheet, placed a skillet, blackened side up, on the pillow. It was an old device, but in a darkened room the simulation might draw fire and expose the shooter.

I couldn't see the beach, just the shoreline marked by scatters of light foam. Any time now, I thought, and took a chair to the far corner on the shack's entrance side. Before I sat down I unscrewed the overhead lightbulb. Earlier, I'd dismantled the tripline because I didn't want intruders alerted. Now I watched the doorway and remembered how Anita had stood there poised as a water nymph, naked and unashamed. I drew the pistol from my belt and laid it on my thighs. I owed her my life, the greatest debt man can owe. I couldn't bring her back but I could try to avenge her murder.

There was no moon, and the darkness seemed impenetrable. It seemed to symbolize my ignorance concerning the Chavez family. When all four were alive had they been close, caring? Colonel Oscar a good father? What was Marie the mother like? Rita, the older sister who went her own way? Compulsive roundheels, or fit wife for an aristocratic jejune Spaniard? Knowing details of Chavez family interaction would help me understand how Anita had fitted—or not fitted—in. But for all her beauty and presumed wealth she had been a lonely young woman, and I realized that her inner need was one factor that had drawn me to her.

I heard a car engine slow as it pulled off the highway, slow to a crawl as it entered the access road. Then the engine died. The killers—or a couple parking for a front-seat quickie? The road was convenient for clandestine love-making—I'd seen used condoms in the sand—but I hoped the killers had arrived. A parked car with a copulating couple would keep others away until the road was clear.

Even though my eyes were well adjusted to darkness I could see nothing on the beach. Presently, clouds freed the moon and I glimpsed the glint of glass atop the dune. Binoculars were trained on the shack; they were scoping before advancing. Even though the interior was unlighted the moored boat told them I was probably inside.

They waited until clouds again blotted the moon, then came quickly across the beach. At water's edge the two men paused long enough to pull off shoes and roll up trouser legs. They waded in, side by side, right arms erect, MAC-10 machine pistols pointing skyward.

Earlier I'd thought of letting them come in and shoot up my bed before firing back, but for some reason I hadn't anticipated automatic weapons— probably because I hadn't any. That changed the equation and I had to take them sooner than planned. There was nothing chivalric in what I was about to do, no Wild West bullshit giving first shot to the black hats. They had too much firepower.

Besides, I reflected as they neared the stairway, they'd given Anita no chance to live. They'd tortured, questioned and butchered a terrified, helpless woman, and for that they were going to die.

Crouched over, I moved to the doorway and lay flat on the flooring, sawed-off in hand. I poked the muzzle toward the stairway, lifted my gaze and waited until I saw the first man on the rise. Waiting that second eliminated any chance the men were deputies, and they were not.

So when I saw head and shoulders I fired the right barrel and as the man screamed and dropped back I rose to my knees and gave his partner the second barrel. The impact knocked him backward into the water, but his trigger finger closed reflexively, sending a long wavering burst toward the shack and me. I pulled out my pistol and looked down at my visitors. The nearest one was crumpled on the stairway, most of his head blown away by the tight pattern of Number Fours. His *compadre* had one arm on the lowest step, the rest of him floated face-down in the water. I kicked the nearest man for signs of life, intending a *coup de grace* shot if he wasn't dead, but my first barrel had finished him. Now I had two corpses and a disposal problem. Their car I could take care of later, removal was Job One.

In turn I collected their billfolds, car keys and MAC-10s, and put them in my boat. With nylon mooring line I tied slipknots around an ankle of each man—both were in the water—and towing two corpses astern, I headed the boat seaward. Looking aft, I saw their bodies turning and tumbling, raising plumes of spray, so I throttled down and the plumes disappeared. Three miles offshore I tossed their weapons overboard, undid ankle knots and watched the bodies float free before sinking from the weight of waterlogged clothing. Soon they'd be below, down where the morays dwelt, down among crabs and scavengers four hundred feet deep.

"Anita," I said to the sea wind, "I pray you rest in peace." Then I shoved the throttle ahead and raced back to the shack.

While stairway blood was still wet I sloshed seawater on the steps and waded to the beach. I collected two pairs of fancy snakeskin semi-boots and carried them to the parked car, a brown, rental Pontiac sedan. I opened the trunk and hoisted my bike into it, closing the lid. The engine started first try and I backed onto the highway. Driving north toward Windley Key, I stopped at a wayside picnic area long enough to toss the boots into a trash bin, and then drove on. When I spotted a pulloff for fishermen I turned into it and parked the car at the far end. After opening the trunk for my bike, I closed it and wiped my prints away. Did the same with the steering wheel and door handle. I left the keys in the ignition, kneed the door shut, got on my bike and rode away.

My blood was surcharged with adrenalin but fast pedaling was metabolizing it. Half an hour later when I reached my shack I was downside, my system drained of energy.

I poured Añejo from pan to glass and drank deeply. Even though alcohol is a depressant I needed a jolt, badly. Overhead light restored, I remade my bed and opened the visitors' wallets. One was soaked—it came from the second man I'd blasted—but the other was dry and undamaged by pellets. I spread the wet contents on absorbent napkins, and while they were drying I went through the first killer's documentation.

His driver's license gave the name of Juan Cantú Santos, and the photo of a face I'd barely glimpsed before it vanished in the shotgun flare. Age thirty-six, born Camaguey, Cuba. Height five-eight, weight one hundred sixty-two—though he'd seemed heavier in death. There were six credit and charge cards, all issued to different names and obviously stolen; rent receipt for an apartment in Northwest Dade, two hundred-dollar bills, and a scrap of paper with the name Claude and a telephone number.

That called for another *trago*, and the Añejo was cool velvet to my tongue.

The second thug's name was Arnoldo Pobrezo Leon of Reynosa, Mexico, age thirty-two. He was slightly richer than his late partner; his wallet produced three hundred-dollar bills, a ten, two singles. In addition, there was a massage parlor card with "Melinda" scrawled across it, and a piece of folded notepaper with Plaza Romana in block letters. That was confirmation I'd been looking for, erasing any doubt that Pobrezo and Cantú had murdered Anita. The prize, of course, was the telephone number linked to Claude, the missing husband.

In case a follow-up team came looking, I re-set the stairway trip line, and loaded my sawed-off, placing it beside my pillow. My hands were trembling from stress and fatigue, so I got on the bed and while I was wondering what to do with the emeralds and bank account list I fell asleep.

Bright sunshine streamed across the floor. I made coffee and swam around the shack to loosen tight muscles before setting my mind to immediate problems. I ought to pack my gear, close down the shack and run the boat to Miami or Key Biscayne, beyond reach of the Monroe County Sheriff. By now, I assumed the brown Pontiac had been noticed by the Highway patrol and a check made with the rental company. That could lead to one of the two killers, unless the car had been stolen, a high probability. I wanted to get my new information to Manny Montijo, but when I phoned, his secretary said he was away and not due back until afternoon.

Midday radio news reported that two members of a Jacksonville motorcycle gang had been detained in connection with the murder of Mrs. Anita Tessier. Names not given. The two men had been seen harassing Mrs. Tessier in an Islamorada bar shortly before her death. Further details when available.

I didn't mind the bikers being hassled by the law—given their aggressive lifestyle they had to be guilty of something—but they hadn't killed Anita. There was insufficient evidence to hold them for more than a couple of days, unless 'ludes or pot seeds had been found in their pockets. But even a novice public defender could quash a possession charge by asserting police search lacked probable cause. So the eraserheads would have a couple days' free jailhouse lodging, then be released with a warning to leave the Keys.

Except for Key West, the Keys were Bubba Redneck country, and although I wasn't crazy about socializing with swamp-buggy, deer-jacking Good Ol' Boys, we had a common dislike of unruly outlanders. Especially the ones with loud hawg bikes, black leather jackets and pink-dyed Mohawks. So the prevailing cultural attitudes were okay with me.

Except for currency and the two driving licenses, I burned the killers' wallets and documents in my charcoal grill pan. While doing it I noticed a state Marine Patrol boat idling in my direction. Normally, they checked for fishing licenses, size of catch, illegal lobsters and so on. But officers had a right to examine my baitwell, so I went down to the Renegade and fished out the jewel bag I'd cached there. As the patrol boat neared, I waved from the balcony and got a wave in return. Inside, I put the bag in my microwave oven, broke out a Coors and drank on the balcony while the patrol boat burbled closer. The wheelman looked young enough to be a Sea Scout; his partner was a grizzled old hand, face and eyes like a Chief Bos'n's mate. He lifted the loud hailer and bellowed, "'Mornin'. Haven't seen you before."

I cupped my hands and called back, "Haven't seen you, either. Looking for something?"

"Nothin' special. Catchin' much?"

"Grunts, grouper."

He nodded. "Mind if we check your baitwell?"

"Help yourself." They'd be looking for illegal snook, stone crabs, undersize lobsters; eyeing the Johnson for polluting leaks, maybe checking my CG registry number with the Miami base.

The wheelman maneuvered their much larger boat alongside the Renegade's stern. The Bos'n lifted the baitwell cover and looked inside, then replaced it. He tapped the outboard and looked up at me. "Lotta power for a twenty-footer."

"Sure helps against a running sea."

"That it would." He nodded at the wheelman who, I saw to my surprise, wasn't a beardless youth but a young woman, whose blue cap, short hair and flat chest had fooled me. Agewise, they could be father and daughter. "Coffee?" I asked.

"Thanks, got some. Well, have a good day."

"I'll try." The boat backed off and moved lazily seaward. They hadn't checked the boat's registry, possibly because the base computer was down, as often happened. I was prepared to deny ownership if it came to that, because the six bagged kilos still taped inside the cubby made a statement all their own.

But now that I knew the now-dead searchers hadn't come for the coke there was no reason to keep the bagged sugar in place. So when the Marine Patrol boat was well offshore and turning south I removed the bags and sweetened the water around the boat.

Phoned Manny again and got the same reply. Rats! When I was an agent there hadn't been anyone in the Miami office I could trust; now there wasn't anyone I knew.

Was Saul Hornstein reacting to my provocation? Even if he didn't share a press conference with the US Marshal to disavow Claude Tessier, his overweening self-confidence might be diminished, to the eventual benefit of the criminal justice system.

Radio news had nothing about Hornstein, but the mother of Anita Tessier had arrived from Europe to claim the murdered woman's body. Mrs. Marie Chavez, widow of the late Guatemalan dictator, Oscar Chavez, said that services would be private.

So private, I mused, that even the widowed husband wasn't likely to show but maybe Hornstein would fill in. Last year, I recalled, he'd gone through an expensive divorce, and being of an age with *Señora* Chavez might turn to her for companionship. Saul would estimate her fortune, weigh pros and cons, and reach a beneficial decision. He was that kind of guy.

I poked around the fridge, slapped together a bologna and catsup sandwich, and ate irritably because Manny wasn't warming his desk when he should have been.

Was Anita's sister, Rita, coming for the funeral? I wondered. I wanted to attend, felt obligated, but I was sure a county deputy or two would be on hand to eyeball mourners. Plus journalists of all descriptions digging for dirt.

And, of course, the two Guat bank reps, Pockmarks and Scarface, would be there to hassle the Chavez ladies, perhaps serve them subpoenas. Then I wondered why a Florida court would issue subpoenas, unless the USA was suddenly in the international bill-collecting business. The Marcoses' legal difficulties flashed into my mind but I couldn't parse similarities and didn't try.

What I did was call Manny again and this time he answered. "I've been choppering," he told me, "west Everglades. Took an arrest team on information about a drug processing camp."

"Any action?"

He sighed. "It was one of those exile paramilitary training camps for weekend warriors. Sleeping sheds and hammocks, a cookstove, target ranges and empty armory. No drugs, no would-be warriors, just a world-class supply of mosquitoes."

"Cuban exile camp?"

"Who knows? Haitian, maybe; Salvadoran. Nothing of DEA interest."

"So you'll downgrade the informant."

"Kick his butt, more likely. You called earlier?"

"I did. With a likely lead to Tessier." I gave him the phone number retrieved from Pobrezo's wallet, and Manny asked, "What am I supposed to do
with it?"

"Pass it along, dummy—FBI or your Marshal pal."

"Care to source it?"

"Nope. Make one up."

For a while the phone was silent. Finally, Manny said, "You're really getting into this, aren't you? Big mistake, Jack."

"Hell, I'm only nibbling around the fringes."

"Why? What's in it for you?"

"Satisfaction. Seeing Claude nailed for murder conspiracy."

"Conspiracy? I thought—"

"Two hirelings did it, Manny. But the sonofabitch ordered it done."

"You sure?"

"Dead sure."

A longer pause. "Jack, I'm dog-tired, mosquito-bitten, and a lot less than
happy with the agent who promoted the morning's search-and-destroy mission
in the forest primeval. Can you understand that?"

"I can. Felt that way myself times past."

"Good. So you won't take it amiss if I conclude this stimulating dialogue
and sack out the rest of the day."

"*Ándale, pues,*" I told him, and we disconnected.

I didn't think he'd do it but if he did, Manny would charge it to Comp Time
or annual leave. He was meticulous about expense accounts and logging time
off. He was a senior supervisor, not an office chief, though with Minority
Preference Manny was going to be. He hated quotas and affirmative action,
knowing that a lot of DEA agents joked how *Cucarachas* couldn't make it
without special help. Only they weren't joking.

DEA didn't hire from the Ivy League. It drew small-town policemen and
sheriff's deputies, INS agents and Army MPs; almost anyone who was physically fit and spoke fluent Spanish. Pay and benefits were attractive, and if an
agent kept his nose clean for twenty years he could retire. Now and then, of
course, an agent opted for early retirement; taking two or three hundred thou
to look the other way. Some got away with it, but most were caught because
the briber fingered them.

While reflecting on my former employer my mind had reached a parallel
decision: leave Islamorada and relocate in the Coral Gables townhouse Melody
and I had shared. My car was there along with personal weapons and most of
my clothing. I'd take the bus to Miami and drive back to clear out the stilt
shack, ending this phase of my life.

*   *   *

From the bus station I taxied to Granada Boulevard and found the door key where we stashed it among the roots of a bougainvillea. Inside, I turned on the air conditioning to vent the musty smell, collected mail and dumped it on the dining room table for later examination. There was cold beer in the refrigerator and a small assortment of frozen meals in the freezer.

The bedroom looked the same, though the bed was stripped. The ceiling mirror that Melody had ordered in an antic moment reflected me as I moved around the room, forcing me to recall carnal episodes of the past. What had been Melody's closet was empty, not even discarded panty hose in the corner, so it was obvious that she'd moved out and left me the premises. Along with our buy-option lease that still had several months to run. So be it, I thought, and got car keys from my bureau drawer.

Under garage lights the pearl-gray Miata showed a light covering of dust, and although I turned the ignition key apprehensively the engine caught on first try; the battery hadn't drained.

So I backed out my car, closed the garage door and returned to the house. From the concealed floor safe I took out ten hundred-dollar bills, and changed the combination before closing the lid again. Melody didn't need money—far from it—but the way her mind worked she might decide to take mine as a final way of screwing up my life. Besides, I intended to stash Anita's emeralds and bank list there pending final disposition, and I didn't want anyone getting them prematurely.

I turned on kitchen and bedroom lights and checked under the bed for my MAC-10 pistol and H&K .38 automatic. Both were loaded, ready-round in each chamber. I replaced them and left the house, locking the door. Then, on impulse, I went back in and dialed Manny's number. Somewhat to my surprise he was there, hadn't taken time off, so I told him I was moving back to Coral Gables in case he wanted to reach me.

"I do," he said, "because that phone number you gave me didn't amount to much."

"Why not?"

"It's a public phone in a rest area on the Tamiami Trail. Ochopee, to be exact."

"Never heard of it."

"Who has? The village is way west of here, near the Big Cypress Preserve."

When I said nothing, he went on. "I was over that way this morning looking for the drug layout that turned out to be a paramilitary training camp."

"Yeah," I said, "we both struck out. Well, better luck next time. Any word on Tessier?"

"Only that he's about to be declared a fugitive. Saul Hornstein has another day or so to produce him before that big bond is forfeit." He paused. "Incidentally, Hornstein went to the Marshal and swore he wasn't hiding Tessier, didn't know his whereabouts. Strange, eh?"

"Covering his you-know-what," I remarked. So my anonymous call had made Hornstein edgy and uncertain, to the eventual benefit of law enforcement I hoped.

"Sure you got that phone number right?"

"I got it right, and just because it's a back country pay phone doesn't mean Tessier didn't use it." Tessier and his hitman, Pobrezo.

"So?"

"Oh, nothing. But if there was manpower I'd tap the phone and surveil the phone booth."

"Dream on," he said tiredly, then, "Any sign of Melody?"

"Negative. Cleared out." I didn't want to talk about it. "Like I'm clearing out of the shack." A thought occurred. "I've got a fishing boat there. You can have it on permanent loan."

"Fishing?" He laughed hollowly. "No time, *amigo*, thanks just the same."

I'd tried, but I was still stuck with it. Manny said, "By the way, there was a memorial service for the lady this afternoon. St. Martha's."

"Press coverage?"

"Photographers tried, but relatives came and went by a rear entrance. Hornstein's limousine whisked them away."

"Mother and sister," I said musingly, "the husband being conspicuous by his absence."

"So it was remarked. Well . . ."

"We'll lunch again," I promised, "soon's I figure out what to do with the rest of my life."

"See you." He broke the connection.

I locked up the house again, got into the Miata and gassed it near the University. Then I headed down US I toward the Keys. Thirty minutes later I took the Card Sound Road cutoff to avoid the main highway's killer traffic. it took a little longer to reach Key Largo, but the road cut through glades and jungle and was pretty scenic until it joined again with dive and souvenir shops, charter marinas, restaurants, seafood markets, tackle shops and convenience stores, legacies of unzoned, unrestricted building.

It was close to dusk when I reached my turnoff, and I drove the Miata nearly to the dune, locked and left it there.

The stilt shack looked the same—unoccupied—and the boat was bobbing below it. I waded out and went inside, treating myself to a cold beer while the sun nudged the rim of the sea.

Anita's treasure was still in the microwave. Disposing of it could wait until I was settled in at the townhouse. I cracked another beer and went to the balcony, reflecting that Hornstein was elbowing into the Chavez family, what remained of it. By the time Tessier surfaced—if ever—there'd be no place at the table for him.

For a time my thoughts drifted from Anita to the killers I'd killed, the Chavez emeralds and bank accounts, and the aimlessness of my own life. I didn't want a nine-to-five job and didn't need one—I had enough funds to cover the next several years—but without goals and purpose I could see myself hanging around bars and going alcoholic. I didn't want that, no way.

Alternatively, I could travel, become a cruise junkie or settle in Spain or southern France, try that lifestyle for a while. I didn't miss Melody as much as I once had, but she'd left a void in my life that Anita briefly filled. I'd never know how things would have gone between us, no sense in speculating on what might have been. Instead, I could focus on putting Tessier out of business, permanently, and seeing Anita's fortune in hands where it would do the most good. I had little faith that the present Guat government was the optimum recipient, for funds entering at the top seldom trickled down. A phenomenon not limited to Guatemala.

The ocean was calm, seabirds skittering across the surface, pelicans solemnly gliding against the sunset in a postcard setting. It was getting too late to drive back to Coral Gables tonight. I didn't want the stress and risk of US I after dark, so I took a vote and decided to stay one last night in the shack, move out in the morning. I skipped dinner, drank a lot of Añejo, and tottered into bed, where I slapped mosquitoes and fought damp sheets until unconsciousness took over.

In the morning I fried bacon, bread and potatoes and added part of a dolphin filet to the hot fat. I laced coffee with Añejo, and ate and drank with considerable contentment. After cleaning up I gathered my clothing, unplugged the microwave and stowed surplus food in a carton for transfer. Weapons I wrapped in a pillowcase and decided to do something about the boat. I could attend to it another day, or now, eliminating another trip from Coral Gables. Shirtless, I made the five-minute run to the marina and after negotiating with the dockmaster brought him back to the shack. I paid a month's advance dock rental and watched him vanish behind a tall plume of spray. I hoped the sonofabitch wouldn't rent out the boat or let my fishing gear get stolen, but life was chancey in the Keys and there were a lot of avaricious people around looking for an easy buck and not caring much how they found it.

So I went up the stairway, packed my radio and cellular phone, and turned to pick up the carton of food.

A shadow streaked across the floor and I looked quickly at the doorway. It was blocked by a figure in white linen slacks and bush jacket. Hands on hips, she took a short step toward me and halted. "So," she said huskily, "you're the rotten bastard who killed my sister."

SIX

SLOWLY, I set down what I was carrying, squared my shoulders, and said, "Come in, Mrs. Castenada, and we'll talk things over."

After a moment's hesitation she took a full step in my direction, halted again, and lowered her hands. "I'm not alone," she warned me, "I have protection. So don't think you can harm me too." There were four rings on her fingers, three large and glinting with encrusted gems. The fourth was a slim wedding band, platinum like the others. Her left wrist was circled with a narrow diamond bracelet, and a small diamond crucifix showed through the open collar of her jacket.

I moved to the window and saw two uniformed rental cops on the beach staring at the shack. "Wise precaution," I remarked, "for anyone with your confrontational style." From the pillowcase I pulled out the sawed-off and placed it on the table. "Now," I told her, "sit down and we'll talk."

Staring at the shotgun as though it were a venomous snake, she lowered herself into the chair farthest from it. I asked, "What gives you the idea I murdered Anita?"

She licked full lips that were lipsticked blood red. Her face was oval like her sister's, her slightly Oriental eyes were set above high cheekbones, and her nose had the same streamlined contour as Anita's. Her bust was fuller and her hips somewhat broader, and I judged her figure to be a size or two larger than her sister's. Dark, almost black, hair was drawn tightly back from her forehead into a French braid that trailed partway down her back. It added an exotic touch to a strikingly beautiful woman. Her lips parted. "Anita called me the night before her death, and told me about you."

"Saying I was going to torture and kill her?"

"Of course not," she said irritably. "Said she'd met the first decent, attractive man she'd encountered in a long time. Described you flatteringly but said there was an air of mystery about you. Thought you might be a fugitive." She glanced around the room. "Holed up in this isolated place."

"All right," I said, "you have nothing to fear from me. Nothing. I was halfway in love with your sister. If she hadn't been killed it might have gone all the way. She told me she was meeting her husband and when I didn't hear from her I got worried. Worry took me to her bungalow and I found her already dead." I got up and poured Añejo into two glasses, shoved one across the table and downed the other. "I read that the Sheriff brought in a couple of suspects. Bikers."

"And let them go this morning—no evidence." She picked up the glass, frowned at it and sipped. "What else do you know?"

"The two men who killed your sister are dead."

Her eyes widened. "How can you be sure of that?"

I shrugged. "Don't ask, Rita, leave it at that." I poured another shot of Añejo and stared at it.

"Why did they kill my sister?"

"They were paid to."

"Paid . . . ?" Her forehead wrinkled. "Who paid them? Why?"

"Ask Tessier—if you can find him." I kicked back the rum. "If you and Anita were in touch, then you must know she planned to divorce him."

"Well—yes," she said reluctantly. "She did tell me that."

"Look, I don't know the ins and outs of your family relationships but Anita said hers was an arranged marriage. To protect your father *and* Claude Tessier."

After a moment she nodded. "There was no love there, you're right. But to have her savagely murdered . . . ?"

"Ever since she was killed I've wondered why. And it comes down to Tessier wanting her to do something she refused to do—like not divorce him. Or she had something her husband wanted, and wouldn't give to him." I knew more than that but I wanted her reaction. "Maybe keeping something for him while he was in prison." I watched her eyes. "Is that possible?"

Her face was expressionless. "Claude is a violent man, but I find it hard to believe he would kill his wife, or have her killed."

"Believe what you want," I said indifferently. "I'm comfortable with what I had to do, and what happens to Tessier is out of my hands." I eyed her as she sipped from her glass. "Did Saul Hornstein say where Claude is hiding?"

"Hornstein?" She stared at me. "What do you know about him?"

"A lot," I told her, "including the fact that he represents Tessier, or did. Saul's too crafty to let himself be dragged down by a client. He'll be wanting to get close to you and your mother, so be very, very careful dealing with him. To Saul, money is an irresistible magnet, and the world believes your father got away with more money than the Marcoses."

"Rubbish," she sniffed. "Anyway, I don't need a lawyer."

I grunted. "You might. If the Guat Consulate lays subpoenas on you and your mother."

She sat forward. "I never thought of that. How do you—?"

"Two repo men from the National Bank visited me. They had questions I couldn't answer, but they're around. Scarface and Pockmarks. They didn't confide their names."

After a few moments she said, "You seem to know a great deal about—everything."

"I'm a listener," I told her. "I listened to Anita, I watch TV, and I read the papers. Those are my sources. There's nothing you can do around here, so my advice is to fly back to Spain before the Guats ask Immigration to prevent you. And your mother."

"They could do that?" She seemed shocked by the idea.

"They could. There's not much sympathy for the Chavez family."

"No," she said, "I guess not." She looked at what I'd packed, and asked, "Leaving?"

"My lease expired," I told her, "so I'm moving back to the mainland."

"Which is—where?"

"Coral Gables, honey." I was tiring of this aloof, wealthy bimbo, and wanted her on her way. Standing, I asked, "Anything else, *Señora*?" She looked up at me. "I'll pay you."

"For what? Killing Tessier?"

She shrugged. "If it comes to that, maybe. But I mean, look out for me while I'm in America, protect me."

"I didn't protect Anita," I said harshly, "so I guess the Chavez family is beyond my competence. Try elsewhere. Sorry."

Pink patches appeared on her cheeks. She wasn't used to turndowns. "You said you cared for Anita. Won't you help me?"

"Please understand I'm not a bodyguard. You've got a pair on the beach ready to do your dirty work. You can hire more, buy anything you want—a castle with impenetrable walls."

She swallowed. "Until now I hadn't thought of Claude as her killer. I believe that now, and I'm afraid."

"Then hop the next flight to Madrid. Your husband is your natural and legal protector."

"Jaime?" She laughed bitterly. "A faded flower. No *cojones*. You know the word?"

"I know the word. Is he a *maricón?*"

"Capon." She shook her head disgustedly, and the tight braid flicked from side to side. "The Colonel's daughters were not fortunate in their men."

"Well," I said, "be that as it may, I'm not available for special tasks." I poured the last of the Añejo and drank part of it. "Y'know, Rita, it's remarkable when you think of it. You arrive unannounced, accuse me of killing your sister and end up offering me a job. Definitely screwy."

"I know, I know, but what did I have to go on but your name? Lovers sometimes kill, and you were . . . lovers."

"She said that?"

"Well—not exactly that way. Anita was . . . I suppose prim is a description. Conservative." Her eyes were welling. From a pocket she got out a small handkerchief and dabbed at her eyes and cheeks. After a while she murmured, "I've managed to keep myself under control for days. Now, I—I don't want to come apart."

"What you ought to do," I suggested, "is go back wherever you're staying, get drunk and cry your heart out. By the way, where are you staying?"

"Cheeca Lodge."

George Bush used to stay there when he came bonefishing. "Under your name?"

"As Ann Cutler. Suite 207. May I have your address?"

I wrote it down for her. "Not for casual use."

"Of course not. I understand."

She didn't, really, couldn't, not knowing my background, but I smiled and said, "Always good for a meal, a drink, and getaway money."

"You live . . . alone?"

"Uh-huh, just me and the roaches."

Finally she stood up in a motion that was more uncoiling than angular. Indirect light shaded years from her stunning features, and aside from her dark coif she could have been Anita in that moment. "Well," she said, and held out her hand, "thank you, and forgive me for being—confrontational."

I took her hand and held it lightly. A hard squeeze would have bruised her fingers against the rings. "Confrontation is okay—when you've got the facts."

I walked her to the stairway, and as she went down the rental cops waded out, joined hands to make a seat, and carried her ashore. Like a queen, I thought, an empress.

Which was what she had been when Chavez ruled.

Between her two guards she walked across the sand and over the dune. Presently I heard an engine start, wheels spun in sand, and her car backed out of the road.

About then I could have used a double shot of Añejo, but the bottle was history and, probably, so was she. For a while I replayed our conversation and wondered if she was really the nymph Manny described so raunchily. There had been nothing to suggest excessive sexuality; in fact, she had come across as an almost perfect lady. I found myself hoping she'd go promptly back to Madrid before anything unpleasant happened to her. And it occurred to me that not once had she mentioned her mother, who had been at the service with her. Well, maybe they didn't get along. Anita hadn't had much to say about Marie, either, so I guessed Mom and her daughters were estranged, or led separate lives. And as I considered my recent visitor I reflected that she projected a more positive, aggressive persona than Anita had. Anita, as I thought back, had displayed passive qualities, an attitude of acceptance; after all, it had taken her two years to decide on divorcing Tessier. Rita, I thought, would have taken faster action. Much faster. Yet—and this puzzled me—Rita was contemptuous of husband Jaime, calling him a capon, yet remaining married to him. Was Jaime the beard? The useful screen behind which Rita carried on affairs? In Europe not an unusual arrangement, only what was her hang-up, and why?

Despite the sisters' strong physical resemblance, their physiques differed. Anita had been a jogger, trim and athletic, where Rita appeared voluptuous, soft and sensuous; much more a viewer of others' physical activity than a perspiring participant. Rita would be found in a box at the bullring, relaxing in a beauty salon, not exercising at a fitness club. I speculated that her figure was maturely curved like Goya's *Maja*, the Hispanic feminine ideal. And although her impact on my senses had been strong, I knew I shouldn't be thinking of her at all.

Gradually I'd been sinking into the quicksand of the Chavez family, and that was something I didn't want or need. Leaving this shack, where so much had happened, would break the Chavez connection. So I picked up where Rita had interrupted me, and began moving out.

Up the beach a ways another gill net rolled in the surf with its tangled kill, reminding me of Anita's tears the morning we first met. I couldn't let my mind dwell on that tragic memory, so I concentrated on work at hand, and carried five loads to the Miata before the shack was cleared. There was no room for my bicycle, so I left it for anyone who wanted it more than I did. Driving north, I passed Cheeca Lodge and thought of Rita in Suite 207, quaffing bottles of Dom Pérignon to ease her sorrow.

And rebuked myself for visualizing her naked.

The next two days I cleaned house, changed a/c filters, placed roach traps, watched TV, stocked the bar with liquor, the refrigerator and freezer with easily prepared food, paid bills, called the yard man to tidy up lawn and plantings, got the Miata checked and lubricated, and generally acted like the bachelor I was.

Over ensuing days I had cable TV installed, and established an account with Miracle Mile Video Rental, taking out half a dozen movies per visit. When Melody and I were together we found exciting things to do, and never even considered TV entertainment. Now, things were different. Ribs delivered from Tony Roma's and pizza from the place on Ponce de Leon enabled me to watch movies almost uninterruptedly. I was finding a different level of existence, adapting to a video cocoon that insulated me from outside happenings. From the *Herald*, however, I learned that Tessier's bond had been forfeited and an international search was under way for the fugitive. Saul Hornstein applied to the court for permission to drop his client, a motion the judge reluctantly allowed.

In the afternoon I kept an appointment in South Miami with the orthopedist, who X-rayed my shoulder and admonished me to continue rehabilitation with regular exercise. Inwardly I scoffed at that because I was well down the road to becoming a couch potato, or was one already.

Driving back to CG, I stopped at Miracle Mile Video for another load of tapes, and bought a telephone answering machine at the nearby Radio Shack. After installing it I settled back in the recliner and watched *How the West Was Won* until it was time to phone Kentucky Fried or Domino's for my evening intake of high cholesterol food. After all, I reasoned, the orthopedist had said nothing about dieting, so I felt free to indulge base desires.

After dinner I left the recliner to wash hands and face and floss my teeth. I stepped on the bathroom scale and frowned at the lighted digits: I'd gained five pounds since leaving the stilt shack. Obesity faced me, but I wasn't so far gone that I couldn't fight back. Fruit, vegetables and seafood were the answer, plus long fast walks or a regimen of jogging. Facing myself in the mirror, I vowed to get squared away—tomorrow.

Meanwhile, there was a quart of praline ice cream that ought not be wasted through freezer burn, so I dug out a luscious bowlful and settled back with a large spoon for the finale of a truly great movie.

After rewinding it I looked through other tapes, and noticed one the clerk had recommended—*Green Ice*: a story of emeralds in Colombia—and was instantly reminded of the emeralds stashed in my secret safe. I hadn't thought about them, or the bank listing, for at least two days, and appraised that hiatus as a gain for mental health. Because imbedded in the back of my mind was the uncomfortable realization that I was obligated to do something about Anita's hoard. She'd entrusted it to me—temporarily or permanently, I'd never know—and I ought to determine to whom the fortune belonged. Neither Rita nor Mama Marie would be disinterested informants, were I so ingenuous as to consult them. Besides, they were back in Europe, and that left the man who really wanted the whole enchilada: Claude Tessier.

Where was he? Mexico most likely; free to marry into a drug king's family. Colombia, Ecuador or Peru, where similar opportunities abounded. Tessier was an animal of the species I'd come to know well during my years with DEA. He was a self-gratifying opportunist, who would marry only for personal security or financial gain. Marrying one of Colombia's Parra women would bring him both, but I suspected that development was down the road a ways. He knew Anita's hoard had been hidden someplace, but he didn't know where. Fortunately, as far as I knew, he didn't know my name or anything about me, so for the time being I was safe. But if I started asking around about emeralds and bank accounts Tessier could learn of my inquiries and start pre-emptive action, with fatal consequences to me. So I would have to act with maximum prudence and foresight.

I could rid myself of the dilemma by simply turning everything over to the Guatemalan Consulate, but I didn't think that had been Anita's intention, and I had an abiding distrust of bureaucrats. Like Tar Baby, the problem stayed stuck to my hands.

At eight o'clock I went out and walked down Granada to the University of Miami and back up Granada, home by nine o'clock. Between three and four miles I estimated as I showered away perspiration, exercise I should repeat daily, if not more often.

In pajamas I headed for the VCR and noticed the red light blinking on my answering machine. Playback gave only a pair of dings, no message. The hour was late for a call from Manny, so I suspected phone solicitation for a fabulous cut-rate cruise, an opportunity to buy gold or silver futures, or a time-sharing plan featuring some uncompleted New Mexico condo teetering on the verge of bankruptcy. I was grateful I hadn't been home to hear the phone.

It had been weeks since I'd range-fired my handguns, so I decided to drive down to the Trail Glades Range next day and expend a couple boxes of ammo, engage in gun-talk with the regulars and drink beer with the Bubbas. My concealed firearms license was lifetime-valid, a courtesy the state extended to former law enforcement officers, and I'd have to take it to the range. Cops occasionally went down the firing line checking licenses, and it was better to avoid trouble than disentangle. After practice I could continue along the Trail as far as Ochopee for a look at the pay phone where Tessier undoubtedly received word that Anita was dead. But why so far from Miami? I wondered. Unless he had reason to be nearby. He wasn't the type to fish Trail canals for snook, bass or bream, or take airboat rides into the Everglades as a lot of people did. Maybe he was holed up in a nearby motel, waiting. Waiting for what?

On the day Anita was killed Tessier wasn't a fugitive, but he could anticipate the future and prepare for it. I wondered if he had used that pay phone to call Mexico and make travel arrangements. Manny could get a listing of all calls made from that booth, but he'd need a writ to get Southern Bell's cooperation. The Federal Marshal's office could investigate more easily, now that Tessier was in fugitive status, but they'd have to tell a judge the source of their information, and I didn't want them backtracking to a dead man's wallet, and me.

Maybe I'd just let it go. Better that way.

The phone rang, jangling my nerves and interrupting my thoughts. When I picked up the receiver I said, "Yes?" and heard the voice of Rita Castenada.

SEVEN

"**J**IM," SHE said huskily, "I'm so glad you're there. I—"

"Did you call before?"

"Yes, but I didn't want to leave a message. I wanted to be sure only you would get it."

"Good thinking. Where are you, and what can I do for you?"

"I'm at CocoWalk in the Grove." Her words were hurried. "Do you know it?"

"Yes."

"I need to talk to you. Right away."

"I was getting ready for bed, but if it's something urgent, come here."

"It is. I'll be there in twenty minutes."

I turned on the outside portico light, pulled on my worn Academy bathrobe, and filled a bucket with ice. I was sipping Añejo when I heard a car pull into the drive. Moments later chimes sounded and I opened the door for Rita, who came quickly in. Before closing the door I glimpsed her car, a sleek, dark-green Jaguar. After turning off the portico light I faced my visitor.

Her hairstyle was the same as before, but tonight she was wearing jeweled earrings and a necklace of large gray pearls. Her dress was dark charcoal crepe de chine, gathered at the waist and flaring to just below her knees. Sheer, silvery hose and black silk shoes completed her evening costume, and I wondered if she'd been dining with an admirer.

"Drink?"

"Vodka, please, on the rocks."

I poured Stoly over ice and handed her the glass. "*Salud.*"

"*Y pesetas.*" She drank quickly, licked her lips, and sat behind the coffee table. "It's Claude," she told me. "Claude Tessier."

"What about him?"

"He telephoned me, threatened me." Her lips tightened. She sat forward and drank again, "Have you got a cigarette?"

I shook my head. "Slow down, Rita. He phoned you? How did he get your number?"

"From my mother—the idiot."

"And she is—where?"

"France." She grimaced. "She would never believe anything bad about Claude. Or my father."

"He threatened you?"

"Yes."

"Don't make me drag it out of you. What's this all about?"

She breathed deeply, then sighed. "He said if I didn't give him something he'd kill or disfigure me."

"Definitely a threat. What's the 'something' he wants?"

She balled one hand and cupped it with the other. I could see fear in her eyes. "When Claude went to prison he left some valuables with Anita. When he got out he tried to get them back."

"And had her killed in the process." I emptied my glass, set it on the coffee table, and sat down beside her. "You didn't go back to Madrid, Rita, so take my advice and go now, before Tessier finds you."

"But I don't want to go back to Madrid, not just now." Her eyes appealed. "I moved out of my hotel, bags are in my car."

"Then you're safe for a while."

"But for how long?" Her head turned away and I felt a pang of remembrance: her profile was that of Anita. "Did my sister give you anything?" she asked.

"The pleasure of her company." Not strictly a lie. Anita had cached her hoard at my place, hadn't handed it over to me. "Anyway," I said, "by all accounts Tessier is a wealthy man."

"And greedy. Very greedy. For him there's never too much money. He killed my sister, didn't he, for the things he'd left with her? He'll kill again, only I don't want it to be me."

I thought for a while. "If Tessier were jailed again he'd be no threat to you. Any idea where he was when he called?"

"It was a local phone call, not long distance."

"Background sounds, noise?"

"I—I was too frightened to notice."

"Understandable. If he thinks you have what he wants, or can get it, he'll have to give you a way to turn it over. You've left your hotel so contact is broken."

"I should have called you for advice before checking out, shouldn't I?"

"We're all experts after the fact," I remarked, "but since you don't have his valuables and he can't reach you by phone I'd say you're plenty safe. Unless you contact Mom again."

"Oh, no, I can't trust her. I—I just don't know what to do." Her gaze roved the room. "Could I—would you let me stay here until I get organized? At least tonight?"

"Sure. It's easier to sort things out by daylight. Bedroom's back there, I'll take the sofa." I got up and she held out her empty glass. "To calm me."

After building our drinks I took her keys and brought in her luggage from the Jaguar. Three matched pieces from Hermès, each heavy enough to make my shoulder ache. I carried them back to the bedroom, where she was removing her necklace and earrings. She glanced at the mirrored ceiling, smiled slightly, but said nothing.

"This morning I changed the sheets," I told her.

"Yes. I see that you're a good housekeeper. And this place is so different from that island shack." She stepped out of her shoes. "Are you naturally a recluse?"

"I just don't enjoy crowds."

"And what do you do for enjoyment?"

"Fishing, shooting, movies."

She took her glass from the bureau and drank deeply. "I'm very grateful to you, Jim. Taking in an almost-stranger."

"Glad of the company, and we have a common link."

"Anita, yes." She looked down. "I miss her terribly, will always miss her. To me she was very special. Much different from me but I loved her. We had—so much in common." Her face lifted and there were tears in her eyes. "Being the Colonel's daughters wasn't easy, and Mama was seldom around, so we depended on each other." She sat on the rounded edge of the bed and her shoulders slumped.

"Go to the same schools?"

She shook her head and the tears overflowed. She wiped them away before saying, "Anita went to Cal after I'd been sent to a convent school in Oregon. Punishment for rebellion." Her lips twisted in bitter remembrance. "It didn't work. I stayed rebellious."

"And your father forced Anita to marry Tessier."

"The least of his cruelties." She breathed deeply and lay back exhaustedly. "Promiscuity is a means of revenge—isn't that what the shrinks say?"

I nodded. Her skirt hem had risen, showing beautifully molded thighs. I was glad to have her with me if only for company, a break in my solitary routine. But the longer she talked, the longer she stayed, the deeper I was being drawn into the complexities of the Chavez labyrinth. I wasn't ready to tell Rita about the emeralds because she would probably want them returned to Tessier. And I'd begun thinking that the hoard could be used to bring Tessier out of hiding, where I could get to him. If I succeeded, that would end my Chavez connection.

But as I looked down on Rita's tranquil face and closed eyes, the curve of her hips and thighs, I could not think when, if ever, I had been as close to so beautiful a woman. And I felt I was being disloyal to Anita. "If you can't sleep, there are pills in the bathroom closet. See you in the morning."

Her lips moved soundlessly. I left the bedroom and got sheet, pillow and blanket from the linen closet, carried them to the sofa. More drinks would give me a morning hangover, so I canceled the thought, and slid a rental tape into the player. *Doctor Zhivago* was the offering. Heavy stuff, but lengthy enough to tire and relax me into sleep.

As the title credits rolled I turned off living room lights, arranged sofa bedding and pulled off my blue bathrobe before stretching out to watch in comfort. My mind was keenly aware of the gorgeous female down the hall. The sisters had led troubled lives and Anita's had ended early and cruelly. What lay in store for Rita? I wondered. Fugitive from a loveless marriage, alienated from her mother, and menaced by Tessier . . . I wanted to help and keep her from harm as I hadn't had a chance to protect her sister. But at the same time I wasn't looking for intimate involvement. At that point I didn't know what I *was* looking for, but as my mind groped for an answer I concluded that I wanted to right a wrong, bring retaliatory justice to Claude Tessier. Avenge Anita's horrible death.

If I could do that, Rita would no longer have to fear her former brother-in-law; she'd be free to find a new life for herself, and my Chavez connection would be history.

I hadn't really watched the story unfolding on the video screen, so I paused the tape and went to the bathroom for a pit stop. Through the bedroom doorway I glimpsed Rita sleeping under a coverlet, bare arms and the upper part of a flimsy nightgown exposed. Her unbound hair flared out on the pillow in a dark aura that contrasted with the whiteness of her face. I drew the door nearly shut and walked back to my sofa.

Before reaching it I heard a car coming slowly down the street. Passing my house, it went even more slowly, stopped briefly, and moved on. As though the driver were looking for an unlighted house number—mine?—or a vulnerable car. Her Jaguar was a make prized by car thieves, who plagued Miami, and even if the car wasn't stolen it could be stripped in place. One reason I garaged my Miata after dark.

The cruising car gave me a sense of apprehension. I went to the entry closet where I'd stowed my sawed-off and Beretta, and brought the double-barreled shotgun back to the sofa. Suddenly, voices filled the room as the pause interval ended, and I started reflexively. If thieves had targeted the Jaguar they'd want an all-dark house before beginning their criminal enterprise, so I turned off the VCR to oblige them.

It was lonely sitting there in the dark, and it occurred to me that I should call the Gables police. But then I told myself that, realistically, a prowl car would make a single pass and see nothing, radio a negative report to the dispatcher. Besides, professional thieves monitored police transmissions with compatible scanners, and got to work when the prowlies were far away.

But maybe the stealthy car was driven by a disoriented driver. Unlike Miami's grid of numbered streets, the Gables's streets had Spanish names, and you needed a map to locate where you wanted to go. I assumed Rita had rented the Jaguar; even if it wasn't covered by insurance she could easily afford its loss. So why was I sitting up, armed, in the small hours of the morning, waiting for car thieves who, if they existed, might never come? On reflection I decided I'd overreacted, so I laid the sawed-off on the carpet and stretched out to sleep.

What woke me was a sound of scratching. It phased into my dream as a cat clawing carpet, stopped and started again, and I knew it was no tabby trying to get in. Within moments I was fully alert and listening directionally: the sound came from the kitchen door that gave out into the fenced backyard. There it was again.

I picked up the sawed-off and crawled toward the kitchen. Through the open doorway I could see a flashlight beam outside the door. The door was not only locked but deadbolted, so a lockpick wasn't going to open it, unless . . .

The scratching sound I now recognized as the scraping of a glass-cutter as it grated around the door pane nearest the handle. The would-be intruder wasn't a car thief, but a potential burglar, who'd cased the house before I re-occupied it, found it dark when he cruised down Granada, and come back with entry tools.

Still crawling, I closed the bedroom door, and moved back to watch the progress of the break-in. When he came over the threshold into my territory he became my property and my intention was to hold him for the cops.

A grating sound coincided with the disappearance of the glass pane as the burglar withdrew it. A hand reached in and turned the deadbolt knob. Now only the spring lock remained.

I pointed the shotgun at the door.

Heard the slick slithery sound of the plastic card working against the bolt spring. A click, and the door opened inward.

EIGHT

HE DIDN'T come all the way in, but paused to sweep the kitchen with his flashlight. I squinted to preserve night vision and saw that he was tall and large, where most burglars were small, ratty types, adapted to chimneys and a/c openings. Still he didn't enter, and my trigger finger began to itch. C'mon, shithead, I urged silently, let's get it over with. B & E, possession of burglar tools, home invasion . . . five years on a Raiford road gang. *Move, dammit!*

Finally he did. His soles scraped the tile floor and the flashlight leveled from his hip straight ahead. When he was by the table I raised the shotgun tip and poked the light switch above me. The sudden glare startled him, and for a second he stood motionless, tensing for flight. I rapped the sawed-off against the doorjamb and rose. "*Freeze,*" I snapped, and he raised his arms. "Drop the flashlight, get down on the floor, hands behind your back."

As he got slowly down I noticed a pistol butt protruding from the slash pocket of his black leather jacket. I walked around the table and stood a yard from his boots. "Two fingers on the pistol," I told him. "Ease it out and slide it my way." Armed burglary could add another nickel to his time.

"Jesus," he gasped, "I ain't done nothin', man."

"Tell it to the judge." I watched the pistol come out. "If you're thinking gunfight I'll give you both barrels through the back, fire a shot from your gun and claim self-defense. So push the pistol with the back of your hand." I was trying to keep my voice low, minimize sound to keep Rita from waking.

The pistol slid toward me, and I toed it farther from the thief. "Got a partner?" I asked.

"Just me."

"Where's the car?"

"The—? Two blocks away."

"Far to lug a TV, if that's what you came for. You were just going to steal, right?"

"Yeah," he grunted.

"What's the iron for?"

"I dunno—used to it."

"Used to it," I mocked. "Why don't I believe you? Now, get on your side and pull off the boots."

"Whaffor? Whatcha gonna do?" he whined.

"Boots off." I pointed the sawed-off at his head, and suddenly realized I'd seen him before, and where. He was one of the two eraserheads who'd tried to pull Anita from the Osprey Bar & Grill. The recognition baffled me. Had he trailed me from the Keys to blow off my head? "Look at me," I ordered, and as his face turned we stared at each other. "Seen me before?"

"No, man."

"Never? Sure of that?"

"Said it, di'n I?"

"Yeah." I'd talked too much, hadn't been watching his hands at his boots. Suddenly a switchblade clicked open and he lunged like a striking snake, slashing at my legs. I slammed the sawed-off barrel on the bulge of his skull, and his body dropped face down, knife skittering from his hand.

Using a ball of kitchen twine, I looped his bare ankles, circled them four times and secured them with a slipknot. I cut the end with his switchblade—a nice, well-honed Italian model with a bone handle—and tied his wrists behind him. Then I went through his pockets.

One held two one-dollar bills and change. The other, a cheap billfold with car and cycle licenses in the name of Barton Earl Bevins. The long, zippered compartment produced four hundred-dollar bills and an Osprey promo card. On the back, a laboriously printed telephone number, and that was my third surprise of the night. For the number corresponded to the one I'd found in Cantú's wallet. The pay phone at Ochopee, on the Tamiami Trail.

He hadn't come for a TV and he hadn't come to kill me. He'd been paid to frighten, kill or kidnap Rita.

So, we needed to talk.

While I was making coffee he began to groan and thrash. His eyes opened and followed my every move. I sipped, smacked my lips and said, "What's his name?"

"Name? Who?"

"The guy who paid you four skins to come here."

"I dunno." He rolled on one side, moaned, and grated, "Nobody paid me nuthin'."

I smiled tolerantly. "Your chances of seeing dawn are slim and getting slimmer. Who set this up?"

"Nobody, man, like I said. I'm a thief."

"Unquestionably. You followed the Jag here?"

"No."

"Barton," I said, and brandished the switchblade, "you're heading for jail.

But if I hear truth from you I could forget to mention the gun—and this knife. Now, how did it all come about?''

I let him think it over while I enjoyed hot coffee. After a while he said, ''A guy at camp.''

''What camp?''

''In the Glades.''

''Let's try for a name.''

That posed a problem. He wrestled with it before saying, ''Louie—Spanish guy.''

''Louie who?''

''Dunno. That's what we call him.''

I dropped the knife point down. It stuck in the wooden table top and vibrated like a tuning fork. ''Let's try another name, Barton: Claude. Claude Tessier. Familiar?''

''Never heard it before,'' he grunted, but his eyes gave the lie away.

''Okay,'' I said. ''So this Louie paid you to come here and kill someone. Who?''

''Jesus, man, I wasn't gonna *kill* her.''

''Her? That's progress. I thought I was the target, but I feel better now, more relaxed. If not murder tonight, then what?''

He sucked in a deep breath and groaned as he let it out. ''Talk to her, scare her.''

''Why?''

''So she'd give back somethin' of Louie's.''

I nodded thoughtfully. ''Your Louie—my Claude—scared her out of the hotel. Louie-Claude followed the Jag here, or had it done. Right?''

''I dunno.''

''But you were told to look for a parked Jag.''

''Guess so,'' he said resignedly. ''Hell, you seem to know the setup, why ask me?''

''Confirming. Because none of this need come out in court, understand? You'll cut a better deal if it's only B & E, Barton. I'm sure you understand that.''

Nothing from the biker on the floor.

''This camp, where you met Louie. Down the Trail, West Everglades, by the Cypress Preserve. That one?''

''You got it.''

''Where a bunch of fellows get together for target practice?''

He grunted affirmatively.

''Assault weapons, of course.''

''Yeah, and if I had one now—''

"—you'd blow my head off. But I've got iron and you haven't. The camp's a Cuban operation?"

"Some Cubans, mainly Guats."

"Hmmm. Louie's Spanish, or Guat?"

"Speaks Spanish—how the hell do I know? Spiks is all the same."

"Like bikers and rednecks. So it's a training camp, and you're a weapons instructor. Partner, too?"

"Eddie's radio comm."

"Volunteers?"

"Me? Eddie? Hell, no, we're mercs."

Gradually I was getting the scene together. "Louie's the main man."

"Ain't seen no other. He pays, gives orders."

"Preparing for what?"

By now I knew the answer but I wanted it from him.

"Fighting."

"Where?"

"Down south."

"South of Mexico. Guatemala?" I finished my coffee, set the cup in the sink. Claude Tessier was ambitious. He wanted to rule Guatemala as Oscar Chavez had, and was assembling a private army to force the coup. Fifty, a hundred trained mercenaries covertly inserted in Guatemala City could bring it off—unless the government was warned.

I didn't know if the present Guatemalan government was a grand improvement over Chavez's, but if Tessier opposed it, then I had to be for it. I didn't think much of the quality of his paramilitary trainers, but it didn't take an excess of brains to fire an M-14, man a mortar or handle a field radio pack. And, of course, Tessier could be bombing the capital from his plane to terrify authorities and citizenry—it had been done before. By CIA.

To my prisoner I said, "The deal is this. You say nothing about the woman, the Jag, Louie or the camp. I'll keep knife and gun out of it."

He thought it over. "Okay."

"Eddie in the car?"

"Yeah," he said, then swore, having denied it before.

"What make?"

"Olds. Brown."

"Where is it exactly?"

"Corner of Obispo and Sorolla." Both names mispronounced.

"If he's not there the deal's off, you go all the way. A nickel in Raiford is bad enough, a dime's eternity. Your choice."

"Eddie's there," he said sullenly. "Don't say I ratted him out."

"I won't but he'll probably figure it."

For a while I stared at him. "One final thing. That blond at the Osprey you and Eddie hassled—she wasn't a random target. Now, think this over very carefully because our whole deal depends on the answer."

"Whatcha want?"

"Who chose her, told you what to do?"

He sighed, and for a few moments I thought he wasn't going to reply. Finally he said, "Guy at camp."

"Louie?"

"No. Pal of his. Louie wasn't at camp, didn't show until later."

"How much later?"

"Days—week, maybe, I dunno."

He was right about that because Louie-Claude was still in the slammer. "What's the pal's name?"

I could see his throat working as he swallowed. "Arnoldo—somethin' like that, how it sounded."

"Pay you?"

"Yeah. Fifty each."

The instigator would have been Arnoldo Pobrezo, the late Arnoldo Pobrezo. "And for fifty each what were you supposed to do?"

"Snatch the broad, twist her arm until she turned over some things."

"Arnoldo mention her name?"

"Anita."

"Identifiable how?"

"Pink Jeep. Parked at her cottage." He swallowed again. "Where she was killed."

"Why not work her over at the cottage?"

"Wasn't there. Spotted the Jeep at that bar—the Osprey. Went in, had a few beers—you seen the rest."

"Fortunately for the lady. All right. It checks out, the deal stands." I collected his .38 Astra pistol from the floor, checked his bonds and went into the bedroom. After turning on a table lamp, I sat on the bed and gently woke Rita.

She sat up, a frightened look on her features, but I said, "Rita, I caught a burglar and I'm going to call the police. Just stay here, out of sight."

"You—?" One hand went to her mouth. She was breathing so heavily I couldn't help noticing the rise and fall of her full breasts. "Easy," I said. "You don't want to make a statement, be called as a witness, right?"

"No—unless it would help you."

"I can handle it."

"But—"

I reached for the bedside phone and dialed 911. When the dispatcher answered she said, "Crime in progress?"

"Sort of. One burglar apprehended in my home"—I gave the address—

"and an accessory, the wheelman, parked at Sorolla and Obispo in a Brown Olds. Assume he's armed."

"Are you all right, sir?"

"Fine. Everything's cool here, so the neighbors would appreciate no sirens or flashing lights."

"I'll get officers there right away."

"And I suggest they apprehend the accessory first, okay?"

"No problem."

I hung up and turned to Rita, whose eyes were wide with uncertainty. "Is that all?" she blurted.

"Except for a bracer." I went to the bar, dropped ice in two glasses and added vodka. Quite a lot of it. Rita sipped gratefully. "After the police leave you'll tell me more?"

"Depend on it." I patted her wrist, turned off the lamp, and closed her door. I wasn't going to reveal the Tessier connection, that would really frighten her, so I'd tell her how I caught the geek. That ought to satisfy her for now. And I certainly wasn't going to let her know the two thieves were the same hooligans who manhandled her sister at the Osprey Bar & Grill. All that was need-to-know, and as far as I was concerned she didn't need to know.

Before returning to the kitchen I switched on house and yard lights, and found Barton Earl Bevins where I'd left him. Looking up, he said, "I get to keep the money, right?"

"Wrong." I took the four bills from his billfold and pocketed them. Along with the Osprey card and its Ochopee number. Showing him the Astra, I said, "Hot piece?"

"Dunno. Louie had it."

"Then it's probably hot. And all the more reason to keep it from the cops." I sipped my drink. "Barton, I'm going far out on a limb for you and I expect you to keep the faith."

"You got it."

I shoved the illegal sawed-off in a kitchen drawer, and stashed the Astra in the freezer for later disposal. Then I got my Beretta from the closet and put on my bathrobe. By then lights were flashing on my lawn, so I opened the door and admitted four cops with drawn guns.

"You the owner?" the sergeant barked.

"Yeah, and the perp's on the kitchen floor." I held out my Beretta for inspection.

"You shouldn'ta tried to subdue him alone. Call us every time."

"Thanks, officer, I'll remember that." I followed them to the kitchen, where two cops hauled Bevins off the floor and handcuffed him. They cut off his ankle bonds and read him his rights. Bevins gave me a sick look before they marched him off. To the sergeant I said, "What about the getaway driver?"

"Scooped him up first." He eyed me. "Good job, mister. You in law enforcement?"

"Disability-retired." Close enough to the truth.

He handed me a police card. "How about coming to headquarters after noon tomorrow and making a statement?"

We shook hands, the cops filed out, and that was it.

I drank the rest of my vodka while the cars drove off, and then I knocked on the bedroom door. "All clear."

The door opened and she stood there in a short pink peignoir, empty glass in hand. "Refill?"

"Many as you want." Barefoot, she followed me to the bar, her nightgown's swaying hem not entirely concealing the dark apex of her loins. Refilled, our glasses touched, and she asked, "If I'd been here alone—what then?"

"You wouldn't have been here alone. But if you'd heard a burglar you'd have called the cops and they'd have come in minutes, like they just did."

"Maybe—but it's much more reassuring to think you'd be here."

"Well," I said, "I usually am, and that was a really unlucky thief. The place has been vacant until a week ago, and he picked tonight."

"Really." She smiled. Not a sunburst, but a nervous, tentative, hopeful smile and I welcomed it because it was the first Rita-smile I'd ever seen. I told her so, and swallowed more vodka.

Her expression tightened, she took my hand, and drew me to the sofa. Seated beside me, she murmured, "I suppose I've come off as dour, lugubrious, haven't I?"

"As well as mournful and sad." I couldn't resist kissing the lobe of her ear. She shivered but didn't resist. "Truth is I haven't had much to smile about. And losing my sister—" Her face burrowed into my shoulder and quietly she began to sob. I stroked her thick, clean hair until the spasm ended. She dried her eyes on my robe lapel, gazed at me, and swallowed the rest of her drink. "'Nother?"

"Why not? Been a stressful night." And she knew only ten percent of it. As I refilled our glasses I noticed her fingers toying with the hem of her shortie. The liquor was hitting her, and that was all to the good. She'd need a strong hit to sleep again, and as I saw her sitting among my rumpled bedding, I realized that so would I. She looked so much like our lost Anita, and her body was so gorgeously curved and proportioned, that I stood there like a yokel staring at Little Egypt. Her face turned and her eyes took in what must have been my expression of awe. I didn't know what to say—a mumbled apology seemed oafish—so as I collected my thoughts I saw her lips lift into a smile. "What are you thinking?" she asked.

"Ah . . . um . . . how nice it is to have you here." I moved toward her with our drinks. Handing her glass over, I said, "Because if you weren't here then

I'd have nobody to tell about the burglary and how courageous I was throughout."

She tilted her glass and sipped. "But you haven't really told me."

"No? Thought I had." I sat beside her. "Must be the drinks."

"Maybe. But I've been thinking that we're two loners, you and I." Her fingertips traced the side of my face. "Ever feel—incomplete?"

"Occasionally. Now and then." When her fingers touched my lips I kissed them and I could feel her body shiver against me. "That was nice," she murmured. "It's been forever since anyone did so nice a thing." And she moved more closely against me.

Like a sleepwalker in a slow-motion dream sequence I saw my left hand lifting toward her breast. Her eyes flickered at the motion but she didn't draw away, didn't object. My index finger touched her nipple. Hard, erect, and yielding. Her body shivered again and she whispered. "Don't stop. Please don't stop."

So I turned her face to mine and kissed those full and perfect lips. My hand cupped and pressed her breast as her free hand invaded my robe and touched what was already undisguisably erect. Boldly, my tongue thrust into her mouth, met hers and tilted with it. Languorously, she sighed, leaned back, and drew me downward with her.

I felt her thighs part, she peeled off my robe and undid my pajama bottom while our mouths pressed voraciously together. Her pelvis rolled upward to trap me in her inner warmth, and her arms circled my torso as she began to buck and whimper uncontrollably. She climaxed with a muffled shriek that brought me over the top, and then we were moving together, slowly, caressingly, caringly, my lips covering her forehead with kisses of gratitude.

Finally our bodies stopped moving—mine seemingly with a will of its own—and I said, "I didn't realize how much I wanted you."

"I wanted you, too, but I fought it. Then tonight you calmed my fear and I realized you could be gentle and it was going to be all right, whatever happened."

"It is all right, *querida*."

"Then the burglar . . . the way you handled everything . . . so confident, so . . . *male*. It all excited me—beyond what I'd ever known." She placed my hand on her breast and pressed. "I was afraid you'd make love to the ghost of Anita, but then I didn't really care."

"I didn't," I said truthfully. "I made love to Rita—to you."

For what seemed like a long time we lay together, our heartbeats gradually slowing, and then I moved aside to relieve her of my weight. When she spoke her voice was remote. "This is a wonderful dream," she said quietly. "Such a wonderful dream." Then coyly: "Do I have to leave in the morning?"

"Not until you've made breakfast."

She tweaked my nose and giggled. "Chauvinist pig."

"Confrontational female."

We both laughed and she kissed my cheek. "How right you are." Then, as if suddenly aware she was naked, she exclaimed, "Oh! Where is my nightie?"

It was rolled up like a cord circling her throat. I drew it over her head and squeezed it into the size of a golf ball. "Never be the same," I said sadly.

"But I'll keep it—always. A souvenir of—tonight."

"Leaving me with memories."

"If that's all you want."

"No, no, more, much more," I said quickly, and glanced at the mantel clock. "Three forty-eight. Too early to get up, too late to go to sleep."

"Then let's just go to bed." She got up, breasts swaying like twin mangoes, took my hand and plodded ahead of me to the bedroom. I closed and locked the door while she turned on a corner lamp. Then she flung herself onto the bed, rolled over, and pointed up at the mirrored ceiling. "Your inspiration?"

"Previous resident."

"I'll bet it's reflected a thousand naughty scenes."

I liked her upbeat mood, so in contrast to everything before. "Let's add a few more."

I grappled with her, she shrieked, we rolled back and forth until she was on top. She fitted herself to me and glanced up at the mirror. I said, "Splendid view. Awesome. Magnificent buns," and slapped one for effect.

"Enjoy while you can. My turn next." She rubbed her nipples against my chest and began rotating her pelvis excitingly.

An hour or so later we were exhaustedly asleep, her head on my arm, our legs still intertwined.

I woke around nine and closed the blinds to maintain darkness. As I looked at Rita I told myself that she was all I'd ever wanted in a woman, and more. But she was married—how could I keep her?

That was one of the major problems ahead of me, and none could be resolved in a day. Emeralds, mercenaries, Tessier. Couldn't handle everything alone—have to bring in Manny soon.

NINE

"**P**RIMERO," I said to Rita as we finished late breakfast of poached eggs, juice and coffee, "you return the Jaguar."

"Why?"

"I can't garage it, and you won't need it. Parked in the drive it's going to attract more thieves."

Her shoulders hunched protectively. "If you say so."

"*Segundo*, I want you to stay in South Beach until things settle down around here."

"What 'things'?"

"Oh, last night's burglars could have vengeful pals, and I don't want you in any kind of danger."

Her hand reached out and covered mine. "But I need you. How can I do without you—now?"

"We'll be together, I promise, only not here after dark." That Barton and Eddie had been arrested wouldn't stop Tessier from trying again.

"For how long?"

"A week, two, maybe." I hoped it wouldn't be longer. Today she looked even more beautiful than she had last night, and I felt that I was becoming infatuated with her. One night of love did not a lifetime marriage make, but it was an excellent beginning. I lifted her hand and kissed it. "Honey," I said, "for reasons I'll explain, I was living at the shack under an assumed name. An alias."

Her brow furrowed. "Anita was right."

"About me being a fugitive? No. Not from the law, honey, from my past."

She sat back, away from me, sending a body language message. "I have this horrible feeling," she said hollowly, "that you're going to destroy everything. Dawn, and the prince becomes a toad."

"Will you, for God's sake, just listen?" I grasped her hand and Rita looked away. "I'm not much of anybody," I told her, "a guy from Chicago, whose dad was killed in a mill accident when I was four. Mom kept me clean, dressed and in school. An old friend of my father's became a Congressman, got me an appointment to the Naval Academy—where that blue robe came from.''

Her mouth relaxed. ''I wondered about that.''

''Naval Aviation. Carrier duty off Vietnam. Married a New York fashion model. We saw each other when I was in port. I realized things were coming apart and requested shore duty.'' I swallowed. ''By then she was hooked on heroin—just a wraith, a ghost of the girl I'd married. She overdosed. I found the dealer and killed him.''

''Oh, Jim—'' Her expression was anguished. ''I'm so awfully sorry.''

''Don't call me Jim. My name is Novak. Jack Novak. Hated drugs, the culture, the fat slobs who got rich off addicts like my wife. Joined DEA. Seven years. Quit, but did contract jobs from my place in Cozumel.'' I reached for a water glass, seeing my hand tremble. ''I broke up too much profitable business for the Mexicans to tolerate me. There was a shootout at a drug hacienda in Sonora, and I took a slug in the shoulder.'' I gestured, and saw her nod. ''While I was hospitalized, Mex authorities expelled me, confiscated my house and plane. I had no place to return to, so I rehabbed where you found me. I used another name to stay clear of enemies who want revenge for what I did to them, their business.''

Her lips parted but I shook my head. ''Let me get it all out, then never again.'' I breathed deeply and went on. ''I'm not poor—I did some confiscating myself before I was put down—but last night's burglar didn't come for my money, he came for me.''

That was the first lie, but I said it to protect her. ''South Florida is crawling with drugs and dealers. I saw the 'burglar' at a bar in the Keys. Until last night I didn't know I'd been recognized—obviously I was.'' I looked away from her, through the window, where a young male cardinal was preening on the security fence. ''I can't have you endangered by my past—I'd rather lose you alive, than dead—so it's essential you not be linked to me, not here where I've been spotted.''

She nodded understanding. ''Anita knew all this?''

''None of it. There—wasn't time.''

She raised my hand to her lips, pressed them there. ''I'll do whatever you want.''

''The break has to be now. Drive to the airport and check your bags. Turn in the Jaguar. Come back for your bags and taxi to South Beach. Check into the Clay Hotel, and from a pay phone leave your room number on my machine. Just the number, nothing more.'' Reaching over, I touched her cheek and hair. ''I love the way you look, the way you are, but I want you to change your appearance, your clothing. Shops there cater to European models—let them think you're one of them—as you could easily be. The hotel will assume the same. Don't use credit cards, pay cash for everything.'' I handed her a thousand from my wallet. That left Barton Bevins's four hundred kill dollars. "When that runs out, there's more."

"I have two bank accounts in Miami," she told me. "One near the airport, the other on the Beach. Money's no problem."

Nor would it ever be, I thought, for the heirs of Colonel Chavez.

"For the immediate future," I said, "we have to have a safe haven where we can be together and make longer range plans. Very slowly I'm getting a line on Tessier and expect to know what he's up to. If I can get the right evidence, the Feds will take care of him. Otherwise, I'll do the job myself."

"As you destroyed my sister's killers," she said in a low, contained voice.

"Fire with fire," I remarked. "Works for me."

"But for how long, darling? You don't want to lose me, I don't want to lose you. You've satisfied Anita's blood debt, can't we just walk away from violence and revenge? Isn't having each other enough? We found each other—how fortunate can two people be?"

I considered while she came around behind and circled my shoulders with her arms. "We're more than fortunate," I said slowly, "but we won't live securely until Tessier's put down. He killed your sister trying to regain those 'valuables' you mentioned. You're next, if he thinks you may have them." I paused to let the thought sink in. "What were they—those 'valuables'?"

I couldn't see her face, but I felt her arms tighten briefly. "Things of my father's."

"Tessier stole them?"

"I—I don't know. But the Colonel trusted Claude, thought of him as a son. So he probably entrusted them to Claude before he—was killed."

"In his own plane, in Mexico."

"Yes." She moved around and sat on my lap, arms circling my neck. She kissed my cheek before saying. "Knowing Claude, I've thought he could have sabotaged the plane—he's capable of it, and probably knew how."

"Must have," I agreed. "But were they estranged? Bad blood between them?"

"That could be, I can't say. Claude envied the Colonel's power in Guatemala, and my father was probably plotting to return." She sighed. "The world hasn't much use for expelled dictators."

"So, if Tessier had designs on Guatemala your father would have been an obstacle."

"Immovable."

"Except the plane crash removed him." I drank the last of my coffee. "Did you go to the crash scene? Talk with the Mexicans?"

"My mother did. She said the crash investigation was amateurish at best, but she was convinced my father was killed in it."

I hesitated before asking, "Was there any identifiable evidence? Remains?"

"Like bones, dental work? Whatever they scraped up my mother had cremated. Took ashes back to France."

"Was any cause for the crash given?"

"Supposedly a combination of pilot error and mechanical failure."

"Engine failure?"

"I just don't know." Her face turned away. "Jim—I mean Jack, you have to understand that I *welcomed* the Colonel's death. I loathed him as far back as I can remember." Her body was trembling. Quickly I said, "Honey, I'm sorry I asked all those questions, but I didn't know how you felt. You have your reasons, I'm sure, and they don't concern me. I was speculating the crash could have been rigged."

"You mean—so my father could get away and avoid prosecution here?"

"Something like that," I said soothingly, "but we have our own lives to get on with, and—"

"That's a frightening thought—that he may be alive." She shuddered. "A monster."

"That's the consensus. Enough of the Colonel. Let's get you packed and out of here." I glanced at my watch. "In three hours I want to hear from you."

She kissed and hugged me for a long time. "You will."

After seeing her Jaguar back out of the drive and turn up Granada toward the airport, I phoned Manny Montijo, and told him there'd been developments we needed to talk about.

"Developments that involve my office?" he asked warily.

"You'll be the judge. I'll buy lunch."

"I brown-bagged it. But—you at the townhouse? I'll be heading that way, so I can stop off for a few minutes. But it can't be long. Gotta meet a plane at Homestead."

Homestead was the largest military air base in Florida. Customs, DEA and INS aircraft customarily used Opa Locka, so someone of importance must be coming in. Or departing. "I'll be waiting," I told him, then cleared away breakfast dishes, changed damp, rumpled bedsheets, and got into a clean shirt before Manny arrived.

"So, *compadre*, what's up?" he asked, closing the front door. No embroidered guayabera today. Brown poplin suit, blue button-down shirt and silk repp tie. An organization man looking his best.

"Starts back here." I led him into the kitchen and showed him where the glass pane had been removed.

"Neat job," he remarked. "Anything missing?"

"The burglar."

He smiled slightly. "Waste him?"

"Naw. Called the cops. After preliminary interrogation."

"Oh, boy. Much left for the cops to haul away?"

"Enough to serve substantial time. Wheelman, too."

"You foiled a burglary. Why should that interest me?"

"Oh, Manny. These guys didn't want my cufflinks and TV, they had a contract on me." I wasn't ready to tell him about Rita; I wanted to withhold that for the present.

He sat down. "Mean that?"

"Tessier paid them." I produced the four hundred-dollar bills.

He grunted. "Always turn a profit when you can, don't you?"

"The glazier'll take one of them for a new pane."

"Hell, I'll do it for fifty."

"I don't employ scab labor."

He looked at his watch. "So, the missing Tessier has a hard-on for you. Should that interest me? DEA?"

"Dunno. But last night's hooligans were trainers at that 'Glades camp you surveyed. Weapons and radio instructors. Add that to Tessier's background, his association with Chavez, and what's the sum?"

He shrugged. "Sounds like another private army. Jack, you know as well as I how these Latin exiles live with the dream of returning—at the head of a conquering army."

"Castro did it."

"But his opponents failed."

"A wretched chapter in our history."

"So it was—is. You know the areas of DEA interest, Jack, and exile activities ain't among them."

"Unless there's a drug connection."

"I'm listening."

I sighed. "Under Chavez, Guatemala was a prime transshipment point for drug cargoes to the US, right?"

"Right. But Chavez is gone."

I smiled. "Tessier's still around. Not too long ago this country invaded Panama to knock out Noriega and keep that country from facilitating the flow of drugs into the US. That effort was costly and bloody. Let's project six months, a year from now: Tessier stages a coup and takes over. In forty-eight hours the loads from Medellín and Guayaquil start flying in, and we've got a problem far beyond DEA's resources, a problem only the military can solve. The same bloody way."

His lips twitched as he stared at the table. Finally he asked, "Did the hitman mention narcotics?"

"Not a word. But I wouldn't expect the boss to confide in anyone that far down the chain of command. Training first, invasion second, drug pipeline third.'' I grunted disgustedly ''We can't get the Mexicans to shape up, do the right things, and they're supposedly a friendly country. I can envision top level cooperation between Mexico and a drug-oriented Guatemalan dictator, can't you?''

''Yeah, but that's strategic thinking.''

''It's logical.''

''And far above my station.'' He looked at his watch. ''Any ideas?''

''Have the trainees rousted, the camp leveled. Have INS check for illegals. That'll slow preparations a few months. Hell, Tessier could even be netted.'' I unfolded a road map of south Florida and smoothed it on the table. ''Exactly where is the camp you visited?''

After peering at it, Manny made an x-mark with his pen. ''Approachable by road, about there.'' He drew a thin line. ''Also by water.'' He indicated a cluster of mangrove islands hugging the coastline. ''Stone Crab country. Plus sharks, snakes and alligators. I'd leave it alone.''

Turning from the map, I looked at him. ''What are you going to do?''

He shrugged. ''I'll try to decide what I *can* do, Jack, but it won't be an easy call. Interagency relations haven't improved since our last go-round. Everyone wants the prime time sound bite but nobody wants dirty hands getting results.'' He began walking from the kitchen. Following him, I asked, ''Who's the VIP you're meeting?''

''Assistant Director Doremus. We're phasing into another Strike Force, Jack.''

''Strikeout Force's more accurate.''

''You said it, not me.'' He opened the door and started out.

''Guard your pension rights,'' I told him, and watched Manny get into the office Ford, identifiable by its distinctive radio antenna. When would they learn? I wondered. When would they ever learn?

I made coffee and wandered back to the sofa, where last night's lovemaking had unexpectedly begun. Rita Chavez de Castenada dominated my thoughts, and though I missed her presence I knew that relocating her was the sensible thing. By now she ought to have checked into the Clay, and for her youth, wealth and tastes, the South Beach Art Deco scene was just right. High fashion shops, four-star restaurants and scores of beautiful young women like herself. Far different, I reflected, from Madrid's stodgy Gran Via.

As I sipped coffee I realized I'd been too involved with my story and her reactions to bring up her husband, but we'd cover that in good time. Along with where to settle, and how many children to raise. Subjects still unexplored. But we were in a phase of mutual discovery and I didn't want to rush it. Nor, I suspected, did she.

I phoned a mobile lock-and-key outfit, and arranged to have the door pane replaced, as well as the spring bolt that had yielded to Bevins's plastic. Maybe an alarm system was in order. Why not?

I extracted more cash from my safe, secured it and replaced the concealing serape. I'd glimpsed the emeralds inside and realized I still hadn't come up with a solution. Well, things had intervened. Important things. Specifically Rita, whose welfare was top priority.

When door chimes sounded I assumed it would be the windowpane replacer, so I unbolted the door and opened it.

Two men in dark, tropical-weight suits, white shirts and ties. "Mr. Novak?" He flashed a Bureau credential. "FBI. Can we come in?"

"Sure." I stood aside while they filed inside. After I closed the door each handed me an official namecard. Special Agents Doak and Ferre. I stuck the cards in my shirt pocket and gestured at the sofa. "What can I do for you?"

They sat and crossed their legs simultaneously. I eased into my recliner and studied their faces. SA Doak said, "Last night you foiled a burglary and apprehended a burglar."

I nodded. "And it's reassuring that the Bureau is following up house crimes."

SA Ferre glanced at his partner before saying, "Not exactly, sir. One of the arrested men is a Bureau informant."

"Not Barton Earl Bevins, the eraserhead with the body temperature IQ?"

Doak managed a smile. "No, his partner. Now, Mr. Novak, we ran your name through the files and learned you were with DEA, so you'll understand the meaning of confidential official information."

"How could I forget?" I eased forward. "Eddie the getaway wheelman is your informant?"

"Edward Rollin Zagoria. Bail has been posted for him so he can continue his usefulness."

"So this call," said Doak, "is in the nature of a courtesy because we're asking you not to raise any questions about his release."

"Courtesy to me? Sounds more like a favor to the Bureau."

"Well, putting it that way," Ferre conceded, "Eddie will disappear, you won't see him again."

I grunted. "I first saw him and Bevins in a Keys saloon, mauling a young woman. They're both pieces of shit."

"Agreed," Doak said stiffly, "but right now Zagoria is involved in a Federal investigation."

"Of what?"

"Sorry, can't go into that."

"How often I heard that in the bad old days of DEA-Bureau infighting, and it's still the same: everything for you, nothing for me. Well, my impulse is to tell you guys to fuck off, but I'll restrain myself if you tell me one thing."

"What's that?"

"Did Bevins and Zagoria have a chance to talk together after their arrest?"

The agents looked at each other. Doak said, "I'd tell you if I knew, but I don't. It would be Bureau procedure to keep them separated but how Gables cops handle multiple arrests I can't say."

"You can ask Zagoria."

Ferre said, "He's out of range. No contact for a week."

"Well, can someone ask him then?"

"If it's important to you."

"You could even ask the Gables booking officer."

Doak shook his head. "Coming from us a query could be counterproductive, know what I mean?"

"I'm grasping at it."

Ferre got up, followed by Special Agent Doak. "We have nothing else, sir. Appreciate your cooperation."

Ferre smiled. "Bevins was complaining you pinched his money. Wants you charged with theft."

"The nerve of some people," I remarked. "The way out is straight ahead, door's unlocked."

I bolted the door after them, relieved that for the moment no law enforcement agency was aware of Tessier's quest for the emeralds, or Rita's involvement with me. Zagoria would be giving the Bureau info on the exile training camp; several Federal agencies liked knowing about such things. But my hope was that Bevins had not been given an opportunity to tell his partner what we'd been discussing while Barton was trussed on the floor. I didn't want that information getting back to Tessier, who would then know how much I knew about his plan and operation. When the time came I wanted him to find out in person.

After a while door chimes sounded, and this time I made sure the caller was the repairman. After I'd shown him the window we discussed alarm systems and he gave me brochures to compare and consider. While he replaced the cut pane I made coffee for myself and watched him install a new deadbolt with no beveled edge. Two keys came with it. I paid him a sum that seemed large enough to cover a child's summer camp tuition, and he left by the back door. I was double-locking it when the phone rang. Four times more before the machine cut in, and after the ding I heard Rita's voice on the monitor: "Three zero two. Repeat, three zero two." That was it.

I pulled on a nylon shoulder holster and filled it with my H&K .38, put on a striped seersucker jacket, and secured the house before leaving. The Miata was ready to go, so I backed out of the garage and headed for the Dolphin Expressway, MacArthur Causeway across Biscayne Bay, and the international Art Deco yuppieland of South Miami Beach.

TEN

THE REJUVENATED Clay Hotel was faced with pinkish stucco and white stone trim. It had Moorish archways, balcony and barrel-tiled roof, all overlooking Española Way, where carefree, scantily-clad girls and boys demonstrated their roller-skating skills and styles to bench-warmers, young and old.

Rita's suite comprised sitting room and bedroom with large double bed. The décor was Spanish rustic, or possibly Moorish, for all I knew. Cool interior colors prevailed; there was nothing visual to jar the senses.

When the suite door opened I thought I'd mistaken the number. For the woman in a see-through black negligee had short auburn hair. High-heel pumps matched shiny black fingernails. Her lipstick was glossy black, and for a second I thought she was either a practicing witch or dominatrix. "Yes?" she breathed, and before I could step back she pulled off black wraparound shades and giggled. "Oh, Jack, you should *see* your face!"

"Damn!" I exclaimed. "What a reception!"

"Well, you said to change my appearance." She pulled off the auburn wig and shook out her dark hair. "I did, didn't I?"

Door closed and bolted, I moved close and took her hands. "You certainly did." I parted the negligee down to her navel and kissed her nipples. She shivered, and said, "I always wondered what it would be like to wear something like this, but I never had the opportunity. Then, I noticed this little boutique called Decadence." She spun around and the lace flared high. "You like?"

"I like it for the boudoir. How does it feel?"

"Whorish—I guess. Liberated. *Insouciante.*"

"And decadent. Now stay where you are, don't leave. I can get you a thousand bucks for an hour's congenial work."

She struck my cheek lightly, bit my ear lobe. "You'd live off my earnings, too, you user. Men are such bastards."

"And women are such bitches." I grabbed and hauled her to the sofa, bent her over my knees and spanked her buns. The first slaps brought a yelp, then her body relaxed and she began squirming erotically. "You're not supposed to enjoy this," I told her, and stopped.

"Teaser."

"We'll see." I stood up, sprawling her on the rug, pulled off jacket and gun, stripped shirt and trousers, and pinioned her to the floor.

The foreplay had excited us both. She was dripping wet, and I was bone hard. We made love quickly and aggressively, and when I rolled aside she asked, "That's all?"

"Just to clear our heads. Main course later." I got up unsteadily. "Anything to drink in this joint?" I demanded.

"Try the fridge, dear."

It was built into the wet bar and held four cold bottles of Dom Pérignon. I popped one, guzzled foam, and waved the spurting bottle back and forth over her body. Rita screeched, got on her knees and grabbed the bottle. She tilted it and drank deeply, returned the bottle to me. "We're savages, aren't we? I love being so uninhibited." Black makeup was running down her face, spotting her breasts. "Back in a moment, don't leave." She disappeared through the bedroom doorway, I heard the shower spattering and presently she came back, fluffy towel wrapped around her body. Makeup gone, she looked fresh, sweet and clean. "That's my girl," I said approvingly, "though the other was pretty seductive. Shall we engage her again?"

"Whenever you like, darling." The towel dropped away and she stepped into the needle-heel pumps.

"Centerfold quality. Miss April, sure enough." I popped a second bottle, found glasses and filled them. As hers touched mine, she murmured, "I love this, darling, I don't ever want it to end."

"Doesn't have to," I said and stopped. My expression told her what I was thinking. Her fingers gently touched my cheek. "Marriage has been a convenience for me," she said quietly. "When the Colonel was expelled I was living in Spain—I have a hacienda in Asturias . . . hills, some cattle, a river, cork and almond trees . . . I know you'll love it. As a gesture to the new Guatemalan government the Spanish Foreign Ministry canceled my visa and gave me two weeks to leave. My attorney said marriage to a Spaniard was the only solution, and produced Jaime de Castenada. Old family, nearly broke. Sixty-four and in poor health. I paid him—never mind how much—thinking he wouldn't last long, and he won't. Some days he can't get to Parliament, where he has a seat. My money pays his bills, keeps up the Madrid home, and he's happy. In return I have a diplomatic passport as his wife, and total freedom. Now—do you understand?"

"Can you pay him for a divorce?"

"Not in Spain, never. But he'll be agreeable to an annulment . . . that can be expedited, too."

The marriage and the annulment were typically European solutions, I reflected, that ordinary people couldn't afford. I didn't like the arrangement, but conceded it was a sensible one, given her circumstances at the time.

She tilted my glass and sipped. "It's my problem, darling, and I'll deal with it. Meanwhile, as far as you and I are concerned, Jaime does not exist."

I drew her down on the sofa beside me, glanced at my shoes and socks and thought how ridiculous they looked. After getting them off I said, "You didn't return to Madrid when I suggested it, said you weren't ready to go. Why was that? What kept you?"

"You," she said simply. "I felt strongly drawn to you, a compulsion to find out more, learn if you were the unique male my sister described. Now"—she looked away—"I couldn't leave even if you rejected me."

"That's not an option, never was."

She laid her head against my shoulder like a little girl. "I feel loved, secure—what else should a woman want?"

"A husband, children . . ."

"Those things, too. If you don't like Spain we can live wherever you like." Her head lifted. "I mean that."

"I think I'd love living there. Asturias sounds far from drugs and violence and rioting."

"It is."

I gestured at my holstered pistol. "That's been too much a part of me for too long."

"In Spain it won't be needed. When can we go?"

I thought it over. Tessier was a major threat to both of us, but I didn't want her to know that, or why. If I gave him the emeralds and account numbers, he'd have profited from Anita's murder, and he wouldn't just go away. For him it would be easy to locate her hacienda, send a hit team to finish us off. Then turn full time to capturing Guatemala. "Soon," I replied.

"*How* soon?"

I stroked her hair, scented its cleanliness. "A few weeks. So why don't you leave now, settle with Jaime, and I'll join you as soon as I can."

"Don't want to," she said in a muffled voice. "Don't want to be so far from you. No one knows where I am, I can't possibly be found. Darling, don't make me go. All alone I'd be miserable—and worried."

From her limited viewpoint it was a reasonable argument. I couldn't think how to refute it without giving too much away, so I kissed her forehead, and said, "All right. But if danger develops I'll put you on the next plane."

Silently she nodded, and the deal was made.

* * *

We had dinner at Antonini's, a trendy two-star on 13th Street, a few blocks from the hotel. Rita was wearing her wig, a low-cut white blouse, dark shades and tight purple shorts. She was tarted-up splendidly, like the mass of young females, and thus entirely inconspicuous. We shared antipasto, creamy salad and robust Italian red wine. Over espresso I said, "Saul Hornstein will be disappointed if he doesn't get to see you again, so how about a visit tomorrow?"

"Why should I do that?" She looked at me suspiciously.

"It's 'we,' darling. We will ask his advice on disposing of Anita's possessions."

"Did she have any?"

"Foremost, a pink Jeep."

"What on earth would I do with a pink Jeep?"

"Donate it to a charity of your choice. Have Saul arrange it."

"You're so devious, darling. What's the real object of our visit?"

"Find out what he knows about Claude Tessier."

She stirred her coffee with a tiny spoon. "He's not Claude's lawyer anymore. Or is he?"

"That would be worth learning. Along with how badly Tessier wants his missing valuables." I finished my espresso. "Do you know what those valuables are?"

She hesitated before replying. "Anita had a number of cut emeralds, at least half a million dollars' worth."

"Sizeable sum. But Tessier must have banked many times that amount."

"He did. In foreign banks."

"So, what's his problem?"

"He gave Anita the account listing," she said heavily. "Without it he can't collect the money. Jack—my sister never told you this?"

"Would I be asking you? What you've told me suggests bait for a trap."

"I'm afraid I don't understand."

"Tell Hornstein you'll return Tessier's valuables. Show Saul imitation gems and a made-up account list. Hornstein will figure a percentage for himself and bring Tessier out of hiding to get it."

"Imitations . . . ? Suppose it doesn't work?"

"Then we've lost a few bucks, big deal."

She sighed. "The conspiratorial mind. But I thought you don't want me exposed to Claude."

"You won't be. Say you have to return to Spain, I'll act for you."

Her hand covered mine. "If it will end things sooner."

One way or the other, I thought. So before we left I had her call Hornstein's office from a pay phone. The message Rita left on his machine asked for a midday appointment and said she would call in the morning to confirm.

That gave us the night to ourselves, and we took full advantage of the bouncy bed and the Dom Pérignon.

Very late that night the sound of fire engines woke us. They were blocks away, but sounded close enough to startle us both. Shivering, Rita held me close, and after I'd calmed her she said huskily, "If you weren't here I'd have panicked." She nuzzled the side of my neck. "Being lonely is a terrible thing. I don't suppose you've ever felt that way."

"I have. Very much alone." I stared up at the dark ceiling. "After Pam's funeral I came back to our place, turned on the lights and looked around. It was the same; furniture, paintings, everything there, but my wife. She'd given life to the surroundings, illuminated them. Without Pam the rooms were vacant, almost hostile. Wandering through them, I felt as though I were moving through display rooms in a furniture store, and I realized how totally alone I was, that she was gone and somehow I'd have to go on without her. Took me days to gather her things together, and everything I touched had meaning, renewed memories . . ."

"Oh, Jack," she said softly, "I'm so sorry. I can feel how tragic it was for you."

Can you? I wondered. Can anyone really comprehend the emptiness of another's despair? Then nothing more was said, the fire engines went off into the night, and in each other's arms we let sleep return.

In the morning I left Rita asleep and had a continental breakfast at a place down Española Way. From there I drove to downtown Miami and left the Miata in public parking near the Seybold Building, the center of Miami's custom jewelers, most of them Cubans transplanted from old Havana. Inside, I went from one shop to another, asking about simulated gems, until at my fifth stop the elderly proprietor nodded, adjusted his yarmulke, and brought out a lined tray of glittering semi-precious stones. "It is a mounted ring you are interested in, gentleman?" he inquired politely. "Loose stones," I replied. "Emerald look-alikes. For show."

He nodded thoughtfully. "From nature I have nothing, but I can show you an assortment of *faux*-emeralds. Manufactured." And from his safe he brought over a second tray that held perhaps thirty stones, all deep translucent green and cut in a variety of styles. "Just what I had in mind," I told him, and began selecting nine stones resembling the emeralds cached in my safe. When I'd set them aside he studied my face. "You don't ask the price, gentleman?"

"I figure you're an honest craftsman. How much for the lot?"

He produced jeweler's scales and weighed each stone, noting carats on a pad. He put aside the scales and looked at his notations, calculated price, and said, "For so many, a discount price."

I nodded. "Bottom line?"

"One thousand six hundred dollars." His expression was apologetic. "Plus tax."

"You pay the tax, okay?" I counted sixteen hundred-dollar bills from my wallet and handed them over. "And a carrying bag if you have one. Or a piece of cloth."

"With pleasure." From under the display counter he brought out a small velvet bag with a gold cord drawstring and I dropped the stones into it. "Thank you," I said, and turned to go. "No, gentleman, thank *you*. My first customer of the day. A good sale is a good omen."

"For both of us."

"*Shalom*," he said, and I left him to his wares, the gem bag in my pocket.

In the street-level arcade I downed a tiny paper cup of Cuban coffee and phoned Rita's room from a pay phone. She answered sleepily, and I told her it was time to phone Hornstein and confirm a twelve-thirty meet. "If there's a problem, call me at the house. If not, meet me at noon. Corner of Española Way and Collins Avenue." She repeated the instructions, and murmured, "I miss you, wish you were here."

"So do I. *Ciao*."

"*Ciao*, yourself." She hung up. From there I drove west on Flagler as far as Bird Road, where I turned south and entered the Gables, finding my house undisturbed. After shaving I changed into wiseguy clothing I'd acquired in undercover work, hung a gold chain around my neck and clasped a gold Rolex to my wrist. My shirt was Italian-cut faded blue denim, pants baggy gray cotton, bare ankles and black Magli slippers. The costume made me look like the type of client Hornstein was comfortable with.

I opened the safe, got out the bank account card and copied portions on a trimmed card from my Rolodex. I printed the city abbreviations, but altered digits in each account number, before including it with the simulated stones in my velvet bag. Then it was time to leave.

Rita was waiting when I pulled up, got in beside me, and said, "Twelve-thirty it is—and he sounded eager to see me. But you—what have you *done* to yourself? Is this the real you?"

"Not hardly." I placed the velvet bag in her lap, and when she opened it she gasped. "They look real!"

"Real enough to hook Hornstein," I said. "And Tessier."

We drove south on Collins, turned west for the causeway, and south again to Brickell Avenue. Hornstein's office occupied two floors of a new high-rise with underground parking. The elevator whisked us to the twelfth floor, whose corridor window provided a sweeping view of Biscayne Bay.

Oak double doors had polished brass handles and a brass nameplate: Law Offices. Saul F. Hornstein, Esquire.

The reception area held a broad magazine table and an oak desk that supported a multiplex phone system. Behind the receptionist, a computer console and a large oil portrait of the boss. On each side of it framed newspaper clippings featured Hornstein victories; other walls were hung with bold-colored modern oils.

The receptionist was a zaftig binzel in a flimsy peach top, with a demure smile and an oversize chest. She took Rita's name, spoke inaudibly to the intercom, and announced, "It'll be a few minutes. Coffee?"

"Please," Rita responded. I shook my head, no. The girl excused herself and came back with a silver tray bearing sugar and cream, coffee in a patterned Spode cup with saucer. We seated ourselves, and the receptionist asked, "Anything else?" and looked down at me. "Anything at all."

"I'm sure," I said softly, and got a hard look from Rita. "But not right now, *gracias.*"

"Whenever," she said silkily, and palmed down her hips as though stripping off water. She returned to her desk and replaced her headset. Rita eyed me irritably, said in Spanish, "You're allowed one letch per month, and that was it."

"*Sí, querida,*" I said contritely, and lovingly stroked her thigh. Rita ignored it and finished her coffee. For five minutes no one spoke, then a flush door opened and Saul Hornstein himself came in. He was wearing a beige silk shirt with puffed sleeves and open collar, through which showed a gold chain with large links and a Star of David. Beltless matching linen trousers, whose bottoms smothered white leather shoes. His face was tanned and healthy. Thick black eyebrows and flowing mustache were neatly trimmed, and his mouth opened to show apposite rows of perfectly capped teeth. "*Señora,*" he exclaimed, "so sorry to keep you waiting. So good of you to come."

Rising, Rita said, "It's I who should apologize for so little notice. But I'm leaving for Spain, and it was now or never."

"Then let's not waste more time." He hadn't included me in his remarks, or acknowledged my presence with a glance. But I was now standing beside her and he could no longer ignore me. Hand on my arm, Rita said, "This is my friend, José Menéndez."

"Call me Pepe," I said genially and thrust out my hand. Reluctantly he took it, muttered, "Saul Hornstein," and led the way to his office. His glass-topped desk was about eight feet wide and backed by a tall leather-padded chair. The silver-gray carpeting was springy underfoot and covered the considerable expanse of his thirty-by-thirty room. His desk was flanked by flags of Florida and the USA on display standards. The wall behind was covered with framed diplomas, hand-decorated achievement awards and testimonials, and large photographs of Himself with a chronological progression of Presidents, governors and senators, as far back as JFK. Another wall consisted of built-in bookcases filled with law books. The wall opposite the desk was inset with a

four-by-four TV screen, and below it the façade of a VCR. As Hornstein sat
in his CEO chair he pointed to an antique French provincial sofa and invited
us to be seated. After tenting his fingers and propping the tips under his chin,
he spoke to Rita. "You've had a terrible time, and I'm very sorry about the
loss of your sister. Is there anything I can do to make things a bit easier?"

I looked away from his earnest face. Here in the belly of the beast I reaf-
firmed what crime was all about. Crime paid impressively well. After experi-
encing Hornstein's suite, who could doubt it?

"There is," Rita replied smoothly. "I feel something should be done with
Anita's possessions—whatever she had."

He nodded. "There was some clothing, I understand, a watch, a bit of jewelry—all probably still lodged with the Monroe County Sheriff. Do you know
of anything else?"

"She had a vehicle—a pink Jeep. It was parked behind her bungalow."

"And should be reclaimed. What do you want done with it, *señora*?"

"I believe my sister would want it given to a worthy charity that could use
it in their programs, or sell it for the money."

"Very generous," he responded. "Do you have a particular charity in
mind?"

"Salvation Army?"

"Excellent choice."

"Can you—will you make the arrangements?" she asked.

"Happy to. Now, what to do with the personal items?"

"Perhaps they could be sent for—there's no hurry—and Pepe could claim
them for me." She gave me a loving glance, to show Hornstein how matters
stood.

"Yes, that can be attended to, no problem." He hated looking at me because
I represented an obstacle to a possible conquest of Rita and her fortune, but
he had to when he asked, "Your phone number?"

"I stay loose," I grinned. "No fixed abode. I'll check with you, okay?"

His sour expression changed as he turned again to Rita. "Is there anything
else?"

She nodded. "Were you representing my father?"

His lips pursed. "During extradition litigation. And had he been brought
here I was prepared to continue the representation."

"And Claude Tessier?"

"For a time I was his attorney, yes, but that relationship no longer exists.
He deceived me, deceived the court, and is a fugitive from this jurisdiction."

She sighed. "That's disappointing."

"See," I said, "told you, didn't I?"

Rita patted my arm.

"Perhaps—" Hornstein said, and left the thought unfinished. Rita breathed deeply. "Well, it concerns some valuables Claude left with his wife, my sister. I have them, and to unburden myself I want to return them to Claude."

"May I know the nature of these valuables?"

From her purse she drew the velvet bag and handed it over to Hornstein. He undid the drawstring and spilled stones across his desk, gasped as he saw their glitter. The card came out, too, and he eyed it. "Emeralds," he said thickly. "One, two—nine emeralds." He swallowed. "Must be worth a great deal."

"Worth a damn big fortune," I volunteered. "Yeah, and she's crazy to give them away."

"But I have more money than I'll ever need, dear." She smiled and touched my cheek roguishly. "Besides," she said to the lawyer, "I have reason to believe Claude would resort to violence to regain the jewels, and I don't want that sort of thing. Not at all."

"Me neither," I interjected. "Money ain't worth a life—and he's a lifetaker, from what I hear."

Hornstein licked his lips, touched a mustache tip. "You have something in mind, *señora*?"

"I thought that if you and Claude are in contact you could mention the emeralds—and that card, whatever it is."

He picked it up, scanned it, and from his expression I knew that he grasped the numbers' significance. Or perhaps Tessier had told him. "You are prepared to convey these . . . items to Mr. Tessier?"

"In return for peace of mind. You see, I know a good deal about my former brother-in-law, how inclined to violence he is. I just want these things off my hands and out of my life."

"I see," he said thoughtfully, and began restoring the stones to the bag. The card went in last. "How can I be of assistance?"

"Even if I were remaining here I would not want to deal with Claude face-to-face. He can be very frightening." I squeezed her hand comfortingly. "But if there is no way to contact him . . ." She reached over and reclaimed the velvet bag. It vanished in her purse.

"Suppose—for the sake of argument—that Claude does contact me. What should I say?"

"That the valuables will be returned to him under certain conditions. Pepe will have them, he'll decide what to do."

He didn't like my keeping the emeralds, preferring himself as the temporary—or permanent—custodian of same. And couldn't resist saying, "I have a vault, perfectly safe and secure."

"That could be dangerous for you, I'm afraid. No, Pepe will take care of everything." She smiled sunnily at me. "Until I return. Won't you, dear?"

"Right," I said. "That's how it is. Uh—got a camera around here?"

He nodded. "Several, I believe."

"Then take a snapshot of the jewels. If Tessier calls, tell him you've got a photo. That oughta hurry things up."

"Excellent idea. I should have thought of it." He spoke to the desk intercom, drummed fingers on the desktop. Presently a shy young fellow floated in, Nikon strapped around his neck. Hornstein explained what he wanted done, and Rita handed back the bag. The photographer placed everything on a sheet of white paper, and flashed three times. "Include the bag," I ordered.

He flashed again. "There, that is everything. Develop now?"

"No hurry," Hornstein told him. "Thank you, Ronald."

Ronald drifted out as silently as he'd arrived, and while Rita was scooping everything into the bag, the lawyer said, "Of course, I have no idea when or if Claude will make contact."

"I understand," Rita said evenly, "but we'll hope." Standing, she offered her hand to Hornstein across his desk. "Thank you so much, sir. Shall I pay outside?"

He waved a hand dismissively. "No charge, *señora*. Glad to be of some small service, under the circumstances." As I rose he said, "It could expedite matters if I had a means of reaching you, sir."

"Pepe. Pepe Menendez," I said cheerfully. "Won't hurt Tessier to wait a while, right? Just think of what he's getting. Anyway, some things can't be hurried. I'll call every now and then."

"And," added Rita, "I assume this matter will be treated in strict confidence."

"Absolutely. Not even my closest associates will know." And Ronald, I felt sure, was the soul of discretion.

Hornstein led us to the door, clumsily kissed the back of Rita's hand in what he hoped was a reassuring gesture, and we made our goodbyes. As we passed through the reception area Rita spoke to the receptionist. "Get a life, kid," she spat, and we went out together.

In the corridor she hissed, "I *saw* how you were stripping her with your eyes, you bastard."

"And I saw how Saul was salivating over you. But don't fret, darling," I said soothingly, "I'm all yours."

Driving back to the Hotel Clay, we laughed over the act we'd put on for Hornstein until Rita sobered and said, "I hate to think of the danger when you meet Claude."

"I've got too much to live for to take unnecessary risks. Trust me."

She laughed thinly. "Where have I heard that before? Promise me you won't be in any danger."

"I promise."

So I drove down to Crawdaddy's on the farthest point of the Beach, where we had a splendid lunch with numerous tequila cocktails while enjoying the sea breeze and the slow, majestic passage of cruise ships through the channel. Then we repaired to her place and made love in air-conditioned comfort for the rest of the afternoon.

ELEVEN

THREE DAYS later I phoned Hornstein long enough to hear him deny contact with Tessier. Okay. Either the con would work or it wouldn't; I had plans for both.

Meanwhile, Rita and I were living a lovers' idyll and were hardly ever apart. At the Trail Glades Range I gave her basic pistol instruction and taught her to shoot from combat crouch. Driving to and from the Range, we'd stop beside a promising-looking canal, flip in a shiner or live shrimp and hope a snook would strike. She'd done fly-fishing in Spain for trout and salmon, and though spinning tackle was new to her she adapted fast. But over a week's trying we hooked no snook at all, though we brought in a lot of bream and crappie, and five average largemouth bass. I released them all because her suite had no cooking facilities, and I didn't want her seen at my place.

Almost daily she'd urge me to abandon the hunt for Tessier and come to Asturias. And she telephoned her Madrid lawyer to arrange the annulment. Paying off Jaime was a mere matter of price, and although ecclesiastical approval also involved pesetas, the Madrid diocese moved slowly in such things.

Next time I called Hornstein he told me Anita's bags had been delivered to his office and I could claim them from his office manager. I said, "I'll leave them there a while, in case Mr. Tessier wants them."

"Suit yourself, Mr. Menendez," he said irritably, "Claude—"

"Pepe. Call me Pepe."

"Claude is not likely to contact me."

"Then maybe after thirty days I get the emeralds."

"Don't even think of that," he warned.

"Or we could split them. Rita's in Spain, she'd never know."

"That's a shocking suggestion. Shocking. And highly unethical."

I smothered a laugh. Hornstein held the state record for charges from the Florida Bar, a companion record for beating every one. On technicalities. "Hey, man, I'm sorry. Forget it, huh?"

"Never mention such a thing again," he said severely, "and now I have other things to do. Goodbye."

I smiled as I left the pay phone. Hornstein was forming a clear concept of me as a not-too-bright self-promoter with flexible standards and criminal inclinations. He'd pass that misinformation to Tessier, giving me a potential psychological advantage.

I had a pretty good idea where Tessier was hiding out, and sensed he wouldn't break cover if he could avoid it. For all I knew, he might never telephone Hornstein, sending all my planning and waiting down the tube. Maybe Rita was right; I should break off and settle in Asturias to lead the life of landed gentry. Objectively she couldn't be faulted, but she hadn't found Anita's bloody, tortured body, seen the death glaze in those once lovely eyes. I had, and the memory haunted me, propelled me on.

But when I joined Rita in her suite I was halfway ready to surrender. She kissed me, and asked, "News?"

I shook my head.

"I thought not, you look so dispirited. How can I cheer you up?"

"You really need to ask?"

"But I'm dressed to go out—we have lunch plans."

"Now you're sounding like a wife," I said grumpily.

"And you sound like a husband who wants sex on demand," she retorted.

"Unlike Jaime," I said cruelly. "Oh, shit, honey, I shouldn't have said that. Blame it on my mood. I'm mad and frustrated because nothing's happened. We baited a trap and the rat hasn't even sniffed it."

"That's not your fault, darling, and you're forgiven for what you said. It was uncalled for and it wasn't nice."

"Apologized, didn't I? Sorry, I was wrong. There." I splashed Añejo in a glass, added ice.

"Drinking alone?" She came over to the bar where I was standing.

"Old habit. Same for you?" I made her drink and we touched glasses. "Suppose we had the real emeralds, the real account list—what would you do with them?"

"Use them to bring Tessier to justice," she said firmly.

"Leaving out Tessier—what then?"

"Do something for Guatemalan children: money for food, medicine, clinics, help their mothers. Jack, you don't know how miserably those people, especially the Indian families, live—I mean exist. It's pitiful. And the Colonel bears a lot of responsibility—he and his cohorts, men like Tessier, enriched themselves while the poor starved."

"He wasn't the first looter, and won't be the last. But I've seen what you describe—gone in from the Chiapas border through the Petén, Quezaltenango ... heart wrenching." For an instant I was going to give her the real emeralds, tell her the full story, but I checked myself. It would be dangerous knowledge for her to possess, while giving her a powerful reason to have me leave Tessier alone. Those were the negatives, besides which I wanted time to hook Tessier and bring him to gaff.

"Still," she said quietly, "it's a wonderful fantasy."

"And I love you for it." I kissed her cheek. "Let's go lunch at Christy's and forget problems while we can."

That evening we took a dinner cruise along Indian Creek, the boat gliding past Miami Beach's condo/hotel wall on one side, magnificent estates and their moored yachts on the other. The view was supposed to compensate for the mediocre food, although Rita was impressed by the softly lighted *palazzos* we passed. To that I said, "Some were bought with dirty money."

"Drug money?"

I nodded. "And some were confiscated by DEA, resold to legitimate buyers."

"I could be a legitimate buyer."

"You've got a spread," I remarked. "Maybe more. I don't need ostentation, honey, and I don't think you do, either."

"Still, it would be nice to have a place here when hacienda life gets boring."

"With you I don't think it could ever be boring. Besides, we don't want Hornstein as a neighbor."

"He has one of those?" She gestured at the shoreline.

"I've heard. Glitz adds to his image."

"A repellent man," she said with a grimace.

"But useful, if he establishes contact with Tessier."

"Pepe Menendez," she laughed. "You were marvelous, know that?"

"I think he bought it, but we'll see."

So after the boat docked we returned to the hotel and turned on the TV. I was pouring cognac, when I noticed Rita staring fixedly at the set. I watched the story until I realized it concerned child abuse, father-daughter incest. "Hey," I said, "that's pretty depressing, let's—"

"Depressing, yes. It happened to me." She burst into tears.

I turned off the set and sat beside her on the sofa, held her in my arms while she wept. After a while she said brokenly, "I was going to have to tell you sometime but I didn't know how to begin."

I kissed her cheek and forehead. "You don't have to tell me anything, ever."

"But I do." She began drying her eyes. "I was thirteen, Jack. The Colonel was drunk, came to my bedroom and raped me."

"God! Where was your mother?"

"In France, visiting relatives. Every night he forced me until she came back, then only when she wasn't around."

"Didn't you tell her?"

"She preferred not to believe me, called me a lying little slut who was probably fucking the servants." She broke down again and I held her tightly until the spasm passed. Exhaustedly she said, "He wouldn't leave me alone, always after me, pawing me, fingering me . . . After I threatened to kill him he sent me off to the convent school . . . My baby was born there, the nuns saw to everything, wouldn't let me kill myself. I named him Rafael, a sweet little child but"—her voice quavered—"when he was less than two I realized he wasn't—right. Nothing to be done. He's thirteen now, lives with me in Spain." Her eyes searched my face beseechingly. "I'm afraid, afraid you can't accept that."

"He's part of you, and he needs a father, a real father." I stroked her head consolingly, my mind filled with a mixture of rage and sorrow. How could a man do that to his own daughter? If Chavez wasn't already dead I'd want to kill him. Handing her the cognac, I said, "Drink it down, all of it." After she'd swallowed I did the same.

In a muted voice she said, "I had therapy, Jack, years of it. I seldom saw the Colonel but Claude came now and then. He wanted the same thing the Colonel wanted—I let him, because it was a way of getting back at the Colonel, don't you see?"

I nodded. "And Tessier married your sister."

"Yes. While I was in the convent the Colonel raped her, too, used her as he'd used me."

"Jesus, what a bastard! And your mother . . . ?"

"Moved away to avoid acknowledging the situation." She breathed deeply. "I think she and Claude were lovers. No, I'm quite sure they were. Now you understand why I loathed my father, why I hate Claude Tessier—and my mother."

"I understand." The Chavez quagmire was deeper and more sickening than I'd begun to imagine. Killing Tessier would clean things up—a little. As I looked at her face I could visualize a handsome boy playing happily in the broad fields of Asturias, tended by a devoted niñera, innocent of life as it really was.

I went to the bar for refills, and while I was there Rita asked, "Are you ashamed of me?"

"Hell, no. I love and admire you more for all you've gone through—and for keeping Rafael with you." Handing her the glass, I asked, "How much does your husband know?"

"He knows I have a son, not who the father was."

"But Tessier knows?"

"He knows. Sometimes I wondered if he used that knowledge to blackmail the Colonel—except that the Colonel could easily have had him killed." She sipped lengthily. I gave her my handkerchief to blot her cheeks. Looking away, she said, "Once I stole something from a Paris shop—a scarf. I was arrested, paid for it, and my psychiatrist said it was a sexual thing I'd done."

"Kleptomania," I nodded. "So they say."

"After the theft was explained to me I never did anything like that again. But until you, dear, I never knew real sexual love, what it could be like. It's opened me to you—completely."

"I'm glad, and grateful."

"You'll never leave me?" she asked in a childlike voice.

"Never."

"We can have a happy life, Jack, don't you think?"

"I know we can. And have children of our own."

"I want that, too."

So after a while I led her to the bedroom and we lay down together, holding each other like survivors on a raft in a raging sea. My thoughts kept churning until I felt her body relax in my arms, her breathing slow in sleep. Then, I slept, too.

Next day I phoned Hornstein again, and this time he said Tessier had contacted him and wanted to meet with me.

"How soon?" I asked.

"He'll tell you. Gave me this phone number to set things up."

I wrote it down, not the Ochopee phone.

"Got it," I told him. "Anything else I should know?"

"I'm out of it. Regards to Señora Castenada." The connection ended.

I stared at the dead phone. Thanks, Saul, I said half aloud, I'll take it from here.

BOOK
TWO

TWELVE

THE SECRETARY who answered Manny's phone said he was in Puerto Rico attending a regional meeting. Rats! I'd wanted a fix on the phone number I was to call, now I'd have to do without.

Tessier.

He'd made it with Mama Marie, tupped both sisters and had one killed, combining sex and murder. And I couldn't stop wondering if he'd arranged the Colonel's death. Everything Rita told me was further evidence that Chavez deserved to die. An animal, inhuman. Too bad he wasn't going to be with Tessier at our meet; that deprived me of the pleasure and satisfaction of killing them both. A twofer. So I'd settle for one.

I'd had plenty of time to plan for the meet, now I had to prepare for it. Carefully. I wanted to take Tessier when he was alone, where I couldn't be blindsided, and that limited meeting sites to the sea.

I left the pay phone and returned to Rita's suite. Her pale face and vacant eyes showed she was still emotionally racked by last night's revelations and the memories they renewed. I wanted to comfort and reassure her but decided the best course was to stay off the subject and occupy her thoughts with Hornstein's news. After I'd told her she seemed to draw herself together. "What now?" she asked in a dull voice.

"Why, I meet the man."

"Yes, but then . . . ?"

"Don't worry about it," I told her gently. "The less you know, the less involved you are. And that's important to me."

"You mean," she seemed to shiver, "if something goes wrong."

"Nothing will. But in the unlikely event it does, you know nothing." I sucked in a steadying breath. "Then you'll go back to Spain and resume life as it was."

"Hardly an attractive picture," she remarked, got up from the sofa and came to me, circling my neck with her arms. "I don't think I'd want to live if . . . anything happened to you."

"Nonsense. You have Rafael to live for, and many other reasons. Just don't worry about me. I've dealt face-to-face with big-time drug creeps and always came out on top."

"But you were shot—in Mexico. Right?"

"Shoulda ducked," I told her, "and I'm okay now. Right?"

She smiled vaguely. "Certainly are. Now when are you meeting Claude?"

"Won't know until I talk with him. I want to meet tonight, have done with it, and fly off to Spain with you."

"My fondest hope," she murmured. "Will you come here afterward?"

"Of course."

"When? Can you give me an idea so I won't go crazy?"

"Let's say midnight, one o'clock, thereabouts." I kissed her forehead. "We'll talk about it then."

Her eyes searched my face. "All of it?"

"All of it," I lied, and looked at my watch. "Tessier may be waiting." Then, after a long, close embrace, I left her and went down to my Miata. From South Beach I drove to the Gables and my place.

After collecting mail I got out my heavy, zippered scuba bag and put my MAC-10 into it, along with a spare mag. Then the trusty sawed-off and a nearly full box of Number Four high-base shells. I checked the Beretta magazine, chambered a shell, and fitted it back into its nylon holster. With that arsenal, if I failed to kill Tessier I deserved to die.

I itched to phone Tessier, but whatever time I gave him before the meet would enable him to make plans of his own. On the other hand, I reasoned, Hornstein could have suggested I was a jolly-jack, letting Tessier believe I'd be easy to take. In theory, he wanted only emeralds and account card, and had no reason to kill me . . . but killing was his way of doing business. So why not eliminate Pepe Menendez, the simpleton? Cleaner for him that way.

The bag of simulated emeralds was in my pocket, ready to show Tessier if things got that far. There was nothing else needed from the house.

So I drove down US 1 to the marina where I'd left the Renegade, and parked the Miata near the office. At the adjoining marine supply store I bought a halogen spotlight and screwed it to the decking that covered the forward cubby. Checked gas and oil; both okay for the short run ahead: battery fully charged. Ready for fight or frolic.

There was a saloon about fifty yards away. On my way to it I scuffed over crushed coral and the harsh sound reminded me of trudging to the Plaza Romana that hot and dusty afternoon. Were the killers with her then? I asked myself. If I'd opened the door would I have saved her life? Tessier would know but there'd be no time to ask him.

At the bar I killed a short Cuba Libre, sucked in lungsful of cool air and braved the heat again on my way to the outside pay phone.

I dialed the number carefully and counted the rings. Five before a voice answered. "*Señor* Tessier?" I asked politely.

"Who wants him?" In Spanish.

"Pepe . . . Menendez. Saul's friend."

"I'm Tessier. Talk."

I hesitated. "Ah . . . *señor*, I'm at work now, can't talk from here. See—I needed to make sure you were at this phone number." I paused again. "I'll call later."

"What the—" he began angrily, but I broke the connection. Let the bastard wait, and sweat, I thought, knowing he would, because he believed I had what he wanted, and repo time was near.

I weighed calling Rita, decided in favor of it, and dropped another quarter in the slot. When she answered, her voice was low and breathy, as though she'd been crying. "Things are moving along," I told her. "Everything's A-OK."

"Oh, Jack, I'm so afraid—please don't see him. We'll leave tonight. *Please.*"

"Nothing to be afraid of, honey. I'll tie up loose ends and be with you later. Just don't stray far from the phone, okay? And you might change into those beguiling pretties you bought at Decadence."

"If—if you still want me," she said uncertainly.

"I do, always will. Now don't worry. We'll be in Spain before you know it."

"Promise?"

"I promise. Love you." I hung up and wiped perspiration from my face, thinking that because we hadn't made love since her tearful confession she was probably assuming I regarded her as tainted. Well, we'd straighten that out later—after I'd consigned Claude Tessier to the deep.

While on the phone I'd heard a car pull into the side lot but hadn't seen it. Not until I'd entered the bar again and taken a booth did I realize a Sheriff's patrol car had arrived. With two deputies who knew my face. They were standing at the bar holding glasses of what looked like Coke, and so far they hadn't noticed me. Corporal Rafe and Private Jesse. Smiley and Goober. If I left now they might look around, so I decided to stay put and hope. I signaled a waitress, and ordered fries, a cheeseburger and a large Coors while avoiding their line of sight. While I was doing that, Smiley and Goober accepted refills. *Shit*! The two Bubbas were taking their time cooling off. I raised the stained menu and held it myopically close to my face until the waitress brought my order.

"Dessert?" she asked.

"Think not, just the bill." I raised the beer stein and took a long pull. The waitress scribbled on her order pad, tore off a chit, and laid it on the table. "Enjoy," she commanded, and waltzed off with the menu. Not a day under sixty, but Smiley and Goober watched her haunch movement with overt approval. Jesus, I thought, they must really be hard-up, and in that moment Smiley glanced at me. His eyes widened, and he tapped his partner's shoulder. I kept stein at mouth until they left the bar and came toward me.

Arms folded, Goober stared down at my face. "Seen you before, mister."

"Possibly." I lifted the greasy hamburger bun and bit into it. The taste was worse than I'd imagined.

"Yeah," said Smiley, "you was the guy found the Tessier broad. Right?"

I chewed for a few moments and swallowed. "Who?"

They exchanged glances before Goober spoke. "What's your name?"

"Novak."

"Yeah? Where do you work?"

"Until Braniff folded I was in maintenance. Now unemployed." I drizzled catsup over my fries and chewed one. Greasy as the burger. Yechh.

"Got ID?"

I took out my wallet and extracted my driving license, placed it face up. Smiley examined the photo, then my face. Goober pointed at my right hand. "Mech? Don't look like no mech's hands."

"Well," I said, "it's been a while since I worked, but when I did it was avionics. Solder burns now and then, no grease."

"What else you got?"

I produced pilot's and concealed weapons' licenses for their inspection. They eyed them, turned them over, and finally returned them to me. Reluctantly. Goober asked, "Whatcha doin' here?"

"Having lunch, officers, and a beer. Being of age."

"I mean like being here, on Matecumbe?"

"I keep a boat over there." I gestured toward the marina. "Small boat. For fishing. After lunch I'll take it out for a spin, maybe catch a grouper. Okay?"

"Reckon," Smiley grunted. "But I still figure you was at the Plaza Romana."

I took another bite of cheeseburger. Swallowing gave me time to concoct a reply. "Sounds like a massage parlor," I remarked. "Here in the Keys?" I replaced the three licenses in my wallet, slid it back in my hip pocket. I didn't want them shaking down my Miata; they'd come across the MAC-10, and for that weapon I had no license. So I smiled amiably, and after a few moments Smiley and his partner returned to the bar. Before they got further ideas I decided to leave. So I laid money on the bill and walked slowly out of the bar. From there I went directly to my boat, started the motor and cast off. What I'd eaten formed a cold, hard greaseball in my stomach, made sour by the beer. I kept the boat offshore until I saw the green-and-white patrol car pull out of the bar's parking lot. Then I headed in and bought two ice bags and three liters of Evian water for the cooler, feeling lucky the deputies hadn't hauled me

down to the Sheriff's office for further examination. Things could have gotten
unpleasant, and I'd have missed my date with Tessier.

After opening the Miata's door and letting out heated air I drove north to
Tavernier and parked at the end of the bridge over the creek. From the hump
of the bridge I shaded my eyes and looked north across Florida Bay. The old
Navy bomb-run marker was still there, about a mile offshore. When new it
had resembled an oil drilling rig, but most of the superstructure was rusted
away. Now it was marked on charts as a navigational hazard and painted red
warning blinker maintained by the the Coast Guard. Excellent. It was the ref-
erence point I needed for my night's work.

At five-thirty, after workers stopped working, I phoned Tessier again. Testily, he said, "That you, Menendez?"

"Me. Uh—*Señor* Tessier, it's important you understand that I'm not involved in this—just doing a favor for *La Señora.*"

"I understand."

"But I have to protect myself."

"What's on your mind?"

I hesitated, cleared my throat, and said, "I want to turn over what's yours,
but I'm not a brave man, don't want trouble."

"So?"

"So just the two of us meet, okay?"

"Where?"

"Offshore. Take a small boat, open so I can see it's just you, and I'll meet
you at eight tonight."

He thought it over, said irritably, "Where, dummy?"

"A mile north of Tavernier Creek there's an old iron structure in the water,
got a light on it. I'll be there, you be there, and I'll give you what's coming
to you."

"Lot of trouble for us both, dummy. Let's keep it simple. Why not cars?"

"Ah . . . um . . . can't see inside cars." My tone was apologetic, humble.
"My way, or—"

"All right, all right. Mile off the creek mouth, you say."

"That's it." I sighed loudly with relief. "Blinking light, can't miss it."

"Listen, with me going to all this trouble you better be there, Menendez."

"Oh, I'll be there, *señor*, and it'll be worth all the trouble." My trouble,
not his. I broke the connection and went back to my car. Sitting in it, I reviewed
the rendezvous plan and wondered what could possibly go wrong. Greed would
drive him to the meeting point, and if he was convinced I was a dummy he'd
be off guard and vulnerable. The way I wanted him. The bag of fake emeralds
felt heavy in my pocket, but in a few hours I wouldn't need them.

From the distance four sportfishing boats were coming in, broad wakes behind them. End of an active day for the fishermen, and my action was just

beginning. To the left, the sun lay about twenty degrees above the horizon, another two hours' light. After that I'd need only the old marker's blinker, and my spotlight.

From the bridge I drove six miles to the Crack'd Conch and ordered Añejo on the rocks to settle my growling stomach. When I felt better I munched a small order of smoked marlin, then three conch fritters, and requested a side of sautéed yellowtail, thanks but no fries. As I ate I kept track of the time, and afterward I drove back to the marina.

This time I stowed my weapons bag in the boat, returned to the Miata and locked my wallet in the glove compartment. After applying an anti-theft bar to the steering wheel, I locked the car and got into the Renegade.

Even in fast-fading light, following the coastline was easy. I throttled down off Tavernier Creek and looked around to see if Tessier's boat had arrived. Not yet. I opened the weapons bag and set MAC-10 and sawed-off on the duckboards out of sight, put on the holstered Beretta, and concealed it under my lightweight jacket.

Quarter to eight. The sun was way down, silhouetting mangrove islands offshore. Okay, I was going to kill Tessier and make a new life with Rita, but I hadn't resolved disposal of the real emeralds and the Colonel's bank accounts. Only God and the bankers knew how many looted millions were involved; I had no claim to them and Rita didn't need them, so she was the logical recipient. If she decided to turn over the loot to the Guat bank reps, I wouldn't object. But I preferred her idea of doing direct good with the money, helping the wretched Indians for whom it had been intended. That would make up for some of the Colonel's savageries.

At five to eight I ran west at moderate speed before turning back toward the marker, whose blinking light was clearly visible. I didn't intend to tie up there and lose mobility so I eased into neutral a hundred yards away.

Eight o'clock. Where the hell was Tessier? Should be able to see his boat's red-and-green running lights, assuming he had enough savvy to turn them on. East, a party boat was moving into the bay for night fishing: snapper, grunts and grouper. Thirty dollars a head for possibly three bucks worth of fish. But it was sport. Affordable sport, an evening away from wife and kids.

Five after eight. I kept scanning toward shore as the party boat chugged off in the distance. Picked up the MAC-10 and switched to full auto. Sink his boat, too, I thought, as the Renegade had been sunk. Hatred for this murderer, this debaucher of women, this mother-fucker, raised bile in my throat. Coughing, I spat overboard, and when I raised my head from the gunwale I saw tiny red-and-green lights heading my way. In profile, the boat was lighter than the sea as it came toward the blinking light. It had a center console and a powerful inboard engine. A man stood at the wheel, guiding it toward rendezvous. With no lights showing I swung the Renegade toward the yellow warning light just as the other boat reached it. From fifty yards away I turned on the spotlight, caught man and boat in its glare. He waved at me to cut it off, but I kept coming, wanting to get within sure-kill range before I fired the automatic. He was wearing a light guayabera, no shoulder holster. I saw him pull the throttle and his engine died. Cupping his hands, he shouted, "Come alongside and give it to me. And turn off the light."

Twenty yards away I bent over and picked up the submachine gun. That gave him the opportunity to jerk a pistol from his belt and point it. "No need for that," I called, keeping the auto out of sight, "you'll get it."

He fired a shot so close to my boat's hull that water splashed over the coaming. "Tie the bag to a lifejacket and I'll pick it up," he ordered, and shot out my spotlight.

Dammit, I hadn't figured on a shoot-out but the play was far from over. My night vision was high, but for another minute his would be close to zero, thanks to my spotlight. Ducking down, I grabbed a lifejacket and tied it to the velvet bag. When he went for it I'd have my chance. "Coming," I called, and tossed the jacket toward him.

In that moment he fired a distress rocket upward, and when it burst, a parachute flare descended. For a hundred yards around us the sea was light as day. I could see every detail of his face; Tessier without question. And, of course, he could see me. His pistol began to flash and bark and bullets hit the hull, but waves were rocking my boat. I dropped out of sight, MAC-10 in hand, while he kept firing. Two more bullets impacted, a third whistled over my head. His magazine should be empty, I decided, and peered over the coaming. Just then I heard the heavy flutter of chopper blades and saw a big one rise from sea level to hover fifty feet above my head. From it bullets sprayed my boat and water fountained through the duckboards. I fired a burst at the chopper, which banked away, and looked for Tessier. He was out of sight, but I fired the MAC-10 where I thought he was lying, and suddenly the chopper was overhead again. I gave it another burst but my bullets weren't jacketed, and the chopper was armored. When the receiver locked back on Empty I pulled out my Beretta and kept firing at Tessier's boat. I could see the impact holes but not Tessier, and while I was focusing on him there was a solid thud behind me and I turned to see a man releasing the chopper's ladder with one hand, while pointing an Uzi at me.

THIRTEEN

"**D**ROP IT," he snarled, and I let the Beretta fall into water that was flooding my boat. My sawed-off was already submerged. The chopper veered over to Tessier's boat and a man began laddering down. Tessier steadied the ladder for him, and when he was free of it, Tessier handed him a boathook and pointed at the drifting lifejacket. Three tries and he lifted the jacket aboard. Tessier grabbed it, untied the gem bag and probed it with his fingers. I couldn't see stones he brought out but I could see the smile of triumph on his face.

My boarder was wearing jungle camo and black jump boots; extra Uzi magazines were belted to his waist. I gave him a sick smile and said, "He's got what he wanted, I go now?"

"Don't be a comedian. He's got questions for you."

"So, let him ask. But it better be quick or we'll be swimming."

"You, maybe, not me." He waved his left arm and Tessier's boat came toward us. The chopper noise blanketed the sound of his engine. It was giving me a headache—in addition to the disgust I felt over my failed performance. Tessier's boat bumped gunwales with mine, and the Uzi-man said, "Get out and get in. Now." The Uzi poked my ribs menacingly, so I climbed over and got into the boat I'd intended to sink. Tessier appeared not to notice me. He was sitting down, eyeing the gemstones one after another, his man at the wheel. I saw him extract the trimmed Rolodex card and tuck it away. Then he looked at me. "Hornstein said you were a dummy, but I think you fooled him." He poked his pistol into my belly. "Didn't you?"

I shrugged.

"You and that Chavez whore." He stood and gestured the chopper away. "Where is she?"

"Spain."

"No," he said. "I phoned her hacienda and she hadn't been there in weeks. Where is she?"

"Maybe they lied to you."

"The kid wouldn't lie, not smart enough. A real dummy." He laughed coarsely. Over his shoulder I saw the parachute flare drop into the sea, its light extinguished. He'd been ahead of me all the way.

After telling the helmsman to take the boat to base Tessier gazed at me again. "Know why the kid's a dummy?"

I swallowed. "Didn't know she had a kid."

"Well, she does, and it's the Colonel's. He had a good thing going with his daughters, but only one conceived." He laughed again, nastily. "My late wife was too young—so she told me." Lifting the green stones in his hand, he said angrily, "Whose idea was this?"

"Idea about what?"

"These cheapies. This shit." He flung them overboard, and I looked horrified. "Wha—why'd you do that?" I blurted. "That's what you wanted."

"Oh, no," he said levelly, "I wanted the real ones. Where are they?"

I furrowed my brow. "That's what Hornstein gave me, *Señor* Tessier. If they were copies he must have the real ones."

"Horn—?" He stared fixedly at my face and for a few moments said nothing. "Hornstein told me Rita had them, gave them to you."

I swallowed. "Not exactly. Hornstein asked to keep them while she was in Spain, said he'd give them to me when needed. This morning he did. Believe me," I said humbly, "I wouldn't try to cheat you. I've been afraid of you all the way."

"Why?" he snapped.

"Things Rita told me. Said to be very careful when I met you."

He grunted. "So you came armed. I think you planned to get me out here alone, kill me and keep the stones for yourself."

"Would I risk my life for fake stones? I didn't start the shooting, only shot after you began firing at me."

He stroked his beard thoughtfully. The waves were higher out on the open bay, thumping under the hull, making balance difficult. "Something in that," he said. "Hornstein had you all wrong, maybe on purpose. So he could have switched stones." He scratched the side of his face, wet with spray. "We'll see."

I grabbed the coaming to steady myself. "Where are we going?"

"Where I can keep an eye on you while questions get answered." He looked forward beyond the wheelman, then back at me. "That was your boat?"

"Borrowed." I looked dejected. "I'll have to pay the guy."

"Machine gun yours?"

I shook my head. "The man lent it to me. He . . . he brings loads in now and then."

"So I'd say he's out of business for a while. What's his name? Maybe I know him."

"Pedro. Pedro Ramirez. Works out of Marathon."

"Maybe you won't have to pay him."

"Why's that?" I asked, knowing what the answer would be.

He shook his head. "Death cancels debts. Remember that, Menendez." The smile was vulpine. He was in charge and he was enjoying it. Someone tried to give him a fucking, and got fucked instead. Thanks to his superior brain and instincts. My boat was gone but I was alive—so far.

"You're not Cuban," he said. "What are you?"

"Mexican," I lied. "Reynosa, border town." We were out of sight of land, a sliver of moon showed we were heading northwest, across Florida Bay. The next landfall, if I lived to see it, would be somewhere along Cape Sable. I wondered where the chopper was, why he hadn't boarded it for a faster ride to destination.

"How'd you meet Rita?" he asked abruptly.

"Waiting tables."

"Where?"

"Chauveron, North Miami." I licked lips that were already dripping spray. "She came in alone, took a liking to me and made a date."

"Ever meet her sister?"

"No."

"Or hear her mention Jim Nolan?"

I shook my head. "Who's he?"

"A guy I'll take care of, when I have time. Knocked off two of my shooters who went after him. They never came back." He frowned. "One guy, and the assholes couldn't take him." His gaze lifted to me. "You been living with Rita?"

I nodded.

"Where?"

"Cheeca Lodge. That's Islamorada."

"How'd you get from there to your restaurant?"

"She drove me—nice green Jaguar. Then she moved to the Coconut Grove Hotel."

He nodded. "Left there, too. Know where she went?"

"No." So far he hadn't mentioned the eraserheads he'd sent after Rita, and that was a plus. Tessier said, "Getting back to the fake stones, I don't think you had the brains to set up the switch. But Hornstein could have. Saul would know where to get fakes, then send you out here with them, while keeping the real ones for himself." He paused and thought for a few moments. "Or Rita did it. Where was she last time you saw her?"

"Hornstein's office. Just before she left for Spain."

"Before she *said* she was leaving for Spain." Again he pawed his wet beard. He was developing a theory that might or might not be helpful to me. "But I can't think why she'd stay in the States. Any ideas?"

"No. Seemed anxious to go home, said she'd send for me when she could."

"You believed her?"

"I wanted to believe her. Still do."

He laughed unpleasantly. "Forget it, Pepe, she's gone. You haven't enough class for her—a waiter." He shook his head pityingly.

"Well, it's a four-star restaurant."

This time his laugh was more of a sneering grunt. "She used you, dummy, pushed you at me and got away. Like her mother. Marie's not as smart as Rita but plenty smart just the same. Oh, I know them all. Now, the Colonel—he was getting ready to shove me aside, but I struck first. No more Colonel."

"She said she was glad he died."

"Bet she was. The old bastard couldn't get enough of her. Then she went away to have her kid, and little sister was next. A man like that—he deserved to die."

"Absolutely."

"And I got a kick out of killing him."

"Good job."

Pistol in hand, he got up and stood beside the helmsman.

"What's our speed?"

"About twenty knots."

"So, how much longer?"

"Half an hour."

"*Mierda.* I should have taken the chopper." He began unbuttoning his guayabera and pulled it off. Where I expected to see bare chest or a T-shirt a white bulletproof Kevlar vest was strapped to his body. He undid Velcro retainers and shrugged off the vest. Looking it over, he said, "You hit me. Twice," and pointed at two lead stains where bullets had impacted a few inches apart. He laid the vest across his seat and put on the guayabera. "I didn't totally trust Hornstein, thought he might be staging a rip-off, so I wore protection. I don't trust anyone." He grinned unpleasantly and waved the pistol at me. "Ever in military service?"

"Army, two years. Medical Corps. No combat."

"Didn't think so—the way you shoot."

I shrugged. "Make love, not war."

That got a belly laugh. Gradually I was diminishing in his eyes. "Sit down," he ordered, "we've got a ways to go," and produced a bottle of white Bacardi. He downed a long swallow and passed the bottle to me. "Thanks," I said, and sat on the transom seat. Rum had never tasted better, and I needed it to settle nerves that had become frayed by defeat. I drank again, and passed the bottle back. He handed it to the helmsman, who drank his share and shook himself. Wind cooled our spray-wet clothing. Arizona air-conditioning.

For a long time nothing more was said. Covertly I watched Tessier's pistol, hoping for a chance to grab it and shoot them both, but Tessier had covered men before, probably more than I had, and opportunity never came.

It was only a half-moon that emerged from the horizon and cloud cover blanked the stars, so the night was dark. I thought of Rita alone and fearful, waiting for my return. Not tonight, *mi amor*, I thought dispiritedly, and maybe never. Vegas would give me no survival line. What odds did I give myself?

He hadn't killed me when he could, and I'd created enough uncertainty that he wanted me on standby while he put Hornstein's feet to the fire. That reprieve could last a day or two. At least Rita was safe; I'd done well to get her out of circulation when I did. That was the only accomplishment I could think of.

Suddenly a rain squall struck like the blast from a fire hose, pelting deck and windscreen with the force of hail. Tessier and I had our backs to it, but the helmsman had to shield face and eyes with one hand. The downpour smoothed the water and slightly increased our speed.

Florida Bay was stippled with mangrove islands, too small to be named or marked by warning lights, and I was nourishing hope that the helmsman would smash into one, or tear out the bottom on an oyster bar. A crash, a sinking would be an equalizer, giving me a chance to escape. Turning around, I screened my face and peered into liquid darkness. Was that a light to starboard? I squinted and focused. There it was again; either the Cay Mosca light, or East Cape Sable. The latter marked the divide between the bay and the Gulf of Mexico, where seas could get a lot rougher than in the relatively sheltered bay. The other men hadn't noticed the light, and I wasn't going to mention my find, or its significance. Let them be brave mariners, whose victory derived from an armed gunship. Without it, Tessier couldn't have taken me, I was certain of that, but he'd outsmarted me, ambushed me, and the realization stung.

Truth was I'd underestimated him, pictured Tessier as a semi-literate *campesino* with a gun. A *bandolero*. And that was because I'd let hatred and passion form my picture of him. I'd forgotten that Tessier was a skilled pilot, a man who'd helped Chavez rule Guatemala for close to a decade, and survived. He'd even managed to kill Chavez, then his own wife when she wanted to leave. During the hour I'd been with him I'd gained a clearer picture of the man.

He had the arrogant self-confidence of a cobra, who'd strike without warning, indiscriminately. Strong, supple build, a face not handsome but brutishly masculine; cold, steely eyes; a leader, not a follower, capable of pursuing a single goal despite obstacles. And he exuded an aura of authority that women found attractive. He was my enemy.

As suddenly as we'd entered the rain squall we came out of it and the drumming of its droplets ended. Clouds had cleared away and stars were visible. So was the occulting light I'd noticed.

The helmsman saw it, too, and pointed it out to Tessier, who got out the

Bacardi bottle again and passed it around. As I drank I scanned the sky for Polaris, found it off the starboard bow, and figured that despite darkness and rain-blindness the course held true. Starlight illuminated the ghostly outlines of mangrove islands, enabling the helmsman to avoid them while maintaining speed.

From his seat, Tessier pointed the pistol at me. "I blame you for this misery, this waste of time. You tried to be smart, meeting me back there, when a reasonable man would have met me ashore without complications."

"I was only trying to be cautious, preserve my life."

The pistol waved. "And what did it get you?" He grunted. "What did it get me but a bag of pretty pebbles? For that I should kill you."

Was it coming now? I turned from him, cowered. "Kill Hornstein, not me," I blurted. "Put blame where it belongs."

"Maybe," he said vaguely, and then the helmsman called, "There it is, chief, we made it."

"Good man." Tessier got up and punched his shoulder. "Too bad it was all for nothing."

When I looked around I could see dark shoreline, two white lights toward which the boat was turning. Where the hell were we going? Nothing but swamp in there.

The two lights marked the mouth of a narrow stream. The boat entered slowly, passed between the lights, and the engine died. In silence we glided to a small wooden dock thrust out from a screen of bushes. The helmsman snubbed the bow with a line, came aft and snubbed the stern. "You first," Tessier said to me and gestured. I got out on dock planking and found myself swaying slightly, still in rhythm with the boat. "Where are we?" I asked.

"Dangerous knowledge," Tessier replied. "Don't ask again." He waved me ahead with the pistol, and I followed the helmsman down an overgrown trail that seemed to lead nowhere except more dark jungle. The trail paralleled the creek, if that's what it was, and moonlight reflected on the water showed it widening. I was stumbling along through undergrowth when I heard a distant shot, then a second. Rifle, from the sharp, cracking reports. I halted, but Tessier prodded me ahead. "Alligator poacher," he remarked. "I don't bother them, they don't bother me. Keep moving."

Another two minutes and we entered a small clearing, whose creek side had a dock some ten feet square. Floating beside it was a good-sized airboat, rotary aircraft engine and propellor in a protective wire cage, raised high above the boat's metal bottom and set aft of the driver's seat and controls.

The helmsman climbed into the driver's seat and I dropped into the boat, Tessier behind me. "Noisy but fast," Tessier commented. "Ever ride one?"

"Never," I lied as the driver waggled the control sticks and twin vertical rudders responded. He flipped the starter toggle and the propellor began turning, slowly at first, until the engine caught with a loud burst of exhaust flame. "Sit down and hold on," Tessier ordered, and stuck the pistol in his belt. Over the roaring he shouted, "If you want to leave, go ahead, but there's no place to go," and gave me that gloating grin once more. "Hey," I called back, "I'm happy to be alive."

"Enjoy it," he said sardonically, and cast off the snubbing lines.

The airboat didn't head back to the bay as I'd expected, but moved deeper into the creek channel. Presently the creek gave out, then the driver throttled ahead and, driven by the pusher prop, the airboat surged into a sea of shoulder-high grass.

From his height the driver could scan the moonlit wilderness and steer around occasional hummocks and dead trees. The airboat accelerated until it was speeding along at maybe forty miles an hour, deep into the Everglades.

Often as I'd flown over the 'Glades it had always been by daylight. Now I had the sensation of flying at ground level over moon-silvered reaches of tall wheat, where long-dead trees with skeletal limbs and fingers clawed eerily at the sky.

When I glanced at Tessier his arms were folded and his face was fixed in grim concentration. My watch showed close to eleven PM. Had disaster struck only three hours ago? Seemed a lifetime. I clutched the vibrating metal bench and held tight as the driver, like a mad coachman, spurred our hybrid vehicle endlessly on.

From time to time the bottom crashed over ridges of solid land that jerked and shook us, then smooth water again, sawgrass, hyacinth and tule. Egrets and white herons fled our noisy onslaught, taking lumbering wing that silhouetted them like prehistoric flying reptiles against the sky. We skimmed across sluggish streams and weed-choked waterways, always bearing slightly west of true north until, finally, the grass ended at the placid waters of an inland lagoon.

Trees rimmed the shoreline, ancient oaks and cypress were draped with Spanish moss that hung like spectral beards of long-dead men. The airboat slowed because we were running among the stumps and trunks of a drowned forest where the risk of capsize or holing was very real. Then we were beyond the obstacles and speeding over lily pads and water hyacinth again. The great grass savanna covered the south and east. We were penetrating northward into what resembled Amazon bywaters; trees on either side arched branches that nearly touched above us. Foliage so thick that only snakes and panthers could get through.

And alligators.

Our wake washed over them as they lazed along the narrow shore, sending them scrambling into the water behind us. Huge saurians, larger than I'd ever seen, gorged and fattened on garfish, snakes, birds and the flesh of their young. The old .30-.30 lever action racked just behind the driver's seat didn't put out enough foot-pounds of bullet impact to kill an animal that big. Unless you drilled an eyehole to the brain.

The noise of prop and engine was deafening. Tessier didn't try to talk, and I was relieved he stayed mute. Never thinking I'd be captured, I hadn't prepared a cover story; what I'd supplied Tessier had been spur-of-the-moment lying inspired by desperate desire to stay alive. But if he tortured me I knew I'd crack. I had before, in Guadalajara, and knew my limits. But lying, inventing, was better than staying silent—or trying to—and if I lasted through tomorrow Rita would have time to get far away.

I thought of the emeralds in my safe, the account numbers that could yield Claude Tessier great riches. And I thought of the mercenary force he was raising to retake a country that was not even his own.

His eyes were closed; he seemed asleep but I was not persuaded. He was planning, scheming, dreaming . . . a mind restless as his never tuned out; it nurtured the primal imperative to stay alive.

To him, I mused, my dead Anita had been a toy, a convenience, and before the end, an obstacle to be eliminated. Self-love was all he knew, had ever known. A soulless creature in human frame.

When he opened his eyes they stared at mine, and I felt chilled as though my grave were being dug. He must have sensed my reaction because his mouth formed that predator's smile and I thought of hyenas with foul, dripping jaws.

Abruptly the airboat turned right, heeling over toward a dark inlet. The engine slowed, prop noise diminished, and Tessier glanced at the illuminated dial of his watch. Then from shore a spotlight caught us in its blinding beam.

FOURTEEN

THE ENGINE died and we glided shoreward. In the sudden silence I could hear shooting beyond the mass of mangroves. Automatic weapons. Spurts of fire, answering bursts. Tessier waved his arms above his head and the spotlight beam moved to a wooden dock. The driver steered toward it and three uni- formed men materialized from the darkness. They tossed lines across the water. Tessier caught one, I grabbed the other and secured it to a gunwale cleat. The airboat bumped dock fenders and was still. Our voyage had ended.

Tessier was first out, then me and the driver. The reception party wore lightweight jungle camo, billed caps and AK-47s, sheath knives in their belts. In rigid formation they saluted Tessier, who acknowledged them with a casual gesture. I stood facing them, listening to the *pop* of mortar shells punctuate weapons fire until Tessier spoke to me. In a low voice he said, "If you talk to anyone don't mention the phony stones. Better still, talk with no one."

I nodded, he shoved me ahead, the three *soldados* stood aside, and I followed a spongy trail marked by a low railing of trimmed branches. It gave out into a clearing bordered by a number of palm-thatched, sideless structures under which hammocks were slung. At the far end stood a wooden shack roofed with tar paper. Thin smoke drifted from its stovepipe chimney. Through the almost continuous sound of weapons I could hear the chugging of a heavy generator. Its electricity supplied lightbulbs strung around the camp's perimeter and in the jungle barracks. This was the camp Manny and his expectant crew had visited and found uninhabited. Well, I thought, it was inhabited now and the inhabitants were armed and dangerous.

"What's going on here?" I asked Tessier, to indicate ignorance of the site and its purpose.

"Training," he said gruffly. "Right now it's a night exercise." He grunted. "If lucky we won't lose more than two to three to friendly fire."

I nodded as though I understood. "Cubans. What the papers call weekend warriors, right?"

He shrugged. "Don't get too curious, Pepe, men have died for less. You're here, you're still alive, be grateful."

"Hey, sorry I asked."

We were approaching a stockade fashioned from branches trimmed into stakes with sharpened points. The door was chained shut, held by a padlock. A *soldado* with an M-30 carbine came to attention and presented arms. Tessier told him to open the door. Nervously the guard fumbled with the key, got the padlock open, and the door swung on squeaking hinges. "Any trouble?" Tessier asked.

"No, *jefe*, no trouble tonight."

Pointing at me, Tessier said, "Here's another *cabrón*. Food, water and a hammock." He looked at me. "Ever sleep in a hammock?"

"Acapulco," I replied, "but not alone."

That made him smile briefly. "The two men there decided they didn't like it here, wanted to leave. Now they're thinking it over." He eyed me. "If you were any kind of shooter I might give you a chance to join up."

"Join what?"

"I call us Conquistadores. Modern Conquistadores. Like the old Spaniards, we seek a better life."

"Hell, I'd go for that myself."

"Unfortunately, there's no time to train you, so you'll wait here while I put some questions to Hornstein." His face turned grim. "The son of a whore backed out on me, after all the money I paid him."

"The legal profession doesn't run on gratitude."

His face relaxed; he liked that, too. "All right, Menendez, maybe we'll talk tomorrow, maybe not."

I scratched my neck. "Got any mosquito repellent?"

"No, but there's plenty of mosquitoes." He was turning away when a slight, uniformed figure came running around the stockade, calling, "*Claudito!*" No cap over shingled blond hair, a bosom that pushed out the camo jacket, and spike-heeled shoes. She grabbed Tessier and covered his face with kisses, as he tried to disentangle himself from her clutching arms. "I've missed you, *amor*," she exclaimed, then noticed me. Stepping back, she blurted, "Who's this?"

"A *pendejo* who was fucking around with Rita. I'll tell you about it later."

"I want to know now!"

"You'll hear it when I'm ready." He slapped her rump, put an arm around her shoulders and walked her away. Until then I hadn't had a clear view of his back, but light showed a large, colored quetzal painted on his guayabera. The quetzal is a parrotlike bird with an exceedingly long feathery tail. In the jungle it gives out mournful cries that help blowpipe hunters locate it. The bird is the national symbol of Guatemala, and its monetary unit as well. Tessier didn't seem to me like a man given to wearing patriotic painted shirts, but there you are.

I watched him and the uniformed female until the guard growled, "Inside," and I went in.

The roofless enclosure measured about twelve-by-twenty feet. A double row of vertical four-by-fours supported five slung hammocks. Set in the middle was a crude picnic-type table with benches on both sides. I noticed a trench latrine's stench permeating the hot and humid air.

Two hammocks were occupied by men in camo uniforms. They watched as I looked around but said nothing. I did the same, then tested the farthest hammock's cords, a precaution I'd learned as a midshipman. It was late, I was as tired as I could remember, and my injured shoulder ached. I eased onto the hammock, lay back and stared at the starry sky. What a day, I thought, and what a disastrous night it had been.

By now all gunfire had ceased, and I judged the trainees were taking a break before the next night maneuver. I wasn't sure how much sleep I'd get but more gunfire wouldn't help.

At the dock there had been two other airboats, both smaller than the one that brought me. Manny had said the camp was approachable by road, so it was logical that personnel and supplies arrived by truck. A way in equaled a way out, I reasoned, and it was up to me to find it. No one was going to help me get away.

My thoughts turned to the blond woman in uniform. She was on intimate terms with Tessier, and I wondered how much her presence was resented by the *soldados*. Tessier had taken care of himself, why couldn't the other campers have comfort troops to assuage their *machismo*? Of course, they didn't understand the special relationship, but I thought I did.

Her blondness, light complexion, voice, and the set of her eyes, chin and mouth gave her the appearance of Anita grown old and blowsy. She had to be the girls' mother, Marie; widow of Oscar Chavez.

What was she doing in camp? Keeping a jealous eye on her lover? Financing an invasion that would re-establish her as Guatemala's First Lady? Or merely curious? On second thought, there would be a short limit to mere curiosity; pampered living hadn't prepared the onetime showgirl for the rigors of jungle camping. She wouldn't like the food, the accommodations, the rain, bugs and snakes, so there had to be a stronger motivation. Tessier had no monopoly on sex; in Europe she could bed any male she wanted even if payment was required. So she was checking on her investment and staying close while her *Claudito* attempted to secure additional funds.

As I considered Marie's unexpected presence, I wondered how much she knew about Anita's death, Tessier's role in her murder. If she knew the truth, how could any mother with a spark of humanity cling to her daughter's killer?

Having asked myself that question, I remembered how Marie had tolerated her husband's rape of their daughters. Hadn't objected, just gone away. Copped out. Some mother. Some maternal figure.

Except for the relentless chugging of the camp's generator the night was still. Oh, a few bullfrogs barked and bellowed by the water and gecko lizards chirped and squeaked in the nearby trees, but there were no dogs baying at the moon, no roar of highway trucks, and best of all, no gunfire.

Tessier hadn't searched me, so I still had my Boy Scout knife in the sock where I'd transferred it. Big deal, I thought, against assault rifles and mortar rounds. Just then one of my fellow inmates began to snore. For that the old shipboard remedy was slashing hammock cords, but I wasn't going to get involved with the two mercs. If the three of us survived Tessier I didn't want them able to recognize me. And I didn't want to be displayed to the *soldados* at morning formation. More than one of them, I figured, had narcotics backgrounds and might remember me from a bust in Miami, Houston or Mexico. Doubtless Tessier had done some quiet recruiting during his prison stay; that kind of trash would flock to his banner so long as money was involved. That being the definition of mercenary.

Within the next day or two Tessier would be confronting Saul Hornstein and not getting the answers he desired. Either he'd believe the lawyer's disclaimers or he wouldn't. Tessier could walk away and torture me for the truth, or kill Hornstein for personal satisfaction. However it went, my time was limited.

By no standard was the stockade a secure prison. It was intended to separate malcontents from reliable troops, the camp location itself—between water and jungle—being the best personnel retainer.

The crude wooden stakes that formed the enclosure had irregular spaces between them. They were sunk into soft, spongy earth that was not unlike peat, and held together by laundry cord that ran in and out serpentine fashion. I'd only seen the one guard, and aside from him the three helpers on the dock. So the bulk of Tessier's army was off in the boonies making like soldier boys.

If I was ever to get away it would have to be at night, when few campers were about.

Tessier and Mama Marie were off in their lovers' bower; but I didn't know where the three dockers had gone. Maybe their detail was guarding the three airboats. Where were the camp trucks? They'd be guarded, too, and I was a good many miles from anything resembling civilization. The prospect of trudging a dark jungle road with snakes, gators and mudholes was a major challenge; the prospect of being killed by Tessier even worse. So, what was I waiting for? My *compañeros* were deep asleep. I slapped at mosquitoes on my hands, wrists, neck and face, and got out my knife. C'mon, Novak, you've had enough siesta. Time to haul butt.

I eased quietly off the hammock and approached the trench latrine, whose stench made me hold my nose. Going there tested whether the hammock occupants were watching. I turned and eyed them. Four eyes closed. I tiptoed to the door and peered through a crack. The guard was sitting on a stool a few feet away, back toward me. His head was down as though dozing. Was he? I improvised a little test. I coughed loudly and the guard didn't stir. Good. Better than good. I moved back to my hammock and watched the sleepers before going to the stockade's far side. In a crouch I sawed through the lowest cord, then the higher. Tension drew the ends free and three stakes sagged inward, making a V-shaped opening. I pushed through and was out. Before leaving, I pulled the stakes upright and positioned them firmly in the humus. Then I breathed deeply to slow my pulse and decided a diversion was needed.

The sound of the generator suggested a target. I itched for a firearm, any kind, but taking the guard's was too risky. Instead, I'd rely on stealth.

I stayed low as I made my way toward the generator sound, keeping just beyond the camp's lighted perimeter. Found a narrow footpath and followed it until I came to a lighted zone a hundred yards away. The generator was there, feeding from a fifty-gallon gasoline drum. It was a big mother, big as a tractor's engine, and beside it was a horizontal stack of drums.

Just beyond the lighted zone I saw an RV trailer hitched to a Ford pickup whose outside wheels and high springs made it a swamp buggy. Inside the trailer shades were drawn, but I could see dim light leaking from one of the window cracks. The top-mounted air conditioner hummed and throbbed, cooling Tessier's love nest.

It took me five minutes to work around to the point nearest the generator. Concealed by trees, shrubbery and shadows, I waited and thought things through. At any moment troops could return to camp, the guards change, making escape impossible. I had to act now.

I was getting ready to sprint to the generator when the trailer door opened and a female stepped outside. Naked, she raised her arms and gazed at the moon. At that distance her lush figure resembled Rita's, except for the somewhat sagging breasts. Belly-bulge and cellulite-dimpled thighs completed the picture of an aging female. I could see the swelling of her thorax as she inhaled, and then she turned, went back in and closed the trailer door.

My future mother-in-law, I told myself disgustedly: a shopworn old bitch!

After the window light went out I crossed to the generator. I was searching for the fuel supply valve, when I heard a sound behind me and looked around into the barrel of a gun.

"Freeze, asshole!"

My gaze lifted from the gun to a face streaked with black greasepaint. "You!" the man blurted. "What the hell you doin' here?"

Eddie Zagoria.

"Keep your voice down, Eddie," I snapped.

"Why should I?"

"Because I let Agent Doak spring you from jail. Help me or I'll tell Tessier you're an FBI stoolie."

His mouth opened and closed. "Don't think I wouldn't," I warned, "because my life's on the line. Yours, too."

"Wha—whatcha want?"

"Silence. What brought you here?"

"Patrol. Perimeter patrol." He swallowed and licked his lips. "Whatcha gonna do?"

"Get away," I told him, "while this thing blows. Got a lighter?"

He fumbled in his pocket, brought out a Bic. I took it from his hand. "Where are the trucks?"

He gestured over his shoulder. "Back there, but Tessier keeps the distributor caps."

I touched his AK-47. "I need this. Get another."

He goggled at me. "How?"

"You're a thief, Eddie, steal one. Don't fuck with me." I pulled the weapon from his hand. "Where's the armory?"

"The weapons?"

"You know what I mean. Where is it?"

"They use a big van. It's locked and guarded."

"I want some grenades."

"Aren't none left."

I gritted my teeth. "How many guards by the airboats?"

"Two—three—I dunno exactly."

"All right. When this baby blows you run to the dock, get the guards here."

"How? How can I?"

"Say Tessier's in danger, his broad, too. They'll come."

He shook his head uncertainly. I said, "You'll do it because if you cross me you'll die, got it?"

He nodded.

"Get moving."

He turned away and disappeared into darkness beyond the trailer. I didn't care if he ran all the way to Miami. I had his weapon.

Over the steady pounding of the engine I could hear weapons firing resume. Volley after volley rent the night. Good. I found the fuel valve and loosened its connecting flange from the copper feed line until gasoline began to dribble around the engine base. Enough was still flowing through to keep the engine going, but a pool of volatile fluid was collecting below.

I went to the reserve gas drums and found the tool that opened their caps. I unscrewed one until fuel began to spurt out, and then I tore a long strip from around my shirttail. I laid one end in the gasoline pool and lighted the other. Then, carrying Eddie's weapon, I retreated into darkness beyond the perimeter and headed for the airboat dock.

Against an opportunity to kill Tessier I had to weigh my own survival. Even if I riddled the RV with bullets the son of a bitch could be wearing Kevlar again and escape death. Too, I didn't feel right about endangering Mama Marie. Much as I detested her, she didn't deserve the fate I planned for her lover.

So, I was going to get away and try to kill him another day.

I was running, stumbling, half-tripping down the trail when the generator blew. With the gas drums it exploded like an Iraqi ammo dump, hurtling flame and debris hundreds of feet high. Shock waves slammed through the jungle, fanning my face with invisible force and sudden heat. Ahead of me I heard startled voices. Eddie was at the dock urging the guards to fight the fire. I veered into the jungle, waited ten feet from the path as the four *soldados* ran by. I paused to catch my breath as detonations erupted far behind me, and wondered if the RV had been hit. Well, Marie had put herself in harm's way and had only herself to blame. Her greed and ambition.

I continued toward the dock, more slowly than before, holding the AK-47 upright to keep branches from my face. Nearing the water, I slowed, kept to one side of the trail, and peered ahead. Ripples reflected the red-gold hues of the burning sky. The garish light illuminated the dock and three tethered airboats.

For almost a minute I surveyed the scene, didn't move on until satisfied I was alone. Then I ran the last twenty yards to the nearest airboat, one of the smaller two. The gas gauge registered low, the other's tank was two-thirds full. I untied lines, climbed into the driving seat, buckled the strap across thighs and chest, and found the ignition switch. But before I touched it I paused. Should I take the big boat, the one I'd come in? No, I reasoned, its gas could be low, and it would be harder to maneuver than this one. So I hit the switch and behind me the prop began turning on battery power. No ignition, so I waited a few moments and tried again, hoping gas had been sucked into the ignition chambers. Again the prop turned, and with the report of a shotgun blast the engine finally caught. I revved it and used the control stick to steer the craft from the dock into the main water. Stick between my knees, I sighted the automatic rifle at the big boat's gas tank and fired two rounds. The tank was holed but no explosion. I sighted on the other boat and fired a short burst into the tank. Before I could lower the rifle the tank detonated with a sheet of flame, and seconds later the big boat exploded. Heat and debris slammed past me, bits of metal clattered into my boat, bounced off the prop cage and singed my left hand. I sucked the burn, gazed at the flaming wrecks and said, "Catch me if you can." Then I shoved the throttle ahead and the airboat accelerated down the stream.

There was no compass to set course by, but plenty of stars and moonlight for direction. Anyway, until I reached the open 'Glades I could only follow the creek. I kept the engine at half-speed to conserve gas and avoid obstacles. Tessier's driver had known the route but I didn't, so I ran slowly through the sawgrass sea, the drowned forest and the tree-arched river, my hearing numbed by the prop noise just behind. The return trip was taking much longer than before and I fell into a kind of motion hypnosis, not noticing herons, gators or anything else. The banging and thumping of the bottom was monotonous. I tried tuning it out, realized I was half asleep. I was thirsty, too, hadn't swallowed liquid in hours. My mind visualized chilled bottles of Evian that had sunk with my Renegade and that made me even thirstier. But I had to go on.

The tall grass around me seemed endless; even from my raised seat I couldn't see over it, though occasionally I came across flattened patches that marked the way we'd come. I was beginning to think I'd never find the outlet when I saw a hummock rise nearly dead ahead, and veered away. Atop it grew a lone cypress that I remembered passing before, so my course was relatively true.

Finally the savanna ended and the long waterway began. I throttled down even more and began searching for the dock where we'd disembarked from Tessier's boat. There was a chance of drinking water aboard, maybe a swallow of Bacardi, and I was desperate for any fluid at all. I saw the boat first, then the dock. I cut the engine and steered to the boat, tied the airboat to it and got aboard.

The Bacardi bottle was lying on its side, topless. There was an ounce or so left, and I swallowed thirstily. Then I began looking for water. Nothing in the engine compartment but the fumes of gas and oil. No water in the cubby, either, but plenty of cartridge cases on the deck from Tessier's shooting. I could see where I'd holed the side with my MAC-10; the punctures were well above waterline.

The Bacardi was making me light-headed. I was so tired I could hardly keep my eyes open. The cushioned transom looked heaven-sent, so I lay back on it and closed my eyes. After what seemed only minutes later, but was more than a real-time hour, something prodded me. I reacted slowly, opening my eyes and sitting up before becoming conscious of danger. What prodded me was the barrel of a rifle, held by a man who was staring down at me.

FIFTEEN

HIS HAIR was black and shaggy, long enough to touch the shoulders of his color-striped shirt. Age wrinkled his coppery face, but his eyes were clear and unblinking. The shirt was loosely bloused over faded blue denims, and its open throat showed a necklace of alligator claws. A Seminole Indian. "You okay?" he asked.

I sighed in relief. "Just taking a nap." I flexed my arms and stood up. He drew back the rifle and I saw that he was standing in a wide canoe hollowed from a cypress trunk. Its bottom held the carcasses of three alligators, each about seven feet long. Near them was a hand-held spotlight, useful for jacking deer or finding the chatoyance of gator eyes. By some laws he was a poacher but the Seminoles regarded 'Glades wildlife as their own and I wouldn't argue against them. "This your boat?" he asked.

"It is—now. Ah—got any water?"

"Some. Can you pay me?"

I dug into my pocket, found two crumpled dollar bills and handed them over. He bent down and brought up a plastic gallon jug with a Publix label. "Help yourself."

I sat down and tilted the bottle to my mouth, drank, swallowed, and kept drinking. Water had never tasted so good. I set the jug on the transom while I gulped air and rested. The old man regarded me with curiosity. I drank again. He watched, finally saying, "That's two bucks' worth."

"Okay, okay." He had his rifle in hand, my automatic was on the airboat out of reach.

"I'll trade the jug for gasoline."

I glanced over the gunwale and saw a small, ancient outboard clamped to his stern. "Got a hose? Take what you want."

From his boat bottom he produced a length of garden hose, unscrewed the boat's gas tank cover, and began sucking gas into his outboard. When his tank overflowed he withdrew the hose and replaced the gas tank cover. "Much obliged."

"Want the boat?"

"Burns too much gas. Want some gator steaks?" He gestured at his lifeless victims. Each had been shot cleanly through the skull. "Thanks, but too fishy," I told him, and looked at my watch. Daylight was on the way. I wondered what the scene was like at Tessier's training camp. There'd be some heavy cleanup to do and a possible mutiny by recalcitrants who objected to manual labor.

If I could reach a telephone in the next couple of hours I could keep Rita from leaving. By rounding Cape Sable to the east I could reach Flamingo in an hour or so; civilization's nearest point.

"Got anything to eat?" I asked.

He opened a blouse flap and brought out a flat, thin piece of something reddish brown. "Deer jerky," he said, "smoked," and gave it to me. The dried meat was tough and stringy but I liked the salty taste even though it renewed thirst. But I had the jug now, and everything was going to be okay. Gravely he extended one hand, we shook, and he began poling his boat away. Ending, I thought, my first contact with a Native American in his own habitat, and each of us had gained something worthwhile.

I couldn't think of a way to transfer boat gasoline to my airboat's higher tank, so I decided to sink Tessier's boat and avenge the sinking of mine. Under the deck hatch I found a petcock valve where it ought to be. Sunk, the boat would clog the waterway and bar passage to boats that drew more water than the Indian's. I opened the valve and water began fountaining in. I could have holed the bottom with my automatic, but ammo was scarce and I wasn't yet home.

Taking the water jug, I climbed into the airboat, untied the line, and slung the AK-47 over one shoulder. Then I strapped into the driving seat and hit the ignition. The still-warm engine barked into life, reminding me of my Fairchild's in-line Lycoming engine now serving some rapacious Mex. For years I'd nursed that plane along, cared for it like a baby, only to have it taken away. On reflection, I missed it as much as my confiscated house. There'd been a time when I'd shared it with Melody. Now some fat Mexican colonel possessed it, and the injustice rankled my memory.

Carefully I guided the airboat out of the inlet, through the marker lights I'd seen on the earlier trip. Was Tessier alive? I wondered. Mama Marie? Eventually I'd hear.

Early dawn helped me follow the coastline south; along the way black-feathered cormorants preened atop channel markers, indifferent to my noisy passing. Brown pelicans drifted, rose and dove, engulfing fry in their capacious beaks. Silver tarpon rolled offshore, and I lusted for a rod to lay tempting baits before them.

Another time, I told myself, momentarily forgetting I had no boat to fish from.

Pre-dawn sunlight silvered an arc of horizon off the airboat's port bow. Soon I would be heading toward it, but for a while longer my course was southerly, paralleling the Cape.

Rita, I thought, had probably spent a sleepless night. She'd wait until noon for my call, then check out and head for the airport and Spain. I'd follow as soon as I could, taking the emeralds with me for her disposal. But I was going to call her from Flamingo so maybe she wouldn't have to travel alone.

According to the gauge there was a quarter-tank of gas remaining, more than enough for another hour's running toward Flamingo, but nowhere near enough fuel to get me across the Bay to the marina where I'd left my car. And how to get from remote Flamingo to Miami? Once ashore I'd talk with locals, work something out. Like borrowing a car and leaving the airboat for security.

Having destroyed Tessier's two airboats and sunk his boat I hadn't considered pursuit. Then, suddenly, I saw a line of small splashes in the water just ahead of me, bullet holes pocked the airboat's nose, and I realized I was under attack.

Looking back I saw the chopper, a man firing from the doorway. A bullet pinged on the wire cage just behind my head, and I swung the airboat left, pushed the throttle ahead, and raised the AK-47. Above, the chopper was following. Too dark last night to tell, but now I saw it was an Iroquois. I triggered a three-shot burst at the shooter, but missed. He disappeared inside and the chopper banked away. Using my knees I pressed the control stick hard right and the airboat heeled over. The Iroquois turned back and firing resumed. Muzzle flashes were bright against the chopper's dark interior, and his fire was getting more accurate. There were bullet holes in the thin metal bottom and water was coming in. I couldn't last long in the open, had to get to the mangrove shore a hundred yards away. Shortage of ammunition kept me from wild firing at the chopper, so with the automatic across my thighs I steered an evasive serpentine course toward the mangroves, praying for an opening where I could hide. A bullet glanced off the back of my metal seat but didn't penetrate. The next rounds got through the protective cage and splintered the wooden prop. The whole airboat shuddered violently, and I cut the engine before it wrenched loose. Now I was gliding shoreward, the prop's convulsions fading. I expected to crash into the mangrove thicket, then glimpsed a dark opening, and steered toward it. Branches battered me, snagged the prop cage and gave way. The boat hit hard and stopped, but the chopper couldn't see me under the thick, leafy canopy. I slid down from the seat into four inches of water flooding the bottom, and began looking for the chopper. It hovered above the airboat, giving the shooter a steady platform. He must have been able to

see the prop cage because bullets were tearing it apart. I moved to the prow
and sighted through an opening in the branches. I could see the man's camo
uniform, the AK-47, whose magazine he was changing. I got off two shots at
him and saw him duck backward. Then he was firing again, bullets ripping
through the dense tangle of branches, vines and creepers, showering me with
green confetti.

His rounds were striking the airboat, punching holes everywhere, but the
airboat was grounded and couldn't sink. I got off into dark, thigh-deep water
and moved to where I could get a clear view of the chopper. Then I sighted
carefully at the rotor gearbox and fired until the magazine was empty. Sparks
jumped where my jacketed bullets hit, and oily smoke appeared. The rotors
slowed and the chopper began banking away. The shooter fired a parting burst
at the airboat, and the gas tank exploded, slamming me face down against hard
mangrove roots. I managed to turn my head and look upward. Suddenly the
rotors froze, the Iroquois bucked and whirled madly, spun by the tail rotor,
then plunged into the sea.

Behind me the stench of burning oil and gasoline. My nostrils filled with
smoke and fumes. I tried to get up but pain flared through my chest. My left
arm was numb. I opened and closed my hands, thinking that everything had
gone wrong—except for one thing; I was still alive. The chopper had overtaken
me unnoticed because the airboat's strident noise had covered the loud beating
of the chopper's blades. And I'd gone blissfully along . . .

Pain had me breathing in shallow gulps. Something salty covered my lips;
blood. If I didn't move I'd die there, never be found. My legs felt like jelly. I
rolled to one side, gasped from pain and rested. I was getting light-headed. I
touched my forehead and felt a painful bump, sticky with blood. Mosquitoes
were swarming to me, had to get out of the swamp. Bracing myself with
branches, I stood and oriented myself. The airboat resembled smoking junkyard
metal. The explosion had dropped the engine across the driver's seat where it
hung at a crazy angle. I took a tentative step and water swirled around my
thighs. Another. Blood was hammering through my temples. Sudden nausea
made me vomit what was in my stomach. I splashed water over my face, rinsed
my mouth and spat, nearly fainting from that slight exertion. I clawed at another
branch, and froze. Less than a yard away were the open white jaws of a cot-
tonmouth moccasin, its dark body wrapped around the branch. As my arm
jerked back the snake struck, its fangs closing on empty air. With a yell of
horror I plunged aside, praying the snake wouldn't drop down and pursue me.
But when I looked back I saw the bulbous eyes and narrow snout of a gator
swimming toward me. I yelled again, splashed water at him before turning to
where I suddenly glimpsed open water. Confused by the splashing, the gator
slowed. I moved as fast as I could, recalling that gators were riverine creatures

that abhorred salt water. Presently I was clear of the mangroves and staggering exhaustedly into the clearer, salty waters of the bay. Behind me the gator stopped and sank below the dark, brackish water of the swamp. I kept moving.

To the right there was a partly submerged sandbar, water rippling across it. I couldn't swim, my left arm was next to useless, so I kept forcing one foot ahead of the other, wading toward the sandbar where I could sit and rest or lie down. Eventually, I thought, some fisherman would notice me, bring help. Only, when would that be? Maybe if I rested a while I'd gain strength enough to go on. I was exhausted, and still a dozen feet from the sandbar. Current eddied against me, the water was getting deeper. Suddenly it rose to my chest. It made my body lighter, a bit easier to move. I sculled with my right arm as I floundered onward, finally felt the bottom slope upward to the sandbar. On my knees I clawed the sand, pulling myself to the highest part, where I flopped onto my back and saw the morning sky revolve.

Passed out.

SIXTEEN

RHYTHMIC THROBBING awakened me. I heard the steady slosh of water and opened my eyes. The sun was much higher. I was in a boat, strapped to a Stokes litter. Beside me a voice said, "Hello."

I turned my head just enough to focus on a young woman in Marine Patrol uniform. She was sitting beside me. "How you feeling?"

"Not good. Where are we going?"

"Marathon, the hospital. The Chief thinks you've got a concussion, so do I." Her short hair and youthful face seemed familiar. Sensing my thoughts, she said, "Haven't I seen you before?"

"Maybe."

Her fingers snapped. "Got it! That stilt shack. Right?"

"If you say so."

"Yeah, that's it. A while ago, right?" She got up and I watched her go into the wheelhouse, talk to an older man, the Chief. Sure, they were the pair who'd stopped by and checked my baitwell, declined coffee; I'd wondered if they had something going. The Chief looked back at me and nodded. The mate returned and sat down under the awning that shaded me. Sea breeze cooled my face, helped my breathing. She said, "Want to talk about it? What happened?"

I licked dry lips. "Water," I croaked.

"Coming up." She opened a cooler, got out a plastic bottle and brought it to me. "Sorry, no straws." Then she raised my head so that she could trickle water into my mouth. Cold, it was even better than the Indian's. Slowly, I drank at least a pint. "My ministering angel," I said as she took the water away. She gave me an appreciative smile and came back from the cooler. "How'd you find me?" I asked. "I thought high tide would wash me away."

"Well, we got there first. The fire station ranger at Sable saw an explosion, called it in and we were sent to look for survivors." With a gauze swab she blotted perspiration from my face. "More than you?"

"Just me."

"We were afraid . . . Anyway, we have to report what happened." She paused. "That airboat's totaled."

"I know."

"Hate them," she said. "So dangerous. You're lucky to be alive."

"I'm sure of it." I tried shifting on the litter but pain stopped me. "Got an aspirin or two?"

"If you need it."

"I need a lot more," I told her, "but I'll settle for whatever you give me."

From the wheelhouse she brought back a large first aid kit and doled out two aspirin. More water, and I thanked her.

"We carry morphine," she said, "but the hospital will want to know where you hurt." She gazed at me for a while before saying, "Once we got the muck cleared off you didn't look so bad." So far she'd said nothing about the chopper. The ranger must not have been looking when it went down, and I wasn't going to mention it. Let the sea keep its secrets. "Anything broken?" I asked.

"You tell me."

"Ribs feel like hot wires when I move." I flexed my left hand; some of the numbness was gone. "What time is it?"

"After nine. When did you crash?"

"Dawn. Hit something—maybe that sandbar—lost control, and plunged into the mangroves."

"What we figured. At low tide that section's a menace. Bet you didn't know that."

"No. And a tough way to find out." I thought I'd embellish the story a little. "Friend lent me the airboat, said the best tarpon fishing was close to dawn." I moistened my lips again, realized they were puffy. "It'll be a while before I try that again."

"Yeah." She left me and went to the wheelhouse, took the helm, and the Chief came back to me. "Lucky man," he said. "Shoulda stayed in that stilt shack." His leathery skin was covered with a half-inch white beard. Good protection from the sun. "I appreciate your help," I told him, "and I feel pretty stupid."

"You were damn lucky that explosion didn't kill you." For a few moments he watched two pelicans flying by. "Guess my little sea-bunny told you the boat's finished."

"Sea-bunny?"

"Diana, my mate. She tell you?"

"She did."

He looked at his watch. "We got about an hour to go, why not grab some more sleep?"

"Good idea."

"Want anything? Water?"

"Got enough, thanks." He went down the companionway and after a while brought up two china mugs with coffee. Carried them to the wheelhouse. With an attractive young mate like Diana, I thought, the Chief must find patrolling pretty good duty.

The monotonous throbbing of the engines and the cool breeze combined to put me to sleep again under the awning. When I woke, the boat was docked. Two white-uniformed attendants lifted my stretcher into their ambulance. Diana and the Chief waved goodbye and then the doors closed.

At Fisherman's Hospital my clothing was removed, chest, head and arm X-rayed. A shot of painkiller made me drowsy, but I managed to give my name and address, said I could pay for services after I got my wallet from the car. Then I asked for a phone and dialed the Hotel Clay.

Rita's room didn't answer. The clerk said she'd just checked out. Damn! But she was following instructions. Tomorrow I'd call her hacienda, close up my house and get on over to Spain.

A doctor came in holding X-rays. "Couple of bruised ribs, Mr. Novak. You took a good bang on your skull but no fracture. Facial lacerations . . ." He sorted out another X-ray, peered at it. "How's the left arm?"

"Better than it was. Some numbness, tingling." The sort of thing that would wear away.

"Your forehead needs a couple of stitches, okay?"

"Okay."

"And I'm ordering IV fluid for dehydration. You'll feel better."

"Anything that makes me feel better I want."

He smiled. A young Latino doctor whose mustache added a couple of years to his olive-skinned face. "You'll do okay. Ready?"

They wheeled me in to a small operating room, fed me a twilight sleep anaesthetic along with the IV sucrose, and the doctor, now wearing mask and surgical gloves, stitched my forehead, cleaned and bandaged minor cuts, and wound tape around my ribs.

After that, I phased out, and when I woke I was in a small, two-bed room, alone. I rang for a nurse, who cranked up my bed and gave me a waterglass with straw. I sipped while she was getting my wristwatch, and as the anaesthetic wore off I realized I was feeling a good deal better.

The time was now noon. I phoned Manny's office and learned he was back from PR but lunching. I left my name and number for callback.

After a while the young mate, Diana, tiptoed in and stood at bedside. "Hello," she said, "how are you feeling?"

"Didn't you ask that once before?"

"Hours ago. You look heaps better than when we pulled you off that bar."

"Did I say I was grateful? Express appreciation appropriately?" My tongue was so thick I could hardly enunciate the syllables sequentially.

"I think you did. But we never really got your name. For the report," she added, with a slight blush.

I gave it to her, and she wrote it down along with my Gables address. "If you need it for insurance you can get a copy of the report."

"I don't think I'll want it," I told her. "Makes me look like the fool land-lubber I am."

"Oh, even experienced boaters run aground. That happens all the time. Pappy and me—he's the Chief—just winch 'em off and no problem."

"Draw up a chair," I suggested, "pass some charity time with a wounded man. Is that asking too much?"

She didn't reply, but dragged over a chair and sat. "Anything I can do for you?"

I nodded, felt a twinge of pain. "A sisterly kiss would do wonders for me."

Her smile was impish. "Sisterly it'll be." She leaned over and planted a cool kiss on my swollen lips. When she was seated again I noticed that her cheeks were flushed. "I could use more of that, Diana."

"So could I, but, well, I've got a man."

"Pappy?"

"Uh-huh. We're together so much we might as well be married."

"So?"

"He's got a wife. In a place for alcoholics."

"Well," I said, "I'm sorry about that, but life doesn't seem to sort things out very well."

"No," she said morosely, "it doesn't," and looked at me. "Married?"

"No. But I've got a relationship. She's married, and just left for Europe."

"So?"

"Chances are we'll get together. For keeps. What's your last name?"

"Neville. I'm at the barracks, mostly, or on patrol. But now and then I get time off."

"Enough to see a movie?"

"Uh-huh, even grab a burger and a beer."

"Sounds good. When I'm looking less like an AIDS victim I'll call."

"Look forward to it." She blushed again and stood up. "Pappy's waiting to finish the report."

I took her hand and held it. "Thanks again—and please thank Pappy."

"I will . . . Jack." She left the room, paused at the doorway for a backward glance, waved her fingers, and was gone.

Her visit brightened my day. I never expected to see her again, but I thought our conversation had been good for both of us. Diana was modest, attractive, hard-working and unpretentious. How many women had I known with all those attributes? Very damn few. I was remembering her slim figure and firm bottom when the nurse came in waving a small card. "Lady left this for you." She plopped it down beside my hand and left. It was a hospital appointment card, on the back of which was printed a telephone number; below it: "Diana N." in feminine script. So, she wasn't kidding about movie, beer and burger. Must be less committed to her relationship than I was to mine. Maybe she didn't like being called "sea-bunny"—if she knew. I re-examined the card and laid it on my pillow. Then I closed my eyes and slept until telephone ringing brought me awake.

Manny exclaimed, "Fisherman's *Hospital*? What the hell happened, Jack?"

"A lot," I told him, "and from none of it do I come out looking particularly well. You're back from the San Juan fleshpots, are you? How about getting down here for the sorry tale?"

"Ummm. Are you likely to pass away immediately?"

"Hope not."

"And you'll be there a while?"

"So they tell me. Manny, remember that exile training camp you visited?"

"Hell, yes, I do. And last night it blew to hell. Started a damn forest fire that . . ." His voice trailed off. "You—?"

"C'mon down, *amigo*, and hear the whole wretched tale. And pick up a flask, will you? I've got ice."

"Añejo?"

"What else?"

SEVENTEEN

I FUDGED a little telling Manny how Tessier had managed to kidnap me; hell, I fudged a lot. But the Añejo loosened my tongue while Manny listened. When I paused to refresh myself he said, "There were two bodies at the camp, but as far as I know neither was Tessier. Or Marie Chavez." He spilled rum into his glass and looked at it. Through window shades I could see early evening outside. The heat of the day was gone. Manny sipped, sighed and said, "No report of a chopper crash."

"There were two in it, maybe three. Tessier could have been the third."

"You hope."

"It's possible. These days I clutch at slim possibilities."

"Like confronting Tessier and getting out alive."

"Like that," I agreed.

"So, if he wasn't in the chopper he could be anywhere."

"Anywhere." And Rita was in Spain. In the morning I'd telephone, re-establish contact, make plans.

He loosened his tie. "Anita's killer was never found, was he?"

"Killers. Two of them. No, the authorities never found them."

He eyed me over the rim of his glass. "Someone did?"

"Justice was done."

He nodded thoughtfully. "That's good to know."

"Partial justice," I amended. "Tessier is responsible for the crime."

"Let it go, Jack. He may never be heard from again."

"That wouldn't bother me too much," I remarked. "Then again, I'd like to settle a growing score. Or scores." My tongue was losing coordination with my thoughts. Añejo and residual anaesthetic were to blame.

He shook his head disapprovingly. "I always said you were too damn persistent and it's got you in deep stuff time and again."

"I thought impulsiveness was my basic character flaw."

"Not mutually exclusive."

"While I juggle that inner meaning, tell me: you've got family in Spain, right?"

"Burgos. A grandpa, aunt and cousins. Why?"

"I'm going over there. Glad to take gifts, money, whatever."

He shook his head. "Jack, you've got this stereotype of me coming from an adobe hut, no lights, no plumbing. In actual truth my family owns vineyards, olive and almond orchards. They live very well indeed; by some standards they're wealthy." He grunted. "Gifts and goodies come from Spain, not the other way."

"Jeez, Manny, a thousand pardons," I slurred. "How could I be so mistakenly wrong?"

"Ah, forget it." He stood up. "There's not enough left of Tessier's camp to spit on, but he can find another."

"Harder to sign up more recruits."

"Might be. According to fire-fighter reports about eighty trainees took off—down the road, through the swamp. Bullshit aside, Jack, that was a good night's work."

"Pepe Menendez did it all."

He smiled. "Gotta get home. You'll be out tomorrow?"

"Guess so."

"Don't rush it," he advised. "Concussion's nothing to fool with."

"Thanks for coming, *compadre*." I raised my good arm and we shook hands.

After he'd gone, dinner arrived: limp salad, chicken-fried steak and boiled carrots. I wolfed the steak and drank a half-pint of chocolate milk. Before the attendant removed my tray I had him crank down my bed and turn off the ceiling light even though I was tired enough to sleep on a bed of thorns.

In the morning I made my way to the bathroom, stiffly and painfully, saw my bandaged face in the mirror and grimaced at it. My taped ribs ached but my left arm was usable again.

The nurse said my release depended on the doctor and he wouldn't be around until ten. Well, a couple more hours' rest could only be beneficial, so I sacked out again and watched a *Bonanza* re-run until the door opened and Diana Neville came in.

"Morning," she said shyly. "How you doing?"

"Good morning to you, and I'm doing well enough to get out of here."

She was wearing tight bluejeans and a loose shirt-blouse with vertical blue stripes. Her previously windblown hair was combed and set, her eyebrows were lined and the healthy glow of youth suffused her skin. She looked absolutely delicious.

"Except for my father," she said, "I've never taken anything to a man in a hospital. But I thought you might like these." From behind her back she brought a small pot of violets tied with a velvet bow. "Why," I said, "they're lovely, and just what I've been wanting." I placed them on the tray and inhaled their perfume with closed eyes. "Terrific."

"You really like them?" She sat and folded her hands on her lap. "Have I ever lied to you?" I asked, realizing I had, and only yesterday.

She shrugged. "Guess not."

"Crank me up so I can really see you. You're not in uniform today."

"It's . . . well, I decided to take some time off, accrued Comp Time. Doesn't count against annual leave."

"And decided to squander it on me."

"I wouldn't say that—I feel sort of responsible for you."

"Do you now? That's very Oriental."

"Oriental?" Her forehead furrowed. "I don't—"

"Out there, Diana, when you save someone's life you assume responsibility for it. So, Orientals don't often want to get involved."

"Never knew that."

"But whatever brought you here, I'm happy to see you again."

"Really?"

"Really." She needed extra portions of reassurance. "Where do you come from?"

"Pahokee—that's on the lake, Lake Okeechobee. You?"

"Chicago. That's on a lake, too. Lake Michigan. How long have you been with the Marine Patrol?"

"Nearly four years. I had to wait until I was eighteen."

Making her twenty-two or so. A little over half my age. Very, very young. But—so was Melody. She said, "I'm glad you were still here—I mean, not that I want you staying in the hospital, but if you'd gone I'd have felt kinda flat."

"I know what you mean. And there were the violets." I picked them up and inhaled again. "Can I plant them in my yard, or do they stay like this?"

She shook her head. "I don't know much about flowers, though I'd like to. What I know about are fish and things, marine animals."

"Like manatees."

"Poor things," she sighed. "Jack, can I get you anything?"

"Well, I'm in a mood for ice tea, how about you?"

"Me, too." She left the room and I found myself a little disturbed by her attachment to me, her vulnerability. She returned with two glasses of ice tea and set mine on the tray. I got out the Añejo bottle and flavored my tea, offered her the bottle. "Well," she said, "it's really early, but I'm off duty, so—why not?" and poured a dollop into her glass. We drank together, and I asked, "What plans for the rest of the day?"

"I—well, I thought I'd stay here, be helpful. Maybe read to you, something like that."

I shook my head. "I find it hard to believe that a lovely young woman like you has nothing better to do than cosset a banged-up bum old enough to be your father. But if that's how it is, I'm grateful."

"Jack, you're not so old." She blushed, and drank from her glass. "Pappy's close to retirement."

"I figured so. Ah—did you drive here?"

She nodded. "Can I take you someplace?"

"Well, I left my car on Matecumbe at the marina, if you feel like running me there."

She brightened. "I'd be glad to—but I better not drink more rum."

"And I'll treat you to beer and burger."

So we chatted back and forth and I learned she was one of six children, her father being foreman in a lakeside sugar mill until his death in a cane field accident. Insurance hadn't amounted to much so everyone went to work when they were old enough. She had a high school diploma but wanted to go to Community College. "And maybe I will when I've saved enough."

"Great idea," I said approvingly, then the door opened and Dr. Peregrino came in. Without being told, Diana went out, and the doctor began squeezing and thumping me. Rib pressure made me yelp. He nodded, and said, "Keep the tape on until you're more comfortable. Give the stitches a week and snip them out yourself." He wrote a painkiller prescription, signed the release form, and said, "The hospital bills you."

I thanked him, he went away, and Diana came back. She watched me walk stiffly to the narrow clothes closet, where my abused clothing hung, and helped me into my shirt. She turned away while I pulled on my pants, then fitted on my filthy stockings and shoes. Holding the pot of violets, I left the hospital with Diana at my side.

Her car was an old dented Dodge that bore patches of unpainted fiberglass filler. "I'll get around to painting someday," she told me as she unlocked the passenger door for me. "Why bother? It's wheels." I got inside, fanned hot air from my face, and she slid behind the wheel. The engine sounded better than the car's appearance suggested, and she wheeled onto US 1 with plenty of reserve horsepower. Took thirty-five minutes to reach the marina, and as she braked beside my Miata she stared at it and whistled. "Yours? What a dreamboat."

"Gets me around," I replied and punched my door's electronic sequential lock. I rolled down windows for ventilation and looked at my driver, whose expression was wistful. "Can you drive all right, Jack?"

"I have to try," I replied, "because I really need to get to my place, but maybe you could follow me."

Her face brightened. "I was thinking of that. And we could stop for a bite at Mac's BBQ."

"Great idea. Let's go." I unlocked the glove compartment, got out wallet and ignition keys and drove onto US 1. The barbecue palace wasn't what I'd had in mind, but a stop there seemed the least I could do to repay her courtesies, including the violets. My thought was to say *adiós* at the restaurant, since I was anxious to get to my house and start phoning Spain. But while we were gnawing spicy ribs and downing beer, she said she was curious about Coral Gables, and would like to see my place, if I didn't mind. I could hardly refuse, so for the next hour her Dodge followed my Miata into the Gables. I parked in the drive, she left her heap at curbside and joined me at the front door.

Inside, she wandered around admiring my furnishings (Melody's, actually) while I poured Daniels for her and Añejo for myself. My message machine was red-lighted, and I wanted to get to it but politeness forbade. Anyway, I expected she'd have her drink and leave.

After a jolt of rum I went to the bathroom and pulled off minor bandages to air cuts, and swallowed four Tylenols to dull rib pain. Driving all that distance had been plenty uncomfortable, and using my left arm had brought back a throbbing ache. As I left the bathroom Diana slipped in and closed the door. After turning on the a/c I stretched out on the sofa to ease my ribs, and thought about Rita. By now it was night in Spain, a good time to catch her at the hacienda, assuming she was there. I heard the toilet flush, and presently Diana returned, stopping at the bar to freshen her drink. "How's yours?" she called.

"Fine." Ice clinked in her glass as she walked to the sofa and sat down beside me. "You have a very nice place, Jack," she remarked, "and I'm glad you let me see it." There was high color in her cheeks. "Live here long?"

"About two years. I own it with a young woman who's in Europe."

"Spain?"

"A different one."

She smiled. "So, two of your women are abroad."

"Ah—the joint owner isn't my girl any longer."

"But the other one, in Spain, is?"

I nodded and my shoulder twinged. She read my face and murmured, "Poor Jack."

"Lucky Jack."

"Very." She was bending over, as though to give me a compassionate, sisterly kiss, when the telephone rang. "Shall I answer?" she asked.

"Just help me up." I trudged to the phone and picked up the receiver. "Yes?"

Not Rita's voice, but a male, saying, "Mr. Novak? Special Agent Doak. I left messages on your machine, but—got a minute?"

"A short one."

"Okay, here it is: that informant, Zagoria, passed a crazy story about that exile camp burning down."

"So?"

"It burned, all right, but Eddie says you did it."

Damn the shithead! "You're asking me?"

"To confirm his story."

"Do I need a lawyer present?"

"I can't advise you on that," he said stiffly, "but Federal land was involved, giving Bureau jurisdiction."

"I'm sick," I told him, "been in bed. I'll call when I'm feeling better." I replaced the receiver.

As I returned to the sofa Diana looked up, expression curious. "The guy who lent me the airboat," I explained. "I'll deal with it later." I lay back, and Diana said, "Where were we?"

"I forget."

She sipped from her glass, and planted moist lips on mine. It was no way a sisterly kiss. It was full of expression and meaning. I turned away and said, "What's happening?"

Sitting erect, she smiled. "Yesterday morning when I saw you on that sandbar you looked like a heap of old clothes. It never occurred to me I'd want a relationship with you."

I swallowed and said nothing. She was so damn *young*.

"Jack, don't you recognize seduction in progress?"

"What about Pappy?"

"Visiting his wife. What about your girlfriend? Don't see her around."

"Because she's in Spain visiting her son, and expects me to behave myself."

"Ummm. I gave you violets but I guess you don't know the language of flowers." I wasn't going to encourage her by asking violet symbolism, but she was going to tell me anyway. "Violets mean desire."

The time had come to be firm. "Diana," I said, "this is crazy, now back off and let's be friends."

"We're already friends, Jack, and don't say you don't like me. Yesterday I saw it in your eyes, and today even more. If you didn't want what I want you shouldn't have asked for that 'sisterly kiss.' "

"My mistake."

"But you liked it."

I was getting aroused. "You know damn well I did. Do. Hey, stop that!" The palm of her hand was stroking the bulge under my fly. I'd heard about the aggressive young female generation and now I had unwanted proof. Not . . . entirely . . . unwanted . . .

She opened my fly and said throatily, "Real men wear boxer shorts, like you," and tenderly grasped my membrum virile. "Are you going to tell me to stop?"

"No. Uh-uh. No. What the hell . . ." Conscience had drained away. She unbuttoned her blouse, bent over and licked me. Then she looked up with large, moist eyes. "I know you're wounded and in pain but I just gotta try. I'll do . . . everything." She peeled off her blouse. No bra, because she didn't need one. Her breasts were mounds with tiny pink nipples. I touched one and she shivered. "Hope you're not a man who demands big tits."

"I take what comes," I told her, "with pleasure." Then we kissed for a long time, and the tip of her tongue entered my mouth, challenging mine to do likewise.

After a while she got up and pulled off her jeans and panties. Then, very carefully, drew off my trousers, shoes and socks. Naked, she looked even younger than I expected. Not an ounce of excess flesh on her trim, boyish figure; buns that looked and felt as firm as peaches. She padded over to her purse and brought back a sealed condom. "Not that I think you've got AIDS," she explained, "but I don't want to be an unwed mother." She tore out the condom and sheathed me. Lithely she got astride my hips, fitted things into position, and with a gasp leaned forward and pressed her lips on mine. "Oh, Jack," she whimpered, "do it. Do it to me," while from her throat erupted guttural sounds of pleasure. Injured as I was, she was giving me the ride of my life. Bucking and rotating, pinching her nipples, sucking her thumb and grasping my shoulders, she demonstrated how they did it in the country, or on the briny sea. She wailed her climax and that brought me off just seconds later. "Oh, Jesus," she husked, "oh, God!" and fell forward on my taped chest. I clenched my teeth to keep from yelping, knowing I deserved pain for fucking this delectable, horny child. A lot more pain for infidelity to Rita. But it was done, and few regrets. Had Ol' Pap polished her technique, or had she learned from teenage schoolmates? What difference did it make? None at all to me.

I held her tightly while our breathing subsided, feeling strong contractions that prolonged pleasure. Yoga stuff. Where had she learned it? Who cared?

Affectionately I stroked her flanks, her smooth back, lifted her chin and kissed her lips. "You're something," I told her, "really something."

"You like?"

"Know damn well I do. Now build us some drinks."

"I have to drive back," she reminded me, "unless I stay over."

"Really shouldn't, Diana, I have to make some calls."

"I won't be in the way—I promise." She detached herself and went to the bathroom, returning with a warm washcloth and a Kleenex for the condom. After ablutions, she made fresh drinks and sat beside me. "Couch potato," she charged.

"Sorry."

She shrugged. "I liked the way we did it."

"Improvisation."

"Whatever." She drank more Daniels and traced my lips with her finger. "If you hadn't come on to me yesterday I'd never have come on to you today."

"I think you had it in mind all along."

"What about you?"

"It was a momentary thought, but I never expected anything to happen."

"I did. Decided to *make* it happen. Anyway, when a guy buys dinner he expects something from a girl."

"I'm the exception."

She laughed. "Oh, Jack, you *know* you had ideas about fucking me. Because I had them, too."

"Okay, it's been mutual." I kissed the nearest nipple and she stroked my shriveled wand. We were getting along just fine.

With a deep sigh, she said, "I'll take a shower and you make your calls. Knock when you're through."

"I'll do better than that, I'll join you."

So she went off to shower and I got Rita's phone numbers from my wallet. Hacienda La Torre. After I dialed there was the usual wait and transatlantic screeching, and finally a male voice asked, in Spanish, who was wanted. "*Señora* de Castenada," I replied.

"Not here."

"Isn't she expected?"

"Can't say, sir."

"Is she in Madrid?"

"I really do not know."

"Well, if I can leave a message, Pepe is well and planning to join her."

"The message will be delivered."

Disappointed, I hung up, then dialed her Madrid residence, thinking Rita might well have stopped there to rest after the flight rather than continue on to Oviedo, the nearest Asturian town of any size.

The Madrid telephone was answered by a similarly-voiced male who said the *señora* was not there, and as far as he knew, not soon expected. I left the same message and broke the connection. Where was she? I phoned the Hotel Clay to verify her departure yesterday and again was told she had checked out.

Rats! I didn't want her to go on thinking an evil fate had befallen me, but what more could I do? Of course—check phone messages.

Hers was the first of three, and she said she was frightened because I hadn't called the night before, but was leaving as I'd instructed. She had decided not to fly directly to Spain, but to stop over at a place whose name she didn't want to give by phone. And she would call soon. End of message. I felt frustrated but relieved that she was going to call. That was the good news. The bad news was that hearing her voice gave me a load of guilt because of what had just transpired on the sofa, where the two of us first made love.

The next two messages were from Special Agent Harloe Doak, who left his phone number and requested I call. That had been taken care of, and I wasn't planning to respond again. But as I left the answering machine I wondered where she had gone—or taken refuge, as the case might be.

Carrying my glass, I went to the bathroom door, knocked, and Diana let me into the steam-filled room. "That took forever," she said with an edge of irritation. "I'm half boiled, but let me scrub your back."

Afterward, we made love in the bedroom, Diana giggling at our raunchy reflections on the ceiling mirror. "Oh, Jack, I look so gross, don't I?"

"You look gorgeous."

"Stop that—I don't want anyone staring at my behind."

"Then lie on your side—that's the way." We arranged ourselves comfortably and pleasured each other extravagantly, no condom needed.

After nightfall I sent out for Shanghai-style Chinese, we warmed the containers by microwave, and I tried showing Diana how to manage chopsticks. She tried gamely, then set them aside and used fork and spoon. "Where'd you learn, anyway?"

"I was in Asia for a while. Ate local chow when the carrier was in port."

"You were Navy?"

"Aviation. F-14."

"Why, Jack, that's wonderful. I knew you were something special. And you tried to pass yourself off as a landlubber. Your very word."

"That was a long time ago," I said reminiscently, "and I never had airboat instruction."

"So, what do you do now?" She forked lo-mein into her mouth.

"Not much. Semi-retired."

"Disability?"

"Ummm. Investments."

"In *these* times? You *are* lucky—or very smart."

"Lucky. As in having you rescue me from the sandbar."

"Fantastic."

I thought she was describing the moment of my discovery but she was only praising a succulent segment of Peking duck.

Afterward, while Diana tidied the kitchen, I drove down Miracle Mile, rented videos and replenished stocks of Daniels and Añejo.

When we were seated on the sofa munching buttered popcorn and watching the start of a late Gene Hackman movie, Diana exclaimed, "This is living, Jack. What I've been missing! Can I—come back when it's, well . . ." She stopped and began again. "What I mean is sometime when you might be lonely and it's—convenient."

I put my working arm around her shoulders and she snuggled up to me. "I'll let you know."

"Promise?"

Lately everyone wanted me to promise; another wouldn't hurt. "I promise."

The alarm woke us at five-thirty. I scrambled eggs, made bacon and toasted English muffins, while Diana showered, dressed and made ready to drive back to Marathon for patrol duty.

Half dressed, I walked her to the Dodge, kissed her a long time, and said, "Thanks for everything."

"Jack, *thank* you!"

"And don't give my regards to Pappy. I covet you."

"That's nice. Prove it by calling."

"I will."

She got into her duster, the engine fired, she blew me a kiss and drove away.

As I stood there, a neighbor lady passed by with a tiny Chihuahua on a rhinestone leash. She was wearing a salmon wrapper, floppy bedroom slippers, silvery wig and a disapproving frown. "Morning, ma'am," I said cheerfully, and heard a muffled grunt as I turned and walked tiredly to my house. The pert little sea-bunny had kept me active a good part of the night; the years had taken their toll and I needed compensatory sleep. As I passed through the living room I lifted Diana's violets from the coffee table, inhaled the scent and carried them to the bedroom. Naked, I found an opening in the tangled sheets, and slid in. The aroma of her body lingered pleasantly, and while thinking of the many explorations we'd accomplished, I prepared my mind for sleep.

But then I heard the breathy beating of a chopper in the distance. The sound recalled the Iroquois that captured me, the one I'd managed to shoot down. And that led to a chain of thought involving Tessier, escape and Rita.

Rita. Where was she? When would she call? I hadn't silenced the phone ringer as I often did when sleeping in, but when the phone rang it was after ten and the voice I heard wasn't Rita's.

EIGHTEEN

M ANNY SAID, "You're there? *Bueno*. How you feeling?"

"Groggy. Too much sleep or not enough. What's—?"

"TV news flash. Hornstein's dead."

"No kiddin'."

"So I thought of you."

"Ease off," I told him. "Dead how?"

"Bullets in head and chest. Body found in the parking garage under his office. Initial speculation is some dissatisfied client killed him."

"That's what the newsies always say. Medellín cartel, right?"

"Possibly. Ah—you weren't around?"

"Last night I was entertaining an attractive young person, but Tessier's a possibility. Manny, there won't be a dry eye in the courthouse."

He grunted. "There's plans for an office party here—by way of celebration. The consensus is: whoever did it, good job."

"I suppose they'll round up the usual suspects."

"Slowly. Very slowly. They deserve equal time to get away."

"They do indeed." As suggested to Manny, I felt Tessier was a leading candidate. Hornstein had set up the meeting with me, and I'd destroyed Tessier's camp. That was in addition to Hornstein's putative responsibility for the fake emeralds. Apparently Saul hadn't argued his case persuasively enough, or Tessier became impatient with denials and terminated the attorney. Of course I couldn't convey my theory to Manny because that would have led to a bunch of other things he didn't need to know. "Who's got jurisdiction?" I asked.

"Murder's a state offense, but Tessier's a Federal fugitive so it's mixed. So far Tessier's name hasn't been mentioned."

"But it will be."

"Very likely."

"Then we'll watch developments, right?"

"And assist as able. Wait a second, a police report is coming in . . . Okay, a witness, the garage watchman, said he saw a car come in—man and woman. That was before six this morning. Doesn't know where the car went and heard no shots. Car left about six-thirty, same couple in it. He was making his final rounds before going off duty at eight, and spotted Hornstein's car—a cream-colored Excalibur roadster with gold trim—in its slot. He went over to admire the car and found Hornstein behind the wheel."

"And by this afternoon the watchman will have lost his memory. Won't be able to describe the man and woman or the car they came in."

"Might even claim he was never there. Yeah, you got it right. Witness amnesia avoids reprisals. Say, you were going to Spain?"

"Soon," I told him. "Ah, Manny, I'm feeling a little rocky, so—"

"Gotcha. Later."

After replacing the receiver I looked around the bedroom and remembered my Pahokee Playmate with affection. Today, things might be a little strained between her and Chief Pappy.

I swallowed four Tylenol tabs with morning coffee and decided I ought to fill the painkiller prescription the doc provided. That meant a trip to the pharmacy—when I felt up to it.

In the shower I let hot water ease joint and muscle pain, shaved, and put small Band-Aids where needed. I was dressing and thinking about food when door chimes sounded. So, in pants and Navy robe I went to the door. "Who is it?"

"Special Agents Doak and Ferre."

"What's on your minds?"

"C'mon, Mr. Novak, we got things to talk about. Open up."

"Got a warrant?"

"No."

"Then you don't come in." I opened the door and eyed them. "Talk."

They looked at each other. SA Ferre said, "Looks like you've been fighting."

"Mugger. Next question."

SA Doak shifted his feet and leaned forward. "Information developed since I spoke with you suggests that exile training camp was run by Claude Tessier."

I ran a hand through my hair, looked puzzled. "The place your informant, Zagoria, was at?"

"That's the one."

"Which Eddie says I burned." I scratched my chin. "You know how reliable your informant is. If he says Claude Somebody ran it that's okay with me."

"Tessier. Claude Tessier, a fugitive from Guatemala."

"That Zagoria," I said, "was an accomplice to the burglar I apprehended. At your request I didn't press charges against him, and now you're asking about things he must have made up. I don't like it." I paused. "Maybe I'll retain Saul Hornstein and go after you guys for harassment."

Doak laughed unpleasantly. "Hornstein's dead."

"No kidding?"

"Gunned by some pissed-off client."

"Yeah? When?"

"Last night. Anyway, I'm sorry you're not cooperating, Mr. Novak."

"I contribute what I can," I replied, "without making up weird tales like Zagoria. And Hornstein's death still leaves a lot of lawyers who'd love to represent me against the Bureau." I frowned. "Are you guys really looking for someone who set a bonfire in the 'Glades? Isn't there more important work to be done?"

Ferre was about to reply when Doak nudged him. "Thanks for your time, Mr. Novak, we appreciate it." They turned and went down the walk to their Chevy Caprice. I watched them get into it and then I closed and locked the door. That damn Zagoria, I thought. I'd let him live and he didn't appreciate it.

After dressing I drove to the pharmacy for my prescription, stopped at Publix for food and drink supplies, and returned to my house. My answering machine showed a red light and I played the message, hoping it was Rita. Instead I heard Diana Neville saying, "We're about twelve miles off Spanish Harbor looking for Cuban rafters, but I wanted to say thanks again for a really great time. Sorry you weren't there. 'Bye."

Just as well, I thought, as I re-set the machine, because I didn't want her figuring a one-nighter as the beginning of a steady thing. Sorry, Diana, it's Rita I want to hear from.

After stocking the refrigerator I put ice in a glass and added Añejo, swallowed two prescription capsules, and decided I ought to pack a bag, get ready to leave for Spain as soon as Rita called.

Until then I was going to stay close to the phone, become a hermit again, a semi-prisoner.

My thoughts turned to the emeralds in my safe, and the bank account numbers. Somewhere, someone had a list of the bank names, unless that list was burned with Chavez's body in the crash. Tessier might have it, and with both lists could tap into that enormous looted wealth. He'd discarded the fake emeralds, but kept the account card I'd made up with altered numbers. To him they might look valid, but would gain him nothing at the Swiss banks if he tried. Until Rita told me of her parents' estrangement I'd considered Mama Marie a logical holder of the bank list, but seeing her with Tessier convinced me that if she'd had it her lover would have it now.

It would have been shrewd of Chavez, I mused, to split the bank account information and avoid betrayal by one sole holder. Well, he was crafty and conspiratorial; he hadn't been able to seize and rule Guatemala by practicing stupidity. And to succeed him Tessier needed funds more desperately than ever. His training camp was in ashes, his trainees dispersed, and he was in hiding again.

Not having witnessed Hornstein's murder, I couldn't be certain Tessier had killed him. From time to time Miami drug lawyers were knocked off by clients to whom they'd promised and failed to deliver case dismissal or short sentences. Bribery was notoriously rampant among the local judiciary, and any judge who pocketed a bribe had better deliver. Because what corruption surfaced came usually from resentful defendants who fingered bribe-takers to the FBI.

That's where Special Agents Doak and Ferre ought to be concentrating, instead of investigating swamp fires and bugging me.

That train of thought led me to contemplating, as I occasionally did, the enormous governmental machinery involved in suppressing narcotics. The cost was incalculable and involved our defense establishment and every aspect of law enforcement. To that add the subsidies (bribes) paid to Andean drug-producing countries, total it all up and compare with the negligible result obtained.

Why not, I thought, as in the case of Prohibition, declare victory and make narcotics legal? Repeal of the Volstead Act hadn't made us a nation of alcoholics, and I suspected that drug availability wouldn't swell the sale of syringes. Without their enormous profits from illegal narcotics the Mafia and the Medellín and Cali cartels would abandon trafficking, and Andean peasants would return to growing maize, rice and beans instead of coca, poppies and marijuana.

Manny didn't like hearing that kind of talk, accused me of advocating the easy path, to which I responded it was the practical path and the only one that hadn't been tried.

Still, as long as drug enforcement laws were on the books they had to be obeyed, a point Manny raised, and with which I agreed.

In Spain it was now late afternoon. Should I phone Madrid and the hacienda again or rely on Rita's promise to call? That Tessier was still on the loose worried me plenty. He'd tried to get at Rita before, and in Spain it would be a lot easier than here because I wasn't there to protect her. Of course, he had no way of knowing she'd left Miami, and for now his ignorance was her shield.

At noon I drove to a men's shop on Miracle Mile and bought a white nylon money belt for the emeralds, hurried back and checked my answering machine: no messages.

I microwaved leftover chicken lo-mein and made a meal of it, turned on the TV and watched midday news reports. Local news-hens were clucking over Hornstein's murder, and there was footage of the crime scene, sans corpse. Hornstein's custom-built Excalibur was a long, beautiful cabriolet with a tan canvas top. To me it symbolized the profitability of crime while you were alive to enjoy it, and I was cheered up by the thought that I might have played a role in hastening the lawyer's end.

From the closet I selected clothing to take to Spain. The province of Asturias was located between ocean and mountains and would be cooler than the high central plateau of Castile-Madrid, so I packed for both climates. Briefly I considered trying to smuggle my H&K .38 into Spain, but decided the risk was excessive. Besides, Rita's hacienda would have shotguns for *perdiz* shooting, probably fine Spanish Eibars or Sarasquetas that could serve for defense.

After opening my floor safe to remove passport, five thousand dollars and Anita's emeralds, I handled and fondled my .38, and remembered the loss of my prized Beretta Parabellum three nights ago—along with my MAC-10. To the cache I added Barton's .38, the one supplied by Tessier; a throwaway piece was sometimes useful to have. Then I locked the safe and covered it with a serape.

I was in the garage dusting off two suitcases for my journey when I heard the telephone ring. I raced in, caught it before the machine did, and to my astonishment heard the voice of once-beloved, faithless Melody. "Jack," she purred, "you're actually there—I'm so glad."

"Are you? Why?"

"Oh, Jack, don't be difficult."

"I'll change the question; where are you?"

"Salzburg."

"For the Mozart Festival?"

"It doesn't start until August."

"Then you're at the head of the line for a seat, or seats. Paolo with you?"

She hesitated before saying, "Well . . . no. He stayed in Como."

"The lake or the town?"

"The town, silly, that's where we've been living. Jack, I think about you, worry about you—are you all right?"

"I wasn't, sweetest, but now I'm okay, and I'm glad we're in touch. I'm paying mortgage and tax bills on this place, and I've wondered what your intentions are."

"Well—since you ask, that's one of the reasons I called. See, I'm thinking of coming back, and—"

"With Paolo?"

"Umm. I think not."

"Trouble in Paradise?"

"Jack—*please*. You can be *so* cutting." This from the young lady who'd cut me like an old boot from a fishline.

"So, what are your travel plans?"

"They sort of depend on you. I mean, I wouldn't want to barge in and find you had . . . company."

"I see, and I appreciate your consideration. Right now our joint lovenest is—how shall I put it?—occupied. But I can unoccupy it in, say a week. Suit you?"

"Perfectly. But I wouldn't want *you* to feel you have to leave."

I breathed deeply and exhaled. "Honey, you've been gone a year. You found *Signor* Perfection in Barcelona, clasped him to your bosom, and I became excess baggage. I suffered, *signorina*, but that's history. If you've been contemplating return to the status quo ante, I don't think you're being realistic. To reprise our relationship: when you were barely Of Age you deceived me into taking your maidenhead, and we went on from there. So I see myself as a fixation of your extreme youth, one you've outgrown in many ways. Even though," I added, "legend has it a girl fondly remembers the guy who copped her cherry."

"Jack! You can be so disgusting!"

"Always. So, tell me—is this break with Mr. Fettucine final, or a cooling-off period?"

"With your attitude, I don't feel I should tell you anything."

"Better if you don't, then there'll be less to retract."

"You don't want to see me," she complained.

"I'll always be glad to see you, Melody, and if you come next week feel free to enjoy the place."

"I'd enjoy it a good deal more if you were there," she pouted.

"I understand that, and I'll even authorize you to use my car. Just pay for any body work, okay?"

For a while I heard only electronic humming. Finally she said, "You're being very cruel."

"I don't think so. But I want to avoid becoming an alternate *amico*, with you bouncing back and forth between Paolo and me."

"If you'd really listened to me you'd understand I'm through with him."

"I always thought you could do a lot better than a guy who couldn't even win a bronze to your gold."

"It was a source of friction," she admitted, "and his not having a job, or even seriously looking for one, just added to it. Uh—I guess your new . . . relationship is satisfactory."

"So far, though we haven't been at it long. Listen, there was a break-in, nothing taken, but if you're moving in I'll have a security system installed."

"Darling," she trilled, "that's so thoughtful of you."

"And I'll leave a key in the usual place."

"Once there, I'll miss you all the more."

"Umm. Very hot here. How's Salzburg?"

"Delightful. The mountains are wonderful."

"Enjoy the breeze," I said, and replaced the receiver.

Well, that was a surprise, but my leaving and her arriving was going to work out just fine. I found the security system brochures left by the glazier, and phoned to request a home security analysis. The dispatcher said she'd have someone there in two or three hours if that was okay. I agreed, and freed the phone for incomings.

After he'd surveyed the house the tech recommended a system suitable for the Uffizi Gallery at a correspondingly cosmic cost. I got him down to a reasonable figure and paid a deposit, figuring Melody could pay the balance after moving in. Work was to begin next day.

After nightfall I broiled tender *fajita* and consumed it with salad and Coors. Since Melody's call the telephone hadn't rung, and in Spain the hour was like two in the morning so I doubted Rita would be phoning. At the video rental shop I returned the movies I'd shared with Diana and selected five others for myself. It was going to be a lonely wait, though I hoped not a protracted one.

Two men worked half a day installing the alarm system that flashed house and yard lights when violated, and emitted piercing screams until turned off. Doors, garage and windows were rigged against intrusion, and the workmen's parting act was to paste warning decals on my windows, calculated to frighten off thieves.

Now I felt enveloped in an electronic cocoon and less vulnerable to villains like Barton Earl Bevins, who, I hoped, was still behind bars and would continue in that status for numerous years. Hornstein was no longer practicing the kind of law that would get him out, though an inspired public defender might succeed.

Manny phoned to say that Hornstein's murder topped the local list of unsolved crimes, and without clues of any kind the Metro Police were helpless. The Miami Bar Association posted a ten thousand dollar reward for information leading to arrest and conviction, but so far no takers. The garage watchman, as anticipated, had developed amnesia. Confronted with his earlier statements, he denied them and grumbled about police harassment.

"It's a dry well," I remarked to Manny. "They'll never identify the perp."

"Don't I know it, though we're giving the cops a list of known cartel hit men." He sighed. "Still going to Spain?"

"Definitely." I remembered Melody's call and told him about it. His comment was, "I knew she'd want to come back, all's forgiven."

"After a year's absence," I said musingly. "Well, no accounting for the female mind."

Next afternoon Diana phoned from the patrol boat and we talked for a while. They were off the Dry Tortugas, she said, and asked if I was into scuba. I said I was, and that led to her suggesting we dive Pennekamp reefs together. I gave her a pleasant temporizing reply, she said Pappy wanted the radio telephone, and ended transmission.

So my diminutive Venus was bouncing around the briny with Pappy as duty required, but I had to admit her presence would have been more than welcome. I felt hemmed-in by the house, and lonely as I'd never felt at the stilt shack before Anita came jogging by. There I could swim and fish; here I had movie tapes and microwave popcorn. The quality of life was deteriorating while I waited for the absent Rita's call.

Where, in thundering hell, was she?

The following morning, before I was fully awake, the phone rang and I picked it up eagerly, sure it would be Rita. Instead, my caller was Manny Montijo.

NINETEEN

"**G**OT A flash for you, Jack. Tessier's been spotted."

"Where?"

"Mexico City airport."

"Arriving or departing?"

"The airport watcher said he was picked up by a stretch Mercedes and driven away. That was yesterday morning."

"Tessier alone?"

"Watcher didn't say—and didn't have wheels to follow."

"Where did Tessier fly in from?"

"Not known; his name wasn't on any passenger list, so he was traveling under alias."

"How about Marie?"

"She's not on our watchlist so some bean-counter would have to check a couple thousand arrival names. Is it important?"

"Guess not, I'm just curious." The good news was Tessier was in Mexico, far from Rita. On the downside he was still loose and able to reach Spain in half a day. "Well," I said, "for now I don't need to worry about reprisal. And Tessier can rest easy under the benevolent protection of the cops."

"Yes—it would be hard to make a move against him. And given Mex sensitivity I'm convinced we'd never get authorization for a snatch." He paused. "Say, how come you're not in Spain? Waiting for Melody?"

"No way. Just—circumstances," I finished lamely. "Anyway, thanks for the travel report."

I made mid-morning breakfast: Canadian bacon, scrambled eggs and English muffin, washed down with coffee and juice. While I was stacking the dishwasher the phone rang again, and I answered, hardly daring to hope it was Rita.

But it was.

There was a cautious edge to her voice as she said, "Jack? Oh, I'm so glad you're there. I've been terribly worried . . . How are you?"

"Fine. I called the hacienda and Madrid trying to reach you, but—"

"I'm in Zurich taking care of some personal things. When can you join me?"

"Let's say tomorrow. I'm out of here as soon as I can book a flight. Been packed for days." She hadn't asked the state of Tessier's health or how our meeting had gone but I laid that to caution. It wasn't hard to eavesdrop on transatlantic calls. "And I'm bringing something you'll be very glad to see."

"Tell me. I hate surprises."

"Sorry, this'll have to wait. Where are you staying?"

"The Baur au Lac. Suite 619."

"Alone?"

"Of course. Jack, you didn't think—?"

"Just kidding. Honey, I've really missed you."

"And I'm longing to see you—so phone me when you land. Dial zero one, two two one, sixteen, then fifty. The hotel will send a limo. And, darling, don't be surprised if it's a Rolls."

"Silver Cloud, I hope. And you'll be wearing . . . ?"

"The Decadence trifles, of course. So don't delay."

After saying she loved me Rita ended the call and I made a note of her hotel phone and suite.

Years before, during DEA apprenticeship, I'd tailed a Peruvian money courier from Miami to Zurich's Union Bank and waited while he deposited a suitcaseful of currency. As he was leaving I braced him and made him cough up deposit slips. I couldn't arrest him but he didn't know that, and he fled with his empty suitcase. Next day, after tellers had counted his two million green, I withdrew the money by cashier's check and flew back to Miami.

So I'd only been overnight in Zurich, and my lasting impression concerned the excessive cost of my hotel room, taxis and meals. Returning would be under different circumstances.

I phoned Hornstein's office manager and asked to have Anita's suitcases sent by courier to Señora Castenada at my Gables address. The office was too disorganized to raise questions, and the manager agreed as soon as I said I'd pay delivery charges.

My next call was to the Apollo travel agency on Coral Way. After checking departures the agent said I could fly American Airlines at eight o'clock but I'd have to be at airport check-in by six. First class seating was available. I said I wanted it, and needed the ticket delivered; payment in cash.

Going through the house I turned off lights, adjusted the a/c to eighty degrees for Melody's benefit, and buried a front door key among the roots where I'd recovered it. In the kitchen I printed a sign: *Handle With Care*, and stuck it under the Miata's windshield wiper for Melody's attention. I was locking the garage door when a delivery van pulled up and the driver stepped out. "Castenada?" he called, and I nodded. With that he hauled out two matching suitcases and carried them up the walk. I paid and tipped him, and lugged the suitcases to the bedroom, where I opened both and began going through them. Cosmetics, running gear, swimsuits, numerous pairs of slacks and matching blouses, an ornate leather box with earrings, necklaces, bracelets and rings; tampons and pump jogging shoes. That was one suitcase. I set aside the jewelry for Rita.

The other suitcase held ten pairs of shoes and an equal number of folded dresses; panties and pantyhose. A Gucci leather manicure kit was the largest single item. Its metal items were gold-plated. Four purses, none containing change or bills. Legal tender customarily disappeared when detectives pawed through a victim's belongings.

As I touched things that had been Anita's I felt a remembered intimacy, and sorrow. So young to be destroyed; her life was only beginning . . .

I closed both suitcases and stored them under a tarpaulin in the garage where Melody was not likely to notice them. As far as I was concerned they were Rita's now.

My airline ticket was delivered by motorcyclist. In the living room I paid the boy plus five for his trouble. He wrote out a receipt and wished me a good flight.

I took a shower, shaved and stuck a Band-Aid across my forehead stitches. Then I called a taxi and finished dressing.

It was five-thirty when I activated the alarm system and left the house. The taxi driver took LeJeune Road north to the Expressway and west to the airport. After checking in I placed a call to the Baur au Lac but Rita's room didn't answer. I left my flight number with the concierge, who reminded me that in Zurich it was after one.

So Rita was asleep. She would get my message when she woke, and we'd breakfast together. The first of many.

At the duty-free shop I learned I could take a liter of liquor and a bottle of wine into Switzerland, so I paid for on-board delivery of Añejo and Dom Pérignon. In First Class I was welcomed with a glass of undistinguished champagne and a dinner menu. As I considered selections the plane began rumbling toward the flight line, where it braked for a final run-up check. Presently it moved ahead, accelerated and rose smoothly into the air. Below I could see chains of light from cars crowding the expressways. They diminished as we gained altitude. The plane banked gently eastward, and we crossed over the long spit of Miami Beach, with its glittering high-rise towers, to the dark ocean. Above it I glimpsed the first evening star, and was reminded of guiding the airboat by stars and moon over trackless reaches of water and grass.

But all that was behind me, I told myself, along with the violence, death and fear I'd lived through so recently in the past. I was done with it, and ahead, on the far side of darkness, a new life was taking shape for me. Beginning with the dawn.

BOOK THREE

TWENTY

SHE LAY beside me on the canopied bed, her naked body turned from me in sleep. Her bottom was cool, her breathing light and rhythmic. How long since we'd made love? The Meissen clock over the fireplace showed two hours since I'd arrived.

Our bed was antique four-poster, the mattress buoyant eiderdown. Chairs and sofa were patterned rose damask, the wallpaper flocked in blue *belle-époque* designs. I remembered part of my flight, the filet mignon dinner, wine, and cognac before asking for a pillow. Almost at once fatigue had overwhelmed me; the stressful events since our parting finally drained my strength and forced surrender.

The flight attendant let me sleep until Kloten airport was in view; still groggy, I went through Customs and found the waiting Rolls, dozed during the twenty-minute ride, and woke at the hotel.

Rita came to the door in a translucent peach peignoir over the South Beach scanties. I tipped and dismissed the porter, then we were in each other's arms ... only two hours ago?

I left her sleeping, opened a bag and got out shaving gear; showered in the huge tiled double bathroom with its bidet and thick warm towels. My rib tape itched badly and I wanted it off, forehead stitches, too, before we appeared in public.

So far there'd been no time to talk but I was curious over the seemingly endless interval before Rita called me. Had she been in Zurich since leaving Miami? What business brought her here?

In turn, I'd have to explain my bandages and how I came to possess the emeralds and bank account list; neither explanation could be entirely true.

Unnoticed, Rita came from behind and circled my shoulders with her arms, pressed her body against me. "Ummm—you smell so good." She kissed the nape of my neck, wiggled sexily. "I've missed your loving. Am I hurting you?"

"No, but I want the tape off. Got scissors?"

"Let me get the house physician. Please?"

I shrugged. She used the wall extension phone to call the concierge and make arrangements. Replacing the receiver, she said, "Now, what got you so bruised, darling? And when am I going to see my surprise?"

"Why don't you," I suggested, "order us some breakfast? Coffee loosens my tongue."

"If that's what it takes." While I finished toweling she spoke to room service. I left the bathroom and presently heard the shower.

I pulled on shorts and flannel slacks, opened the money belt I'd worn across the Atlantic, and took out Anita's nine emeralds. I set them on the night table, made a separate pile of Anita's jewelry. The doorbell rang, I crossed the sitting room and let the doctor in.

After explaining what I wanted done I lay on the sofa while he cut through the tape with blunt scissors and pulled it off. He snipped my stitches and drew them out with tweezers. That done, he applied an antiseptic swab to the cut and had me hold it in place while he wrote out the bill. I paid in dollars, he wished me good-day, and was gone.

Hardly had the door closed than the breakfast cart arrived attended by two immaculate waiters. After they'd set everything out on a white linen tablecloth and flourished the fluted napkins, I told them we could manage alone, signed the bill, and filled two cups with steaming coffee. On impulse I placed the emeralds on Rita's plate and covered them with a napkin, arranged the jewelry on mine.

Rita appeared, wearing a fluffy white robe with black and orange flashes, hair still damp, no makeup. After we kissed she murmured, "In the shower I kept thinking of you, the wasted time apart. Let's not have it happen again." She touched my ribs' purple-yellow contusions. "I assume you met Claude. What happened?"

"He outsmarted me. Wasn't fooled by the fake stones. Shanghaied me to a camp in the 'Glades where he's been training a private army to retake Guatemala."

Her eyebrows lifted. "That's very interesting. But you got away."

"I cooked his camp, and in the confusion stole an airboat. Got to open water and crashed in the dark." I sipped from my cup. "A patrol boat picked me up, took me to Fisherman's Hospital . . ."

"Oh, Jack!" She squeezed my hand possessively. "Thank God you survived. But I told you Claude was a formidable adversary."

"I know, honey, and I underestimated him."

"Did he—Is he—?"

"Alive? 'Fraid so. In Mexico City."

She inhaled. "At least he's far away. Jack, was it worth any part of what you've gone through? The danger . . . ?"

"Guess not," I replied, and thought back. "All I saved from Tessier was my name. Far as he knows, I'm Pepe Menendez, your gofer and gigolo." But he was still looking for a certain Jim Nolan.

"While Jack Novak is my fiancé." She smiled. "I'm so glad of that. And I'm dying to see my surprises."

"*Voilà!*" I uncovered Anita's jewelry. She said, "Oh!" as one hand lifted to her mouth. "Where did it come from?"

"Her suitcase."

Picking up a bracelet, she held it so the gemstones glittered and said quietly, "I remember when Anita bought this. Thank you, dear."

"And now this." I lifted her napkin and the stones blazed with green fire. She touched one, drew back. "I—I'm speechless," she said huskily. "Her suitcase too?"

Rather than speak the lie, I nodded. "Now take care of them, darling, they're yours."

"Jack, you deserve them." She sat down slowly, tears in her eyes.

"We'll discuss that another time. But while we're here, let's use a hotel strongbox for safety."

"Of course." She dried her eyes, and I sat across from her. "You haven't told me why you came to Zurich."

"Because it involves Jaime, money and the annulment. He came here, signed papers at the nunciature, and I paid him off."

"How soon before you're free?"

"A month, two at most." She seemed to rouse herself. I served eggs and sausages and said, "Being here with you, knowing we'll marry, makes everything worthwhile, darling. And now I'm eager to see La Torre, meet Rafael."

She reached over and covered my hand with hers. "Tomorrow soon enough?"

I nodded. "I'm not crazy about Zurich. It's stodgy, like the Swiss, and everything's money, money, money."

"Isn't it the same everywhere?"

"Haven't been everywhere." I dripped honey onto a warm croissant, discovering how hungry I'd become. "I guess you know most of the world's gold is buried under the Bahnhofstrasse."

"Isn't that just a legend?"

"Maybe. But part of it secures the Chavez bank accounts."

"The Colonel's," she said quickly, "not mine."

"What about your mother, Tessier?"

"Very likely."

I brought out the laminated card. "This was in a suitcase lining."

She took the card, scanned it and put it down. "In Zurich there are dozens of banks, Jack, scores of them."

"I know."

"Shopping, I've noticed the banks of Ticino, Vaud, Luzern and Valais . . ." She spread her hands. "Asking at random would be useless."

"And there's the Union Bank of Switzerland; I once did brief business there. It's not an institution that would welcome casual inquiries."

"Nor any other." She fingered the card again. "You're sure the bank names weren't somewhere in Anita's belongings?"

"Pretty sure."

She laid down the card and sipped coffee. While I was refilling her cup she said, "The information must be somewhere unless it's been destroyed."

"Would your mother have it?"

She shook her head. "The Colonel would never have given it to her. They were barely speaking."

"But she saw the Colonel in Mexico just before his death."

Her eyes narrowed. "How do you know that?"

"You told me."

"Did I? I don't remember it."

"Incidentally—or not so incidentally, Tessier told me he'd sabotaged the Colonel's plane, bragged about killing him."

She sighed. "As we suspected. Did he say why?"

"The Colonel was an obstacle to Tessier becoming Guatemala's next *Lider Máximo*."

"It had to be something like that . . . power . . . ambition." She gazed morosely at her plate. "I don't want all that money, but Claude mustn't get it."

I studied the card. "Two numbers begin with eighteen, two with forty-seven, and three start with ninety-four. Those would be digraphs identifying three banks. Anyone can remember three banks, but still needs account numbers to do business." I flashed back to my capture. "Tessier deep-sixed the fake emeralds but kept the phony card."

"Then he'll surely come to Switzerland," she said dully. "Oh, Jack, I wish you'd killed him."

"God knows, I tried. But he was wearing a bulletproof vest I hadn't counted on." It was humiliating to remember how many other surprises I hadn't anticipated but I was keeping them to myself lest Rita lose confidence in me.

For a while we concentrated on eating, and when the coffeepot was empty I said, "Tessier can't get at the money, so let's forget about him. The only small problem I know of is getting from here to Hacienda La Torre."

She nodded. "We fly to Madrid and change to a smaller plane that will take us to Oviedo. I'll have a car meet us for the rest of the trip." After touching Anita's jewelry, she said, quietly, "I could never bring myself to wear these things."

"I understand."

"If I had a daughter I'd keep them for her. But—"

"Maybe we'll have one."

She smiled. "A wonderful thought. But these emeralds have caused death and sorrow—I'll have them appraised here, maybe sell them and use the money for helping people. Unless you'd like it, Jack. As I said, you deserve all of it." She touched my hand. "Do you realize I have no idea if you're rich, poor, or in-between."

"I have enough to do pretty much what I want over an average year."

"I wouldn't want you ever to feel you were being kept by me. As Jaime said yesterday, even though our arrangement was strictly financial he resented my money. I resented his avarice." She shrugged. "We compromised. He's getting his payoff, I get my annulment."

"Okay. And we'll keep the account numbers somewhere safe. Who knows? The bank names may come along one day."

Her eyes twinkled. "Before we're old and gray."

Hand in hand we strolled from the hotel up Bahnhofstrasse and across the Paradeplatz where—as Rita told me—serious shopping began. By serious she meant high-priced, of course, and after I'd checked out a few window displays I knew she was unarguably right.

Bijoux Brevoort was an old, very serious establishment. The white-haired jeweler designated to appraise our emeralds was turned out in charcoal morning coat, grosgrain vest, stiff gates-ajar collar, pearl stickpin in light gray cravat, and opal cuff links. He had the bushy eyebrows of C. Aubrey Smith and the supercilious accents of John Gielgud, but he was a tradesman *au fond* and regarded the emeralds covetously.

He spread a square of black velvet atop a glass display case, inserted a loupe and examined one of the gems. "Emerald, indubitably," he pronounced, "and apparently of good quality." He measured with a small micrometer, sniffed and set the emerald with the others. "Colombian, madame?"

"I believe so," Rita replied, "a gift."

He nodded. "Appraisal will take at least half an hour, depending on your wishes. By which I mean wholesale or retail value."

"Wholesale, I suppose," Rita told him.

He nodded again. "If a certificate of appraised value is required the fee is accordingly higher."

"That won't be necessary."

"Very well. If you care to wait there is an enclosure where coffee, tea and chocolate are served. Your name, please?"

Rita supplied it, adding that she was staying at the Baur au Lac. He gathered the display cloth by its four corners and carried the emeralds to the rear of the store and out of sight.

We went to the waiting room, which contained five comfortable leather-covered chairs and a dark mahogany coffee table that held a neatly arranged assortment of financial magazines in French, German and Italian. From warm urns I poured coffee for Rita, hot, syrupy chocolate for myself. We then settled down to wait. After a while Rita said, "I wonder how much the emeralds are worth?"

"No idea," I responded, although Manny had mentioned more than half a million.

"Why don't you keep them, Jack, or sell them? As a wedding present."

"Because I have nothing comparable for you."

She sipped, frowned slightly, then brightened. "You'll give me yourself."

"I plan to. And not subject to exchange."

She kissed my cheek. "Or substitution. Perfect. See how easily our problems dissolve?"

"May it be always so." I picked up a trilingual brochure relating the history of the House of Brevoort and scanned it. "Founded in 1597," I said conversationally, "by a Dutch immigrant from Ijmuiden. So it's a pretty stable place."

"The Swiss are a pretty stable people."

"But they don't seem to enjoy life very much. They ski, yodel and make money from other people's money." I replaced the brochure. "Boring."

"Not if you were Swiss. Besides, you've had an adventurous life. Will you perish of boredom on the hacienda?"

"Uh-uh. There comes a time when every man wants peace, quiet, love and affection, and that time has come for me. The old life I left behind in Miami."

She kissed me again. "I hope so."

And, I thought, the only worrisome factor is that Tessier's still alive.

After a while the appraiser returned with the emeralds in small plastic bags numbered one through nine. He placed them on the coffee table before us and drew up a chair. Seated, he consulted a list in his hand. "I give you the appraised values sequentially in thousands of Swiss francs." After clearing his throat, he said, "Twenty-two, fifty, seventy, twelve, ninety, sixty-five, twenty-eight, thirty-six and fifty-three." He glanced at us for reaction. Seeing none, he continued, "To a total of four hundred twenty-six thousand Swiss francs."

I turned to Rita, who asked, "In dollars?"

"Six hundred seven thousand dollars."

"Sizeable," I remarked, and Rita nodded.

"Unlike diamonds, whose value emeralds outrank," the appraiser told us, "flaws and shadings enhance the worth of emeralds." He gestured at them.

"Yours, madame, would be more valuable if the cutting and polishing more closely approached professional standards."

"Still," I remarked, "they're not macadamias."

He spoke to Rita. "As the gentleman says," and produced a bill written in Spenserian script. Fifteen hundred Swiss francs. Not bad for a half-hour's work. Rita said, "Thank you," and began putting the bagged emeralds in her purse. Pausing, she asked, "I wonder if Brevoort would be interested in purchasing them?"

He thought it over. "Possibly. Our senior gemologist would have to decide."

"At the appraised value."

"Less taxes."

Rita continued collecting the stones. "Ask him," she instructed. "I'll stop by later."

At the cashier's cage Rita presented the appraisal bill and paid in cash. "Now," she said, tucking away the receipted bill, "let's see about flying home."

TWENTY-ONE

$\mathbf{B}$Y THE time we got back to the hotel our suite had been tidied and afternoon sunlight streamed through open window blinds. From the sitting room I could see the juncture of the Limmat River and the Zurichsee that was not a "sea" but a calm blue lake cradled by the Alps. Beyond cathedral spires white sails dotted the lake. From behind, Rita said, "It's a lovely view, isn't it, Jack?"

"I won't say priceless because everything in Switzerland has a price. But it's certainly impressive."

"Did you ever visit Lake Atitlán?

"Flown across it. Very deep, very blue."

"Little Indian villages all around it," she said nostalgically. "When I was small I'd visit on horseback, but the people were frightened by my body-guards."

"With reason."

"So—I never got to know those people and I'm sorry about that." She looked away. "Maybe someday we can go there together."

"Maybe." From the table I picked up the Union Bank draft issued by Bijoux Brevoort for the nine emeralds. Made out to Bearer, its sum was four hundred and twenty thousand Swiss francs. More than half a million dollars. "You can do a lot of good with this, honey."

"Or you." She stepped out of her shoes. "I want no part of it."

"At least Tessier didn't get it," I remarked. "With it he could buy himself another training camp. Anyway, I was impressed by the way you stood up to the gemologist."

"Imagine, offering so much less than his own appraiser's valuation." She shook her head, rolled down her panty hose. "The taxes took enough as it was."

"He certainly underestimated you."

"Didn't he, though? Thought I was just another Latin rich-bitch feather-brain. Now they'll think twice when the next Latin lady comes into their store."

"Exactly. And now I'm ready for a little refreshment." I opened the bar's refrigerator for the Dom Pérignon I'd brought from Miami and Rita got out chilled glasses while I wrestled with the cork. *Pop*, fizz, and I filled our glasses. Rita lifted hers. "To a new life together."

"Together," I echoed, and we drank. We sat on the sofa and looked at each other as couples do when they realize they are alone and deeply in love. As I drew her to me the door buzzer sounded. "I'll go." I detached myself reluctantly, and walked to the door. "Who's there?"

"Travel agency—airline tickets." A deep voice with an unfamiliar accent. We were expecting ticket delivery so I opened the door. The man who stood there, ticket envelopes in hand, was a shade under six feet. His full head of silver-white hair surmounted a deeply tanned face and he wore a tailored suit of light gray silk. This was no messenger, I thought, but the owner of the travel agency, or a chain of them. His tanned features gave an Italianate impression, but Greek was equally likely. Below a flourishing white mustache projected a cleft, obdurate-looking chin. His eyes were blue, teeth too even and too white to have been there very long, and his overall appearance suggested a wealthy Mediterranean yachtsman who spent plenty of time taking the sun. But I sensed a core toughness at odds with the fine clothing and expensive crowns. His head turned and I saw his eyes moving to peer around me. When our glances met he said, "Madame Castenada?"

"I'll take them," I said brusquely, and reached for the tickets.

"But—"

"Madame is occupied," I grated, "now give me the tickets."

"Certainly, sir." His head bowed slightly and I saw a sardonic twist on his lips. "I merely wanted to be sure." He released the envelopes, I said, "Thanks," and closed the door. Returning to Rita, I said, "At the travel agency did you see anyone who looked like Cesar Romero?"

"Why no," she laughed, "did you?"

"Or a fellow resembling Niarchos in his younger years?"

"I didn't know Stavros Niarchos in his younger years."

"Hmmm. But you know him?"

"We've danced," she conceded. "Now, what is this all about?"

I sat beside her, planted the tickets on the table and shook my head. "The delivery boy wasn't a boy but a full-grown man in expensive clothing. He was trying to get a glimpse of you, honey. Have you got a fan club here? Give out autographs?" I sipped from my glass, added more champagne.

"What on earth are you talking about?"

"Okay, here's what he looks like." I described him, and asked, "Anyone you know?"

"Not remotely." She shook her head.

"For a moment I thought it might be your husband."

"Jaime? He's skinny—bluish complexion and balding."

"Mysterious," I remarked, and sat forward. "Unless the guy's a private eye—I suppose they have them in Switzerland. Could Jaime be trying to build a case to squeeze more money out of you?"

"Oh, I don't think that's likely. It was hard bargaining but he got what he wanted."

"Could be he wants more. I don't know how the Church works internally, but couldn't a credible charge of adultery delay your annulment?"

"Perhaps," she said moodily.

"Giving Jaime heavy leverage to extract more pesetas from you."

After a while she said, "It's a disturbing idea but right now I don't want to deal with it." She drained her glass and moved over to the telephone stand. I heard her ask the hotel operator to place a call to Spain, then gave the hacienda phone number. After replacing the receiver she came back to me. "It takes a while to get through. Even in Madrid phone service isn't great. At the hacienda we can be without service for days at a time."

I was still thinking about the incongruous deliveryman. "Around here are you known as Chavez or Castenada?"

"I never use Chavez, the name is like an obscenity." She looked over at the sunlit windows, the distant snowcapped mountains.

"But a connection could be made."

She sighed. "I suppose so. What's worrying you?"

"I remember the two Guat bank reps who visited me looking for Anita. She's dead, so is your father—I mean the Colonel—so the account's still open. Suppose the delivery guy is one of their investigators? I don't like it at all."

She frowned. "I don't understand your concern. What's the problem?"

I took a deep breath. "From personal professional experience I know that the Swiss have become cooperative with foreign governments seeking to recover embezzled funds and dirty money from Swiss banks. I don't like to think about it but there is a possibility you could be extradited to Guatemala for trial."

"I see," she said slowly. "How great a possibility?"

"Can't say. But the first move would be to locate you."

"My location has never been secret, Jack. Besides, I'm a Spanish citizen."

"In Spain that probably protects you, but not here."

She thought for a few moments, then said, "Until now I've never really considered the possibility that there are those who want to do me harm."

"They just want their money."

"It's not theirs," she said fiercely. "What I have came from my fa—the Colonel's estate on his death. I have no direct knowledge how he acquired that money."

"But we can guess," I remarked, "and if Guat courts are anything like Mexican they have no scruples where money's concerned."

She nodded slowly. "I'm afraid you're right, but we'll be in Spain tomorrow and—" The telephone rang, she went to it and spoke with Francisco, La Torre's major domo. Reading from our tickets, she told him in Spanish that we would be flying to Madrid and taking the three o'clock feeder flight to Oviedo. "Be sure to have the car meet us, and Rafael, if he wants to come." She listened a few moments and said, "Very well, then, I'll see you tomorrow when we arrive. Oh, Francisco, have the guest room made up, the one next to mine. That's right. And if Rafael is there I'd like to speak to him . . . Swimming? Is Juanito with him? Good. You know I never want him swimming alone. Tell him I love him. *Gracias. Adiós.*" She replaced the receiver and I said, "I thought you might be using Castilian accent."

"Except around Madrid, it's considered snobbish. Especially in the north of Spain where Basque is the popular tongue." She refilled her glass and drank. "For centuries the Basques have struggled for a separate state. Their political organization is known as ETA—*Euzkadi Ta Azkatasuna*, Basque Homeland and Liberty—that's also their slogan. ETA action teams bomb and kill people even in Madrid."

"Like the IRA in Ireland."

She nodded. "Where we are, near Basque country, they don't kill much; instead they exact tribute from businesses and landowners."

"Like you."

"I pay tribute to whoever comes around to collect. I never see who comes; Francisco handles it as he does everything on the hacienda."

"He's Basque?"

"And probably a sympathizer. But it's well worth what I pay to live without fear."

"And the Guardia Civil?"

"Are you kidding? They don't want to know about it. They live *and* sleep in fear."

I looked at my watch. "Stores are closing pretty soon, and I want to get something for Rafael before jet lag pulls me down."

"That's nice of you, Jack. Whatever you take him my son will be grateful." Her eyes met mine. "So will I. And while you're gone I'll visit the hairdresser." She scanned her spread fingers. "And manicurist. I love La Torre but we lack urban amenities."

I finished my drink. "Hungry?"

"Not really. Let's have an early dinner—the Grill Room is adjacent, marvelous food. Then to bed—we have a full day tomorrow."

Before leaving the hotel I asked the concierge to recommend a toy store. He wrote down the address and I showed it to the taxi driver. "Speak English?"

"Some."

"Take me to this travel agency." I showed him my ticket envelope. He nodded, and swung out of the drive. At Paradeplatz he turned right onto Poststrasse and pulled up in front of the travel agency. After telling the driver to wait I went in to the desk of the travel agent who had arranged our reservations. In her early forties, she wore jet black hair fringed across her forehead, thick glasses and a man's white shirt with black bolero tie. She turned from her computer and smiled pleasantly as I sat down. "Is there a ticket problem, sir?"

"Not at all. But the messenger you sent to deliver them—I neglected to tip him, and I'd like to do so now. Is he here?"

"He should be, I think all today's deliveries have been made. His name is Heinz. I'll call him." She spoke into an intercom and presently a blond teenage boy in blue-gray messenger uniform strolled toward us. I got up and met him away from the desk. Showing my ticket envelope, I said, "You were to take this and one other to the Baur au Lac, Suite 619. The name was Castenada, remember?"

"Yes, sir."

"But you didn't. Why was that?"

"Because a gentleman—a foreign gentleman—said he was a friend of Madame's and wanted to deliver it." The boy swallowed. "You got the tickets?"

"Yes, but where did this foreign gentleman intercept you?"

"Did I do wrong?" He licked his lips. "I don't want to lose my job."

"Just tell me what happened." I got out ten francs and gave them to him in case the agent was watching.

"The gentleman was here when the agent instructed me. He followed me outside and told me he was a friend of Madame Castenada and wanted to surprise her."

"And tipped you."

He hung his head. "Yes, sir."

"Had you ever seen him before?"

"No, sir."

"Or since?"

He shook his head. "Please don't tell the agent."

"Anything else?"

He swallowed again. "When you and the lady came in I saw the gentleman walk past our windows. At least I think it was him."

I grunted. "With that white hair and tan face who else could it be? How many look-alikes do you see in a day, a week?" I stared at him. "And later when he met you outside you didn't think it strange that he didn't come in to greet her?"

"I—I don't know foreign customs, sir. But it occurred to me he wasn't entirely sure who she was."

"And could make sure by delivering the tickets."

He said nothing.

"Well, Heinz, I have a piece of advice for you. Your employers pay you to make deliveries. Don't betray their trust." I smiled for the agent's benefit and left the agency, angry at the messenger and sick with the realization that Silver Hair had been following Rita. From our tickets he knew our itinerary. How was he going to use the information? Keep Rita from leaving Zurich? And how much should I tell my fiancée?

As I got back into the taxi I felt that the man probably worked for the Guatemalan Central Bank. Rita had been in Zurich for days, giving the Guat consulate plenty of time to complete paperwork to have her held for extradition.

On the other hand—and this was my hope—consular bureaucrats worked at the slow, Latin pace. In Bern, where extradition requests had to be approved and issued, the Swiss Foreign Ministry might work just as slowly. There must be fifty countries, I reflected, trying to access embezzled funds, and tying up Ministry manpower in the process. But I couldn't be sure how much time we had before the exit door slammed shut, so it was best to assume we had no time at all.

The toy store on Bahnhofstrasse was two blocks from Brevoort's, and named Tivoli, a good international name. I selected a flying Piper Cub model with gasoline engine and radio controls, and asked to have it sturdily packed for shipment. The salesman said the three-foot wing was detachable, facilitating packing. He recommended a can of special fuel, and I had it included, along with extra batteries for the controls. After paying for it I asked for a sporting goods store, and he said the Zugspitze was farther down the block, adding it was very reliable and offered a wide selection of sporting items.

While the Piper was being packed I went to Zugspitze and examined the fishing tackle display. I chose three identical French spinning rods, a light-weight tackle box and an assortment of freshwater lures, hooks and spoons. From the counter I moved to the arms counter and was shown a Hämmerli air pistol with an oiled walnut forend and grip. Its .177 pellet, the salesman assured me, had great penetrating velocity. Six pumps of the lever would send the pellet through an inch of white pine. I told him I'd take it, along with a holster, two large tin boxes of pellets and a sheaf of paper targets for fifty-foot handgun range.

The rods, minus their reels, were protected in heavy cardboard tubes. I had the reels packed with the Hämmerli and its gear, and the three rod tubes taped together for easier handling.

I paid what seemed an enormous bill, compared to Stateside prices, but this wasn't the States, and I was acquiring the first gifts for my stepson-to-be. Rita hadn't told me the degree of Rafael's impairment, but if he was able to swim, then he was probably able to fish as well as shoot. Whatever the cost, it was going to be worth it.

The salesman helped me get my purchases into the taxi, and the driver followed me back to the toy store for the model plane. I found it boxed in heavy reinforced cardboard that could take knocking around, thanked the salesman, and had the driver place the box in the taxi's trunk. Then we drove back to the hotel, where I had the concierge store it in the baggage room for early departure.

Rita hadn't returned from the beauty parlor—that could take considerable time—so I began packing my clothing, reflecting that I'd unpacked a scant twelve hours ago. I had everything put away except shaving gear, when Rita came in looking absolutely radiant. In place of the usual French braid, her hair was coiffed over forehead and shoulders. "Like it?" she asked gaily, turning to show the back arrangement, then saw my almost-packed bags. "Jack," she exclaimed, "what is this? Are you leaving?"

"We're leaving," I told her. "Trust me, sweetheart, we have to get out of Switzerland as soon as possible. And that means tonight."

"But—"

"You've been watched, followed. I'm pretty sure it's the Guatemala bank guys." I told her how the agency messenger had been diverted, and my fear that she could be prevented from leaving. "So, get your things together and we'll head for the airport."

"What about dinner?"

"There's a restaurant at Kloten, or we can eat on the plane. Tell the cashier to send up your bill so we won't have to hang around the lobby. That white-haired bastard may be watching."

"If you say so." Glumly she picked up the phone and gave instructions to the desk. Then she opened closets and began emptying them. As I watched I saw that she'd done enough shopping to fill two new suitcases. She packed quickly and efficiently, and while she was doing that I discovered our champagne was flat, so I poured Añejo into two iced glasses, and we drank together. When a bellboy arrived with the bill I took the elevator to the lobby and, after looking around for White Hair, spoke with the concierge. "What I need," I told him, pressing fifty francs into his palm, "is an invisible departure. Have a limousine meet us around back, with our bags already loaded."

"How soon, sir?"

"Immediately."

"And where shall I tell the driver to take you?"

"The Hauptbahnhof," I replied. The main railway station.

"Very good, sir. As soon as the limousine arrives your luggage will go down by the baggage elevator. You and Madame will then follow."

"Splendid. And be sure those boxed items over there go with us."

"I guarantee it."

As I left his desk I glanced around again for White Hair, strolled to the sundries shop and bought a newspaper. Then I took the elevator to our suite.

Rita had almost finished packing, and needed me to sit on a suitcase while she locked the clasps. Her face was drawn with stress, so I made fresh drinks and told her our getaway sequence.

"What do you suppose the concierge thinks?"

"He'll assume we're avoiding your husband—or my wife. This is Europe, honey, where domestic entanglements are the norm. Finished?"

"There's a coat and hat but I'm wearing them."

Dusk was falling over the lake. The cathedral spires were lighted, and lights were going off all over the city as stores and offices closed for the day. Cars moved slowly over the quai bridge to the eastern side of the city, its Old Town. The lake itself was already dark; mist gathered above it. Zurich was tucking in for the night, and I found myself envying peaceful townspeople going their unhurried ways.

When I answered the door buzzer two porters came in with baggage carriers. After they'd loaded everything we followed them to the service elevator at the end of the corridor. I tipped them and said we'd be along shortly. While waiting for the elevator's return I took Rita in my arms. "Long time since I kissed you, darling." "Too long," she replied, and tenderly returned my embrace.

Despite concierge assurances I checked the trunk to make sure Rafael's presents were loaded, and they were. When we were seated behind tinted windows Rita said, "I think you're taking too many presents, Jack. Rafael will be overwhelmed."

"I only got some things I remember wanting at his age." Leaning forward, I slid aside the privacy panel and told the driver to take us to Kloten Airport. He nodded although he'd expected a short drive to the Hauptbahnhof. "And on the way," I added, "tell me if you think we're being followed."

He nodded again and I closed the panel.

Rita linked her arm with mine. "If I didn't love and trust you completely I'd think all this secrecy and urgency was unnecessary."

"Maybe it is, but it's better to be safe than sorry."

She smiled. "Old American adage."

"Old universal adage." I lifted her hand and kissed it. "We need to take the next flight to Spain; Madrid, Barcelona, wherever. Then the earliest morning flight to Oviedo."

"There's only one, unfortunately, and that's the one leaving Barajas at three."

"Damn! White Hair knows we'll be on it."

"But what difference can it make? We'll be out of Switzerland and safely in Spain."

"You're right," I said after a moment, "but first we have to get there."

Because of evening traffic it took us half an hour to reach Kloten. After I paid the driver he brought over a middle-aged porter to transfer our baggage and I explained we lacked reservations and would have to apply at different airline counters, starting with the nearest. He loaded our baggage onto a large wheeled carrier and led us into the airport.

British Airways offered a midnight flight to Barcelona, but that meant a five-hour wait and I wanted to leave sooner. The ticket agent checked his computer and came up with an Iberia flight to Madrid leaving at nine. That was only two hours away.

At the Iberia counter we exchanged our tickets and checked all our baggage to Barajas. As we left I said, "Is there a Holiday Inn or something at Barajas? Sheraton?

"There is. Iberia will fax ahead for reservations."

"No, I'd rather arrive unheralded."

"You *are* cautious."

"With reason."

In the restaurant we began with a cold bottle of German hock and ordered *geschnetzeltes Kalbfleisch* after the waiter explained the dish was sautéed veal in a cream sauce of white wine and mushrooms. He recommended *Rösti*— hash-brown potatoes—as the natural complement, but Rita said, "I'll pass on those. Just a small salad, please, oil and vinegar." After the waiter refilled our glasses she said, "It's exciting to be with you on the run like this."

"I hope it doesn't get too exciting."

"But what could happen? We're practically there."

I mumbled something noncommittal rather than admit that Tessier's ambush had pared away much of my naturally cautious optimism. Even though I'd destroyed his training camp and routed his mercenary recruits, the memory of his cunning stuck in my throat like a fishbone. Always there, always irritating.

So we dined in the staid commercial atmosphere of the airport restaurant, and after thick Swiss coffee, we went to the boarding gate and were ushered to our seats.

I didn't feel secure until the big plane lifted above the dark lake and I could see the city and the glitter of its dividing river below. I felt reasonably confident that we'd evaded White Hair and any watchers he might have deployed to trail or intercept us. Even now, without knowing his intentions, I was glad I'd kept him from seeing Rita. For whether his employer was her husband or the Guats I was sure he threatened our tranquility.

Then as I held Rita's hand I thought about the Chavez fortune we were leaving behind. The secret accounts backed by bricks of gold in steel vaults deep below the streets of Zurich. Rita seemed indifferent to that tainted wealth, but gaining it before Tessier did was a challenge I couldn't ignore. It was hers—ours—if I could claim it, and I still had the account card Anita entrusted to me.

Hidden under the insole of one shoe.

I looked at her smooth, lovely and untroubled profile, lifted her fingers to my lips and pressed them there until lag exhaustion surged over me. The plane's even, monotonous vibration lulled me and I felt my body relax as sleep dissolved reality.

Rita woke me. The plane was motionless. I could see terminal lights beyond the windows. "We're here," she told me, and kissed my forehead as she rose. "We're safe, we're together, and from now on everything is going to be fine."

As I got groggily to my feet I hoped her prediction would endure. But Tessier was alive, mobile and driven by obsessive avarice. If Rita had forgotten him I had not. Someday, somewhere, I'd face him again, and one of us would go down. That was inevitable as the rising of the moon.

As unavoidable as Death.

TWENTY-TWO

EVEN THOUGH we were late arrivals the airport hotel had suites available and we chose one with the large (matrimonial) size bed. The bellboy brought ice, we had an Añejo nightcap, and undressed for bed. Made love and fell asleep.

After room-breakfast, Rita phoned La Torre and reconfirmed our Oviedo arrival to Francisco, then spoke affectionately with her son, apologizing for being away so long. Rafael had things to tell her and after listening she asked about his pet cockatiel, rabbit and kid. They chatted a while longer, and when she hung up I could see her eyes misting with tears. I put my arm around her and kissed her forehead. In a strained voice she said, "He's a dear child, a wonderful gentle boy, and I've done all I can to make him happy."

"Then he should be very happy."

"In his world, he is." She turned away. I told you he was born retarded—and specialists say he'll always remain a child of six. So I want him to live undisturbed by the harshness of the outside world." She looked back at me. "I could send him to a special school where he'd be with children like himself, but that seems so cruel. Or am I being selfish wanting him with me?"

"You're being maternal, don't think otherwise."

"That's consoling," she murmured. "I never asked anyone but Anita."

"And what did she say?"

"Just what you did. Soon I'll have to try to explain to him why *Tía* Anita won't be visiting him anymore."

"Or say nothing," I suggested.

"Maybe you're right." She nodded thoughtfully. "Tell him only when he asks about her. Yes, that's how it will be." She smiled wistfully. "More and more I rely on you, darling."

"As it should be," I told her. "I'll cherish and protect you both forever."

"And in time perhaps you'll be able to care for him, treat him as a son."

"I'm sure I will."

"He'll be enchanted by your presents, Jack. Overwhelmed. You'll see."

*   *   *

After a while she used hotel stationery to draw a map of La Torre showing the residence, pastures and outbuildings, the pond, the river near the western reach of her land and its tributary brooks where horses and sheep watered and grazed. There was a garden for table vegetables and a deep, unfailing well. Only a few years ago had electric lines reached the hacienda, replacing a diesel generator that was always breaking down. "Now if we lack electricity it's because the ETA have cut the lines for reasons of their own."

"Not easy to understand terrorist philosophy," I remarked. "Blow up your neighbor's house, spread misery, for what?"

"Publicity, I suppose; defying the government. Peru, El Salvador . . ."

"And Guatemala."

"Yes. And I think the guerrillas would fight any invaders Claude Tessier might send in. They fought the Colonel, they'll fight anyone associated with him."

"I wonder if he considered that. Mercenaries aren't always a match for True Believers." My coffee was cold but I drank it anyway, noticed the ballpoint hotel pen she'd been using, and pocketed it, not having one of my own.

"I wish there were an earlier flight but there's only the one. Now that we're in Spain I can hardly wait to be home."

I gestured at my money belt that held the Brevoort check. "No money problem—why not charter a plane?"

"I could, but at Oviedo that would cause comment. The ETA might decide that if I could afford charter flights I could afford to pay more tribute to their collector—a lot more. In the long run it wouldn't be worth saving a few hours now."

"I hadn't thought of that. But how are we going to explain me to Rafael?"

She breathed deeply. "I've thought and thought. How about a good friend? A long-term visitor? Estate manager? Can you come up with something?"

"How curious a boy is he? I mean, is he likely to ask . . . questions?"

"Not deep ones. All we need is a cover story for you that will last a few weeks. Then at the wedding he'll understand we've become man and wife."

"Well, we don't have a lot of time to fabricate a story. What about the servants? Any problem there?"

"Basques can be quirky and unpredictable. All the hacienda servants are deeply moral, but they're also loyal and protective of Rafael and me. I just don't want to be obvious and ruffle their sensibilities—so ostensibly we won't be sleeping together. That ought to be enough."

"They'll know but they won't know, that it?"

"Something like that. And they don't gossip."

"What about Jaime—do they know him?"

"He's visited only twice. He dislikes Rafael and my son dislikes my . . . husband. And Jaime doesn't care for the countryside."

"Honey, I don't mean to pry, but I ought to know who Rafael thinks his father is."

She thought that over, too. "I've managed to be vague about that. Juanito is his caretaker and companion and there's a strong bond between them. I think he views Juanito as a father figure and I've encouraged that. Rafael may not even be aware of fathers as such. I mean, that children have fathers as well as mothers." She brushed strands of hair from her forehead, and because displacement activity signals stress I decided to ease up. Anyway, her responses had outlined a situation into which I'd have to fit myself as things developed. Wasn't going to be easy, but something worth having never was.

After checking our baggage for the Transair flight to Oviedo we strolled around the large, unattractive terminal while Rita bought gifts for her son: a video game, jigsaw puzzle, video cassettes of *Pinocchio*, *Treasure Island*, *Red Riding Hood* and *Batman*; shirts, trousers and Reebok sneakers. Then two decorative boxes of Rafael's favorite candy, *turrón*—hard nougat filled with nuts and candied fruits, made in Gijón. "Can you think of anything else, Jack?"

"I think you've covered it. How's the liquor supply?"

"We drink mostly wine, but—"

"My contribution." At the liquor shop I selected cognac, Añejo, vodka and Red Label scotch, paying elevated Spanish prices.

Our aircraft was a ten-seat Fokker with twin prop engines. There were only four other passengers, so the flight attendant let us use the spare seats for our parcels and bundles. The plane's interior was hot, and almost immediately we were perspiring. Finally, the engines fired and the plane trundled out to the flight line, wisps of cooler air coming from the laboring a/c system. Other, larger planes took off but we stayed where we were. Our flight attendant conferred with the crew and reported to us that bad weather at Oviedo was delaying departure. Fanning her flushed face, Rita said, "We're so near the coast that we get touches of ocean weather. The rain is marvelous, except when you're trying to fly there."

Passengers began verbalizing their discomfort, the attendant passed around paper cups of something suggesting lemonade, and after half an hour he checked our seat belts and we were ready to go.

Over Madrid we rose on a northwest course that took us across Castile's hot, barren plateau, above the snowcapped Guadarrama range to a flat landscape of rivers, cultivated fields and isolated forests. As altitude cooled the cabin Rita dozed beside me, her cheek on my shoulder. The flight was scheduled under two hours, then an hour's drive to the hacienda, so I was glad she could rest before an unavoidably stressful arrival: presenting me to the staff, then her son. If enough daylight remained I could take him to the fields and fly the Piper by way of ingratiating myself.

Lulled by the engines' steady drone, I dozed, too, waking when air pockets bounced the little plane, then lapsing into sleep again.

Then we were on the ground, bumping to a halt on the rain-puddled tarmac before the little airport building. After helping Rita off the plane I watched our baggage being transferred to a baggage cart, and saw a young man in loose blue trousers and open-collar blue shirt trot toward us. He went to Rita and spoke effusively until she returned to me. "This is Antonio, who drives and repairs our cars and machinery. Antonio, *Señor* Juan."

"*Mucho gusto, Señor.*"

"*Igualmente*, Antonio." We shook hands, and Rita showed him our baggage.

After a while he loaded the rear of a dark blue Volvo station wagon and opened the passenger door for us. Our seat was behind his, and when we were on the two-lane road Rita asked about her son, staff members, rainfall and hacienda details. After that she enumerated her employees for my benefit. "Francisco is *mayor domo*, his wife Paquita is the *encargada*, responsible for the household. Pilar, the cook, is her cousin, and the two maids, Victoria and Encarnación, are somehow related. Isidro, the *capataz*, runs the hacienda and oversees Esteban, the groom, the *estableros*, Raúl and Manuel, and the field hands, Miguel and Pedro.

I laughed. "How do you keep track of them all?"

She smiled. "Don't even try. I just delegate."

The sloping foothills of the mountains were behind us. Ahead, the narrow road wound over bridges and streams bordered with pines and willows. Cattle and sheep grazed peacefully in pastures bordering the road. There were patches of mist from the recent rain, and ahead the setting sun was obscured by gray clouds that threatened more. Antonio slowed as we passed a roadside Guardia Civil post. The duty guard, in his glossy tricornered hat, waved us on, and I noticed a semiautomatic rifle slung from one shoulder. Another mile and I saw a tumbled-down castle in the distance, ruined legacy of Moor or Crusader. Across the landscape there were only a few crude dwellings; whitewashed mud-brick sides and conical thatched roofs with irregular enclosures for occasional cow or goat. Then nothing but unplowed fields, here and there a copse of ancient oak or pine breaking the desolate flatness.

Ahead, another bridge. This one arched over a rocky stream, and as we neared I saw a makeshift barricade across it. "Antonio, was the *barricada* there when you came this way?"

"No, *señor*."

"Then be very careful." To Rita I said, "Better get down, honey. Could be trouble."

"If it's only money—"

"We'll see." I tapped Antonio's shoulder. "Brake for the *barricada* but don't get out."

"Maybe I should drive through." His face was chalky.

"No, I don't want any shooting."

The Volvo slowed, took the rise of the bridge and stopped short of the wooden barricade. Beyond it the roadway was sprinkled with trihedral spikes; we couldn't go far with punctured tires.

Then from the far side of the bridge two men came toward us. They wore red berets, and below-eye-level red scarves masked their features. Each had a white armband. One carried a revolver, the other a sawed-off shotgun, both weapons pointing at us.

Rita gasped. I said, "Stay down, stay calm."

As they reached us one kept his revolver on Antonio while he opened the passenger-side door. He slid onto the seat beside Antonio, and I heard his partner opening the tailgate. I was fumbling in my pockets for anything resembling a weapon, touched only my ballpoint pen. Gripping it, I kept my hand down behind the seat and spoke to the *pistolero*. "What do you want?"

"*Dinero.*" Money.

To Rita I said, "Open your purse," and watched the shotgun holder lift a bottle from my liquor sack. "Many things here," he called to the *pistolero*, "we'll take it all and kill them."

The *pistolero* turned to see what his partner was doing, so he couldn't see my right hand. I whipped it up and drove the ballpoint into the side of his neck. He screamed and I snatched the revolver from his hand. While he was clawing at the ballpoint the tailgate bandit had leveled his sawed-off at me. Before I could react I saw the cocked hammer fall—*misfire*. As he cocked the other hammer I swept the revolver around and fired over the baggage.

The heavy bullet slammed him backward but he didn't drop until I fired again. I got out fast and dragged the *pistolero* to the road. He'd jerked out the ballpoint and blood was spurting from his severed carotid. "Watch him," I told Antonio, and went around to where the other man lay. He was alive, but barely. I picked up his sawed-off and tossed it onto piled baggage.

Shakily, Rita called, "Can't you help them?"

"Help them? If they live their *compadres* will come after us." I toed the fallen man's arm to expose red letters inked on his white armband: *ETA*. Blood welled from wounds in his upper chest and stomach. Breath rattled in his throat. The piece in my hand was an old British Webley, bluing worn bare in places. A heavy First World War model but still plenty serviceable. I stuck it in my pocket and hauled the dying man to the side of the road. Then I went around to where Antonio was staring down at the *pistolero*. His teeth were chattering. "Pull this *cabrón* aside," I told him, "drag the barricade out of the way, and clear the spikes."

"*Sí . . . Sí, Señor.*" When he was moving I turned to Rita, who sat numbly in her seat. "It's all over," I said gently. "Those *hijos de puta* were going to kill us—remember that."

She swallowed. "Oh, God . . ." Clutching my arm, she began sobbing hysterically. I shouted to Antonio, "Faster, let's get moving! *Ándale!*"

The barricade had been shoved far enough aside that the station wagon could get by and he was crouched over, picking up spikes and tossing them into the rain-swollen stream below. I went back and closed the tailgate, noticing the vodka bottle had smashed when the bandit dropped it. We could have lost a lot more, including our lives. The Guardia Civil lads could have been helpful, if they'd been around, but the bandits had chosen a location far from possible help.

I went over to the *pistolero* and saw the death dullness of his eyes; his heart no longer pumped blood. Around us mist had gathered and thickened. I beckoned Antonio behind the wheel and said, "When something like this happens, act fast before the bandits can organize their thoughts."

He nodded quickly.

"And if word of this—*any* word—gets out I'll hold you responsible. *¿Entiendes*, Antonio?"

"*Sí.*" He licked dry lips, glanced at bloodstains on the seat behind him.

"As soon as we reach the hacienda, get rid of those traces. And act normally." I got in beside Rita. "Let's go."

As the car moved over the crest of the bridge she murmured, "I . . . I don't know what to say. It was so . . . sudden—so bloody."

"They strayed from the paths of righteousness," I observed, "and had to expect what they found." I pressed her hand between mine. "Or would you prefer us lying dead back there while the barnyard commandoes drove away?"

"Of course not."

"Then you have to accept how I reacted; can't have it both ways."

She was still breathing jerkily, as though suppressing nervous sobs. "But we left them there—they won't even get Christian burial," she complained.

"Maybe they will, though they didn't seem religious types. Red scarves and red berets don't signify Papal guards." I looked aside at the darkening fields. "One alternative would be to report the incident to the Guardia Civil, which might not view my resolution sympathetically. You'd be involved as a witness, and Antonio." I looked back at her troubled face. "Or we could stretch them across the hood and drive them to the hacienda for burial. Of course, everyone who works for you would know, and word would get back to ETA. To maintain good order and discipline in their ranks they'd have to destroy us—all of us, and Rafael."

She shuddered. "I'm . . . sorry. I was being emotional, not thinking. You saved us—that's all that matters."

I kissed her cool forehead. "Try to get it out of your mind." I wanted her to think of other things, regain composure before reaching the hacienda. "Did we decide on a cover story for me?"

"I thought you were going to."

"Maybe the fewer explanations the better. Say I was a friend of Anita's and I'll be staying at the hacienda for a while." I looked at her face and saw color returning to her cheeks. "Okay?"

"Okay."

I gestured back toward the bridge. "This sort of thing happen before?"

"I—I guess so, but never to me."

"The fundraisers are getting pretty bold."

She looked away from me. "I never even saw their faces."

"Better you didn't—less to remember. Now, tell me things I should know about the hacienda. Is there a lake?"

"It's called a lake, but it's really a large pond."

"With fish?"

"Some," she nodded. "And there are fish in the river."

"How about wild animals? Boar? *Jabalí*?"

"Yes. And foxes, gray foxes."

"Game birds?"

"There are *perdices* and wild ducks. Woodcock . . ."

"Hunting dogs?"

She shook her head. "Never needed them."

"I'd like a Viszla or two; Weimaraners, maybe. Or German pointers. Rafael can help me train them."

She turned to me, misty-eyed. "That would be wonderful, dear. You think of everything."

I kissed her again. "That's a generous compliment but undeserved. I didn't anticipate the possibility of highwaymen and so I had no weapon, not even a knife. Next time out I'll have more than a ballpoint pen, believe me." For a time we rode in silence before I said, "When I first saw the barricade and the armed men I thought it was a Tessier setup. Or an ambush arranged by that strange character who delivered our tickets yesterday. He knew our flight schedule, remember, and could figure we'd be driving this road from the airport."

She nodded soberly. "But the robbers didn't seem interested in you and me, who we were—just our valuables."

"That's true, so it must have been random; rob any vehicle that came along.

Yes, that makes sense, but let's not discount deadly intent.'' I thought of the two shooters Tessier had sent to the stilt shack; they'd been more professional than the ETA robbers but they were just as dead. No, Tessier hadn't gotten to us. Yet.

Off to the right I saw an ancient stone postern gate. Atop it in wrought-iron script the words *Hacienda La Torre*.

''At last!'' Rita exclaimed joyfully.

Antonio slowed, steered off the macadam through the posterns and onto scraped dirt road. Beyond the rise I could make out the top of a distant building with three chimneys.

This was going to be my home, I reflected, and I was responsible for protecting it from threats, invasion and all those who would disturb the tranquility of our lives.

As I held Rita's hands a boy appeared over the rise, running toward us, followed by a running man.

TWENTY-THREE

$\mathbf{A}$s the distance closed I saw that the boy was wearing khaki shorts, short-sleeved white shirt, athletic socks and sport sneakers. His wavy hair was dark and his handsome face was set in determination as he pumped energetically toward our car. The man following was slim and young. He wore blue shirt and trousers and his face was smiling. I turned to Rita. "Rafael and Juanito."

"How nice to be greeted. Antonio, stop the car." Stepping out, she received the perspiring, red-faced boy in her arms. Juanito slowed to a walk while mother and son embraced emotionally in an outpouring of affectionate welcoming words. When they drew apart the boy's companion said, "Welcome back, *señora*, you've been missed."

"Thank you. Your idea to run all this way?"

"No, *Mamá*, I saw you from the treehouse and couldn't wait." Rafael wiped perspiration from his face, and I saw how closely his features resembled those of his mother's and Aunt Anita. A handsome boy.

"I'm so glad you came. Now, everyone in for the ride back."

Juanito got in beside Antonio, Rita next to me, and then Rafael. Closing the door, he glanced at me, and his mother said, "*Querido*, this is my friend, Juan. He was a friend of *Tía* Anita and he'll be staying at the hacienda."

Forthrightly, he thrust out his hand and we clasped in a firm handshake. "Do you play games?" he asked.

"I try. What games do you like?"

"Hide-and-seek. Basketball, football." He paused. "I like swimming, too."

"So do I."

"*Mamá*, can we go swimming now?"

"It's late," she said mildly, "and we have a lot to show you. Tomorrow will be better."

"What did you bring me?" He glanced back at the packages. "For me?"

"All for you," she replied. "We'll open everything inside."

We pulled up to a circular drive before a columned portico. Several servants formed a row at the top of the steps, and when Antonio braked a gray-haired man of late middle-age came down to the car. Francisco, the *mayor domo*. He wore jacket and tie, opened the door for Rita, and bowed in a courtly way, welcoming the hacienda mistress. Rafael ran around back and opened the tailgate. He and Antonio began carrying presents inside, three female servants took suitcases, and Francisco and I lugged up the rest.

On his knees, Rafael was tearing open packages, exclaiming happily at each discovery. Juanito used his knife to pry open the model airplane's box and when he lifted out the Piper Cub Rafael looked up at me, tears in his eyes. "I always wanted this," he said, rose and hugged me. "Thank you, thank you, Señor Juan."

"I wanted one when I was a boy, Rafael, so I got it as much for me as for you. We'll fly it together."

By then Juanito was getting out the fishing rods, and while Rafael was handling them I produced the Hämmerli air pistol, pumped it twice, and had Rafael pull the trigger. The gentle *pop* delighted him. I displayed targets, pellets and reels, enjoying his surprise and boundless appreciation. Then Rita introduced Francisco to me, and brought over his wife and the rest of the residence servants to exchange introductions.

Paquita carried in a decanter of red wine and served a glass to everyone assembled, including Rafael. They toasted our arrival, and we thanked them by toasting in return.

The room we were in was to the right of the main hallway, which led to a broad staircase. It was a reception room with Victorian mahogany furniture, dark red velvet upholstery and starched antimacassars; light played over us from a gleaming chandelier. The opposite room, Rita told me, was the music room. Rafael was learning to play the recorder, and she accompanied him on the stately old grand piano.

Despite the age of the furnishings, nothing was worn or unpolished, and the servants seemed genuinely glad at *Doña* Rita's return. My initial impression was of a warm, caring household, one in which I could relax and find enjoyment in quiet living.

After the servants dispersed Antonio handed me a paper parcel and whispered, "The *escopeta*." The sawed-off shotgun. I thanked him and asked if the bloodstains had been removed from the front seat. "All of them," he nodded. "I told Juanito I'd had a nosebleed." He bowed out, and I asked Rita if there were other firearms around the hacienda. "Several shotguns," she replied, "but I don't know of any handguns." Her face was troubled. "Why? Do you—?"

"Just want to know our assets."

"They're over there." She pointed to a gun cabinet in the far corner. I stepped around Rafael and his mounded presents and opened the cabinet door. Two shotguns were double-barreled, 12-gauge Galibondos; the single-barrel was a Merkel 10-bore goose gun. All were seventy to eighty years old with

ornate cocking hammers and patches of rust. The ammunition drawer held
cleaning rods and a scatter of shells whose brass was green with verdigris.
Their black powder loads were suitable for the old gun barrels which I doubted
could take modern smokeless loads. I unwrapped the sawed-off, ejected the
two shells, and stood it in the cabinet with the others. When I returned to Rita
she was seated on the floor with her son who was trying on his new Reeboks.
He watched me attach the wing to the Piper fuselage and install batteries in
the controls. "You know how to do everything, don't you, Señor Juan?"

"He does," said his mother smilingly. "He amazes me every day."

"Too bad it's so dark outside, but in the morning if it doesn't rain we'll fly
this baby."

He clapped his hands together. "I can't wait for morning."

"Anyway," I said, "if it rains we can go fishing. You won't mind fishing
in the rain?"

"Not if you show me how."

"I will," I promised. Rita said, "I badly need a bath before dinner. Jack,
I'll show you your room. Rafael, you need a bath, too. *Ándale.*"

He bounded up the staircase, and we followed tiredly. At the top we turned
down a corridor hung with oil paintings of hacienda scenes, stopped at the
master bedroom, where Rita showed me the canopied bed, settee and writing
table. And pointed out the connecting door that opened into my adjacent room.

Servants had unpacked my bags, hung clothing in the wardrobe and put my
shaving gear in the bathroom. I took the old Webley from my pocket and laid
it in the night table drawer. Rita kissed me, and said, "I'm so relieved and
grateful that things are working out, darling. You're wonderful with my son,
and I think he's going to worship you."

"I'll go slowly, don't want to disturb his relationship with Juanito. But
please tell him to drop the '*Señor*' and just call me Juan."

"He does it from politeness, you know."

"Of course. Honey, I got so much satisfaction from seeing him with those
presents. Won't be long before I'll think he's my own son."

That brought tears to her eyes. She hugged me and went quickly away,
closing the hall door. I went over to the windows and saw nothing but darkness
outside. I pulled down the curtains, shaved and bathed—it had been a long
time since I'd used a bathtub—and after toweling dry I found a tray had been
set out with ice, glasses and a charged seltzer bottle. I got out my Añejo bottle
and drank, thinking it had been a day of change and surprises, not all of them
welcome. I hoped Antonio would keep his mouth shut because if the ETA
didn't get me, Spanish justice would. And Spain still used the garrote to execute
its condemned.

Tired, my shoulder throbbing again, I stretched out on the soft bed and slept
for two hours until Francisco woke me for dinner.

*   *   *

The dining room was the largest room in a large house. Its walls were painted soft rose, and from them hung large oils of knights and long-dead Spanish royalty. The high ceiling was relieved by two crystal chandeliers that lighted the room and our long mahogany table. Rita sat at the head, Rafael on her right, Juanito beside him. I was on Rita's left. Overseen by Paquita, Encarnación and Victoria served us from antique silver platters. Attentively, the major domo poured wine and signaled when another course should be served.

The main dish was lamb, roasted and flavored with herbs, Spanish style. There was fluffy rice, asparagus, salad and crisp, freshly made dinner rolls. Rafael seemed to have no difficulty handling a knife and fork, so apparently his motor functions were unimpaired. From time to time he asked about my life, where I came from, what I did, and accepted simple answers. He reminisced with Juanito over what they'd done that day, and repeated endearingly to his mother how much he'd missed her while she was away.

Dessert was a simple flan served with small sugar cookies. Afterward, Rafael and Juanito excused themselves and went off to the new video game. Rita and I took black coffee in fragile Haviland cups, and when we were finally alone she asked, "What do you think?"

"Marvelous dinner."

"I mean—Rafael."

"I see him as a fine, sensitive boy."

"And?"

"Maybe a bit overprotected."

She said, "I've wanted your opinion, Jack. If that's your feeling, will you unprotect him, try to make him less dependent?"

"I'll certainly try, but it will be very gradual." I added coffee to my demitasse. "Physically he seems quite normal. What's the principal problem?"

She sighed. "Abstract ideas, arithmetic beyond simple addition and subtraction. He gets frustrated very easily, has a fleeting attention span. He can read simple stories, but has to be prodded to read more than half a page at a time."

"From what I gathered from you, honey, I didn't expect him to read at all." I looked up at the portrait of a grim-faced Spanish Don. "How long since he was tested?"

"Four years," she sighed, "and it was a harrowing experience for us both. That was in Madrid."

"You might consider further testing," I suggested. "Psychologists are forever trashing one theory and adopting another. And current chemotherapy is worth looking into."

She seemed transfixed. "You mean—that he could be helped? Long ago I abandoned any hope, decided to provide a calm, untroubled life, but—"

"Look, don't be overoptimistic from what I've said, darling, I'm not a child psychologist but I think he should see one, four years having passed."

But she persisted. "I want to believe you, but you've never had children, how do you know about these things?"

"Learned about mind-altering drugs in DEA, mostly the bad ones. Or the good ones that have bad effects in quantity. Also, I've had friends whose children were early burn-outs but changed through psychologists or pediatricians with chemotherapy." I was thinking of Manny's elder daughter, Rosario, whose IQ and behavior improved dramatically on a prolonged regimen of Ritalin. Graduated from high school into community college. "If you'd like I can put you in touch with a highly respected pediatrician in Miami. It's an oriental-sounding name . . . Chong, Bong . . . Met him once on a fishing trip for marlin."

Flashback to Diana who aspired to community college, someday . . .

"Jack, you've given me new hope—I never dared think of before." She shook her head slowly. "If he could be helped toward normalcy with new techniques, drugs, how could I forgive myself for not exhausting all possibilities before?"

"You did what you thought best, relied on evaluations that seemed conclusive—maybe they were. It's just that there may be possibilities, treatment, that wasn't available four years ago." I took her hand. "From here you can telephone, consult specialists you know, ask for referrals to other professionals before you decide anything."

She gazed at me steadily. "You don't know how much this means to me. I'll do as you say, dear."

"Meanwhile, his life goes on as before, with a few new interests."

"That I thank you for—and for so many other things."

We strolled into the music room where brandy and snifters had been set out for us. "Today," she said, seating herself on the sofa, "when you risked your life to save us from robbery and possible death I was overwhelmed by the violence. Only when I saw you with my son did I realize how gentle you can be, how unique a man you are. And I'll never love anyone as much as I love you." She lifted my hand and kissed it. I smiled. "So you'll definitely marry me?"

"Where else could I find a protector, a lover and a stepfather for my son?"

"I love you," I said, "and it's time we went to bed."

We stopped at Rafael's room to find him engrossed in the video game he was playing with Juanito. Rita blew a kiss to her son, who called, "Goodnight, Mamá," and then we continued on to our rooms.

Half an hour later, when the house was still, I opened the connecting door and joined Rita in the canopied bed. We made love as though it were the first time for both of us, with the desperation of lovers who might never make love again.

I woke in my own bed, went down to breakfast and found Rafael holding the Piper Cub, eager to see it flying in the nearby field. "Is your mother awake?" I asked him.

"Not yet, *Señor* Juan, but can't we go without her?"

"Sure," I said, "the noise will wake her and she'll watch from the window." So I swallowed coffee and went with my stepson-to-be and his companion to the field, where the little plane droned and banked, dived and climbed into the blue sky like a swift-soaring gull.

After the trial flight I showed them how to fuel the plane, and gave the controls to Rafael, who said doubtfully, "I'll hurt it, make it crash."

"No you won't—and if that happens we can fix it or get another. Now go ahead, trust yourself."

He did, tentatively at first, then with concentration and determination, and Juanito looked at me in silent appreciation as his young charge maneuvered the Piper through the sky. And I reflected that the more I saw of Rafael the more difficult it was becoming to think of this gentle, handsome youngster as having been sired by so evil a creature as Oscar Chavez. What I remembered of Chavez's photographed features were absent from Rafael's. The boy resembled aunt and mother so closely as to have been created through parthenogenesis.

When Rafael landed the plane safely I felt an apple-size lump in my throat. This, I thought, was the beginning of an enduring friendship. For once in my life I'd followed intuition and managed to do something right. Congratulations.

Leaving the flyers in the field, I returned to the house and found Rita in dressing gown, breakfasting at a patio table, where I joined her. "Morning," she greeted me. "I've been watching, and Rafael is captivated with his plane."

"He pilots it well, too."

"So I noticed. It never occurred to me to get him something like that. I'm afraid he's missed a lot with only an unimaginative mother. But, now you're here." She smiled and asked Encarnación to serve me.

After an omelette prepared with chunks of hot, spicy *chorizo* I said, "Today's program includes target shooting and afternoon fishing. Then I'm going to ask Antonio's help cleaning the shotguns."

"He'll be eager to do whatever he can, Jack. He admires you enormously. And while you're with my son I'm going to start the telephone survey we discussed last night. If I get encouraging answers I'll want to follow up in Madrid and possibly Miami."

"Will you see Jaime?"

She shook her head. "No need to. Anyway, I thought you might care to go with me."

"Or perhaps I should stay here and continue building rapport." I gestured at Rafael, rapturously stunting his plane. "Whoever goes ought to pick up a couple more models." And some ammunition, I thought, the Webley having only four unfired cartridges in its cylinder. Francisco came over and inquired if everything was satisfactory in my room. I said it was, and asked if shotgun cartridges could be purchased nearby. "My recollection," he said, "is that hunters reload their shells, but I am sure new cartridges are sold in Oviedo."

Rita said, "If you like I can have Antonio drive to Oviedo for them."

"Not for a while," I demurred. "That road—"

"Of course, I'd almost forgotten." She filled my cup from a graceful silver coffeepot. "After I'm dressed I'll show you around. Do you ride?"

"Not well."

"Esteban, the groom, will give you a docile mount. There's so much land to see. Suppose we take a picnic basket?"

"Great."

An hour later, wearing riding togs, Rita walked me down to the stables and introduced Esteban and the stable boys, Raúl and Manuel, all of them in work clothing and knee-high mucking boots. I poked around the smelly compost pile with a pitchfork and uncovered nests of fat worms suitable for angling.

While the groom was adjusting our English saddles a large, unshaven man with black mustache and bushy eyebrows came over, removed his beret and spoke with Rita. After replying, she introduced Isidro, the foreman, to me. His hand was rough and strong and he seemed to glower at me. I asked, "How was the *perdiz* hatch this spring?"

"Poor," he replied, "due to the hard winter. And the foxes." He looked at Rita. "The *señora* won't permit me to dig out their dens."

"The foxes," she said reprovingly, "are necessary to limit the wild pig that injure cattle and sheep."

"*Capataz*," I said, addressing him by his title, "perhaps you'll show me the dens sometime; we'll count the fox population."

"*A sus órdenes.*" He replaced his mud-stained *boina* and as he walked away Rita said, "Now there's a real Basque. Truculent, but hard-working and responsible."

"And not a fellow to cross on a dark night."

"Oh? I never thought of him that way."

"Just my sensitive nature," I explained as Esteban positioned my stirrup. Rita mounted lithely into her saddle, and with our horses at a walk we followed paths that took us along fields of hay and alfalfa, beside cherry and apple orchards, over slow-moving creeks on to pastures of grazing cattle and sheep.

Finally we crossed over a ridge, and beyond it stretched the still waters of a spring-fed pond that was close to a hundred yards long and half that in width. Dismounting, we let the horses water, and as I was stroking my saddle-chafed thighs, a flock of mallards burst from behind a clump of tule, quacking in protest.

Rita unstrapped the picnic hamper from behind her saddle and set it in the shade of a willow. Without comment she undid her jodhpurs and pulled off her white silk blouse. I unhooked her bra, and she went swiftly into the water. I stripped and followed her, gasping at the sudden chill. She breaststroked away, keeping her hair above water, and called, "Isn't it glorious?"

"Glorious," I chattered, and made my way back to shore.

The hot, dry breeze absorbed droplets from my body, and while Rita was gamboling I broke off willow branches and stripped them into flexible switches. After that I set our wine bottle in the water and waited.

When Rita emerged her nipples were erect, lips blue from cold. "I'm freezing," she called.

"This'll warm you." I brandished the switches, and with a shriek she fled. I caught up and laid the willows across her rump. The first stroke drew pink marks that blended with others until both buns showed a furious blush as she ran from me. "Oh, Jack," she begged, "no more," and stopped abruptly. Turning, she rubbed her bottom tenderly with both hands. "You've set me afire, you bastard."

"So you won't feel the cold."

"And made me want you." She came to me, rubbed her nipples across my chest. I dropped the switches and lifted her so that she was straddling my hips. Her legs locked behind me and I shoved her back against a tree trunk where we made love. Arms around my neck, her cheek pressed to mine, she murmured, "You're full of surprises, darling, do you whip all your women?"

"Only those who need it." My knees were dissolving and my back ached. Slowly I released her until her feet touched ground.

"And I needed it?"

"Uh-huh, I was getting tired of Doña Rita, mistress of this vast domain; I wanted my girl again."

"Jack, I'll admit it was exciting, but how can I sit on the saddle?"

"The wine will help," I told her, and we wended our way back to where the horses were guarding our clothes.

There was cheese and Spanish *galletas* in the wicker hamper, chicken breasts, olives, red grapes and oranges, all washed down with cool Paternina white. And when we'd eaten the last grape and sucked the last juicy orange, we dressed, and rode slowly—in Rita's case, uncomfortably—back the way we came.

After siesta I went with Rafael and Juanito to the flying field, where Juanito fixed targets to fenceposts. I showed Rafael how to load and charge the air pistol, fired it to demonstrate grip and sighting, then had him pump, load and fire.

After twenty rounds his grip was contracting, so I put up a fresh target and had him fire again. No longer nervous and uncertain, the boy held with a relaxed grip, pulled smoothly and soon was hitting the black center circle. I put up the next target at fifty feet and showed him how to sit and steady the pistol on his knees. Rafael adapted quickly and we complimented him. When he tired, Juanito shot for a while, and then I got off a few, freehand, and left them to practice.

Rita was at the sitting room telephone desk, making notes on a pad as she talked. She nodded at me as I went to the gun cabinet and got out the three house shotguns and my confiscated sawed-off. I carried them to the patio breakfast table, and returned with cleaning gear. Then I found Antonio in the barn working on a tractor engine. He produced a can of light oil and some steel wool, and went with me to the table I'd commandeered. As I suspected, he had no experience with firearms, so I showed him how to clean the guns' fouled bores with bronze bristles and oily pads. Then set him to work on barrel rust with steel wool, there being no rust-removing compound. The sawed-off's twin bores were the only ones without corrosion, but I oiled them lightly anyway, and did the locking and firing mechanisms as well in order to keep them rust-free.

While Antonio was at work I brought down the Webley, ejected cartridges and empty cases, and cleaned and oiled the weapon. Aside from the sawed-off it was the only piece I could rely on.

When asked, Antonio said he thought he could buy a few shotgun shells at a neighboring hacienda, so I gave him corroded samples to take with him and pesetas for the buy. Then I said, ''Antonio, remembering yesterday's unpleasantness, I want to know of any handguns around the hacienda. I'm not going to confiscate them, I just want to know what's available.''

''I—I've never seen any, *Señor*, though Isidro may have one hidden somewhere.''

''Good. And don't tell him I asked.''

''No, *Señor*.''

I left him to his tasks and returned to the sitting room, where Rita was writing rapidly on her pad. Several pages were already covered with notes. Not wanting to interrupt a project I'd encouraged, I found my way to the kitchen where plump Pilar poured me a large glass of fresh orange juice. I complimented her on last night's dinner and said how much we'd enjoyed the picnic lunch. At that she glowed, and said she would consider it a privilege to provide whatever the *señor* might desire. I suggested a glass for the *señora*, and carried it back to where Rita was at work.

"Jack, I think I'm getting somewhere," she said happily. "There *are* new tests and medications." She riffled her note pages. "I talked with three neurologists, four clinical psychologists, two clinics and a professor at the University of Madrid Medical School. I think that's where I should take Rafael, after I've consulted in person."

I handed her the juice glass. "When are you going?"

She looked down at her pad. "I've lost so much time that I'd like to go tomorrow. Will you go with me?"

"Wouldn't it be better if I stayed here? There's a lot of bonding with Rafael to do, and I'm not fond of big cities, even Madrid."

"We'll stay at the Palace and dine at Botin's," she coaxed.

"Invitation I can't refuse. While you're with the shrinks I'll pick up some things for Rafael."

"And I'll see my lawyer, perhaps go to the nunciature to encourage faster action." She sipped from her glass. "Plane leaves Oviedo at nine; I'll phone for reservations."

Toward twilight I rigged the three spinning rods and went with Juanito and Rafael to the compost pile to dig out a can of wiggling worms. In the hacienda Land Rover Juanito drove us to the pond where I'd lunched and made love with Rita. I selected a spot away from the willows, and demonstrated how to cast a spinning line. After four tries Rafael was able to cast without tangling his line, so I baited his hook with a big night crawler and watched him cast toward the center of the pond. Standing behind him, I told him how to retrieve with jerks of the rod, and presently the rod tip bowed and he'd hooked a fish. But he reeled in too energetically and the hook pulled free. "We learn by trying," I remarked, and had him bait his hook and cast again.

There was a small feather lure on my line and I dropped it beyond the tules where ducks had risen earlier in the day. After two rod jerks I felt something tug the lure. I set the hook, and saw a dark fish break water. Rafael shouted encouragement as I played the fish, and when it was landed I saw that it was a smallmouth bass. I unhooked it and returned it to the water as Rafael begged me for my rod.

While he was casting the feather lure, Juanito tried his luck with worms and presently brought in a half-pound perch. A bass hit Rafael's lure and he yelled delightedly as he played the acrobatic fish before bringing it to shore. "Can I keep it, Juan?" he pleaded.

"To eat?"

"If I can't show it to *Mamá* she'll never believe I caught it."

"Then we'll keep it. The fish are biting, so keep your lure in the water— they won't come ashore for it."

By nightfall we had a string of bass and perch and a six-pound barbeled catfish that I assured Juanito would be excellent eating.

At the hacienda the servants exclaimed over our catch, and Rita told Rafael how proud she was at his success. In the kitchen I cleaned and fileted the fish, Paquita and Pilar watching, and recommended lime juice marinade before baking with herbs and oil.

Rita and I celebrated cocktail hour in the sitting room, and Rafael, still enthusiastic over his catch, joined us for a glass of wine. After Rita told him we'd be a few days in Madrid, I tried to ease his disappointment by promising him another plane. That lightened his mood and he went off to watch *Pinocchio* in his room.

"What a change in my son," Rita said quietly. "In just a day you've worked miracles."

"And there's lots of time for more." I finished my third scotch and got up. "How's your bottom?"

"Warm." She wiggled on the cushion.

I smiled wickedly. "Lady Chatterley never had it so good."

"That's because Mellors had no imagination. So you do read naughty books."

"Only the classics," I told her and went up to bathe and change for dinner.

In the morning we had breakfast before seven, and left the hacienda with Antonio at the wheel. When we reached the bridge I saw that the wooden barricade was gone and there was no trace of the dead *guerrilleros*. All the way to Oviedo airport I kept the Webley in easy reach, and turned it over to Antonio before leaving the Volvo with our baggage. Rita told him she'd phone our arrival from Madrid, and after he was gone we had coffee at the waiting room bar until our flight was called.

Beside me Rita talked optimistically of what might be done for Rafael, but already I was regretting the trip. I didn't like leaving the hacienda, because Tessier was free and able to come at us where we were most vulnerable. But I didn't verbalize my concern to Rita, not wanting to dampen her upbeat mood—a misguided kindness I was to regret.

BOOK FOUR

TWENTY-FOUR

BY NOON we were unpacking in a Palace Hotel suite. Our windows over-looked a park that bordered lanes of fast-moving traffic separated by a wide median strip planted with trees and flowers. To the right, a broad plaza whose centerpiece was a fountain depicting Neptune. From the plaza rose a gentle incline toward the Gran Vía, Madrid's combination Fifth and Park avenues.

The hotel itself was a venerable monument to the Belle Epoque when vis-iting royalty favored it and lodged with their retinues. Now the Palace catered to the world's financial royalty, and as we checked in we were followed by a group of well-dressed Asian businessmen, their wives and children.

After freshening up Rita telephoned for appointments and told me she ex-pected to be unpredictably late returning. "I'll snack somewhere," she said, "and as for dinner, *Madrileños* seldom go out before eleven. And stores close between two and four." We kissed, and she was gone, having hired a car and driver for our stay.

Armed with directions from the *conserje*, I left the hotel's coolness for the city's heat and brilliant midday sunlight. A taxi took me up the Gran Vía to its crest, from which I could view a large section of the city. Freed of Franco's long burden, Madrid had erupted into a frenzy of construction that placed tall, dazzling office and apartment buildings where tenements and ancient ware-houses had been for generations. Men and women in casual short-sleeved attire walked briskly along the sidewalks or paused to window-shop at pricey stores. This was the New Spain, I reflected, no longer retarded by bitter legacies of its tragic Civil War.

At Juguetes Castellanos I selected four working models for Rafael: Tiger Moth biplane with a four-foot wingspan; Cessna Skylane with three-foot wing-span; and a two-foot Chaparral speedboat advertised to exceed 200 mph. Also a *Spirit of St. Louis* balsa and tissue paper kit that I looked forward to building from scratch with Rafael. As in Zurich, I asked to have the models sturdily boxed, with fuel and batteries, and was told everything could be delivered the following day.

From the toy store I followed directions four blocks down and east to the Armeria Los Venados, in whose cool, shaded interior I admired imported and Spanish-made firearms, and settled for a box of Webley .455 revolver car- tridges, two boxes of 12-gauge shotgun shells, and one box of 10-gauge for the old goose gun; all low base shells. Carrying my purchases in a string bag supplied by the store, I strolled down to the Plaza de la Cibeles and stopped at a sidewalk café for an iced wine *spritze*. Seated in the shade of an awning, I scanned the busy streets and thought how different it must have been half a century ago when the city was encircled by Nationalist troops and under con- tinuous artillery fire. There had been starvation and disease, and some of the heaviest last-ditch fighting had been around University City, where Rita was conferring with specialists about her son. Whatever they and consultants yet to be seen told her, she would forever have the satisfaction of having explored the range of professional opinions, and no mother could do more.

I looked at my watch. By the time I got to the Prado the museum would be closing, so I'd postpone the visit until tomorrow while Rita was away. I drained the last of the *spritze* and made my way cautiously across the plaza, feeling like a Pamplona *aficionado* as I risked my body in the rush of moving cars.

Back in the suite I took a refreshing shower and honored the Spanish siesta custom. I woke at five, hungry, and lacking word from Rita, had a steak sand- wich sent up along with a half-bottle of Marqués de Riscal red. Toward six Rita arrived looking hot and tired, drank the last of my wine and said she'd gotten mixed opinions but was still hopeful, and was going to return with Rafael the following week. Tomorrow she had further medical appointments and one with her lawyer after four, so we'd miss the three o'clock flight to Oviedo.

After she showered and changed we left the hotel in her hired BMW and drove up the hill to the barred pedestrian street that was already crowded with *Madrileños* of all ages sampling *tapas* and drinking small beakers of wine. These snack bars adjoined each other in rows on each side of the narrow street, fronts open for access to passersby. Uncovered pans of *percebes, bacalao, acedias* and other Spanish delicacies were banked so customers could add to their plates with ease. Rita was fond of anchovies in red sauce but I settled for fried squid that resembled onion rings. The flesh was rubbery but tasty and the house wine no worse than cheap Chianti.

Lights came on illuminating the colorful *tapeo* scene as we strolled hand in hand, pausing to sample here and there, paying a few *pesetas* to each server. Even after dark the air remained hot, but its dryness evaporated perspiration.

After reaching the end of the street we turned back and had the driver take us five minutes away to Casa Botin. The renowned old restaurant was located off the Plaza Mayor at the foot of a stone-paved alley, and because the hour was early by Madrid standards we were seated without delay on the street floor, comfortably far from the ovens. Above us heavy rafters were blackened from a couple of centuries of smoke. Tiled walls and floors, ancient dark oak tables set with spotless napery. We ordered the house special, lamb roasted in terra-cotta casseroles, and a bottle of Murrieta *tinto*.

Most of the patrons were tourists or visitors, like ourselves, who preferred dining before midnight. After a glass of wine Rita took me down to the caverns where huge hogskins of wine hung from rafters like carcasses in an abattoir. The walls were lined with giant tuns that looked centuries old and had worn wooden spigots whence the wine was drawn. Back at our table the smoky atmosphere seduced our appetites, and when the *corderito asado* was served we ate without regard to *tapas* already consumed. "Always wanted to come," I said, pushing back from the table, "ever since reading that renunciation scene Hemingway set here."

"Saw the movie," Rita remarked. "Tyrone Power and—somebody. Rita Hayworth?"

"Ava Gardner. Filmed in Mexico, not Spain." I paid the bill, we walked back to the car, roused the driver, and returned to the hotel.

Undressing, Rita said, "My first appointment is at nine—early for Madrid, then others until two. Can you avoid boredom that long?"

"I've heard it takes a couple of days to tour the Prado properly. Goya, Rubens, Velázquez . . . but I'll meet you here at two; we'll lunch in the Palace garden."

She yawned. "Sorry. I'm exhausted and stuffed with too much food. Let's go to bed."

In the morning after Rita left I was reading *El Pais* for the peculiarly Spanish slant on world events, when Juguetes Castellanos delivered my purchases, strongly boxed as requested. At ten I crossed the Recoletos to the Museo del Prado—Spain's Louvre—a neo-classic temple of six facing columns surmounted by a wide triangular frieze. As I approached the entrance I noticed on the left an imposing bronze statue of a seated figure: Velázquez. Inside I paid a small entrance fee and bought a museum guidebook to its treasures. A sign in multiple languages announced that photography was forbidden and a clutch of Japanese reluctantly surrendered their cameras to the checkroom.

Many of the paintings were displayed in separate, well-lighted rooms or alcoves off the main viewing galleries. Following the guidebook, I located El Greco at once, then a two-room Veláquez exhibit. Rubens was in the rotunda, and the second floor appeared entirely dedicated to the works of Goya. After viewing his group portrait of the royal family I studied his two portraits of the Duchess of Alba, one clothed, the other nude. That one had become the most scandalous painting of the age, and I much preferred it to the other.

Toward noon I suspended viewing Goya's brutal drawings of Napoleonic massacres and visited the museum cafeteria for hot chocolate and *churros*— fried, sugared batter, a common breakfast snack.

At one I surrendered to eyestrain, promising myself to return after lunch and siesta for the French and Italian exhibits, the statuary collection and Picasso's *Guernica* housed in the museum annex.

After a refreshing shower I stretched out on the bed and napped until Rita woke me after two. "Ready for lunch?"

"Almost." I dressed while she summarized her consultations. "On the whole, Jack, they've been so positive I'm planning to bring Rafael for testing next week."

"Terrific."

She was rinsing her face with cool water. "Another thing, they agree it's a good idea to have him with other children—what was the phrase? Inter-relating." She dabbed water from her face. "So, it turns out I was wrong about that, too."

"But you're on course now, both of you."

"Thanks to you, darling." At the mirror she applied light pink lipstick, the shade reminding me of Anita's Jeep.

I knotted my tie and drew on a lightweight seersucker jacket. "I'm ready."

"And I could use a good, stiff drink."

"Let's go."

The open-sided garden area was covered by a translucent cupola, tables surrounded by banks of ferns and growing flowers. After vodka marts we shared a jumbo-size shrimp salad, served with palm hearts and garlic toasts. Raspberry sherbet, coffee, and luncheon was a pleasant memory. Over a coffee refill Rita asked what was in the packages, and when I told her she said it was too much, I was going to spoil Rafael. "I'll enjoy the boat and planes, too, so we'll be equally spoiled," I told her, "and if Rafael doesn't go off to school I want him to have an exercise room."

She smiled teasingly. "Which you'll also use, no doubt."

"No doubt."

"Possibly a swimming pool?"

"That nearby stream could be dammed. Save money that way, and give the servants some pleasure, too."

She nodded thoughtfully. "Keeping the pond for ourselves."

"Absolutely."

We finished our coffee and returned to the suite where Rita placed a call to the hacienda. When the phone rang she had me pick up an extension, saying Rafael would want to hear from me, too.

When Francisco responded, Rita told him we'd be returning the following day, and to have Antonio meet the plane. "And now, I want to speak with Rafael."

"Rafael? Ah, *señora*, it must have slipped your mind that he's gone to visit his grandmother."

Her face went white. "My mother? I never agreed to that. When did he leave?"

"It was yesterday after lunch. She arrived, told us she had your permission, and so we allowed the boy to leave." Stiffly he said, "*señora*, who are we to question the words of your mother?"

Eyes dull, she seemed to shrink into herself. "I don't blame you, Francisco, but it was very wrong," she said hoarsely.

"Francisco," I said, "was there anyone with Señora Marie?"

"I think there was only a driver."

Sobbing, Rita eased heavily into a chair.

"Listen to me, Francisco, we're leaving for Oviedo as soon as we can charter a plane." I looked at my watch. "Have Antonio there no later than seven."

"*Sí, Señor*. And, *señora*, I'm terribly sorry we did wrong."

"Oh, God," Rita wailed after I hung up, "couldn't he have called me here? What's she going to do to Rafael?"

"She's not going to hurt him," I replied, "that much we know. Now, pack and I'll lay on a flight." I wanted her active, not thinking of Marie and Rafael.

By phone I explained to the *conserje* that a family emergency required immediate departure, and asked if he could arrange for a charter flight from Barajas to Oviedo. He said he could and would call back at once.

Dry sobs erupting from her throat, Rita emptied drawers into her bags, yanked dresses from hangers and filled the remaining space. I had fewer things so I caught up with her quickly, and we were ready to leave when the *conserje* called.

An Aer Cantabria plane was waiting our arrival at Barajas, he said, and our hotel bill was prepared.

Until we were in her hired BMW we spoke only a few words, then pent-up emotion broke and she cried hysterically while I tried to calm her down. Finally, she dried her cheeks and eyes and said, "Without you I don't know what I'd do."

"First," I said, "you're not to worry about Rafael. I'm sure he's safe."

"But my mother—why would she *do* this thing? Kidnap my son?"

"We won't really know until she makes contact, and that could be very soon."

"How soon?" Again, tears were welling in her eyes.

"Perhaps tonight."

"I'm going to bring in the police."

"Not now," I said. "Not until we've heard from Marie. Besides, they won't look on it as kidnapping—she's his grandmother."

"I—I'm afraid you're right. But she never cared what the Colonel did to me, to Anita. She's never cared for Rafael, ever."

I sucked in a deep breath. "This isn't a good time for it but I have to tell you something I didn't feel was important until now."

"What, Jack? Why is it important now?"

"It goes back to when Tessier had me in his training camp. Marie was there, staying with him."

"Oh, my God! You saw her and didn't tell me." She looked away. "And now you think Claude is behind this. Yes, that's what it has to be." Abruptly she covered her face with her hands and began to weep, rocking back and forth beside me. "To think that animal has my son."

"Not for long," I said soothingly. "He doesn't want Rafael, he wants the money. All right, he gets the account numbers, we get Rafael."

Looking up, she managed a weak smile. "You give me such confidence, dearest. But for you I'd be completely apart."

"Just hang on," I told her, and then Barajas terminal was in sight.

The plane was a twin-engine Cessna six-place. I'd flown the aircraft in multi-engine transition and could have gotten us to Oviedo but I was glad a pilot was available. He knew the routes and mountains as I did not, and set us down a little after seven.

As before, Antonio loaded the Volvo with our baggage, and handed me the Webley revolver I'd given him the day before.

"Fast, Antonio," Rita said as she got in beside me. "Drive as fast as you can."

I knew she wanted to be at the hacienda when Marie—or someone—telephoned, even though they'd be sure to call again. And although I'd tried to assure Rita that her son would not be mistreated, I remembered Tessier's scorn for "the dummy," as he called Rafael. Okay, he was going to get the account numbers; it was up to me to get Rafael back unharmed. Forget all that hidden wealth, let Tessier build his army, retake Guatemala; Rita, Rafael and I had a life to build far removed from Central American politics and violence. I spoke those thoughts to Rita, who nodded and said dully, "I don't at all blame you for not telling me my mother was with Claude. I suppose you wanted to shield me from her shame, but I knew they were lovers."

"Did the Colonel know?"

"Except for a loss of pride I don't think he would have cared. But he wouldn't trust Claude as much as he once did."

Ahead of us the sky was darkening. By the time we reached La Torre there would be no light in the surrounding fields. Ideal conditions for Tessier and an armed band to invade and enforce his demands.

Rita's arm was linked with mine as the car sped over the two-lane road. I prayed there would be no barricades or Basque brigands before we got to the hacienda; I needed to concentrate on Tessier, anticipate his moves despite my previous failure. This time there was more at stake—the life of a terrified boy.

Rita, I knew, would do anything to have him safely back—so would I—but I didn't want her involved in negotiations or nearby when I faced Tessier, maternal impulses being unpredictable.

When we reached the bridge where we'd been ambushed I looked at her face for any reaction but it was impassive, eyes staring at the road ahead. She was silent, rigid, in a kind of stupor induced by stress. Then in a flat, distant voice she murmured, "How devastating to fall from hope to despair in only a few moments. If my son is harmed I won't want to live."

"You will, because I need you. And when we reach La Torre I want you to tell the servants I'm in charge, they're to do as I say without question. Will you do that?"

"Yes. Of course I will."

The road was bumpier now, each pothole slammed and jarred us, shifting baggage behind, the presents for a boy no longer there. Antonio switched on headlights, sent chickens flying as we rounded a curve.

In Houston and San Diego I'd worked hostage-kidnap situations but always with a trained team. Now I was alone, responsible for the lives of innocents. I could arm Antonio and Juanito, Francisco and Isidro, the *capataz*, with shotguns and hope they wouldn't have to fire the old weapons. But Tessier would expect a primitive defense and his automatic weapons could cut us down like the sweep of a scythe.

I wondered if Tessier would wear his Kevlar vest, and said, "I think he'll act tonight when we're least prepared."

"Jack," she clutched my arm, "don't try to kill him, just give him what he wants."

"He has to give us the boy."

"Yes. He's all I want."

Antonio turned off without slowing, sped through the postern gate, and up the drive toward the lighted hacienda. From it a figure came running toward us. Antonio braked, a cloud of dust swirled over us, and through it I saw the tense face of Juanito emerge. "*Señora*," he choked, "come in, come quickly. Rafael is on the telephone for you!"

TWENTY-FIVE

I<small>N THE</small> sitting room Rita snatched the phone from Francisco, and I picked up the extension earpiece. "Rafael, *querido*," she cried, "are you all right? Where are you?"

"With *Abuela* Maria, *Mamá*, and I'm fine. We're—"

"That's enough, child," Marie cut in. "Now, Rita, that was to assure you Rafael is in good hands."

"Mother," she said wildly, "bring him back to me. You have no right to him. He's my child, I love him."

"I'm sure you do," said the widow of Oscar Chavez, "and to regain him you will follow my instructions."

"Yours or Claude's?" she said bitterly. "Tell me what to do."

"Good. I'll call again."

"But I must speak to Rafael—"

"Later." Marie broke the connection. Rita stared at the telephone and turned to me. "You heard?"

I nodded. "Rafael is well and they're ready to negotiate. That's good. Now I want a word with the servants."

Rita swallowed and spoke to the major domo. "Get everyone here. *Señor* Juan is to be obeyed without question."

While Francisco was rounding up the servants I took the shotguns from the gun cabinet and opened my bag for new shells. After loading my Webley I loaded all four shotguns and laid them aside. Servants had crowded in, and I said, "As you know, Rafael has been kidnapped. The *señora* and I will be negotiating for his return, but because there may be danger I want all female servants in their rooms until dawn. Eat now and disappear." I turned to Francisco. "You, Antonio, Juanito and Isidro each take a shotgun. Two of you stay inside, two patrol outside. Shoot anything that moves."

Francisco cleared his throat. "The *capataz* is not here, *Señor*."

"Why not?"

"He is attending the funeral of a nephew. The young man was found dead on the road to Oviedo."

I glanced at Rita, who nodded her understanding. "All right. Francisco, inside with me, Juanito and Antonio, start patrolling. Separately. Quietly. Take your guns." I handed more shells to each of them, and told Francisco to guard the rear of the house.

When we were alone Rita asked, "Is all that necessary?"

"We don't know Tessier's plans, so we plan for the worst."

"You think he might try to kill us?"

"He won't want any interference when he goes for the bank accounts."

"But we wouldn't do that."

"Try convincing him."

She touched the Webley. "I can use this."

"If there's a direct threat. Now, they'll have to meet us for the exchange. You agree but say you can't drive the Volvo, Antonio will drive you. Only I'll be Antonio."

Her eyebrows lifted. "Claude will recognize you."

"He'll recognize Pepe Menendez, but it won't matter." From my bag I extracted a shoe and pried up the innersole to take out the laminated card. "Copy these numbers exactly," I said, "and hide them."

She took the card, sat at the desk and began following instructions. When she finished she looked up at me. "Claude must have the bank names."

"He's always had them," I told her. "Stole them from the Colonel before killing him. But his mistake was giving the number card to Anita when he went to jail. Ever since he's been trying to get it." I touched the card. "He gets it now."

"After it cost Anita her life," she said heavily, "and by threatening my son." She got up and handed me the copied sheet. "Where shall I keep it?"

"That vase on the fireplace mantel." I rolled the paper and inserted it. Then I drew her to me and held her close. "Everything is going to work out, darling. So close to success Tessier will be focusing on that. He'll expect you to be so helpless and so frantic to get Rafael that he could go for a straight exchange without any deception. Now, show me Juanito's room."

It was upstairs, next to Rafael's, with a connecting door. From his closet I took heavy blue trousers and an unpressed blue work shirt. The dresser yielded a dark blue neck bandanna and a black *boina*. I changed there and went down to where Rita was waiting by the telephone. Her face was distraught as she asked, "When will they call? I can't bear this waiting."

"They'll call," I said soothingly, and left her while I went out to make sure Antonio and Juanito were following orders. I apologized for borrowing Juanito's clothing, he said it was nothing. "Señor Juan, it was a terrible thing to take the boy. Why did she do it?"

"It's complicated," I replied, "and now we have to get him back."

"We are very glad you are here, *Señor*," Antonio told me. "We don't miss the *capataz* so much." He eyed me knowingly.

"Funerals are a family obligation," I remarked, and let his implication ride. I went around the front drive to the Volvo and placed the sawed-off shotgun under the driver's seat, where I could reach it in case of gunplay. I was hoping for an above-board deal, but Tessier was as unpredictably devious as any criminal I'd ever known. Undoubtedly Marie would come along to calm the boy, who would be far from understanding what was going on. Aside from that would she be help or hindrance to her lover?

The sky was cloudless. A half-moon silvered distant mountain peaks. Around me the cool night air bore the fresh scent of grassland. I breathed deeply and in my nostrils it was sugar-sweet. For a few moments I lingered to watch stars in the indigo sky, and then I went back in to Rita.

Except for low shielded lights in the sitting and music rooms the house was entirely dark. Francisco was back in the dark kitchen, an old and unfamiliar weapon across his knees. Night vision could be crucial if invaders came.

Rita was sipping cognac. I wet my lips from her glass and sat down. Before her on the writing desk the Webley revolver lay next to the telephone. Twenty-four hours ago I'd been looking at her across our dinner table, and I reflected how our lives had seemed unobstructed, so many obstacles cleared away. Rafael was going to be helped . . . but even then the boy had been delivered by his grandmother into the hands of her consort. What fools we'd been to leave him.

Rita turned her head. "That's a heavy sigh, Jack."

"Oh? Tired, I guess."

She gestured at the telephone. "Maybe the line's been cut."

"Check it."

She lifted the receiver, listened, and replaced it. "Working." She shivered. "God, I can't stand much more waiting . . . I've never felt so close to death."

"They're torturing you, trying to wear you down so you'll agree to anything. Don't let them get to you."

She nodded uncertainly. "If only the phone would ring."

"It will. Now put the revolver in your shoulder bag with the number card. I want to deliver the card to Tessier. If he insists you do it, say you're afraid of him—"

"That's true, God knows."

"—and Antonio will deliver it, unarmed."

She left the desk and picked up the leather shoulder bag from where she'd dropped it, carried it back, and emptied its contents on the desk. Then she put in the card and revolver and closed the flap. Seated again, she said, "After what she's done how can my mother ever face me again?"

"She's not planning to. She'll be busy counting money with Tessier, living the golden life far, far away. She's never been a decent mother to you. After tonight she's out of your life forever."

"Thank God." Her lips trembled. "Poor Rafael. I can hardly bear to think of how frightened he must be."

"Confused, yes, frightened?—he'd have to understand the situation to be frightened." I pressed her hand. "I've been thinking about Tessier's getaway. Once we have Rafael he's got to worry about being followed and forced to stop. So he'll probably shoot out our tires. If he does, don't let it frighten you. No one's going to keep him from leaving."

She sipped from her glass, passed it to me. The cognac was like cold fire on my tongue. I wanted more but I had to stay alert.

The mantel clock struck ten-thirty. It must have been striking before while we sat waiting but I hadn't heard it.

Rita smiled weakly. "I shouldn't have given up smoking. I've never needed a cigarette so badly."

"This is—" I began, and then the telephone rang.

Rita stared, and reached for the receiver. I lifted the earpiece and nodded. The voice we heard was Marie's.

TWENTY-SIX

R AFAEL'S GRANDMOTHER said, "Listen closely, Rita. Follow instructions and you'll soon have Rafael."

"I'm listening," Rita replied in a taut voice.

"Very well. You have the bank account numbers—don't say you haven't—and you'll turn them over in exchange for Rafael."

"I have the numbers, and I'm ready to give them to you. How is my son?"

"Sleeping."

"Is he frightened? Has he been crying?" Rita pressed.

"I tell you he's fine, has no idea he's been—taken." There was an edge of irritation to her voice. "Now write down these instructions."

Rita looked at me before picking up her pen. I nodded and she said, "I'm ready, go ahead."

"Very well. Drive west past your hacienda exactly seven-and-a-half kilometers. Repeat that."

"West, seven-and-a-half kilometers."

"Good. On your right there will be a large open field. It is fenced but there is an open gate. Stop there and flash your headlights four times."

Rita wrote quickly. "Four times. Go ahead."

"You will see four answering flashes. Drive toward them."

"I understand. Rafael will be with you."

"Yes. Rita, have you said anything to the police?"

"Nothing."

"You swear?"

"I swear on the head of my son," she said huskily, "and by the soul of my beloved sister, murdered by your lover."

"Get out of the car and walk toward the headlights. Have the card in your hand."

"And when will I see Rafael?"

"He will be brought near you. When you give me the card he is free. One last thing, Rita, come alone."

"I can't drive the Volvo. Antonio will have to drive me."

There was a pause, while Marie covered the mouthpiece to confer. Presently she said, "Only Antonio."

"He has no weapons, you have nothing to fear from him. When shall I be there?"

"Eleven. Precisely eleven o'clock."

Rita looked up at me, and I nodded okay. The distance was just under five miles. Even on the dark road we could make it in twelve to fifteen minutes. Rita swallowed before asking, "That's all?"

"Eleven o'clock. I'll wake Rafael now. Just don't try any tricks, understand?"

"No tricks."

The line went dead, and Rita began to cry. I made her drink the rest of her cognac, and went to the kitchen, where I told Francisco we were leaving to get Rafael. "But stay on guard," I warned, "let no one in."

He nodded and I went back to Rita. She shouldered the leather bag, dried her eyes, and said, "I'm ready." Her face was a rigid mask.

Outside, I called in Antonio and Juanito and repeated the instructions I'd given Francisco. Juanito begged to go along but Rita refused. She got into the rear seat, I got behind the wheel, checked the odometer, and started the engine. Drove out to the Oviedo road.

We went two kilometers before anyone spoke. Then Rita said, "I wonder where they've been keeping Rafael?"

"Probably in Oviedo. At first I thought of some isolated barn but your mother wouldn't go for rough camping without food and drink."

"Yes, that sounds like her."

Clouds had gathered to obscure the moon. My headlights made the narrow road seem narrower. As I drove I watched the odometer and checked elapsed time. Rita said, "I pray this is the last of Claude Tessier."

"He'll have no more reason to haunt us." We were making good time over the road, too good. I slowed to reach the rendezvous point at eleven, not before.

Rita said, "I know the place. The field hasn't been farmed for years. The owners live in León." She was talking to keep from thinking. I reached down and touched the sawed-off shotgun, hoped I wouldn't need it.

Ahead, headlights framed a wooden bridge and I slowed to a crawl as its old planks rumbled and creaked under the moving car. Beyond, an antlered deer erupted from darkness and bounded across the road. From Rita came dry sobs.

"Remember," I said, "you're having Antonio turn over the card because you're afraid of Tessier."

"How could I forget?"

"And have Rafael run to the car."

"Yes."

My watch showed seven minutes before eleven. By now Tessier and Marie should be there, waiting. With Rafael. For Tessier it was going to end a long search. Tomorrow in Switzerland he could begin collecting his pots of stolen gold.

"We're nearing the field," Rita murmured.

Five to eleven. The odometer showed seven kilometers run, half a kilometer to go. I turned the headlights low and pulled to the roadside. While the engine idled I reviewed Marie's scenario and tried to think of things that could go wrong. We could be driving into an ambush, but why would Tessier arrange one? I *was* taking a chance he'd recognize me as the man who'd destroyed his training camp but I didn't want Rita close enough to him to be harmed.

Turning to Rita, I said, "Whatever happens, I love you."

"And I love you. Just bring me my son."

"Time to get him." I turned up the headlights and drove onto the road. A few hundred yards and Rita exclaimed, "There's the fence."

"I see it. And . . . the gate."

I turned it and braked. Ahead of us was a broad expanse unbroken except for the distant outline of a tree. Where cattle once gathered, I thought irrelevantly. "Headlights?" Rita prompted.

"Keep watching behind us." I blinked the lights four times, left them off. From two hundred yards into the field came four separate flashes of light. The reception party was in place.

Headlights on, I drove slowly toward the source of the answering flashes. Rita whispered, "Nothing behind us."

"So far, so good." My muscles were tight, neck and shoulder ached from tension. My forehead scar began to throb. I steered to the right of the other car's headlights, not wanting them directly in my eyes. And when I was forty or fifty yards away I stopped the Volvo and turned off the engine to hear final instructions.

After a few moments' wait I saw the other car door open and a woman got out. She was wearing a dark pants suit and her blond hair was teased into the beehive I remembered from the 'Glades.

Cupping her hands, she shouted, "Rita? Come to me."

"I must see Rafael," Rita called back.

"Here he is." She beckoned him from the car until he stood beside her, blinking at my headlights, looking pitifully small. "Now bring the card."

"Come halfway, both of you," Rita called.

From the car stepped Claude Tessier in black turtleneck and black trousers. He stood behind Rafael, both hands on the boy's shoulders. "Rafael," Rita called, "I'm here to get you. Everything's going to be all right."

At the sound of her voice his shoulders began to heave and we could hear whimpering sounds as he knuckled tears away.

"C'mon, Rita," Tessier yelled, "let's get it over with. Bring me the card."

"I—I'm afraid of you," she called. "Antonio will bring it." Over the seat back she passed the card to me. I opened the car door and stood beside it. Tessier didn't like her response and his face twisted into a hard grimace. Finally he said, "All right, we meet halfway. But if he's got a weapon I'll kill the boy."

"No guns, *señor*," I called in imitation of Antonio's voice, and waved the card in front of the headlights.

At that, the three of them walked slowly toward me. I began walking toward them, staying clear of the Volvo headlights to avoid being silhouetted. As Tessier neared I saw something bulky on his belt. Holster? At least he had no gun in hand. Keeping the card at waist level, I approached him. The *boina* was low on my forehead to delay recognition, but Tessier and Marie weren't looking at my face, they were focusing on the card in my hand.

We stopped a yard apart. I said, "Let Rafael go," and when Tessier's hands left his shoulders I handed over the card and grabbed Rafael, pulling him toward me. "Run to your mother," I snapped, and pushed him toward the Volvo. Tessier and Marie were studying the laminated card. "This is it. Marie, we've done it." He tucked the card in a trouser pocket and unhooked from his belt what I now saw as a radio voice transmitter. In a gloating voice he said, "Come in. Come in. We're ready." The receiver crackled acknowledgement, and Tessier replaced the transmitter. To me he said, "She's got the boy, drive her away." Then for the first time he looked closely at my face. "You! Damn you, I should kill you for what you did to me!"

"Pepe Menendez, *a sus órdenes, señor*." I began backing from him.

Suddenly realizing who I was, Marie shrieked and tried to kick me, but I was too far from her. She lost balance in the soft earth and would have fallen, but Tessier steadied her, giving me time to run out of the headlight's glare. He'd called in someone or more than someone—reinforcements—so now was the time to leave. And as I dashed for the Volvo I heard the breathy threshing of chopper blades, and saw a helicopter skimming toward the lights. This chopper wasn't after me, because it hovered over the lighted area and settled to a landing. It must have been waiting for Tessier's signal in the distance beyond the car. I half expected men to jump out and start shooting, but only the pilot stepped out. When I saw an automatic weapon in his hands I yelled at Rita to duck down in the car, raced to it, turned off headlights and grabbed the sawed-off from the floor.

Tessier's exit was cleverly planned. A flamboyant, unexpected departure. He hadn't shot out our tires because we couldn't follow the chopper, and I felt grudging admiration for his resourcefulness. Then I peered at the pilot, saw his pile of silvery-white hair, and recognized him as the ticket messenger in Zurich. He'd followed us all the way, and now he was taking Tessier out of our lives. The three of them were talking. Why weren't they getting into the chopper? Was Silver Hair getting orders to gun us down? I had to find out.

"Rita," I called, "start the engine, get ready to leave."

"Not without you. Get in."

"I have to see them take off."

As I spoke, Tessier and Marie turned and began coming toward us, Tessier in the lead. When I saw the pistol in his hand I realized he wasn't going to let us get away. Unless he killed me first I could drop him with the sawed-off, but what about Marie? She had no weapon, and I couldn't kill her in front of her daughter. I gripped the shotgun and waited for Tessier to come into range.

Movement behind them. Silver Hair was coming, too. I trained the sawed-off on Tessier just as Silver Hair halted beyond shotgun range and brought an automatic weapon to his hip. He was Tessier's backup gun, with firepower that could destroy us all.

Suddenly, Tessier fired. The bullet whistled wide and before he could shoot again I heard Silver Hair's machine gun erupt: *brrrp, brrrp*. I expected the bullets to hit the car, break glass; instead, I saw Tessier fling up his arms, yell, and pitch forward. Behind him, Marie crumpled and dropped without a sound. I could hardly believe what I'd seen. Was Silver Hair our savior, or had he spared us for the pleasure of killing us himself?

I cocked both hammers and aimed, but the gunman knelt beside Tessier's body. He began searching it, found the card, and held it up triumphantly. *Who was he?*

"Jack, get in, let's go?" Rita's voice was urgent, and I could hear Rafael's frightened cries. "All right," I said, but just then Silver Hair trained the machine gun on us and fired a burst that stitched the earth ahead of the Volvo. Rafael screamed, and the man called, "Get out, Rita, I want to see you. It's been many years. You, too, whoever you are." He kept the gun pointing at us as Rita got slowly from the car. "In front of the car," he ordered. "This won't take long. I have to be in Zurich tomorrow."

"That voice . . ." Rita husked as she moved past me. I set the sawed-off on the hood; at that range it was useless. He strolled toward us, kept coming while we waited. As I watched I saw the helicopter in the background; a four-place French chopper that could have him at Barajas within two hours.

Now I could see the well-tanned face, the thick, arrogant lips and dark watchful eyes. Ten feet away he stopped and surveyed us. "Take off the *boina*," he told me, and when I did he grunted. "Novak, eh? Some of my Mexican friends would be glad to see you."

My throat and mouth were dry. Rita said sharply, "Who are you? Why did you kill Claude and my mother?"

"They stole from me and would have stolen more." He held up the number card, and another. "With these I can get what is mine."

"Just let us go," Rita said. "You've got everything."

"Everything," he nodded. "And still you wonder who I am." His smile was sardonic. "You were a beautiful child, you became a beautiful woman."

She stared incredulously, cringed, shrank from him. "*You*," she breathed. "How . . . ? You're *dead!*"

"Am I? My treacherous aide and slut of a wife are dead. *I'm* very much alive."

It was when he began explaining that I knew he couldn't let us go, he had to kill us.

"I'm alive," he went on, "because Marie's maid told me how she and Tessier were planning to kill me. In Monterrey I kept him at my side, gave him things to do while I went to the airport. I had my stand-in ride the helicopter in my place. And as I watched from the roadside I saw it explode and burn." He shrugged. "Never trust anyone. Rita, my child, aren't you going to call me father? I'd like to hear it from your lips."

"I'll never give you that satisfaction," she grated. "You destroyed my life, you *hijo de puta*, and you can't get your money without my help."

"What do you mean?" Breeze lifted his hair, dropped it neatly in place.

"Do you think I'd give Claude the right numbers? I learned deception from you." She tapped her shoulder bag.

"Then give me the right numbers," he snarled, "or I'll kill your idiot son."

"*Your* son, Colonel," she spat, "and I will never tell him."

Angrily he said, "Give me what you've got," and chambered a cartridge. The Uzi was on full auto. "Now. You're wasting time."

"Don't hurt my son," she begged as her hand slipped into the bag.

"And don't try to give me orders. I do what I want, always have."

"Until now," she said, and shot through the bag. Shot again. The heavy bullets slammed him backward, and as he died his hand contracted, firing the Uzi toward the sky. I grabbed the sawed-off and shot both barrels at the weapon, tearing it from his hand. Coolly, Rita approached him, took the Webley from her bag and pressed the barrel to his face. "This is for Anita," she said, and fired. The back of his head exploded. "And this is for me." She fired again, the bullet spraying blood and brain matter in an arc behind his head. She dropped the revolver, turned to me, and began sobbing brokenly. What I could see of Chavez's bleached hair was untouched by blood. Two holes in his face, two in his chest. All the months of cosmetic surgery wasted.

I picked up the matching bank cards where they had fallen and stuck the revolver in my pocket. In the Volvo Rafael was sobbing hysterically. I said, "Take care of your son, both of you get out of here."

She lifted tear-stained cheeks. "How will you get to La Torre?"

"There's an extra car nobody's using, don't worry about me. And—you were terrific, couldn't have done better."

She swallowed. "I never thought I could kill a man, and I didn't. I destroyed an animal."

I kissed her. "Get the hell out of here," and turned her toward the car.

When she was gone I stood alone in the field thinking how close we had been to death. Thanks to Rita, those of us who mattered were alive. I bent over, grabbed Chavez's ankles and began dragging his body to the helicopter. I had to fit it into the pilot's seat before rigor mortis set in. After that, body stiffness was unimportant. I strapped safety belts around him, and fitted the radio headset on what remained of his skull. "*Adiós*, Colonel," I said, and gave his corpse the Italian Salute. His wallet was full of false identification cards, charge plates, piloting licenses for rotor and fixed-wing aircraft, all in the name of Patricio Guzman, Mexican citizen. I left the wallet in his pocket and hefted Tessier and Marie on board. He wasn't wearing the protective Kevlar vest, and his face was fixed in a startled stare through eyes as dull as gray pebbles. Death had aged Marie twenty years. She was a hag in a metallic wig, veins like thick, blue worms on her hands and arms. Her throat uttered a sigh as I lifted her into a seat, and that startled me until I realized it was only air expelled from her lungs.

I seated Tessier last, strapped him in, and reached past Chavez to switch on running lights and ignition. When the rotors began turning, I backed out, dropped to the ground, and closed the passenger door. Then I walked to their car—an old Mercedes sedan—and drove to where the Volvo had been. The Webley's cylinder held two unfired cartridges. I didn't want to use the Uzi, so I left it on the ground and walked back twenty yards and lay prone, facing the helicopter. Gripping the Webley in both hands, I sighted on the gas tank, breathed deeply, held, and squeezed the trigger. The lead slug ricocheted from the metal tank. I breathed and sighted again, and this time the slug went through.

I'd expected an immediate explosion, but when nothing happened I remembered that lead won't spark on metal, and so I went back for the Uzi. I ejected the magazine to see if the high-power cartridges were jacketed, when a shock wave pushed me against the Mercedes. I saw spurting flames before I heard the detonation, and dropped down to avoid flying debris.

The explosion squashed the helicopter to earth, and tore it apart. Rotor fragments were still revolving, caught in the updraft from the roaring flames. This time the body of the real Oscar Chavez was burning in chopper wreckage, but who would ever know?

I laid the Uzi across the car's front seat, and drove away from the hellish conflagration. How Chavez, face-altered, posing as Guzman, had insinuated himself into the job of getaway pilot for Tessier I'd never know. But he'd let Tessier and Marie conspire to extract the number card from Rita, then killed them for it. In those few moments when the three were talking I wondered if he'd revealed himself, then pulled the trigger. It would be like Chavez to gloat before exacting revenge.

Knowing Rita, I didn't think she'd feel remorse for killing her father, and I was going to explain to her that he planned to kill us all. How Rafael would react to all the violence was another matter—extra work for the therapists. Tomorrow we would follow a normal day, flying his new model planes, taking the shiny Chaparral speedboat for long runs on the glassy pond, maybe fishing afterward. Anything to distract his mind from the slaughter he had seen.

Clouds had vanished, the moon was pure silver above the roadway. I looked back at the killing field and saw the red-pink glow of flames, though not the flames themselves. I doubted that the scene would be noticed until tomorrow, perhaps not even then. A helicopter crashed and burned, no survivors. How coldly cruel of Chavez to send his stand-in on a lethal ride from Monterrey. Pronounced dead, he assumed another life, underwent facial surgery, and planned his comeback in another guise. I wondered if he knew Tessier had killed Anita, whether he even cared.

The Mercedes was a disposal problem. A deep pond was a preferred grave, but I didn't think La Torre's pond was deep enough to conceal the car for years ahead. I was too tired to drive to Oviedo and abandon it there, so when I reached the shaky wooden bridge I braked to look down at the dry-bed gully and think things through. If I drove it onto hacienda land one of the servants was sure to spot it. A man with ETA connections—Isidro—would ask questions, and in time the police would come around. For all I knew, Tessier had stolen the car, making it hot, and wanted. No time to take chances.

After turning off the ignition I got out, stretched arms and legs, and listened for vehicular sounds. All I could hear was the occasional distant barking of a dog, now and then the high-pitched squeaking of an invisible bat. After ten minutes I searched the trunk, found only jack and spare, and felt under the seats. My hand touched something soft, and when I pulled it out I saw a brown velvet teddy bear. Rafael's pet, his consolation away from home. I fitted it under my bloused shirt, felt the Webley's weight, and polished prints from the revolver. Heaved it into the gully.

I got behind the wheel and backed from the bridge, stopped and slanted the wheels so the Mercedes would miss the bridge and drop into the gully. I slung the Uzi over my shoulder, closed the door, and through the open window forced the gearshift forward. The transmission shuddered, but the car moved ahead, gathering speed until its front end dropped and the car disappeared. A second later I heard it crash on the bottom. When I looked down I saw that it had landed conveniently on its roof, wheels still spinning. I walked across the bridge, set the Uzi on single-fire and sighted at the exposed gas tank.

One shot did it. As the tank exploded I ducked for cover and saw flame fingers spreading higher than the bridge.

Rafael's cuddle-friend in my shirt, Chavez's Uzi across my back, I took the roadway from the bridge and walked the moonlit blacktop until I could see the arched postern gate of La Torre, and the glow of the lighted hacienda beyond.

As I trudged up the rise I felt as played-out as I'd been after Tessier's chopper pursued me. My pace slowed, the Uzi seemed heavier than a fifty-pound field pack, and when I could see the Volvo standing in the drive, I unslung it and walked to the entrance steps.

"*Señor.*" Francisco, from the darkness.

"*Buenas,*" I replied as he rose, still holding the old goose gun. "*Señor*, Doña Rita had me wait for you. Are you hungry? Thirsty?"

"Thirsty," I told him and went up the steps before him.

He brought ice and water to the sitting room, where I gulped the water before pouring Añejo over ice. After my first sip, the major domo said, "Rafael and his mother are sleeping."

I nodded, too tired to comment sensibly.

"And, *Señor* Juan, permit me to speak for the household: it was a wonderful thing you did to bring back the boy in safety."

I blinked at him. "Give credit to his mother, I only drove."

"And you taught us how to defend this hacienda. Thank you for that as well."

I moved over to the sofa, swallowed more rum, and stretched out. "Do what you can to keep the servants from talking. This was a family matter that should not reach other ears."

"I understand. May I bring you a pillow, a blanket?"

"Just put this gun in the cabinet." I pointed at the Uzi. "Then go to bed."

When he'd gone I closed my eyes and remembered waiting in this room for Marie's call just a few hours ago. I thought of all that had happened afterward, and while I was trying to think of any loose ends I should have tied, my mind blanked over, the glass dropped from my hand, and I slept until morning.

TWENTY-SEVEN

I woke to the sound of music coming from the room across the entrance hall. Piano and wind instrument. Recorder. The melody was *Frère Jacques*. Brother John. I sat up stiffly, tried my joints, and rubbed my unshaven face. Then I crossed to the music room where Rita was accompanying Rafael's recorder melody.

From the doorway I said, "Yes, Brother John *was* sleeping, but I'm awake now. How are you?"

They left off playing and turned to me. "Very well," Rita smiled, "thanks to you." And Rafael said, "I'm fine, Juan. You like my playing?"

"I do. Very much."

"And when can I see my new presents?"

"After I shave and change."

Rita nodded. "I'll have coffee sent up."

As I went up the staircase I reflected that mother and son appeared unaffected by the night's violence. I hadn't expected tranquility this morning, but even if it didn't last it was a godsend.

Before mid-morning breakfast on the patio I opened the Madrid packages for Rafael, the airplane and boat models, and as before, his excitement and gratitude were enormous. After he'd taken the Cessna model to the field, Rita sat across the table and said, "I'm so glad Rafael has things to occupy his mind. I can't say he's forgotten what happened, but I'm encouraging him to ignore it."

"And you?"

She looked away. "How can I forget I killed my father?"

"For years you haven't thought of him as your father, and for the last few as dead. Forget the sudden resurrection and consider the white-haired man as a stranger with a gun who threatened your son and killed your mother." I paused. "ID gave his name as Patricio Guzman, so it was Guzman you killed— and not incidentally saved your son's life and mine."

Her hand covered mine. "You always say such logical things, dear, and your idea sounds just right." She sipped from my water glass. "I'll try hard to follow it." Then with a bitter laugh, "I'm the last of the Chavezes."

"There's Rafael."

"He'll never know." She breathed deeply. "When we got here last night I was sick worrying about you and I had to calm my son. Finally we took sleeping pills—and now, this is another day."

"A much brighter one."

For a time she said nothing and I ate a portion of my eggs and hot sausage. Then she asked. "Are you going to tell me what happened after I drove away?"

"Took care of things so there'll be no inquiries."

"And Claude's car?"

"Disposed of. You have enough on your mind without a lot of details. And I cautioned Francisco not to talk."

"So he told me. At La Torre you're a hero, you know."

"Unmerited. I was passive. You did what had to be done, and I'm terribly proud of you."

"Rafael worships you, dear. This morning he asked if you could be his father."

I smiled. "And?"

"I said it was a possibility, and he was overjoyed."

"Me, too."

"Reminding me," she said as she got up, "I should call my lawyer and apologize for missing yesterday's appointment. I hope he has word of my annulment."

"I hope so, too. Wait." I got out the matching cards I'd retrieved from Chavez, and gave them to her. "Your inheritance."

For a time she gazed at them. "So much blood, so much sorrow," she said absently, "but thank you," and walked away.

I finished my breakfast and went down to where Rafael was flying the Gypsy Moth biplane, Juanito watching nearby. To me he said, "Rafael learns quickly, does he not?"

"So I've noticed. Eager to do what's expected of him. Maybe not enough has been expected of him."

Juanito nodded thoughtfully.

"When he tires of airplanes, take him to the pond with the boat. Help him get started then let him run it."

"*Si, señor.*" We looked up as the little plane executed a graceful, grass-skimming loop. "*Qué maravilla!*" Juanito exclaimed, and I left him with his young charge. Walking toward the house, I was intercepted by Francisco, who asked for a word with me.

"It's the *capataz*, Isidro, *Señor.*'"

"What about him?"

"After the funeral of his nephew he was taken by the police for questioning."

"About what?"

"*Señor*"—he looked anxiously around—"it is said the nephew was killed in an ETA dispute. You know what ETA means?"

"I know. So?"

"As a relative of the dead man, Isidro is under suspicion of ETA involvement." He spread his hands. "We do not expect Isidro to return to La Torre for some time."

I frowned. "Does *Doña* Rita know?"

"I thought it best if you would tell her." He swallowed. "Perhaps she would want to use her influence to secure his release."

"Perhaps she would not want to meddle in a police matter." I patted his shoulder. "Anyway, I'll explain the situation." I walked on and into the house.

In my room I opened my nylon money belt and extracted the Bearer check from Bijoux Brevoort. It represented more than half a million dollars, and although I'd held suitcases and trash bags crammed with millions of green dollars confiscated from drug runners and dealers, this money was mine—if I wanted it.

In the sitting room Rita replaced the telephone receiver and said, "My lawyer says he's hopeful the annulment will be granted within two or three weeks."

"He's said that before."

"And he thought it would be useful if I went to the nunciature with him to press for action. I can do that when I take Rafael to Madrid." She looked at her calendar pad. "This is Wednesday. I thought we'd go Friday, let Rafael enjoy the weekend with us."

"Great," I said, "but right now we have a hacienda problem—no *capataz*." I explained the circumstances as conveyed by the major domo, and Rita shook her head. "That *is* a problem. Isidro came with La Torre when I bought it. I don't know how to go about finding another, even a temporary."

"Could one of the field hands fill in for a while?"

"No, oh, no. He'd never be the same, and a permanent *capataz* like Isidro would have endless trouble with him. Position is very important to hacienda workers, so any replacement has to be an outsider." She tapped a finger on the desk. "As for trying to get Isidro released, I'm afraid Francisco has an exaggerated idea of influence. In his father's day it worked, but I wouldn't even want to try."

"That's what I thought. Anyway, if Isidro is clean he'll come back."

She spread her hands. "Who knows?"

I laid the Brevoort check on the desk. "Before something happens to this I wish you'd take care of it."

"But I've said it's yours."

"All right. Then I can do what I want with it?"

"Of course. What are you leading up to?"

"Very simply an endowment for Rafael. Let the proceeds pay for his treatment and education. Anita would want that; after all, the emeralds came from her."

Tears welled in her eyes. "What a marvelous solution, perfect in every way. And it will be something he'll remember her by."

"So will we. Make arrangements in Madrid to invest at a good, reliable yield."

"My lawyer can advise me," she commented and went over to face the window. After a while she said, "So much has happened since I met you . . . so many things . . ." Her voice trailed away.

"Are you sorry we met?"

"Oh, no, Jack. Some of it would have happened anyway."

"Maybe it all goes back to my meeting Anita. Then she was killed and you were drawn in."

"Fate, I suppose. Destiny." She turned to face me.

"And all the while, behind the scenes, the Colonel was playing a shell game with our lives."

"The master manipulator." She laughed mirthlessly. "And only we survived. Well, from now on I don't want to think about any of it, not him, Marie or Claude. They're gone . . . all gone."

To change the subject I said, "If a *capataz* doesn't show up before Friday I think I ought to stay around, look after things."

"You really want to do that?"

"In Madrid you and Rafael won't be in danger, and I want to learn more about the hacienda."

"Whatever you say. I know the servants would feel more secure."

"Works both ways, so that's what we'll do."

On Friday morning I drove them to Oviedo's airport and saw them safely aboard the Madrid plane. On the trip back I drove five miles beyond the hacienda to the field where Rita's father and mother had died, along with Tessier. I didn't try to turn in to view the death scene because the gate was closed with chains and padlocks. Wide, deep tireprints showed where heavy vehicles had driven through since I'd left it that dark night which now seemed far behind me.

But I paused at the gully bridge to look down at what was left of the demolished, burned Mercedes. Most of its iron and steel had vanished, taken by men with strong backs to sell as scrap, which was all it was. Asturianos valued a peseta as much as anyone.

During the weekend I talked with Rita and Rafael at the Palace, and they phoned the hacienda twice, Rafael wanting to tell me about their half-day visit at the Royal Armory with its suits of armor, arquebuses, crossbows and other ancient weapons. I told him I'd repaired the Cessna's landing gear and damaged wingtip and the plane was ready to fly again.

Esteban saddled up the mount I'd taken before, and I took pleasure in riding the hills and fields of La Torre, noting a gray vixen running furtively toward her den. There were hatches of *perdiz* concealed in bracken, and once I thought I heard the cawing of a pheasant cock.

On Monday I took Pedro and Miguel to the stream, and showed them where I wanted it blocked and dammed with nearby boulders. Using ropes, chains and the Land Rover, we positioned rocks until the stream rose and spread beyond its normal borders. The two young field hands splashed and tugged in the water, enjoying the work, while Francisco watched approvingly from the patio, and by noon there was a usable, freshwater pool available to all.

After siesta I had the major domo show me through the upper regions of the house, found a seldom-used room, and sketched the future locations of wall weights, punching bag and exercise machine to be trucked in from Madrid.

Next day with Juanito, who was at loose ends without Rafael, I fished the big pond, and after we'd brought in a dozen bream and two small bass, I realized that years of neglect had let the pond overpopulate. Too many fish competing for a shrinking food supply, I told Juanito. "I want more bass and fewer bream, so the smallest have to go."

He nodded his understanding and told me he thought he could get some men from another hacienda to net out the smaller fish. "You wouldn't have to pay them, *Señor* Juan, if they can keep the fish."

"They can—but make sure they take only small ones."

That problem resolved, I showed him how to gut and clean our catch, something Spanish men considered women's work, so that in turn he could show Rafael.

The next time Rita telephoned she had good news and bad. Testing at the University had gone well, and Rafael was to be examined by neurologists to devise a chemical regimen for him. "Then I'll look into schools for him— Lucerne, Montreux and Interlaken. And how are you, *mi amor*?"

"Missing you."

"And I miss you, dreadfully. The bad news is the annulment isn't moving very fast." She sighed. "The lawyer says we may have to move the case to Rome—what do you think?"

"It's a way of seeing it lost forever. A Mexican divorce would be faster even if you have to go there—but that's up to you."

"I'll suggest it to the lawyer, let him find out what's involved."

"When are you coming back?"

"Dear, would you mind terribly if I took Rafael to those schools before coming back? Two or three days in Switzerland should do it, but that will mean next week before we're back at La Torre. Or, if you're satisfied with things at the hacienda, why don't you join us?"

"That's a thought—let me know where and when."

"I didn't think things would take this long, *querido*. I'm sorry."

Me, too, I thought, but said, "We still need a *capataz* and I don't want to leave until we have one."

"I understand. Well, I'll phone when some of these medical matters are decided."

After that I called the servants together and asked them to think of friends, relatives and acquaintances who could replace Isidro at least temporarily. They were to telephone freely, and the finder would receive an extra month's salary.

With that stimulus the servants lined up for phone calls, and by the next evening three candidates had arrived for interview. I had Francisco conduct initial screening, after which I talked with each man. One was a boozer, one a drifter, but the third was a well-built man of forty-odd, whose callused hands showed close familiarity with manual work. After I explained the prevailing circumstances he said he would be willing to work during Isidro's absence or replace the *capataz* if he failed to return. His name was Elpidio, and he was eager to leave an employer who paid him poorly and infrequently. "The only problem, *Señor*, is my wife. She is *embarasada* and expecting our child in four months. Can she come, too? Work until the baby comes?"

"Of course." I paid the other men for their time, and sent Elpidio and Antonio in the Volvo to collect his wife and possessions. Then I paid Victoria her finder's fee, and thanked the others.

I was enjoying a nightcap in the sitting room, when the phone rang. I answered, thinking it would be Rita, but instead my caller was Manny Montijo. After the usual jocular fencing he asked when I was returning to Miami.

"No plans," I told him. "Is that a social or professional inquiry?"

"Social, I guess. Melody's bugging me for your phone number, but I wanted to check with you first."

"What's her problem?"

"Hard to tell. Mainly she wants to talk with you." He paused. "You know Melody."

"Yeah. Is she at our house?"

"Said so."

"And the boyfriend—*Signor* Borsalino?"

"No mention."

"She probably totaled my car," I remarked, "and wants to apologize. Well, maybe I'll call her, maybe not. Happens I'm spoken for."

"So I figured. Everything okay over there?"

"Uh-huh. Lot to tell you, Manny, but not by phone. Anyway, you remember that guy who jumped bond?"

"I sure do."

"Well, the Marshals can stop looking for him, he can't run anymore."

"I see." Static and whistling noises came over the line. "Better that way," he said soberly.

"Much better."

"Enjoying life?"

"Yes, and keeping busy managing the hacienda. I like it."

"What will I tell Melody?"

"Oh, tell her I'll get in touch."

"Good, that'll get her off my back."

After ringing off I looked at my watch: six PM in Miami. Might as well get it behind me.

Melody answered after the third ring and said, "I just *knew* Manny could reach you. How are you, Jack?"

"Okay. What's happening?"

"Well, first I'm very lonely here. Most of my friends from the U are in North Carolina escaping the heat, and—"

"*Signor* Zucchini?"

"Who knows? Probably found another *patrona* by now."

"Umm. You wrecked my Miata."

"No, I didn't, not even a scrape. But—when are you coming back?"

"No plans at all."

"Well, I don't want to live here alone, so I guess we should sell the place."

"Good idea."

A long silence before she said, "I—I hoped you'd feel differently."

"Honey," I said patiently, "I have a new life since you left me. I'm practically married—please understand that."

"There was a time when you were going to marry me."

"There was," I agreed, "and you ducked out in Barcelona, remember? We went our separate ways, and now . . . now, things are different."

"But I'll always love you," she said tremulously, "I never stopped loving you."

Women, I thought despairingly. "Very complimentary, honey, but . . . well, why don't you put the place on the market?"

"I've had two offers. But if we sell you have to sign papers."

"Of course. But they can be sent to me." I remembered my floor safe; it held considerable money and a very good H&K pistol. Aside from Manny there was no one I'd trust to open it, and I didn't want Manny to know how much I'd accumulated from our past dealings. That meant going there and clearing out everything I'd left.

"You're really marrying someone else?" she asked in a tone of disbelief.

"I really am, Melody. Now, if that's understood, I'll be willing to come back long enough to clear out my gear and sign the sales agreement. Okay?"

"O-kay," she said grudgingly, "if that's how it has to be."

Ignoring that, I asked, "How are you spending your days?"

"Part-time coaching the diving team—the U wants me full time, but—I haven't made up my mind."

"I've seen some of your cereal endorsements."

"Swimsuits, too, and, oh, lots of other things. I get tons of money."

"Well, I'm proud of you—after all, I knew you when."

"You did. Carnally."

That made me wince as I flashed to a hot afternoon in a sleazy Beach motel. "Don't hold it against me—I was seduced."

"Who'd believe you? Statutory rape, remember?"

"How could I forget? Anyway, get buyers lined up and I'll call you."

I rang off before she could ask for the hacienda number, because I didn't want an incoming from her when Rita was around.

And where was Rita? She hadn't phoned in two days. When we were apart I felt the bonds between us loosening, and I didn't want that, either. By now she could be in Switzerland scouting schools for Rafael. Or still in Madrid while Rafael's response to drug therapy was evaluated. With Elpidio hired, there was no real reason I should stay around La Torre alone. Pond cullers were due in a couple of days, the servants were enjoying the rustic pool, and I was definitely at loose ends.

The next day I phoned the Palace, but Rita was away from the suite. I decided to start building the *Spirit of St. Louis* model without Rafael; he'd be back soon, and could take over. But after I'd assembled half the fuselage I lost interest and walked restlessly around the grounds while I made up my mind to fly to Madrid.

Late afternoon, I phoned Melody, who told me a sale was in prospect though she was bargaining for a higher price. Could she count on my being there for closing? I said she could and I'd stay in touch.

In the morning Antonio drove me to Oviedo airport for the nine o'clock flight to Madrid, neither of us mentioning the ETA ambush we'd survived. Halfway to Barajas a thunderhead bounced the little plane around, one of the passengers vomited, and the sour stench permeated the cabin until on the ground the door opened and fresh air came in.

I'd ridden the Barajas-Madrid road so often I recognized most of the landmarks; counting them off helped pass the time.

At the Palace I had a bellboy carry my bags, and we went directly to Rita's suite. He reached for the bell, but I stopped him with a tip, saying, "I want to surprise the *señora*." So he went away, I rang the doorbell, and waited, hoping someone was there.

There was.

A man in a scarlet bathrobe opened the door. His curly black hair was damp from the shower. In bare feet he stood about five-seven. Black eyebrows, close-trimmed black mustache, olive skin freshly shaved, and a startled expression.

My first thought was that I'd come to the wrong place, so as he stared at me I stepped back to check the number, and yes, this was the suite I'd shared with Rita.

A woman's voice called, "Carlos, what is it?"

I looked over his shoulder and saw her in the bedroom doorway wearing black lace panties and nothing else. The man said, "You can't—" and started to close the door in my face. I jammed it with my foot and pushed in. When Rita saw me she screamed and ran back into the bedroom.

The man called Carlos set his hands on his hips and faced me. "Whoever you are, get out," he demanded.

Ignoring him, I called, "Come back, *Doña* Rita, don't run off like that." Throat through belly, my flesh was frozen and it kept me from throwing up.

Furiously he snapped, "Get out before I call hotel security. Can't you see she's not dressed?"

"We've seen her finer points," I told him, "so what difference does it make? Rita"—I called—"get in here before I drag you."

Angrily Carlos flared, "I won't have you humiliate the *señora*," and then committed a fundamental error; he tried to punch me. I blocked with my left forearm and shoved him against the door. "You're not built for rough stuff," I told him, "so restrain yourself and you won't get hurt. Who are you? Pimp or client?"

He licked his lips. "Carlos Santamaria Alvarez."

"Of the Santamaria Alvarezes? Occupation?"

"Lawyer. I am the *señora*'s lawyer," he blurted.

"I've heard of you," I told him, "but nothing good. Rita"—I called again— "get in here now. I mean it."

Face contorted with rage, Carlos Santamaria Alvarez rushed me, fists flail-

ing. I stepped aside, tripped him and he went down. Hard. His fists pounded
the carpet and whimpers came from his throat. "Stay here," I ordered, and
strode to the bedroom where Rita was frantically pulling on clothing. "As you
were, *querida*. Take it off."

"*You*—you—" she began, then her features softened. "Jack, I can explain."

"I'm sure you can. Take off that skirt and blouse." She glared at me as she
began stripping down to lace panties—the ones from Decadence. I said, "In
the States we have a feeling that lawyers give their clients a fucking. Your
Carlos is no exception."

She stepped out of her pumps and stood before me, legs wide apart, hands
shoving up her full breasts. Lewdly. Defiantly. "You want to fuck me? *Fuck
me!*"

"That was another time, another Rita . . . even another Jack." I took her arm
and pulled her into the sitting room. Carlos was on the sofa, face buried in his
hands. "Where's Rafael?" I asked.

"In—in Lucerne." Her arms crossed over her breasts protectively.

"Carlos," I said, "what's the annulment situation?"

He looked up at me. "What annulment?"

"Fool!" she snarled at him. "Weakling!"

I nodded. "It's all coming together now. No annulment, no marriage . . .
nothing but goodbye. You used me and I let myself be used. I thought you
would be like Anita but you're not. You're . . . well, you know what you are,
and from my point of view this could be worse—we might have married."

Her face was flushed, tears welled in her eyes. Carlos was staring at her but
she didn't look at him. I left her standing there and went back to the room
with the rumpled bed—the one we'd shared not many days ago. Her purse lay
on the bureau. I opened it and took out an airline ticket: Madrid-Geneva-
Zurich-Bern-Madrid. Paper-clipped inside were the matching bank account
cards.

I put the cards in my pocket and replaced the ticket.

She'd watched me from the doorway. "That's what you wanted? That's all
this meant to you?"

"You won't need these—you've got each other." I went to her and walked
her back to the sofa, sat her down beside Carlos. "While it lasted, it was a
hell of a ride, but the ride's over now, and like the *toreros* say, this is the
moment of truth." I took a deep breath to steady myself, my voice. "When I
think back on all that happened I'm going to tell myself everything I did was
for Anita—not you, Rita. And if I'm lucky, in time I'll believe it and everything
will be okay."

Her voice quavered. "What about me? What am I going to do?"

"Do whatever you want. *Adiós* to both of you." I went to the door, opened and closed it, picked up my bags, and walked to the elevator.

As the taxi pulled away from the Palace I flashed back to the night we'd left for La Torre, sick with worry over Rafael. I'd miss the boy and I hoped he could be helped out of his shell into the fullness of life. Her husband was no role model, and from what I'd seen of Carlos Santamaria Alvarez he wouldn't be worth much, either.

My stomach rolled over and I thought I was going to vomit, but not now. Inevitably I'd brood about Rita and how she'd manipulated me into her scheme of things, but this was no time for postmortems. I had to get home and sort things out from there.

I couldn't get a direct flight from Madrid to Miami, so I settled for Madrid-New York, change to Miami. That was the downside. The upside was that the Iberia flight left in an hour, and I was on it.

Across the Atlantic I downed enough Black Label to relax me into drunken sleep, and I was still in a sort of stupor when I went through JFK customs and boarded the American flight to Miami International.

At the airport I noticed an unusual amount of bustle and crowding but laid it to August heat plus Sunday evening arrivals and departures as the weekend ended.

The taxi driver carried my bags to the entrance, and after he disappeared I went around the side and pawed the earth for the door key. Before opening it, I thought back to the alarm numbers, and once inside I punched them quickly.

The bedroom showed signs of occupancy, and I realized that Melody could be around somewhere. But I built a long drink for myself, took a refreshing shower and got into bed.

It was dark when sounds wakened me, and I sat up recalling the night Bevins had broken in. My pistol was in the floor safe, far out of reach, but it was too late to go for a weapon. Now the sounds were in the kitchen, and it gradually dawned on me that Melody had come home.

From the dark bedroom I saw her petite, Venusian figure silhouetted against the hall light, and before she reached the wall switch I shouted, "*Boo!*"

"Oh, God, who is it?" The light went on and she stared at me, chest heaving. "Jack! Oh, you bastard! You scared me half to death." Slowly she came toward the bed. "Why didn't you let me know you were coming?"

"Impulse."

Suddenly she smiled in her bright, little-girl way. "You came to protect me!"

I rubbed a hand across sleepy eyes. "I did?"

"Of course—from a major hurricane headed this way."

"What hurricane?"

"Andrew it's called. I've been fighting shopping lines all afternoon for candles, water, food, ice . . . Jack, you *didn't* come to protect me. That's very disillusioning."

"But on the bright side, you've laid in stores."

"Listen."

I listened. "I don't hear anything."

"That's the point. Everything's still. Birds flown away, no traffic, no planes flying, no wind. Broadcasters call this the Big One we've been expecting for fifty years."

"I haven't been expecting it for anything like fifty years." Getting off the bed, I realized I was naked. Melody eyed me and giggled. "You haven't changed, darling. Not physically."

"I've shown you mine, you show me yours. Oh, Melody, grow up, will you? Are there any storm shutters for this place?"

"Don't think so—unless they're in the garage."

"None there." Outside rain teased the house like the swish of a broom. "Better fill the tub with water."

"We don't have a tub, remember? Shower stall. Where have you *been*?"

"Out to lunch—dinner, too. Okay. There's bottled water?"

"Plenty."

"And liquor?"

"Whatever you laid in—haven't touched a drop. Bad example for the athletes I'm training."

"Open my bag, the cloth one, and hand me my pajamas."

"Say please."

"Please."

She burrowed in the bag and brought over pajamas. "Prude."

"Flashlights."

"Two. I think I'd better unplug the TVs, refrigerator and freezer, don't you? That's what they're recommending."

While she was doing that I opened the floor safe and took out my bulk money and .38 pistol. Unlike the LA police, I was prepared to deal with looters.

The sound of the wind increased, resembling the noise of an outboard a block away. Rain pelted the windows. I said, "Let's wait it out in the bedroom—only one window. Ah—did you sell the place?"

She shook her head. "Deal fell through, insufficient financing."

Wind-flung debris struck the front door. Melody jumped at the sound. "That's the signal to take cover."

So I filled an ice bucket and washbasin with ice, and brought scotch and Añejo to the bedroom along with a jug of drinking water. The Publix label reminded me of buying water from Jimmy Alligator while escaping from

Tessier's camp. "You're not coaching divers now, Coach, so have a drink."

She poured a double shot of scotch, added ice, a few drops of water, and drank. "Ooooooh, good! Long time no scotch."

"*Signor* Zitti keep you on dago red?"

"Jack, we're here together, orphans of the storm, so let's not rub rough edges, okay? By that I mean, we ought not needle each other about detours from the straight and narrow."

"I'm agreeable." Hers was minuscule compared to mine, and if I ever got around to telling Melody how the last couple of months had gone we'd need an uninterrupted week to hear me out.

So we drank and listened to the radio, which was predicting the worst blow in recorded hurricane history, and we could feel the wind pressure increase until the walls seemed to sway. Rubble and debris struck the house at intervals. Outside—palm branches, citrus fruit and street signs were whipping around like projectiles. I poured myself another drink. After Melody did likewise she sipped and stood up. "We're not going to have hot water for long, maybe no water at all, so it's me for the showers—unless you want to go first."

"Had a shower," I muttered. "Go ahead."

The wind was shrieking like a thousand wolves. Through that nerve-grating sound came a bass *sostenuto* that trembled the entire house, and I began feeling edgy. Every now and then lightning whitened the blinds; thunder rolled like an avalanche.

I went to the bathroom door, opened it and was shrouded in steam. "Anyone there? If lightning hits, the shower is a high-risk place to be." From Melody, a frightened cry, and the shower turned off. She stepped from the stall, grabbed a towel and began drying her hair. "No peeking," she admonished, and I noticed her small brown pubic patch. For diving competitions she kept it cleanly shaved, but after the Barcelona Gold she'd obviously let it grow. By contrast, Rita's pubis was black and bushy, a luxuriant, lewdly inviting growth that I no longer cared to remember. Modestly, I withdrew.

When she joined me she was wearing a short, Japanese *happi* coat and zori sandals. She went for her drink, and after sipping said, "You wouldn't have warned me if you didn't care for me, Jack."

"Also, we're co-owners of a substantial property and your welfare is important to me."

She made her way to the bed. "Care to tell me what you've been up to?"

"No—not now, anyway. You?"

She shrugged and the coat slipped partway off one shoulder. "I was a fool—leave it at that. Shake?"

We shook hands. Hers lingered in mine. "It seemed we were apart forever, but now we're under the same roof, that sort of fades away."

I grimaced. "And the roof may go." I put ice and liquor in our glasses. The rain had developed the steady beat of a loud snare drum. Melody said, "I'd be scared to death if you weren't here."

"And you were going to ride out the storm alone."

"Guess I didn't realize how rough it was going to be."

We heard an enormous sound that could only be a big ficus tree crashing down across the street. Lights went out. "So," she murmured, "it begins."

The drumming noise increased in volume until the whole house shuddered. I said, "If anything gives way, we get under the bed. Those ceiling mirrors could be fatal."

"You think of everything." She lay back beside me. I'd heard that phrase from other lips, but from Melody it sounded sincere. "Can I ask one question?"

"Sure." We were both feeling our liquor. "What is it?"

"Who's the Diana who keeps leaving messages on the machine?"

"Diana. Ah . . . well, she's a law enforcement officer who came to my rescue a few weeks ago. What's on her mind?"

"Wanted to warn you about the hurricane."

"Thoughtful," I said, "and in keeping with her generous, outgoing nature. Always thinking of others, seldom of herself."

When Melody said nothing, I added, "She is a very dear child, a very nice young lady, and you'd like her."

"Like hell I would! She said some rather intimate things on the tape. I got furious and erased them. Young, you say? Like how young?"

"Twenty-one or -two, thereabouts."

"At least she's of age," Melody muttered. Lightning struck nearby, she yelped and clung to me. "Too damn close," she chattered, and I found myself hoping Diana wasn't at sea with Pappy, or anyone. She ought to be in a protected bunker somewhere, safe from the raging elements.

We were lying on our sides, spoon fashion, and as Melody moved I realized the short cotton coat was her only covering. Her thighs warmed mine, her tummy molded against my bottom, and I began recalling erotic delights we'd known in this very bed, under the now-dark, invisible mirrors. Very softly she asked, "Are you going to marry anyone?"

"No commitments."

"Me neither." She snuggled closer and her arms circled me. "Mmmmmm, this is nice. Like old times, just the two of us."

"Honey, know what you're doing to me?"

"I know what I *want* to be doing to you." Her voice was low, throaty. "Mind?"

"What a question." Outside, sudden noise sounded like a jet crashing in the front yard. Both of us jumped and Melody began whimpering. I turned so we were facing, kissed and stroked her reassuringly. Her thighs parted, she reached down, and in the utter stillness while the hurricane's eye was passing over, we began making love.

Morning was gray and rainy. The sun came out, disappeared, and for an hour or so it rained. Downed trees were everywhere, making streets impassable. Flights of small parrots with bright green plumage preened and quarreled in the fallen foliage, and the noise of backyard generators was loud across the land.

Listening to radio damage reports got increasingly depressing, so we noshed and drank and made love and slept and repeated the cycle until power was restored four days later.

During that isolated time we talked of many things, including her vivacious mother, the twice-widowed, thrice-married Delores, whose unappeasable avarice and successful pursuit of matrimonial largesse continued to astound. She was, Melody told me, even then cruising the Greek islands with a Turkish art collector, whose eye had fallen on her at a Monte Carlo ball. "I anticipate," I remarked, "a rapid transfer of priceless *objets* to your maternal ancestor; a private museum for the rarities and a vault for the overflow."

"At least I'll never have to support her."

"I used to worry about that," I admitted, "after you and I began fooling around."

"Jack." She eyed me steadily. "Answer me one question: did you ever make it with Mother? Get it on?"

"Hmmmm. No gentleman would respond to such a demeaning question, but in view of our revived romance I'm going to break the unspoken rule. No, we never did nuthin'. Okay?"

"Okay," she sighed. "I used to notice how she looked at you and naturally things came into my mind."

"Naturally?"

"Unbidden."

After that troubling exchange we went outside to look around the property to see what the storm had wrought.

Part of the kitchen wall was stove in by a mango tree, and four windows were smashed, but with all the tales of woe and tragedy flooding in we knew we were extraordinarily lucky.

After viewing the damage I asked Melody if she'd kept up insurance on the place.

"Why, no, I thought you—"

I shook my head. "Fuck it. Let's go find some laughs."

*   *   *

More than anything else the hurricane was responsible for our reconciliation, and we were probably the only two people in South Florida who felt beholden to it. And it wasn't until Melody asked if she could take the Miata to the University that I learned she was registered for classes at the Law School. Her late stepfather, Paul Diehl, had been a Miami lawyer somewhat on the order of Saul Hornstein, but Melody explained that she wanted to learn contract and entertainment law to protect herself from fraud and rapacious shysters, not shield narcotics kings from justice. So I kissed her, wished her well on her first day of classes, and watched her drive off to the U.

In the house I telephoned Manny Montijo to let him know I was back, safe, and so on, but one of the stay-behinds said the office force had been evacuated, with dependents, to Montgomery Air Force Base in Alabama, their return date undetermined.

Next I phoned the Consulate General of Guatemala and asked to speak to Pablo.

"Pablo who?"

"The Pablo who represents your Central Bank. Recovering sequestered funds."

"Oh, *that* Pablo. Pablo Novarro. Hold on."

I recognized the voice when he spoke. In Spanish I said, "Some weeks ago you and your partner came to my stilt shack looking for Chavez money. Right?"

"Who are you?"

"Suppose I could lead you to it? All of it?"

"The nation would be exceedingly grateful."

"And would the nation express its appreciation in a concrete way?"

"I—I suppose so, but I'm not authorized to make such an arrangement."

"Listen to me," I said irritably, "you draw up an agreement by noon, have the Consul General sign and stamp it, and if my percentage is right you'll get the looted funds."

Long silence. "This is serious?"

"Serious," I told him. "And I'm giving you a break. Because if you don't act fast I'll take the money myself."

"What percentage do you want?"

"I'm going for less than the usual ten percent finder's fee. One percent will satisfy me. And if there's no recovery, no fee. How can you lose?"

"That's so," he said after a moment's thought. "All right. One percent of whatever we recover."

"I'll call at noon," I told him, "and we'll meet."

"Why not come to the Consulate? We're in Coral Gables."

"So am I. But we'll do business on US soil—not that I don't trust you fellows . . . "

"I understand. Ah—you would be Mr. Jim Nolan."

"Not really. Leave the name blank and I'll fill it in. You have"—I looked at my watch—"three hours. After which you can go home, triumphant."

I boiled water, made instant coffee and phoned the Marine Patrol base at Marathon. It took a while to get information on Diana's location but finally an officer told me she'd gone PCS to Pensacola in the Panhandle: Permanent Change of Station, so it was unlikely our paths would cross again. Still, the thought saddened me, because Diana was a fine young woman and we'd been good for each other while it lasted. What *had* lasted far too long was Rita's deception. She phoned me that morning, and her voice was soft and compelling as her body. "Jack," she breathed, "I've been trying to reach you but the hurricane—"

"Wires were down."

"I've been worried. Are you all right?"

I swallowed. She still had that effect on me. "I'm fine."

"Then—please listen to me. That was all a dreadful mistake. I wanted to explain but you wouldn't listen. Will you listen?"

"I'll listen."

Moments passed before she spoke. "We've meant so much to each other that I can't bear to lose you—not like that."

When I said nothing, she asked, "Are you listening?"

"Yes."

"I—when I'm alone I get . . . confused. I need reassurance. It's something in me I can't explain, but Carlos was there, and—Jack, I never stopped loving you. Will you believe me?"

"I do," I told her, "and I understand more than you think." I swallowed again, wet dry lips. "When we were getting involved I ran a check on you but I refused to believe what I learned."

"And what was that?" she asked defensively.

"That you're a nymph—a nymphomaniac. Can't control yourself. I can't blame you for that."

"Then—?"

"You lied to me, Rita, and I can't forgive that."

"The annulment, you mean?"

"Mainly—and other things."

"But things would have worked out—I'd have got a divorce somewhere. You have to believe me," she ended plaintively.

I thought for a moment before saying, "Without trust, marriage is only a word. You killed that trust, Rita, and I could never believe you, trust you. You see, every time we were apart I'd wonder. Carlos? Someone else? My life would be wretched and I couldn't endure it. The good things we shared I'll remember—and regret how it ended."

"Jack, don't shut me out of your life. I beg you. I—I'll always love you."

"I think you will—for a time. Then"—my throat was tightening—"you'll find someone else. It's your nature. Try to change it, Rita. Get help. Goodbye." I broke the connection before she could speak; we'd said all there was to say.

Still, her call depressed me because it made me reprise everything I'd concluded and rationalized after the Madrid revelation: she suffered a sickness rooted in her past. Morally impaired, she became promiscuous to purge the psychological residue of debasement inflicted by her father's cock. Accepting that, I could neither hate nor despise her. She was a lost woman as she had been a lost, debauched child. A woman to be remembered with sorrow and regret.

At noon Pablo told me the document was ready. I gave him my address and told him to come alone. He arrived in a Mercury with Consular plates, parked at the curb and came in, carrying an attaché case. He looked as shabby and swarthy as he had the night he held a gun on me, but he was all business now. I printed my name in the blank space of the document that committed the government of Guatemala to pay one percent of recovered national funds. And I gave him the two bank account cards for which so much blood had been spilled. After examining them, Novarro put them in his attaché case. "Can you tell me how these came into your possession?"

"You get the cards, not the story. I suggest you cable your embassy in Bern to begin recovery, and don't try to give me a short count. I know how much is in each bank." That was a lie, but these days I wasn't a trusting soul. We shook hands and he departed. I locked the agreement with its ribbons and wax seal in my floor safe, built myself a drink, and waited for Melody to come home.

Next morning I dropped Melody off at Law School and returned to the house. From the garage I brought out Anita's two suitcases and loaded them in the Miata trunk. Then I drove down US 1, heading south toward the Keys.

All around South Miami the storm's destruction was nearly incredible, and I stopped at the first hurricane relief shelter to donate Anita's clothing for women who desperately needed it, having lost everything. Rita would never send for her sister's effects; she had been interested only in Anita's jewelry and I'd given her that.

So I continued on south through the town of Homestead. Virtually wiped out, it resembled nothing more closely than Hiroshima. The Air Force Base looked as though it had been carpet-bombed.

The farther I drove, the worse the devastation. Road crews had cleared the highway, but debris and shattered buildings hugged the roadsides. It was slow going toward Islamorada, but to my surprise the physical destruction diminished, the eye of the hurricane having come inland just north of the Keys. But when I turned in at what had been my access road I found it blocked by sand, fallen sea grape and mangroves. I picked my way carefully through the tangle to avoid snakes and scorpions until I came to the beach, which had become a mass of twisted trees and storm-hurled flotsam. A few casuarinas were still standing, their remaining branches wind-stripped; without needles they resembled bizarre skeletons. Others were bent or broken, their shallow roots exposed where the barrier dune had been.

Of the stilt shack nothing remained, not even the supporting timbers; nothing but unobstructed water as far as I could see. For a while I lingered there, remembering how it had been that morning when I found Anita weeping by the net, seeing her rhythmic stride as she went along the beach, and then I turned and made my way back to the car. I'd paid final homage to a girl I cared for and who had been so cruelly murdered. And, like the vanished stilt shack and the sand dune, some memories were better obliterated.

It took less than a week for Novarro to get back to me. With two accounts yet to be tapped, more than a hundred and fifty million dollars had been recovered. I told him I'd take payment at the Bern embassy, not wanting IRS to get a handle on it.

So when Melody came home that evening I suggested a weekend trip to Switzerland. "Terrific," she said, "but what's the occasion, and why Switzerland?"

"Honey," I said, and kissed her, "what better place to honeymoon?"